W9-AUP-100

PRAISE FOR *AMORTALS*

"Matt Forbeck takes the plausible and pulls out all the stops in this mind-blowing, high concept thriller. It doesn't get any better than this." JIM LEE

"*Amortals* is an action-packed sci-fi thriller full of fantastic tech and a great ending. 5*****"

SFBOOK.COM

"*Amortals* (to paraphrase another sci-fi writer who, in my opinion, has nothing on Matt Forbeck) blew down the walls of my imagination. It then stepped over the smoking rubble, seized me by the throat and kicked my ass." BILLY CAMPBELL, STAR OF *THE 4400*

"It kicks like a mule and whispers sweet nothings in your ear like Mike Tyson in a boxing match."

BEN TEMPLESMITH

"Matt Forbeck is the writer that other writers aspire to be: his work is unfailingly well-plotted, tightly paced, and imaginatively realized. He juggles humor and pathos with a deftness that defies literary gravity. I'm a huge fan." JOHN KOVALIC

"If you are looking for a great story with action, politics, great characters and an eye toward what might well be our future, Matt Forbeck's *Amortals* is not to be missed!"

MIKE STACKPOLE

"One helluva sci-fi thriller. 4****"

FANTASY LITERATURE

ALSO BY MATT FORBECK

The Marvel Encyclopedia
More Forbidden Knowledge
The Complete Idiot's Guide to Drawing Manga

Mutant Chronicles
Secret of the Spiritkeeper
Prophecy of the Dragons
The Dragons Revealed
Eberron: Marked for Death
Eberron: The Road to Death
Eberron: The Queen of Death
Guild Wars: Fall of Ascalon

MATT FORBECK

AMORTALS

ANGRY
ROBOT

ANGRY ROBOT
A member of the Osprey Group

Lace Market House,
54-56 High Pavement,
Nottingham
NG1 1HW, UK

www.angryrobotbooks.com
Come back

Originally published in the UK by Angry Robot 2010
First American paperback printing 2011

ISBN 978-0-85766-002-2

Printed in the United States of America

9 8 7 6 5 4 3 2 1

Dedicated to my wife, Ann, who makes everything worthwhile, and to our kids — Marty, Pat, Nick, Ken, and Helen — who give our lives meaning.

My deep gratitude goes to the people who were kind enough to offer comments on this book before it went to press, including Aaron Allston, Billy Campbell, Monte Cook, Richard Dansky, Jack Emmert, Richard Knaak, John Kovalic, John Layman, Jim Lee, John Rogers, Scott Sigler, Mike Stackpole, Ben Templesmith, and Jordan Weisman. Also, many thanks to the members of my writers' group, the Alliterates, for many years of words and beers, especially to Troy Denning, Dave Gross, and Johnny Wilson for their feedback.

Even more thanks to all of my family, friends, and fans who have believed in me for so long, especially my parents. You have my undying gratitude. Special thanks to the fine and faithful people at Angry Robot — to Lee Harris, and most of all to my old friend, Marc Gascoigne. No one loves great stories more or treats them better.

Last but not least, thanks to you who pick up this book and brave its pages. I hope you enjoy reading it as much as I did writing it.

ONE

Getting killed always gives me the worst hangover. When I was younger, I thought maybe it had something to do with my soul being forced out of my body and then shoved into the next. Even if I couldn't remember it, that sort of trauma had to leave some sort of mark on a person's spirit, right?

"You ready for this, Agent Dooley?"

I rubbed my baby-smooth chin and leaned forward in the chair, flexing my fresh legs. The techs at the Amortals Project had shaved my face micro-clean, which I never liked, but it would grow out fast enough. "This isn't the first time I've seen myself die, Patrón."

The frat-boy-faced man with the slicked-back hair cracked a shadow of his wide smile. His perfect teeth gleamed in the room's dimmed lights. "Right. I saw the documentary about your first time when I was in grade school."

"The 2132 version is the best," I said, battling a sickening sense of déjà vu. Hadn't we had this conversation the last time? "They went all out for the centennial."

Patrón snorted. I knew he could look right through my bravado. I didn't want to watch this. No sane man would.

"That's *Director* Patrón, by the way," he said. "*Sir* is fine too. You sure your memory's working right?"

Hoping he'd attribute my failure to feign respect for him to revivification sickness, I ignored him. "Just start the show."

Patrón blinked. I'd known him nearly as long as I'd known anyone alive. He had a strong stomach. "It's bad, Ronan," he finally said.

"That doesn't matter," I said. "Does it?"

Patrón shrugged, then waved his hand, and the thrideo leaped to life. The polarizers in my lens implants kicked in, transforming the blurred images into a 3D mirage that looked sharp enough to cut my pupils.

In the thrid, a man sat bound to a white plastic chair in the center of a small, gray room made of cinderblock walls. He was tall and trim and dressed in a navy blue suit, a red tie, and a white shirt splashed with crimson. His ankles were cuffed to the legs of the chair with self-constricting ties, and his hands were bound behind him, likely with the same.

The man had close-cropped, dark-brown hair and a three-day shadow of a beard. He looked young, maybe about thirty, although it was impossible to tell these days. He wore a black blindfold over his eyes, the kind the first-class stewards hand you for overnight flights. Blood trickled down in twin paths from beneath the fabric, framing the rest of his face.

Despite the blindfold, I knew that face well. It was mine, and I did not look good.

Another figure stepped into view. This new man wore the kind of clean suit you see in microchip laboratories, complete with the full headgear and the mirrored faceplate, except it was all black. Loose and bulky, it covered him from head to toe like a high-tech burka.

The new man carried a 9mm semi-automatic Nuzi pistol in his right hand. The safety was already off. He tapped it against his leg before he began to talk.

"I suppose," the new man said in a voice that had been digitally garbled, "that you're wondering what you're doing here today, Mr Methuselah Dooley." I winced at the nickname. The press had slapped that on me over a hundred years ago, and I'd never been able to shake it.

The previous version of me – the one about to die in the thirdeo – grunted but did not say a word. A trickle of blood escaped from his mouth as he tried to speak. The tongue in my mouth recoiled at the ghost of a traumatic memory I didn't actually have.

"Don't answer," the man in the black suit said. "This isn't for you. You'll be dead soon. It's for later, for them."

Patrón glanced at me, but I ignored him. The man in the suit knew exactly what he was doing. We just had to watch to find out what that was.

I knew I could stop the recording to chat with Patrón if I wanted to. I could rewind it, even watch it dozens of times today. My first time through, though,

I wanted to absorb every bit of it without interruption, to see it as it happened.

Something inside of me wanted to turn away, to avoid this horrible spectacle. I ignored that impulse.

The man in the suit snarled, and the man in the chair began to panic. He struggled against the bracelets holding him in place, thrashing about in the chair, straining hard enough to put shining stress lines in the bracelets, even though it only made them bite harder into his flesh. The chair's legs had been bolted to the floor, or it would have gone over for sure. Maybe that's what the man in the chair had been hoping for, although it wouldn't have done him any good.

I stared at the man in the chair as his struggles abated. The bracelets had cut right through his socks, and blood trickled into his shoes. Unable to get free, he gave up the fight and began to weep.

Patrón squirmed a bit in his chair. "That sort of behavior unusual for you, Dooley?"

I ignored the crack. If the man in the chair had wept, it might mean he was trying to tell me something. I'd seen myself die before, several times, and I'd never done anything of the sort.

The man in black shifted his gun to his left hand, then reached out and slapped the man in the chair with a gloved palm. "Get a hold of yourself, Meth," he said. "You'll disappoint your fans."

The man in the chair – I couldn't bring myself to call him Ronan or Dooley or even Methuselah – whimpered at this, but the tears ended, and he did not grunt another word. I felt my fists clench. I wanted to jump up and take out the man in black – tear the life from him with my bare hands – then rescue the doomed guy. It was too late though. Real as the images seemed, I was watching the past. This had already happened.

"This is what the Secret Service does for you, eh, Meth?" the man in black said. "Give them your life, and they only ask if they can have another."

The man in the chair let his head loll back on his shoulders. I wasn't sure he was still alive.

The man in black leaned forward and whispered something into the other man's ear. The audio leaped up to compensate for the difference in volume. I could hear it through the bone conductors tapped into the base of my skull.

"And you," the man in black said, "you give it to them."

The man in the chair flinched at these words, spoken as softly as a promise to a sleeping lover.

The man in black straightened back up again. "You sicken me," he said. "You're like a dog. All those years serving your country and your President. How much did that cost you? Your wife. Your kid. Your grandchildren. Every last one of your lives."

The man in the chair slumped over in the chair, his shoulders sagging, his head hanging low. He'd been beaten in every way.

"You're not even a man," the man in the clean suit said. "You're just a distant echo of the original. A cheap, vat-grown copy. You fade more every time you bounce back into this world. I'd say you'd be nothing soon, but you're already there. Every breath you take subtracts from those the original Ronan Dooley breathed a hundred and fifty years ago."

The man in the black suit leaned in and brushed the other man's sweat-soaked hair back with the barrel of his gun. The gesture would have seemed tender with just about any other instrument.

"You think just because you're amortal you're special. That you can't really die. That it doesn't really matter if you do. It's a great set-up, at least for people like you. One body dies, just go to the whole-brain backup and restore it into a clone. You don't even have to remember the pain of death or the fear it brings. You're like an alcoholic who blacks out before beating his wife. In your head, it's like it never happened."

The man in black knelt down in front of the chair. He swapped his pistol back to his right hand and pressed the tip of his gun against the other man's forehead, then pushed the bleeding man's head up and back until it was level with his own.

"What you forget," the man with the gun said. "What people like you always forget is that a copy is not the original. It may look, sound, smell, taste, feel, and even act like the original, but that doesn't mean it's the same thing. It's a substitute, a replacement, a simulacrum, a doppelganger."

I swore I could hear the man sneer as he continued. "People are not digital files recorded in a meat medium. We are flesh and blood, and we are unique. You may be a perfect copy, but you're still a copy. Somewhere, the fleshless bones of the original Ronan

Dooley are spinning in his rotted grave."

The head of the man in the chair pulled back from the pistol for a moment, then lolled to the side. The man with the gun reached out and grabbed the other man by the shoulder and sat him upright again.

"You're not a man," the man in black said. "You're a ghost made flesh, condemned to haunt this world until the day your number comes up again. Even amortals can only cheat death for so long."

The man in black stood now and placed the tip of the barrel of his gun against the other man's forehead. "Today's the day," he said. "It's time for your run on this Earth to end."

Although I'd never seen the thrid before, I knew what happened next. Despite the fact that I was nothing but a ghost to this scene, watching this little drama from behind the veil of time, I reached out my hand to stop it.

"Aw, no," I heard myself whisper.

"Good-bye, Ronan 'Methuselah' Dooley," the man in the black suit said. "You won't be missed."

The gunshot made me jump. The head of the man in the chair kicked back as if it had been smashed with a baseball bat. If the chair hadn't been bolted down, the impact would have knocked him flat. As it was, the bullet blew out the back of his head and painted the wall behind him an angry red.

The man in the suit stood there and watched the life leak out of his victim. A rivulet of blood ran down from the hole in the dead man's forehead. Far more of it spilled from the back of his skull and onto the floor below, puddling with the fluids already there.

As the dripping stopped, utter silence fell over the room. Then I heard something come from the man in the suit. It sounding like sniffling.

When the man next spoke, his voice came low and raw.

"Good luck," he said. "Whatever you were and wherever you're going, you deserved a lot better than this."

The man then came around to the side of the dead man and shot him three more times in that side of his head. He did the same on the dead man's other side. By the time he was finished, there wasn't enough left of the dead man's skull to fit into my shoe.

Then the man stood in front of the corpse and emptied the rest of his clip into it. The body jumped and leaped under the impacts, jerking about as if it shot through with lightning.

As the echoes of gunfire faded, the body fell still.

The man with the gun removed the clip from it with practiced ease and tossed it aside. Then he did the same for the gun. Each clattered to a rest across the concrete floor.

Then the man turned toward the thrideo camera that had recorded the entire event. He leaned into it, and it seemed as if he was staring straight at me.

I couldn't see his face through the mirrored panel in his mask, though, just the reflections of the twin camera lenses the man had been facing. Staring at them was like looking down the barrels of two guns, one aimed at each of my eyes. For a moment I wondered if they could bark death at me through the screen.

When the man finally spoke, I nearly jumped out of my seat. I felt like I'd been tossed into a frozen pool and couldn't find the hole in the ice that would let me reach the surface again.

"No more Ronans," the man in the suit said through his voice scrambler. "Let the man and all his copies rest in peace."

The thrideo went dark then, and the lights glowed back up. I didn't look at Patrón. I didn't want him to see me shaking.

"Who did this?" I asked. My voice trembled with anger, frustration, and fear.

The Secret Service director made a small cough filled with pity and regret. "We were hoping you could tell us."

TWO

I wrestled with my whirling emotions as I walked out of the private theater and into the headquarters proper of the United States Secret Service. Watching that man murder me – actually violate my body with his gun – made me angrier than I'd ever been. I fought a violent urge to vomit. Had I been someplace more private, I would have given in.

I wanted to strangle the life out of that killer. I wanted to hear him beg for forgiveness. Then I wanted to tear his head off anyway. And if he was somehow amortal too, I'd find every last genetic sample he might have left behind and napalm, bleach, and nuke it from the planet. I'd erase every last indication that he'd ever existed.

And then I'd really get started.

I knew the halls of the headquarters well, and being there lent me some small comfort. I'd served the Secret Service for far longer than this mass of glassteel and reinforced concrete, and with luck I'd still be around when its walls came down. Still, returning to them always felt more like coming home than it did when I strolled into my condo at the Watergate Hotel.

I felt a hand on my shoulder and fought the urge to shake it off and punch the man attached to it. Despite being the longest-serving member of the Secret Service, I knew that Patrón would take a dim view of me assaulting him in the middle of his own headquarters. There's only so much leeway that being reborn that day can earn you.

"I know how you're feeling right now, Dooley," Patrón started.

"Of course you do." I didn't bother looking at him. I kept walking away. I just wanted to get back to my office, reconnect to the world, and get to work. The quicker I found this bastard, the better, and the less time I'd have to seethe over what he'd done to me.

"I've been killed too." I knew Patrón was only trying to sympathize with me, but I wasn't having it.

The other agents we passed in the hall all found something else interesting to look at on the nearest walls or through the closest windows. I recognized some of them, but the set of my jaw broadcast that I wasn't in the mood to chat.

"We've all been killed, Patrón. Every damned amortal one of us. That wasn't murder. That was rape with bullets."

Patrón opened his mouth to say something, then closed it. "All right," he said. "Then let's find the bastard and make him pay."

"'Let's'? As in 'you and me'? Is that option even legally on the table?" I scoffed at him. "Whose jurisdiction is this? Capitol blues? DC? FBI?"

Patrón jogged a few steps to keep up with me and shook his head. "Your body was found in the District of Columbia, so normally DC Homicide would have the first crack at this. However–"

"Always with the howevers."

"The FBI would love to have a crack at such a high-profile case, so they've been pressing to get involved."

"But you told them to– Wait." I stopped dead in the corridor. Surprised, Patrón sailed past me, then spun around to face me again. Sunlight streamed in through the floor-to-ceiling windows lining one side of the hall, and despite the youth of his body, in the bald light of day Patrón looked old.

I glared right into his aged eyes. "How high profile is this?"

Before he even answered, I knew he'd let it spin out of control.

"The killer made that recording and posted it to the web. Then he pinged the major news agencies, and they grabbed it and ran. It's been the top-trending topic worldwide for the past twenty-four hours."

Patrón gave me a "what can you do?" shrug. "Ronan," he said. "It was a slow news cycle. It'll fade."

I brushed past him, leaving him to catch up with me again. A story as juicy as this would have a lot of life in it, I knew. I could just see the headlines: "World's Oldest Man Murdered Again!" "Amortal No More?" "Who Murdered Methuselah?"

The kill-porn sites would get themselves worked up in a frenzy, breaking the thrideo apart frame by frame.

The right-wing establishment would see it as a full-frontal assault on them and their amortal base. The left-wing protesters would recognize a potential hero for their cause in the man in black. It hit enough hot-button topics that every major media faction would try to co-opt the killing for its own pet cause. Among all this, they'd ignore the most important part: I'd been killed, and the murderer was still at large.

"We have full jurisdiction on this one, Dooley," Patrón said as he chased after me, trying to catch me before I reached my office and shut the door in his face. "The President herself has given the order for everyone else to back off and cooperate with all of our requests. You and your partner have the agency's full backing on this one."

I ground to a halt at that and turned to scowl at Patrón. "Partner?" I said. "I haven't had a partner in decades. I work alone. You know that."

Patrón held up his hands and shrugged. He looked anything but helpless. "You've just been killed, Dooley, and in a horrible and nasty and public way. There's the danger you might not be able to think clearly here. You need the help."

"A babysitter, you mean," I snarled. "And no, I don't."

I turned, strode through the door to my office, and slammed it behind me. Many of the other offices in the place had the standard pocket doors that recognized you and – if you were authorized to enter the room – slid aside when you approached. I preferred to put my trust in a set of well-oiled hinges, a thick slab of oak, and a centuries-old lock.

I twisted the deadbolt home, knowing that Patrón couldn't override something so simple, at least not with a simple wave of his hand. I glared at him through the polarizable glass that made up my office's front wall, then turned to see a beautiful woman sitting behind my desk.

"Get out," I said.

The woman smiled at me. She was tall for a woman, nearly my height, dressed in a smart dark suit that nearly screamed "federal agent." She had a perfect, wide smile bracketed by deep dimples. She wore her curly dark hair down to her shoulders, and it framed her flawless olive-skinned face. The bit of gray touching her temples, along with the slight smile wrinkles around her lively brown eyes, told me that she was no amortal. First-lifer, for sure.

She stood and walked around my desk, extending her hand to me. "Agent Dooley," she said. "Welcome back. You may not remember me. I'm Agent Amanda Querer."

I ignored her hand until she put it back in her pocket. "I think you're in the wrong office," I said.

She gave me an understanding smile. Had I not been so furious, I might have admitted she was gorgeous. The hormones pumping through my new body urged me to do much more than that.

"I'm right next door," she said, "so I can see how you might think there could be some confusion, but I've been assigned to help out with your case."

I moved around the other side of the desk and sat down in my chair. She stood behind one of the pair of guest chairs sitting before me.

"I don't need the help."

"I can understand how you feel."

"Can you?" I said, letting loose with my disbelief. "How many times have you been killed?"

"I hardly think that I need to be murdered to dredge up some sympathy for you."

I snorted at that. "I've died eight times now. Three times in the process of saving the life of a President, twice while protecting foreign dignitaries, once in a manner that's still classified far above your level of clearance, and once by accident."

"And this time you were murdered."

"The other seven times someone killed me don't count?"

"Murder requires intent. The people who killed you before – the ones I know of, at least – meant to murder someone, but not you. You just happened to get in the way."

"You have a lovely way of framing my sacrifices."

"I like to keep things as clear as I can."

I opened my mouth to snap at her, then closed it. I reconsidered my words before I spoke. "I'm sure that's just one of the many excellent reasons that Patrón assigned you to this case, but he's just wasting your time. I'm going to figure out who did this. Alone."

Querer shrugged as she walked toward the door. "And I respect your desires. I really do. But I have my orders."

I sat back in my chair. "Ignore them. I always do."

She reached for the deadbolt. I figured she might fumble at it. Most people her age had rarely seen one.

She flipped it without an instant's hesitation. "I'm afraid they come straight from the top," she said as Patrón strolled into the room.

"Thank you, Agent Querer," Patrón said as he straightened his cheap tie. "I'm glad to see that someone around here still knows how to play as part of the team."

I glared at Patrón's tie. Just because our uniform code insisted on clip-on ties didn't mean they had to look like them. Sure, it's wonderful to know that an assailant can't strangle you with a piece of your own clothing that you've conveniently draped around your neck, but they do make them so you don't have to look like you stole your tie from a snot-nosed kid going for his First Communion.

I folded my arms in front of me, leaned back in my chair, and glowered at Patrón. He snaked his way between the two guest chairs and splayed his meaty hands on my desk. He met my gaze. No matter how much I might not have liked Patrón, I had to respect how much of a hard-ass he could be. Licking a few boots might help make you the director of the Secret Service, but it wouldn't keep you there for the seventy-six years and counting he'd put in.

"Do you like living, Dooley?" he asked.

When we'd been chatting in the hallway before, he'd been willing to cut me some slack. The idea that the hallway was private was a thin fiction, of course, but one most agents bought into for the sake of convenience. Here, though, in an office and directly in front of a subordinate, he wasn't about to let me push him around.

"I seem to have grown attached to it."

"Good," he said, allowing a self-satisfied smirk to grow on his face. "Then you know what you need to do to *remain* attached to it."

I cocked my head at him. "You're not threatening me, are you, *sir*?" If he wanted me to pretend to respect him, then I'd do just that – and no more.

Patrón pushed back from the desk and stood up straight. "Of course not. I'm just reminding you that the access you have to the Amortals Project starts and ends with your employment here. If you were to force me to fire you, I'd do so only with the utmost regret, especially considering your long record of service to your country."

"No one has ever served longer or better, sir," I said. I knew where he was headed with this, but I wasn't going to let him get away with an implied threat here. If he wanted to put me in my place, he needed to spell it out.

"If you were to leave your position here, you would lose out on your generous salary."

"What does money mean to me, sir?"

"I read your tax filings every year, Agent Dooley. I know you've made a number of wise long-term investments. They might even come to enough to purchase a revivification policy from the Department of Health and Human Services for you – as long as you weren't fired for cause. In that case, they wouldn't be permitted to sell it to you." He almost seemed apologetic. "By law, you understand."

"All too well, sir," I said. "You're snapping my leash."

"I prefer to think of it as a gentle correction."

I sat forward in my chair and shrugged, dropping the false respect. "It comes down to the same thing. I play the good little agent, or you pull the plug on my amortality."

Patrón raised his eyebrows and gave me a sage nod. "You would be free to live out whatever time you have remaining in this life, of course," he said, peering at my head as if watching the bullets that had blasted my predecessor to death. "However long or short a period that may be."

Querer chose that moment to interrupt. "Since you were just publicly murdered by an individual who demanded you not be revived, the odds that your assailant might wish to become a repeat offender are high."

Patrón had me in a box, and he knew it. It annoyed me that Querer not only knew it too but was willing to help him seal me in.

"All right," I said to Patrón. "I'll do it. I'll take any partner but her."

Neither Querer nor Patrón smiled at this.

"Normally I'd be happy to agree with you," said Patrón, "but Querer was hand-picked to partner up with you if you happened to get killed."

"What jackass made that decision?" I asked.

Querer smiled down at me. "It was you."

THREE

"I'll leave you two lovebirds alone," Patrón said as he left my office.

Querer rolled her eyes in his direction, then sat down in one of the guest chairs and sighed. "He can be such an ass."

"That's a transparent attempt to put yourself on my side," I said. I might have to keep her as my partner if I wanted to keep my job – along with my amortality – but I didn't have to play nice.

"See what you will," she said. "I'm still here to help."

I stared at her. "I don't recall officially meeting you before, much less picking you out as a potential partner."

Querer cracked a wry smile. "It's been a while since your last backup, it seems."

It struck me that no one had mentioned anything about that when they'd awakened me in the rebirther. "What day is it?" I asked.

Querer's eyes flickered to the upper right. "Tuesday."

"The date. What's the date?"

"July 5, 2168."

My stomach twisted as I goggled at her. "You can't be serious."

She gave me a regretful wince.

I clucked my tongue at myself. "So much for my required weekly backups." I'd been ignoring that particular set of regulations since before Querer was born. That was always the worst part of losing so many memories. I had only myself to blame.

"What was I doing?" I asked.

"When?"

I hesitated. "How much have I lost?"

"You don't know?"

"I haven't hooked back into the web yet."

"Ah," she said. She nodded at my desk. "Go ahead. I can wait."

I closed my eyes and concentrated. The nanoservers located inside the artificial lenses implanted in my eyes read my command and leaped to life. The displays went opaque with the OS splash screen for an instant. When that happens with a wall display, I like to close my eyes to avoid the blinding glare, but since this three-dimensional image popped up inside my eyelids, that was impossible. It fast-faded to translucency again.

The data layers sprang up in my favored configuration, transparent bits of information floating in my field of vision. I had a backlog of hundreds of communications sent to me since my death had logged me out. My system had only flagged a few of them as vitally important. I ignored them all for the moment.

I glanced to the upper right, and the time and date

zipped into the center of my view. According to the universal time server, Querer hadn't been lying about the date.

I glanced about the room and engaged different layers, testing out the interface to make sure it was in working order. The shopping layer tagged every bit of furniture in the room with the best price to be found, both locally and online. The colors layer picked out Querer's eyes as mostly a particular shade of mahogany and offered up the PANTONE, RGB, CYMK, and hexadecimal codes to match it. The trivia layer identified the font on one of the awards hanging on the far wall as Decotura.

I peered out the window, and the weather layer showed me the current temperature, barometric pressure, and wind speed and direction. I brought up a radar image and the latest forecast. The skies were clear and sunny for miles around DC, but storm clouds were gathering over the far end of the Potomac. They would break sometime in the next couple of days, but exactly when was anyone's guess. Even modern science had to throw up its hands when confronted with nature's full chaos.

Turning back to Querer, I queried her professional profile. Her résumé flicked into my vision. Graduated George Washington University, with honors, and despite being heavily recruited by other agencies and private firms went straight into the Service from there. Decorated three times for excellence and once for bravery. Not too shabby considering she'd been with the Service for barely a decade.

Her private profile was closed to me, and I opted not to prod it for access. I didn't want to work with her, much less become friends.

I unfocused my gaze and asked after Patrón. An arrow pointed my gaze up, and I craned my neck back to see a translucent avatar of him perched above me. It sat in the wireframe outline of his office, running through its custom work-state animation, indicating he was busy. He had three other top-ranking agents in the office with him, all classified as above my clearance to know more than that, at least as long as they were in Patrón's office.

Subvocalizing the command, I called up my most recent log before today. It was dated Friday, April 1, 2168.

I shut all the other layers down.

"You're kidding, right?" I said, to myself more than Querer. "April Fool's Day is the last I remember?"

"Maybe you saw it as some kind of joke," said Querer.

I thought back about it and realized she was right about the joke, only it hadn't been me who'd made it. I'd developed a habit of not coming in for my backups until they forced me to. Patrón and Dr Juwan Winslow, the head of the Amortals Project, had tricked me into coming in for the backup under the pretense that my previous backups had all been corrupted. As old as I am, I'm willing to risk losing a few months, but a total loss would have meant forgetting about more time on Earth than anyone else had ever amassed.

I didn't find the joke funny, but since I was in the building I went ahead with the backup anyhow. If I hadn't, I would have lost a full six months instead of three. Still, I put my head in my hands and growled at my own stupidity.

"Hey," said Querer. "It's only a quarter of a year. What's that to someone who's two hundred years old? An eighth of a percent of your life?"

"It's not the time lost," I said. "It's what I did with it, which I have no damned idea about. And since it all ended in a spectacular murder, it seems I might have been doing something important."

"Or annoying, at least. To the wrong people, that is."

For someone who'd just partnered up with a man at least six times her age, she showed no inkling of being intimidated. Despite my mood, I liked that.

"I'm not quite two hundred yet," I said.

"Not until November 2. Already planning the party?"

I shook my head. "When you reach that age, no one else is left to celebrate."

"You don't think much of the younger generations, do you?"

I laughed. "I'm the last of my generation, kid. I don't think much of anyone."

She arched an eyebrow at that.

"What was I working on before I was killed?"

"That's classified," she said. "Above my clearance."

But not mine. I called for my mission logs, but nothing came up on my pupil. "My log's blank," I said. "Aren't there any records?"

Querer fidgeted in her seat. "If there are, you didn't seem concerned about sharing them with anyone."

"What about my onboard records? On my last body?"

Querer looked a little drawn. She had words that she clearly didn't want to speak.

"You didn't recover the body?"

Her head gave a tight shake, barely more than a shudder. "No, we found the body and reclaimed it. What was left of it."

I felt a little sick myself then. That explained the blindfold in the thrideo.

"They took my eyes?" My voice came out softer than I'd intended.

Lots of murder victims lost their eyes, along with any other parts that could be stripped for someone else's use. Hair, bones, limbs, skin, kidneys, lungs, liver, stomach, arteries and veins, heart, even the face. Some bod-strip crews were so efficient they left nothing behind but the brain, which couldn't be implanted into someone else. The worst of those bastards even sold the gray matter as a depraved culinary delicacy.

But that had never happened to me before. I was a Secret Service agent, and I was amortal. If I died, someone was bound to notice, and few bod-strippers were willing to risk that kind of heat. There were too many easy victims roaming around the lower levels of American society to make dismembering such a high-profile target worthwhile.

Unless, of course, you were trying to make a point.

Querer swallowed, then answered. "They only got the eyes – and your tongue. The rest of your corpse was intact." She paused a beat. "Other than the damage the bullets did, of course."

A wave of relief washed over me. I realized I was sitting on the edge of my seat, and I leaned back into the chair.

"It happened before the recording," said Querer. "Your optic servers were fitted with last-gen encryption, of course, so the chances of someone being able to access the data in them is close to nil."

"But not actually nil." The sort of people who take the eyes of a Secret Service agent would know hackers who might have a shot at cracking their encryption, especially given enough time. "Did you wipe them by remote?"

Querer had that nauseous look on her face again. "We were unable to make contact with the lenses. They've either been forced offline or destroyed."

"Or cracked and re-encrypted."

She nodded. "There's always that chance. They're designed to wipe themselves if that happens."

I rolled my eyes. People forget that the Secret Service is charged with two missions. The first is to protect high-ranking American politicians and political candidates – from the President on down – as well as any foreign dignitaries on American soil. The other is to protect our currency.

Back when I was starting out with the Service, that meant stopping counterfeiters. This included everyone from kids scanning and printing out new twenties with their home computers, all the way up to hostile nations using top-of-the-line printing presses to deflate the value of the American dollar. As the world moved over to virtual currency, the Service moved with it. We went from raiding downtown print shops to tracking down malicious hackers around the world.

I'd gone back and forth between both sides of the Service. Every time I saved a President and came back, they rewarded me by transferring me back to currency control again. I hated it there. I preferred to protect people instead of numbers. Still, I always understood and went along with it.

The truth was my bosses didn't see the value of putting a high-profile agent in close proximity to a high-value protectee. Pinning a Medal of Honor on my chest made me a juicy media target, and no politician likes to be upstaged by someone who's supposed to be blending into the background. Not even the President. Maybe especially not.

Plus, it made me as much of a target as the people I was supposed to be protecting. There's something about being the world's oldest man that lures the loons off the lake. They start figuring that they can make a name for themselves by snuffing my trick candle, even if only for a day. I'd be perfectly happy to draw fire from my charges, but the thought that a bullet meant for me might find one of them drains all the utility from that.

After a decade or three went by, though, my fame always faded back into a multiply-cited footnote in history. Then my perpetual request for a transfer back into the personal protection side of the Service would finally go though.

This time, however, I'd been killed while working the currency side of the business. I wondered if this meant I'd be moved back to the President's detail soon. First, I had a murderer to find.

"What about the tongue?" I asked. "Why did they take that?"

Querer shrugged. "They command a nice price on the black market. Not as much as the eyes, sure, but enough to make it worthwhile."

I frowned. "But why not render down the rest of me? Why just the tongue?"

Querer took a shot in the dark. "They didn't want you to talk?"

I grunted. "More like they wanted something to prove they'd killed me. A trophy."

Querer screwed up her face, disgusted. "They could have done that with a hair sample or a few drops of blood."

"You don't understand trophy hunters, do you?"

"If you think someone would want to make a trophy out of you, you must think an awful lot of yourself."

I cracked a dry smile. "I have to. No one else does."

I'd seen many things more horrifying than a killer taking tongues. I decided to count myself lucky that it hadn't been worse for me.

Querer looked at me as if I were a purposefully dull child. "Your schedule for the evening contradicts you."

I squinted at her, confused. Then I called up my schedule and saw an event tagged to one of the urgent notices still flashing in my inbox. It read: "7pm: Re-birthday Party at the White House, at the President's Request. Attendance Mandatory."

I cursed. Querer, to her credit, did not blush.

"I don't have time for this," I said.

"We don't," Querer said, "but we will." She leaned forward in her seat, all business now. "I've set up contacts with the DC Chief of Police and the director of his forensics team. They would be happy to meet with us at our pleasure. I've also arranged for access to the crime scene."

She flicked her eyes to her upper right. "I estimate we have enough time to make one contact before your event tonight."

I stood up and headed for the door, not caring if she followed. "Fine," I said, "but I have to make one stop first."

FOUR

The sun still rode high in the sky over Arlington National Cemetery as the sleek black Secret Service hovercar set down near the Eternal Flame. The expansive array of tiny white tombstones stretched out around us in all directions, each like immutable books that told an abbreviated story of the hero interred below. Low green robots that looked like small circular hovercraft mowed the grass between the markers, and a few other visitors roamed among the aisles formed by the white stones: tourists and mourners, some with flowers, others with prayers. One was taking gravestone rubbings of faded numbers and letters with a sheet of vellum and a charcoal stick that had turned her fingers the color of wet ash.

After the autopilot completed its parkdown, the hovercar's hatch released with a soft, pneumatic hiss, and I slipped out of the passenger compartment. I turned around and offered Querer a hand out. She stared at it for a moment before accepting it with a faint smile. We walked away from the car, and the hatch slid closed behind us.

I let my feet lead me down a familiar path that snaked through the markers, taking care not to tread upon the well-trimmed patches of green lawn above the dead. I kept my eyes on the ground as I went, trusting in over a century of habitual visits to steer me toward my goal.

Over all my years, I'd made and lost a lot of friends – and enemies, too, I supposed. Some of them I could barely picture, like candles guttering in the night wind, although I'd worked alongside them for years. Others burned like torches in my mind, illuminating signposts along the road of my life. Colleen Gallagher Dooley – my first and only wife – was the bonfire to which I always returned.

"You realize that this might make you late for your party with the President?" Querer said as she ambled after me.

I didn't even bother to shrug. "They can start without me. They have before. As long as I show up before they cut the cake."

"Ever missed that?"

I smiled to myself. "Just once. Never again."

"What happened?"

I glanced back at her, wondering if she really wanted to hear the story. She gave me a curious gesture that said, "Well?"

"Patrón made it clear that he could and would revoke the unique position of honor I hold in the Service should I ever again neglect to at least feign appreciation for it. I took him at his word."

"But how could you miss a party like that? All those

powerful people gathered to honor you? That could turn a girl's head."

I bowed my head and considered my answer. "The President is just a person. A very powerful person who means a great deal to a large number of people, true. But the party is just another in a long string of photo-ops for her."

"And?"

"And I wanted to spend my first night back among the living with a very un-powerful person who meant very little to anyone else but everything to me."

"So," Querer said, "you always come here? A grave-yard seems like a strange place to celebrate a long life."

I let out a whisper of a laugh. "It only seems that way to the young."

We walked the rest of the way in silence.

When I finally reached Colleen's grave, I raised my eyes and skidded to a halt on the dry green grass. A boy – a young man, really, but then everyone's younger than me – stood there on Colleen's grave, half-leaning and half-sitting on her tombstone.

I had my pistol out before I could think about it, leveled right at the kid's brain.

Querer followed my lead without hesitation. "Secret Service," she barked out. "Freeze!"

In all the times I'd come to visit my wife's grave over the past hundred years, no one had ever been there to meet me. At first, in the decade after Colleen had died, my son Cal had come with me, and for the first few times he'd brought his wife and kids too. When Cal got sick, though, his family rallied around him instead, choosing the living over the dead, for which I could hardly blame them. A couple of the grandkids had kept up the tradition after his cancer took him, but as they got older their visits became sparser and eventually stopped altogether.

Querer dropped her voice another octave and shouted at the boy again. "Get on your knees!"

Once, a woman I'd been dating had come here with me. She'd broken down crying later and soon after had told me she couldn't see me again. She told me she couldn't stand the thought of being just another road bump on the eternal highway of my life. I tried to explain to her that it wasn't anything like that, but she wouldn't listen. Maybe she couldn't.

I understood. It's hard watching the same powerful and popular people in the news looking the same every damn year – better and better, even – while you get older and weaker and fumble your way closer to death.

I always try to stay in the same skin for as long as I can, but some hollow-headed celebrities euthanize themselves every decade or so just to keep themselves looking young and fresh. Some of the most notorious hold suicide parties one day and rebirthday parties the next. Others just live recklessly enough to ensure that they wind up in a new body often enough to seem relevant to the next generation that comes along. When you have the wealth of several generations' worth of your own life behind you, it's not hard to figure out new and dangerous ways to spend it.

Only the rare friend had dared to come here with me since then. Patrón did once, the first time I was reborn after he became director. It made him so morose he swore he'd never repeat it again. But no one had ever been waiting here for me in over a hundred years.

The boy let his legs crumple beneath him. Then he fell forward onto his hands. Querer came around behind him, her gun in a two-handed grip aimed at the base of his skull.

The kid looked up at me, his wide gray eyes pleading for aid. He was tall and rangy with short blond hair, his skin sun-scorched to a burnished pink. He had a twitchy way about him, as if his hide was a hair too tight for him and he needed to stretch it out. But maybe that was just panic from the two loaded pistols trained on him.

"Don't shoot!" he said. "Don't shoot!"

I tapped the law enforcement data layer and requested an ID. My lenses scanned his face, and the response flicked into my vision an instant later. The kid was seventeen years old. He lived with his parents in Alexandria, Virginia, just a few miles away. He was a good student with excellent grades and no history of run-ins with the law. According to his DMV records, he was six feet tall and a hundred and seventy pounds. He had no scars or tattoos, but a slight astigmatism in his right eye that had been genetically corrected at six years of age.

His name was Ronan Dooley VI.

I nearly dropped my gun. "Hold it!" I said, waving off Querer.

I flicked my eyes to toss the ID feed to her server. She gasped, then stared at me, her mouth gaping open.

"Grandpa?" the boy said.

I holstered my gun and helped the boy to his feet. He had grass stains on his knees but was otherwise unharmed. I aimed to see he stayed that way.

Querer lowered her sidearm but kept it in her hand. I shot her a nasty look, but she ignored it.

I put a hand on the boy's shoulder and stared at him. "What are you doing here?" It wasn't a great question, but at that moment it was all I had.

The boy shrugged. "I don't know. I just– I just wanted to meet you." He squinted up at me. "My whole life, I've never seen you once, not outside of a thrid. When I saw the news about you getting killed again, I figured this was my chance."

My first impulse was to gather the boy into my arms for a hug. I fought that. He might have been named after me, but he had sixty-three other ancestors with as much a claim to him as I did. Less than two percent of my blood ran through his veins.

Being suspicious is a Secret Service agent's occupational hazard. You never know what kind of threat you might have to face next, so you guard against everything – especially odd bits like distant direct relatives showing up unannounced.

"Would you like to introduce me?" Querer said.

I realized I'd been staring at the boy for a long while without either of us saying anything. I cleared my throat.

"I would," I said, "but I don't know him myself."

"I'm your grandson." Irritation and frustration welled up in the kid's voice.

"You're my great-great-great-great-grandson," I said. "Six generations removed."

"You say that like it's not far enough," the kid said.

I took my hand from his shoulder and sighed. "It's not personal, kid. I never knew your father or grandfather either. I only met your great-grandfather a few times. We didn't get along."

"So you just cut us all out of your life?" Tears welled up in the kid's eyes, threatening to spill down cheeks flushed red under his sunburn.

I tried to think of something to say. I hadn't cut anyone out of my life, but then again I hadn't made much of an effort to reach out to my descendants either. "It's not like that."

"Then how is it?"

It was my turn to shrug. "Three didn't care much for the government. Those were hard years, and he was out there protesting the Pacific Rim War."

I gazed out over the tombstones spreading away from me in all directions. The cemetery had grown so much since I was a boy. There were huge parts of it I couldn't even see. "He wasn't much older than you, but to him I represented the establishment. He hated me for that, and I never could talk any sense into him."

"Three?" Querer asked.

"That's what the family called him when we got together. Too many Ronans around otherwise."

The kid got up into my face. "What about Four and Five?" he asked. "Why didn't you ever talk with them? Great-grandpa's been gone a long time."

He didn't voice his real question: "What about me?" But I heard it anyhow.

"I–" I started to explain that it was just easier not to deal with it. For a pacifist, Three kept strict control over his kids. I never got to say a word to Four in his entire life. I'd met Five, but just in passing.

None of that really mattered now, especially to the kid standing before me at that moment. To him, I'd been a foolish old man who'd let his family get away from him, and I couldn't really tell him he was wrong. There was only one thing I could say.

"Six." I looked him in the eyes to see how he'd react to that name. A ghost of a grin crossed his lips. "I'm sorry."

The grin grew. He reached out and pulled me into an embrace that made me realize that my new body wasn't all that much larger than his. Apparently my offspring had been breeding well. I hugged him back.

"Hey," Querer said, finally holstering her gun, "if he's six generations down from you, how come he's Ronan Dooley the Sixth? If you're the first, shouldn't he be the Seventh?"

"My son's name was Cal. He named his boy Ronan the Second."

"To honor you?" Querer said.

I nodded. "That was back when the family members who were still alive would speak to me."

She grunted. "I don't think the rest of them hated you as much as you believed."

"How's that?" said Six. "My dad told me to never try to meet Grandpa."

"Sure," said Querer, "but he named you after him anyhow."

FIVE

After Querer finally put her gun away, she insisted on hauling me off to the DC Police Station right away. I went along with that, but only after whispering a few private words over Colleen's grave.

Six begged me not to tell his father about coming to see me. I consented to that, but I made him promise to catch up with me later. "Once this murder investigation is over, I should be able to make plenty of time," I said. "I have something like a decade of unused vacation."

"In the meantime," said Querer, "you have an engagement at the White House tonight, so let's move."

I gave Six a hug. "Thanks," I told him.

"For what?" he asked, as I followed Querer back to the hovercar.

"For being braver than me," I called back over my shoulder.

He stood there and waved good-bye as the autopilot pushed us into the air and sent us scudding away over the cemetery and toward downtown DC. I didn't feel much like talking, and Querer didn't push me. I just stared out the window and watched the city slide by below us.

DC had changed a lot since I had first come to the city back in the 1980s. The zoning code that no building could stand higher than the Capitol's dome, though, had stayed the same for most of that time, despite the fact that the city's population had grown by orders of magnitude since that law had been laid down. For decades, this meant that the DC metro region had sprawled far outside of its original borders. Since the developers couldn't build up, they had to build out. Commutes took hours to get people from the places they could afford to live to the places they worked.

Some architects had experimented with driving their buildings deep into the ground, but when you're dealing with a city that borders on a major waterway like the Potomac, you can only go so far down before you wind up below the water table.

The city planners looked around then and discovered that they'd been looking right at a huge amount of unoccupied real estate without knowing it: the area over the city's streets. They started extending the buildings across the streets to meet each other, burying the roads beneath several floors of housing, offices, restaurants, bars, and stores. Today, there's barely a bit of DC fully exposed to the sky unless it's part of a park or some other open public space like the Mall. Even large parts of the Potomac have been bridged over.

The top of the city, though, is far from a smooth, uniform surface. About forty years back, the city did away with the building height code, and skyscrapers shot up out of the cityscape like sharp silvery blades stabbing through a rotting body. The Secret Service had long stood as the main opponent to skyscrapers in the city's limits, claiming that the new buildings gave snipers too many angles at the White House. The rise of hovercars put a dagger through the heart of that argument, though, and Patrón eventually gave in.

Even in the areas not plagued with sky-blotting towers, some of the lower rooftops in the better parts of town feature acre-large penthouses. As you range farther away, though, squatters take over the flat-roofed buildings, living in temporary structures of fiberboard and corrugated steel that have stood there for decades. That marks where the mortals live, the people who can't afford the pricey rebirth insurance that gives the wealthy as many new chances at life as they like. People like Six and his parents and the rest of his relatives. People like I used to be – and would be again if I ever decided to retire.

The hovercar requested and received permission to set down, then slipped into an open berth in the landing zone on top of the New Daly Building. As the interior door to the berth irised open before us, my directions layer kicked in, and a bright orange stripe on the floor illuminated my path. Querer and I got out of the car and followed the stripe straight to the police chief's office.

When we finally arrived, it was just after 5pm, and I harbored a fleeting hope that Chief Adamson might have already left for the day. No such luck.

"She's in, and she's expecting you," said her administrative assistant, a dumpy, balding man with a silver fringe of remaining hair and a constant wheeze. "She's in the middle of a meeting at the moment, though, and cannot be disturbed."

I ignored him and strode on in. The door gave me a bit of grief for a moment, refusing to slide aside for me. I called up my Secret Service rank on my lens display and flashed it at the door. It hissed out of my way.

I stepped into the chief's office to find Adamson sitting alone behind a massive mahogany desk on top of which not a single item other than her hands sat. She was a trim woman with flawless coffee-colored skin, dark curly hair, and crimson lips framing snow-white teeth. In my youth, I would have figured her more for a model than an eighty-year veteran of the police department. Today, she was just another amortal.

Her eyes were blank, staring into the virtual distance as she held a group thridconference with several people visible only in her lens implants. She continued talking and waved a hand at us, indicating that we should sit in one of the semicircle of six overstuffed chairs opposite her. Querer seated herself, but I continued to stand.

The room looked like a museum display and felt just about as lived in. The walls and ceiling were paneled in dark oak, and painted portraits of former chiefs looked down at Adamson's desk from every angle. Their faces had moved to follow Querer and me as we entered the place, but now they remained fixated on

Adamson, proclaiming her the most important person
in the room.

A wall-sized thridscreen behind Adamson showed a
live view of the Capitol looming over her. It looked as
if it were right across the street, despite the fact it was
several blocks away. The sky over the Statue of Freedom that jutted from the top of the dome had been
doctored to remove any hint of pollution, leaving it far
bluer than it ever really looked, and the American flag
that it held, instead of its traditional sword, snapped in
a non-existent breeze. I'd seen the same thing piped
into other offices all around the city. It supposedly lent
the room a patriotic atmosphere that somehow rubbed
off on its owner. I just found it depressing.

"You'll have to excuse me, Senators," Adamson
said. "I have an urgent police matter to attend to. A
new development regarding the Dooley murder. I'll
make sure to keep your streams fed."

She nodded politely, said her good-byes, and flashed
a winning smile, then ended the conference with a
slap of her hand on her pristine desktop. Her beatific
face fell into a disgusted scowl as her eyes finally
snapped into focus on Querer and me.

"Where have you been?" Adamson ignored Querer
and glared only at me. "I have a police force to run
here, and I can't spend an entire afternoon waiting for
a failure of a Secret Service agent to show up, no matter how famous he might be."

I knew ignoring her anger would only make her
madder, so that's exactly what I did. "So good to see
you again too, Adamson."

"You think you're the only amortal who's ever been murdered, Dooley? Trying to add 'Most Fatal Mistakes Made' to your other world records doesn't impress me."

I raised my hands before me and shrugged. "So now we're blaming the victim. How very cop of you."

"The *habitual* victim. I'm picking out a pattern here."

"At the request of the Department of Homeland Security, the Secret Service will be taking command of the investigation from here," Querer said.

"See," I said to Adamson, "it's not your problem anymore."

She didn't look relieved. "Just you saying that doesn't make it so, Dooley. Does the Service have the staff-hours to devote to solving this? No. So you'll waste my people's time instead."

Querer edged forward on her seat. "We'll try to make this as painless as possible. We all want a quick resolution here. From the President on down."

Tapping Adamson with the President's name sat her back in her chair. "All right," she said with a resigned sigh. "Let's get this over with."

Her gaze unfocused for a moment. "I'm opening our case files for you and giving you full admin access to all aspects of the investigation. The limited resources of the Metropolitan Police Department are available at your request."

"We'll need to see the crime scene," said Querer. My stomach flipped at that. I've seen a lot of murder sites and have even seen my own corpse enough to be jaded to it. After seeing that thrid, though, I had no desire to check out the place where it had happened.

That didn't matter. We had to do it.

I swallowed before I confronted the next unpleasantry. "I'd like to talk with the forensics team and the morgue too."

Adamson's lips pulled back in a wry, fake smile. "Talk all you like. You're not going to like the answers on this one."

She sat back in her chair and put her feet up on her spotless desk, showing off her perfectly sculpted legs. "Honestly, I'm fine with the Service taking over on this one. We ran smack into a wall already. Whoever did this really knew what she was doing."

"She?" I said. The killer had seemed male to me.

"She, he, it – whatever." Adamson threw her hands into the air. "It doesn't matter. You're not going to solve this one."

"You seem awfully confident of that," said Querer, bristling against the chief's claim.

Adamson put her feet back on the floor, leaned her elbows on her desk, and started counting off reasons.

"One: we scoured the room. The only fresh DNA in it is yours, Dooley.

"Two: the voice was professionally scrambled. Our best software can't unmangle it to a state from which we can identify it.

"Three: to top all that off, the murder weapon was registered to one Ronan Dooley."

I grunted. "Sounds like the perfect murder."

"What about gait recognition?" asked Querer.

Adamson shrugged. "The killer has a way of walking, sure, but we came up empty for matches."

"The clean suit could have masked enough of that," I said. "Or he might have just put pebbles in his shoes."

"Olfactory?" Querer asked.

Adamson shook her head. "Only scent in the room came from Dooley."

"What about the clean suit?" I asked. "Any line on that?"

"Sure," said Adamson, "Dozens. Clean suits are cheap, and after that dirty bomb took out the Library of Congress on 4/11, everyone has one."

"Even in black?" I asked.

Adamson smirked at me. "How far in the past do you live, Dooley? Clean suits were a huge fad after that. You can get them in any color you want. Fashion prints too. My great-great-granddaughter has one that looks like LEGO Princess Peach." She shook her head at me. "You never fail to surprise me with how archaic you can be."

That caught me short. I changed tactics. "I was working with the MPD before I died. What was the investigation about?"

Adamson's eyes flew wide, and she goggled at me. "Are you serious? The Ancient Agent forgot to back up his memory for that long?" She stifled a laugh, then turned serious. "How much are you missing?"

"Just over three months," I said.

Her jaw dropped. "So you don't remember any of this? At all? Poking at the Kalis? Them poking back?"

I grimaced with regret.

She smacked her head then gave me a disbelieving smile. "Priceless." Her eyes flicked about again. "Did you back up any of the data you collected? Nothing?"

"The killer took my eyes."

Her grin shivered away. "Right. I'll send you every bit of data from my team, including all of your correspondence with us." She stared at me with a wry frown. "Sadly, you never were any good about writing reports."

A glowing red notice popped into my peripheral vision. The President's chief of staff wanted to know why I had yet to show up to the party being held in my honor and wondered aloud how attached I was to my job.

I tapped Querer on the arm. "We have to go."

Adamson dismissed us with a wave. "Sure. Go shake some hands. Drink some taxpayer-funded champagne." She looked at me with dead eyes. "Not like you have anything better to do."

SIX

By the time I walked into the White House, my re-birthday party was in full swing. The Secret Service uniformed agents assigned to guard duty at the entrance scanned me body and soul and let me through.

I turned to leave Querer at the guard station to cool her heels. "The invite's tagged 'Amortals Only.'"

She cocked her head at me. "Are you going to use that as an excuse to ditch me whenever you like?"

"I'm sure I can come up with something else on the fly." I looked her up and down. "Besides, you're not exactly dressed for a White House party, are you?"

She arched an eyebrow at that. "And you are?"

I looked down at my regulation suit and tie.

"I'm trying to do you a favor," I said. "These events are dull enough to make you pray for an assassination attempt just to break things up."

The uniforms grimaced at my awful joke.

"Are you done trying to dissuade me?" Querer said.

I sighed. "I guess I am." I put out my arm for her, and she took it.

"This doesn't make me your date," she said. "I'm here as your partner."

"Is that what the kids are calling it these days?"

She had the decency to blush.

One of the uniforms, a gray-haired vet named Kingsman, took the initiative to hustle us to the East Room for the event. There are a number of rooms that would have worked for a party like this, but the East Room was the largest on the grounds. My last two re-welcomings had taken place in the State Dining Room, but the White House apparently wanted to step up its game for this one.

I knew the White House better than I knew my condo, and I could have walked to the East Room blindfolded. I hadn't been assigned to the Presidential detail for more than a decade, though, so most of the current White House staff wouldn't recognize me by other than reputation. Letting Kingsman play boy scout for me greased the way through.

An old-timey thrash-swing band was playing a bad cover of "Forever Young" when we entered the room, but no one was dancing. Instead, the guests milled about, chatting idly with each other, while the domestic staff made the rounds with hors d'oeuvres and drinks. As Querer and I entered, Kingsman left us with the Chief Usher, Ben Irvine, whom I'd known for decades. He'd started here back when I was in charge of President Westwood's detail, and he knew I wouldn't want a big entrance.

That didn't stop him for a second. Ben cut the music with a wave of his hand, and the crowd graciously hushed to a murmur.

With my ID layer engaged, I scanned the names hovering over the faces of everyone I could see. With the exception of the servants – and Querer, of course – everyone in the room was amortal. Captains of industry, financial robber barons, media stars, idle Trustafarians: most of them were worth more than I'd made in the whole of my very long life.

Ben cleared his throat, and his voice tapped into the band's sound system. Despite his years, his words rang out strong and clear.

"Ladies and gentlemen! I am pleased to present to you the man whose rebirth we have gathered to celebrate here tonight: the infamous Ronan Dooley!"

The crowd burst into a round of enthusiastic applause. I fixed my best sheepish grin on my face and snapped off a jaunty wave. Over a century of extremely public service had taught me to be on my best behavior whenever the spotlight turned my way, no matter how hot it might feel.

Half the people here were likely recording this moment straight through their optic implants to their onboard nanoservers. Most of them would stream it to the web as soon as they left the White House and were out from under the mandatory media blackout the place labored beneath at all times, press conferences excepted. I knew better than to grouse in front of them.

"Speech," a man I recognized as a recently reborn thrid star said. He'd gone straight to the cosmetic surgeon from the Amortals Project and had himself sculpted into his version of the trendiest look in the land. At the moment, that meant skin that swam with epidermal nanobots that subtly shifted color on the fly to make him look more handsome in any light. That included absolute darkness, in which his skin could swirl and glow.

Others took up his chant, and it spread like a weaponized virus. They were liquored up, bored, and ready for anything to break up the monotony of their night.

"Speech! Speech!"

A note from Ben flashed into the center of my vision: "Not until POTUS arrives. ETA: < 5 minutes."

I wasn't about to upstage the big boss. I'd hoped to arrive after her to cut down on the chit-chat, but it seemed I hadn't dragged my feet hard enough. I swallowed my instinct to get this over with as fast as possible, and I let the chant build for a half a minute before I motioned the crowd to silence.

"Thank you all for coming. I appreciate all the good wishes and warm thoughts that have been flooding my inbox all day long."

I paused for a moment before I lowered the boom and told them they'd have to wait just a bit. Before I could say another word, though, Querer stepped forward and spoke.

"As you might imagine, Mr Dooley has had a very busy day." She flashed me a winning smile. "I'll be happy to release him to say a few words soon, but first we need to get some food in him – and maybe a drink!"

The crowd cheered at that, and the servants burst into action, distributing fresh glasses of champagne for the traditional toast they knew would be coming soon. Patrón stepped forward to shake my hand and drag me into the crowd, making me a part of it rather than the object of its attention, at least for a moment.

"Well done," he said to me. "What's she doing here?"

I glanced at Querer, who did not flinch at the director's bluntness. "She's my plus one."

"The invitations didn't mention anything about guests," Patrón said with the kind of smile alligators flashed when they were hungry. "If they had, my wife would have insisted on coming along too."

"Whose party is this again?"

Patrón nodded. "Fair enough." He finally turned to Querer. "Keep helping him out of trouble like that, and I might think about making this partnership more permanent."

Before I could stifle a groan, I heard Ben clear his throat again. Along with the rest of the crowd, I turned toward him. With a smile on his face, he said, "Ladies and gentlemen, please join me in welcoming the First Gentleman and the President of the United States."

The band struck up a jazzy "Hail to the Chief," and the crowd gathered together a polite round of applause as President Gina Oberon proceeded into the room with her husband by her side. She showed all her perfect white teeth as her hand bobbled atop her wrist in a homecoming queen's wave. Her not-quite-too-handsome husband stood by her proudly, his wide brown eyes only for her as he played the model of the doting spouse.

The first thing about this President that always struck me the few times I'd met her before this was how tall she was. The thrids always shot every President from a low angle, emphasizing their power, no matter what their height might be. In person, though, President Oberon's presence filled the place in a way no thrid could capture. I could actually feel the tenor of the East Room change the moment she walked into it.

She had been a reporter in a previous life – one of the best – and that had brought her the kind of riches that she needed to attain amortality. Couple that with a wealthy husband with political ambitions of his own, and they made an unbeatable team. Rumor had it that he would run to replace her when her current term expired.

He certainly had the experience for it. Despite his apparent age, he was nearly as old as me. He'd held one of the Louisiana senate seats for over eighty years before resigning to help the President run her campaign.

The music ended, along with the applause, and the President launched into her speech.

"Friends and fellow Americans, we gather here today not to mourn the passage of an old hero but to welcome him back into the next stage of his life."

She paused to smile at me as Querer pushed me forward to stand on the other side of the President from her husband. The crowd applauded again.

"Ronan Dooley is a true American patriot. It was

Nathan Hale, America's first secret agent, who said, 'I only regret that I have but one life to give for my country.' Mr Dooley has given his life for America a total of eight times, proving his bravery, his selflessness, and his loyalty each and every time."

The President held out her hand, and Ben stepped forward to fill it with a flute of champagne. Other servants scurried about, making sure that everyone else in the room had a glass of the bubbly too. A white grape sat at the bottom of each drink.

The President held her glass high and spoke.

"Please join me in a toast to Mr Dooley. No matter how many times he may come back to us, he could never be replaced."

"Hear, hear," said Patrón.

We each tossed back the champagne in a single gulp. The grape in the bottom of my glass tumbled into my mouth, where I caught it, ate it, and spit the seeds back into the flute, as was the tradition. The seeds represented the rebirth of one life as the current grape's life came to an end.

Silence held the room for a moment as everyone else joined in.

"Let's hear it for Ronan Dooley," the President said. "America could use more of his kind of hero."

A real cheer went up from the crowd, and I have to admit I blushed. As a Secret Service agent, I don't seek the spotlight. I'm used to blending into the background and protecting my charges while they soak up the glory. Being the focus of so much attention makes me feel like I have a target painted on my forehead.

The President shook my hand, and a message tagged POTUS flashed across my vision: "Say a few words."

I forced a smile onto my face and waited for the noise to die down. I gazed out at the faces in the crowd and saw every eye in the room on me, both mortal and amortal alike. A hush fell across the place.

"Thank you," I said. "Thank you all for coming here and – with the able assistance of the staff of the Amortals Project – helping an old man feel younger than he has in years."

The crowd laughed and clapped for me again. Then the President stepped in front of me to shake my hand once more, signaling that the ceremonial portion of the party was over. The staff burst back into their well-oiled team action, and the guests returned to their drinks and their conversations.

"Well done, Dooley," the President said to me. "It's almost like you've been through all this before."

"More than several times, I'm afraid, Madame President."

She smiled at me. "And I'm afraid I have to leave the festivities early. Duty calls. But I want you to remain here and enjoy yourself for as long as you like. You're to stay in the Lincoln Bedroom tonight."

This was something new. Since I came back the first time, the sitting President had always done something to mark my return, but this was my first invitation to spend the night in the White House as a guest instead of an employee.

"I don't want to put you out, Madame President."

"Say 'thank you,' Dooley. But don't think that this

is entirely altruistic on my part."

"Of course not," I said. "You're a politician after all."

Her lips parted in a real smile at that. They hesitated at first, as if they had almost forgotten how to manage it.

"Director Patrón tells me that DC's CSI technicians are analyzing your place tonight for clues to your murder. I want to give them all the time they need to make sure they gather all the evidence they can. Then I want this case solved yesterday."

I narrowed my eyes at her. "I'm touched by the concern, Madame President. I have every confidence we'll be able to wrap the case up soon."

"That's good, Dooley, because the media spin on this is already tumbling out of control. The most popular position is that your death makes for the worst case of mortal-on-amortal violence in history, and it's conjured up all kinds of vivid revenge fantasies of the sort I cannot have stewing in the public consciousness. I want that meme crushed before any *other* psychopaths decide to pick up on it."

She leaned in as if to speak confidentially, but her volume made it clear that she wanted other people in the room to hear her. "Find this killer, and wipe out every last trace of his DNA. By this time next week, I don't want people to even remember that they forgot about him."

I raised an eyebrow at this. A vindictive smirk curled the corner of the President's deep red lips.

"And yes," she said. "That is an order."

SEVEN

Querer came by the next morning to pick me up and haul me back out to the New Daly Building. Kingsman escorted me from the Lincoln Bedroom straight to her waiting hovercar.

"For someone who had so much fun last night, you look like you're feeling fine," Querer said as I slipped into the seat opposite her.

"One of the many benefits of youth," I said. "Last week, having that much to drink would have put me down for the entire next morning."

"And today?"

I allowed myself a wide smile. "I feel fine."

She gave her head a wry shake. "Must be nice."

As we rose into the air, I peered down at the crowd of protesters massed outside of the White House gates. Protesters always drove me nuts when I was on protection detail. I respected their right to voice an opinion, but putting angry, passionate people that close to the White House forever made me nervous.

"It's such a beautiful summer day," I said as I stared

down at them. "What could they be mad about today?"

"Not 'what?', 'Who?'"

"All right," I said, confused. "I'll bite. Who?"

Querer sighed. "You, of course."

"What?"

I leaned closer to the window to get a better look at the slogan-wavers as we moved away. The thrid displays they toted about – looping images on transparent plastic strung between plastic rods spread over their shoulders – showed a short thrid of me being blown away. It played over and over again. As the life bled out of me, gleaming text flicked onto the screen.

Every one of the signs seemed to have a different slogan. They included:

"ONE LIFE TO LIVE!"

"COPY ≠ ORIGINAL"

"AMORTALS = AMORAL"

"GOD HATES COPYCATS"

"NO MORE RONANS!"

And my favorite:

"ABOUT. DAMN. TIME."

Querer shook her head in sympathy for me. "Don't let it bother you, Dooley. Next week, there will be a whole new crop of lunatics marching out there against something else."

I scoffed at that. "I used to think that. But then I hadn't just been murdered at the time."

"You think your killing was a political statement?"

"Either that or something close enough to be turned into one."

I gestured for the hovercar to take a quick spin around the block. The airspace over the White House and every other important political building in the city was restricted, which meant it was empty but for an occasional congressional or staff vehicle zipping through. Compared to the way the skies over the rest of the DC were clogged with traffic that often blotted out the sun, it made the White House seem like an island of sanity amid all the chaos.

I concentrated on the main group of protesters and blinked. My eyesight zoomed in on the leaders, including a Roman Catholic priest dressed in the traditional black suit and notched white collar. He was an old man, clean shaven with a shock of white hair. My ID layer tagged him as Father Luke Gustavo, a militant papist with a dumpfile of priors ranging from protesting without a permit to resisting arrest.

"Father G," I said. "We meet again."

"You know their leader?"

I looked at Querer. "I was raised Catholic."

She scanned me up and down. "You don't seem much that way any more."

"As they say, I'm a recovering Catholic. I have my first century pin, and I'm going for my second. Not that they would have me back anyhow, even if I wanted to return to the fold."

Querer squinted at me for an instant, than realized what I meant. "They don't consider you to be you. Aren't all amortals automatically excommunicated? Or do they go straight for the exorcism these days?"

Ruefulness welled up in me. "They don't excommunicate us. They believe we're scientific abominations, but they don't blame us – just the scientists at the Amortals Project."

"Hate the sinner, not the sin."

I pressed my nose against the inside of the hovercar's window and stared down at the flock of protesters. The way they clustered together reminded me of a virus in a Petri dish.

"Something like that. Some amortals return to the church after every rebirth to be baptized again and to receive their first communion. As if they hadn't signed revivification orders. As if they were brand-new people who just happen to have the body and mind of someone else."

"And you're not?"

I shrugged. "It sure doesn't feel that way."

I made another gesture, and the hovercar zipped into the buzzing traffic, becoming part of the chaos once more.

When we reached the Metropolitan Police Department Headquarters, we took the elevator straight down to the forensics lab. It was a large, cold room buried deep in the basement levels, lit by scattered pools of dazzling fluorescents that mimicked daylight. Technicians stood hunched over monitors, microscanners, and more, trying to tease clues out of every scrap of data they could collect.

The head CSI technician was Paul Winding, a balding, middle-aged man with a beer belly he'd earned by making a determined effort to drown out what he saw at work every day, like a sack of kittens tossed in the Potomac. I'd never seen him smile. He nodded at us as we came in.

"You made a real mess of yourself this time, Dooley," he said. "I don't know who you pissed off, but you drove him to push the boundaries of homicidal excellence."

"What do you mean by that?" asked Querer.

Paul glanced at her. I could see him scanning her ID to figure out who she was. Satisfied, he answered.

"In my forty years in this lab, I've never seen such a clean crime scene. The killer knew his business inside out. We have nearly zero clues."

I pursed my lips into a doubting shape. "That's what Adamson said yesterday, but I figured you were just feeding her a line to make your eventual triumphs seem that much more impressive."

"I'm not above that," said Paul. "You know that. But that's not the case here."

"Run down the list for us."

"The only fingerprints in the room are yours."

"The killer was wearing a clean suit," said Querer.

Paul speared her with a murderous glare that warned her to not interrupt him to tell him how to do his job. He was being didactic and thorough, but that was how he'd come to run the entire department: by not missing a thing.

Querer shut her mouth.

"The only blood in the room is yours. In fact, the only decent DNA in the room is yours. We vacuumed the place clean and there was nothing in it but bits of you."

Paul seemed to think back on this, then shrugged. "Some far larger than others."

He continued, "We were unable to unscramble your assailant's voice. However, jacking the audio way up past eleven and then refining it allowed us to determine where the crime had been committed. That's how we located the crime scene and recovered your body."

"The killer didn't just tag the thrid?" I asked.

Paul snorted. "All we had to go on was the thrideo, which was released to the public with the geographic information stripped. At first, we wondered if the entire event had been one large hoax. It's easy enough to mock up a show like that using consumer rigs these days. My grandkids could do it. But we were able to isolate very faint background noises and compare them against communications traffic flowing through the city during the same period of time."

"You compared the sounds against every captured audio communications in the city?"

"Just until we found a match."

Paul made a gesture, and a wallscreen behind me leaped to life. Querer and I turned to see a live thrid appear. A DC squad hovercar sat parked in front of a run-down storefront that faced out onto one of the cramped pedestrian malls that snaked through every level of the city. The edges of the storefront glowed yellow on the wallscreen, indicating to any who might see it through lens implants that the place was a crime scene. The police had shot yellow tape across the windows at several odd angles to provide untethered citizens the same warning.

A dead neon sign in one of the storefront's two windows offered the services of "Madame Fate. Fortunes Told. Futures Seen." A virtual sign overlaid the other window, flashing the logo of the real estate agency charged with selling the place. I concentrated on an icon in the corner of the sign, and the place's listing information leaped into my vision. The building had been foreclosed on three years ago and had been on the market since.

"That's Georgetown," I said

Paul gave me a grim nod of approval.

"After we found it, our team went in to collect every bit of evidence we could find, but as I've mentioned, the pickings were slim. Someone let loose a bleach bomb in the place sometime in the past week, and then set a homovorous robot to scour every surface with a UV laser spread to zap away even the germs left behind. Did a good job too and consumed itself completely for fuel in the process.

"Olfactory scans picked up little out of the ordinary for the neighborhood: fuel fumes, cigarette smoke, urine, scents from roaming food vendors. However, we did detect a concentration of certain gastric gases in the room. They indicate that the killer dined on chicken vindaloo sometime within the previous twenty-four hours."

"I like vindaloo," I said. "You sure that wasn't me?"

Paul shook his head. "The autopsy turned up absolutely nothing in your digestive system."

"Killed on an empty stomach," Querer said. "How cruel."

I ignored her. I asked Paul the question I always hated most. I didn't want to do it, but there was no point in putting it off any longer.

"Can I see the body?"

Paul, who had seen more of death than any mortal I knew, blanched. "You don't have to do that, Dooley." His voice was barely more than a whisper. He cleared his throat. "My team has gone over it from scalp to plantar fascia."

"No," I said slowly. "I really think I do."

I needed to do this for a whole host of reasons, one of which – I admitted to myself – was to crank up my sense of righteous outrage at the way I'd been treated. I had to screw it all the way up to the sticking place to make sure my need to follow through on this would never falter. It would be too easy to let this terrify me into letting someone else handle it, and that was something I could not bear.

Paul nodded his resignation rather than trying to argue the point with me. He beckoned us to follow him, then led us down a wide set of stairs that terminated in a pair of institutional-green double doors. The room beyond them was even chillier, but I was too numb at that point to really feel it.

Querer shivered, and I could see her breath when she spoke. "I can do this for you, Dooley."

I didn't look at her.

"Really. I insist."

I ignored her and turned to Paul. He stood before us against a wall lined floor to ceiling and wall to wall with the fronts of massive drawers. He had his hand on one. The glowing label on it read, "Dooley, Ronan."

I really didn't want to see this. It's hard enough to see another human being turned into bullet-tenderized meat, much less yourself. But I'd already watched the thrid. How much worse could it be?

I swallowed hard and shoved all my emotions away, locking them down tight. Then I nodded, and Paul waved his hand in front of the drawer. It slid out silently on blue-glowing hover rails smoother than ice.

Paul hesitated as he put his hand on the pristine white shroud covering the corpse lying in the extracted drawer. Without turning toward me for further approval, he steeled himself and drew it back.

Querer failed to stifle a gasp. I gritted my teeth and forced myself to look.

The remains lay in a convex tray. The mortuary technicians had wiped away most of the blood so they could examine the various wounds, but when it came to my head, there just wasn't that much intact. The skull had been shattered in so many different directions that it reminded me of a cheap vase I'd knocked over as a child. I'd tried to glue it back together before my parents came home, but I'd never been able to puzzle out how the pieces were supposed to go back together.

My face was gone, turned into a ground-up mess. I spotted an eyelid, an ear, and what looked like most of my jaw.

The rest of me was in better shape, but not by much. My skin had that frigid pallor of the dead. I felt grateful that the refrigeration in the room kept me from having to endure the stench of any rot. That, I was sure, would have kicked me right over the edge.

I nodded at Paul, and he drew the shroud back over the corpse again. At a tap on the front of the drawer, it slid back into the pitch-black hole from which it came.

I heard Querer sniffle behind me. Just once.

I had to clear my throat before I could speak. "Any idea how long I was in the killer's custody before the murder?"

Paul clucked his tongue at me. "You hadn't checked in with the Service – at all, much less gone in for a backup – for over a week, so it could have been anytime in that period. Impossible to say for sure."

"What were you supposed to be doing?" Querer asked me, her voice steady and strong.

I'd checked over the logs that Adamson had sent me, plus whatever I'd been able to wheedle out of Patrón virtually while failing to fall asleep in the Lincoln Bedroom last night. I'd been on an undercover mission of my own instigation. Given my record and length of service, Patrón had trusted me to follow my instincts and see where they led me.

Nobody had expected they would take me to the morgue.

"From what I can tell, I was poking around the Kalis," I said. They were the Indian equivalent of the Mafia, straight out of Mumbai, and they ran most of the organized crime on the East Coast. I'd clashed with them dozens of times in my many lives, but never come near putting them down for good. Like the

Hindu goddess they named themselves after, they had many independent arms, and I'd never been able to get a clear shot at the head.

"I'd long suspected them of laundering rupees, rubles, and yuan for the Indian government by filtering it through their operations here in the US. That gave them the added benefit of helping to destabilize our currency by shoving billions of dollars worth of forged funds through our underground economy. The trail ran all the way up to Sharma Patil."

Paul let out a low whistle. "The Indian ambassador? Seriously? He's untouchable, and not in the sense of his caste. You'd need rock-solid proof to frag him."

"Right," I said. "Which is what I might have been after. Maybe I finally got too close."

Querer shuddered. "If so, that's one hell of a 'back off' message he sent you."

"But we can't prove any of that," said Paul. "The only thing we have to corroborate that is the bit of curry gas your killer left behind."

I nodded. "That may not be enough for a court of law, but it's good enough for me."

EIGHT

The hovercar slipped through the morning sky and carried us out over the Potomac. It came to a gap in the buildings covering the river and dove down to the Francis Scott Key Bridge. From there, we jogged a bit to the left and slipped onto the covered portion of 35th Street NW. We hung a quick left on Prospect and came to a rest behind a DC squad car.

When I exited our hovercar, it was like I'd emerged into an entirely different world from where I'd woken up that morning. Georgetown had fallen on hard times about fifty years back, and the university had started selling off bits of real estate to survive. Today, it existed almost entirely online, uniting teachers and students from around the world in virtual thrideo classrooms, but the neighborhood it had inhabited for centuries still bore its name.

The sun never shone here. Organic-glow lightstrips illuminated the streets, all the way up to the blackened ceiling of the tunnel arching overhead. Most people roamed the streets on foot here, but I still saw bicycles,

pedicabs, scooters, and even the occasional car, the
kind that still rolled on wheels. Many of those sat up
on blocks, stripped of any working mechanicals but
still serving as housing for whichever squatters were
bold enough to claim them and tough enough to hold
them.

Trash had been tucked into just about every corner,
fold, or crevice of the street that didn't see enough
traffic to flatten it or shove it out of the way. Disabled
or dying or just drunk beggars sat on every street corner, obeying some kind of unseen territorial system
that kept them from infringing on each other's turf.
Large plasticard box-homes dotted the sidewalks and
peeked out of the alleys, some of them bearing curtains of plastic sheeting over their fronts to give their
occupants a bit of precious, hard-won privacy.

Graffiti covered just about every surface. Some of
the walls had been treated with chemicals that ate any
other paint applied to them, but many of those had
simply been covered with layers of paper or plywood
that took the spray paint just fine. The preponderance
of tags written in Devangari script marked this region
for the Kalis.

Half the people I saw on the street wore flu masks,
hoping to put some kind of barrier between themselves and whatever lethal gunk was doing the rounds
this year. The rest either couldn't afford the masks or
just didn't care.

The mortal life expectancy in the US had dropped
steadily over the years. A huge chunk of the population didn't make it past forty. Once the rich were able

to start over with a new body when they needed it, research into hard-to-cure, fatal diseases like cancer or NAIDS dropped to nothing. Health care in general stalled out. Students stopped going to medical school. The few who did and graduated were hard to find, and if you managed it, you could count on never being able to afford the bill. If you couldn't buy rebirthing insurance, you weren't going to be able to manage health insurance either. Most mortals were stuck with over-the-counter care at their local pharmacy or – if they were lucky – local clinic. Contracting any disease with symptoms more complicated than the pharmacist could handle usually meant a lingering death or euthanasia, often self-administered.

Bullets were always cheap.

I brought the optical frisk layer into my vision. It analyzed anyone I looked at for telltale visual signs of weaponry. Of the thirty-odd people I could see on the street at the moment, about half were carrying a pistol of some sort. Another third had a knife worth calling a weapon.

The criminal history layer showed several priors among the people with nanoserver implants. One had an outstanding warrant for disturbing the peace, but I didn't have the time to pick him up for such a minor infraction. Some of the others, probably most of them, likely had priors too, but I'd have to bring up the facial or gait recognition layers first to figure out who they were. I had other things on my mind.

Madame Fate's stood relatively clean of any vandalism. While there may not have been enough superstition in the area to keep the fortune teller in business, there seemed to be plenty to persuade the local artists to give it a wide berth.

I nodded at the top of a stairwell across the street. "Recognize that?" I asked Querer.

"I don't think I've ever been here before," she said. "I've spent most of my time in the cybercrimes division, attached to a terminal."

"Nothing like actual footwork to help solve a crime," I said as I trotted across Prospect and looked down the stairs. The cement steps snaked down at a steep angle until they reached M street nearly fifty feet below. More glowstrips marked the way down.

"Notice anything funny about this?" I asked.

Querer furrowed her brow for a moment before she realized what was wrong. "There's nobody on it."

"Right. With all the vagrants around here, you'd expect someone to set up shop on one of the landings, at least, but the stairs are empty from top to bottom."

"Why?"

"These are the stairs from *The Exorcist*. The ones the priest throws himself down when he kills himself to get rid of the demon trying to possess him."

Querer stared at me. "In which version?"

"All of the American ones, starting with the original. It became a tradition."

She looked at me with uncertain eyes. "And why are you showing me this?"

"Because despite all our advances, no matter how far we've come, we're still superstitious primitives in our hearts. There's no good reason for one of those vagrants to not set up shop here, but they'd rather fight over other parts of the street than dare to call these stairs home."

I took one look back down the stairs. A fall down them might kill a demon. It could surely kill a man. Maybe there was more to them being empty than simple superstition.

I moseyed back across the street, dodging a trio of pedicabs racing to the west. As I went, I electronically flashed the cop in the squad car my ID, and he activated the speaker system outside his bulletproof window as we reached it.

"Hell of a place to die," he said to me with no trace of irony.

"Where's your partner?" I asked.

"Keeping watch inside. We're just waiting for you. The CSI team's already been over the place. Once you've had your look-see, our work here is done."

"I won't be long."

The cop shrugged. He clearly didn't think there was anything here for us to find, but he had his orders and meant to obey at least their letter if not their spirit. "Take your time."

Querer followed me up to the yellow crime scene tape criss-crossing the front of the building. I put my hands between two strips and pulled them apart, making an opening for her to climb through. I entered right after her.

The lights in the foyer automatically flickered to life as we came inside. A cop with a silver name tag that read "Smithee" stepped out of the back room to greet us. I scanned his ID out of habit, and it came up "Lee Chen." He looked far more like a Chen.

"Right back through here, sir," he said, stepping to one side to allow us to pass him in the hallway.

"What's with the name tag, Chen?" I asked.

The cop blushed. "Just a bit of a joke, sir."

"I don't find it funny," I said. I held out my hand for the tag.

Chen hesitated a moment. I wasn't his commander. He didn't have to go along with me. But he did. I tucked the tag into my jacket pocket.

"Thank you," I said. I jerked my head back toward the street. "Can you step outside? I'd prefer to handle this alone."

"Of course," he said, snapping off a casual salute before making his way outside.

Once he was gone, Querer grabbed my arm. "What's with giving the blues a hard time?"

"Beat cops wear false tags so they can abuse the people who live around here with no fear that it'll come back to haunt them."

"But anyone could scan him and see that it was wrong," she said.

"Sure, anyone with an active tether. Most people around here can't afford that. Something goes wrong, they try to report a cop who doesn't actually exist."

Querer screwed up her face into a skeptic's scowl. "That doesn't sound like much of an alibi."

"It's not," I said. "But when it's the word of an untethered vagrant against that of a cop, it's enough."

"And how does you busting his balls about it help stop that? Are you going to report him?"

I grunted. "For what? His boss wouldn't give a damn."

"Then why bother? He's just going to grab another name tag from his partner and do the same thing tomorrow."

"It made me feel better. Sometimes that's all you get." I opened the door into the back room. "For me, that's enough."

I walked into the room and recognized it instantly from my snuff thridco. The gray cinderblock walls and the cement floor stood splashed with my darkened, dried blood. The plastic chair was still bolted to the floor, and someone had laser-flashed an outline around where my body had been found.

The room smelled like a laundry, the scent of bleach overpowering everything but for a pungent overlay of death. It made my eyes want to water.

"How long were you here before they found you?" Querer's voice was as hushed as if we were in a church.

"According to Paul's report, no more than twelve hours. His team works fast."

"Killed on the Fourth of July."

I nodded. "Who's going to report a few stray gunshots on a day filled with firecrackers?"

I scoured the room for clues, but I knew I wouldn't find anything. There was no way I'd manage to stumble across something that Paul's CSI team had missed. A professional team like that with state-of-the-art equipment would be able to spot a fly's footprints on the wall.

Still, I had one thing they didn't. My perspective.

I sat down in the chair.

"Gah!" Querer said. "Are you–?"

"Yes," I said, cutting her silent. "I'm sure."

I leaned back and put my hands behind the chair, together as if I was bound. I jammed my ankles up against the chair's legs as if they were zip-tied down too. I closed my eyes and tried to imagine what I must have felt like sitting here with the killer babbling at me.

I'd been blinded, my tongue cut from my mouth. The pain must have been horrible. By that point, even I would have been hoping for the sweet release of death, a chance for a fresh start again. That was the only way I was likely to get my missing parts back, after all. Despite the active black market in spare body parts, legitimate transplants were rare. They still depended on twentieth-century technology, as the science behind them hadn't advanced much after the advent of the Amortals Project.

When it became possible to replace your body, vast chunks of medical science had fallen to the wayside. What wealthy foundation would subsidize research that would only help the poor? Better instead to fight for funds that would make amortality available to all.

Of course, that hadn't worked out well either. Backing up your memories wasn't cheap, and neither was force-growing a clone to adulthood. Few people could afford the insurance premiums. Those that could lived like unkillable gods.

The mortals just struggled on the best they could, the world they'd been born into stalling out around them as power and money concentrated itself in the hands of people who increasingly cut themselves off from the world around them. The gap between the haves and have-nots grew to a chasm between the tiny minority who had everything and the vast bulk who had almost nothing.

I'd only found myself on the privileged side of that canyon by a combination of bravery and blind luck.

In 2032, I'd been assigned to protect President Emmanuel during his re-election campaign. When a neo-Nazi death squad tried to assassinate him in the middle of a town hall meeting, I took several of the bullets meant for him. I was a fit and trim sixty-four years old at the time and had been dreaming about retirement right up until the moment I got shot.

As a Secret Service agent, the danger of being killed is part of the job. I'd known that when I'd signed up for it, and I hadn't hesitated to step up when the situation demanded it.

While the President went on video and reassured the country that he was all right, I fought a losing battle for my life at the Walter Reed Army Medical Center. I fell into a coma, and the doctors kept me alive on a ventilator. Everything about me was dead but my brain.

That's when the CIA proposed using an experimental procedure on me to backup my brain and restore it to a clone. They'd suggested it before but always been shot down on moral and ethical grounds. Here they saw their chance. Who could object to taking every measure possible to save the life of the man who'd paid the ultimate price to protect the President?

It worked, of course, and I became the razor-thin edge of the wedge the government would use to argue in favor of amortality. It didn't hurt that the idea of amortality held a lot of appeal for the wealthiest and most influential people in the nation. Within a matter of a few short years, the argument had been won, and the government shoved billions of dollars into the Congressionally approved Amortals Project.

The catch, of course, is that the government was the only organization with the resources to both build and administer such an ambitious and costly program. That placed everyone who wanted into the program at the government's mercy, including me.

I couldn't afford the insurance, of course, and despite being a high-ranking agent, I wouldn't normally have qualified for coverage. As the poster boy for the entire project, though, I couldn't be allowed to die. I was given eternal coverage with one caveat. It only lasted as long as I remained a government employee.

Looking back, I'm not sure I should have agreed to it. I hadn't any choice the first time, of course. That had been up to Colleen to give them consent, but who could have blamed her for choosing to bring me back then? At the time, it must have sounded like some kind of unbelievable fantasy.

Every time I've cashed my chips since then, though, it's been at my own prior request that the Amortals Project cashed me back in. In my lower moments,

I often considered giving it all up, beating Patrón to the punch and quitting before he could make good on his threat to fire me. But if I did that, I'd lose out on the one thing driving me forward today: making sure that whoever killed me each time was brought to justice. So today, at least, I was glad to be back, to be contributing to that cause, to be making a difference. Next week, who knew how I'd feel, but right now I was determined to solve my murder.

"Ronan?" Querer spoke in a worried voice like a child checking to see if her father was asleep but wanting desperately not to awaken him.

I opened my eyes. I tried to imagine the man in the black suit standing there before me, aiming that pistol at my forehead, about to pull the trigger. I shivered so hard I felt the chair shake beneath me.

"Are you all right?" Querer asked.

"No." I stood up and walked toward the door. "But I will be."

NINE

Sitting for so long in the chair in which I had died had made a mess out of the rebirthday suit they'd given me at the Amortals Project. I needed some new clothes and maybe a chance to think.

When Querer and I got back to the street, the squad car was already gone. The DC cops hadn't stuck around for an instant longer than they'd had to.

I walked Querer to the hovercar and told her I'd meet her back at the office later in the afternoon.

"Are you sure? You don't look well."

"Contemplating my own demise does that to me. I just need a good night's sleep in my own bed. Right now, I'll settle for a fresh suit."

As she slipped away, I summoned another hovercar from the Secret Service pool for myself.

I watched the street life while I waited. Nothing had changed. Nothing here had changed in over a hundred years. It just deteriorated.

A grimy man sidled up to me. He'd been sitting in a doorway fifty yards up the street. He was dressed in a shirt that had once been white and still said AN AMERI-CAN ORIGINAL on the front in block letters. He wore cargo shorts and carried an overstuffed duffel bag that likely contained everything he owned. He'd tied his busted flip-flops to his feet with binder clips and rubber bands.

"Hey, buddy? Got change for a hundred?" he said. "I need a twenty for the cigarette machine."

Most people in my social strata didn't carry even a dollar on them. If I needed to pay someone, I just looked into his eyes, brought the right amount up on my ocular display, and authorized the transaction. It was quick and easy, and it kept my pockets clean.

People without a nanoserver, though, couldn't manage this. Some used their phones instead, having you look into the camera lens on the face or just setting up an instant ad-hoc network for the transfer.

Most people only used cash if they had no other choice, and that usually meant black-market merchandise or services. They thought cash was untraceable, but that's not true. It's harder to trace, sure, but most cash registers optically scan the bills that move in and out of them. I can look at a bill, and my nanoserver will tell me its entire life story in a matter of microseconds.

This man, though, didn't really want change. He could buy his cigarettes in any corner store, and they'd give him his change. He wanted to find out if I had any cash on me, if I was worth trying to mug. I waved him off.

He held the bill up in front of me. "Seriously, friend. I just need to turn this into something smaller."

I glanced at the bill, and out of habit, I scanned it. Its history popped up in my lens, and one line of it blinked a bright red. The bill turned out to have been mine. It had left my custody two days ago at a curry shop a few blocks from here, right in the heart of Kali Country. I grabbed the man by the wrist and plucked the bill from his hand.

"Hey!" he shouted. "That's mine!"

I stiff-armed him back. "I just need to look at it."

I flipped the bill over and scanned the other side. Nothing new there. I thought about bringing it into Paul for analysis, but I knew he wouldn't be able to find anything. The bill had been crumpled and smoothed and had probably passed through a dozen hands before finding its way into this man's greasy fingers. Or not.

"Give me my money back!" he said as he came at me.

The man took a swing at my jaw. I blocked it with my left arm and slapped him with my right hand. That set him back. He glared at me with wild blue eyes, then up at the bill I still held in my left hand, staring at it like a starving dog. It wasn't much money to me, but to this man it was worth assaulting a well-dressed stranger and risking having his teeth knocked out.

"Where did you get this?" I asked, holding it in front of me.

The man glared at me, then spit on my tie. "Forget it," he said. "Keep it."

I reached for my badge, and the man cowered as if I meant to go for my gun instead.

"I'm not going to hurt you," I said, showing him my badge just as my hovercar landed behind me. "I only want to know where you picked up that bill."

The badge didn't scare him any less than a gun. "I don't know, pal." He pointedly looked at the ground in a vain attempt to keep me from getting a positive ID on him. "I don't know anything. Swear."

My facial recognition layer picked him out as a likely match for Andre Miandre, no known address. He was only twenty-eight but looked like he was in his early forties. Life in Kali Country was hard. He'd been lucky, strong, or stupid enough to survive this long, but his body had paid for it.

"Look, Andre."

He flinched at the sound of his name. "Ah, no. Don't." The last hint of a backbone slipped out of him, and his shoulders slumped forward. I had him cold, and he knew it.

I held the bill in his face. "Who gave this to you?"

He grabbed the shaggy hair on the sides of his head and knotted his hands in it, then groaned and pulled as if he might yank it all out. "I don't know. Some guy in a hat and a flu mask. I didn't get a good look at him."

"How'd you come by the money then?"

Andre frowned. "The guy gave me that bill and four more just like it. He said I could keep the rest if I gave you the one."

It was my turn to frown. "Me?"

He nodded. "That's right, Mr Dooley."

I glared at him. "And how do you know who I am?"

"I remember you from the thrids I watched in school."

I sometimes wondered how Patrón could ever send me undercover any more. My face hadn't been in the news for a couple decades, I suppose, but it seemed that even guys like Andre had studied my whole life.

"Give me the rest of the money," I said.

He hesitated for a moment, then reached into his pocket and handed over the contents. I scanned the bills and stuffed them in my pocket over his protests. All of them had once belonged to me. As far as the system was concerned, they still did. That meant since they'd left me, no one else had used them in a way that could be tracked.

"You did a good job," I said. I looked into his eyes. No nanoserver there. "Got a phone?"

He fished a grimy roll-up model out of his pocket and held it up in front of me. I looked into the camera lens on the end of the tube and paid him for the bills I'd taken. The glow surrounding the lens shifted from red to green.

"Now get the hell out of here."

He turned and ran off. I had my gait layer size him up as he went. If I needed to find him later, it wouldn't be hard. The pool hovercar arrived, and I slid in and sent it home. It angled down the tunnels toward the Potomac, and as soon as it reached the Key Bridge, it slipped into the sky and followed the river toward the sea.

My place wasn't even a mile downriver, but it might as well have been part of the Mars colony for

how much it differed from Madam Fate's. Despite its
storied history – or perhaps because of it – the Watergate was one of the few private building complexes
that stood open to the sky, without any other buildings bridging out to it. That gave it an unobstructed
view of the Potomac River and Theodore Roosevelt
Island across the way.

The hovercar dropped me off at the rooftop entrance of my building, the Watergate South. It's the
northern of the two curved parts of the Watergate
complex that form a C facing the river, at the south
end of the others. I pinged MPD CSI. Paul's voice
popped into my ear.

"Yes, Dooley?"

"Is my apartment cleared to enter yet?" I asked. I
didn't much care what the answer might be. I was
going in either way. I just wanted to know if any blue
uniforms were going to hassle me about it.

"You should be good. We completed our work there
late last night. Didn't find much of interest, other than
the fact you're a horrible housekeeper."

"That's not news to anyone." I paused to think for a
moment as I stepped into the elevator. "How long has
it been since anyone's been in there?"

"Other than my team? That's hard to say. The car-
bon-dating on the dishes you left in the sink hasn't
come back yet."

"Give it your best guess."

"From the condition of those dishes and the decay
of the garbage in your kitchen, I'd say it had been at
least two weeks, maybe three."

What would have kept me from sleeping in my own bed – or at least from bothering with the dishes and trash – for two or three weeks? With Colleen gone for over a hundred years, I'm a reconfirmed bachelor, but I wouldn't ever let things slip that badly on purpose.

Maybe.

Colleen would have laughed at me. The team of domestic bots that came with the condo kept the place pretty clean. They swept and mopped the floors every night. They washed and folded my laundry. They even kept the bathrooms and kitchens clean and polished. My chores were few. I just didn't always bother with them.

"Did you tidy up for me at all?"

"The Amortals Project return preparation team showed up while we were there, but we told them they'd have to come back after we were done. They should have taken care of you by now."

There were many perks that came with being an amortal, one of which was the return prep team. Despite the fact that an amortal can't recall his own death, it's still disturbing to wake up at the Amortals Project headquarters and realize that your old self must have died. The Project's policy is to send an advance team to pave the way with your friends and family and to do whatever possible to make your reentry into the land of the living cause little more in the way of mental trauma. That included making sure you came back to a clean home.

"Anything else, Dooley?"

"Yeah," I said as the elevator doors opened at my floor. I strolled down the hall. "Do you have any idea why I didn't signal for help when I was captured?"

"Not for sure. If I had access to your logs from that period, there's a good chance I could figure it out, no matter what happened."

There was a "but" attached to that, and I supplied it. "But the killer took them along with my eyes."

"Exactly."

"You're not much help."

"There are just too many answers to a question like that. I could guess, but in my business, that's risky."

"Live dangerously then," I said. "Between you and me."

"You could have wandered into a dead zone for communications signal. They could have knocked you cold before you could initiate the call. They could have set off an EMP or been jamming radio waves. They could have slapped a tin-foil hat on your head. Maybe a HERF gun. It's impossible to know."

"Thanks – wait. A what?"

"Which what?"

"The HERF what."

"High-Energy Radio Frequency. A weapon that generates an EMP, an electromagnetic pulse. Fries sophisticated electronics like the kind implanted in your amortal head. A gun might use a Marx generator circuit. A bomb would probably go with an EPFCG instead."

"Too many letters, Paul."

"An Explosively-Pumped Flux Compression Generator."

"Just as long as it's not a flux capacitor."

"A what?"

"Never mind. Just trading one obscure reference for another."

"I wish I could be more help, Dooley. Just don't go in for a repeat performance of whatever happened."

"If I knew what happened, I wouldn't," I said. I disconnected just as I reached my door, a flat slab of red with the number 616 printed on it. I mimed turning a knob the door didn't have, and it recognized me and slid aside. I took a deep breath, blew it out, and then walked in.

The place sparkled in the way it only ever did when I came back from the dead. The whole condo smelled of bleach and oranges. The floors were so clean it seemed like a crime to have to walk on them. The sun angled in through the auto-polarizing western windows, which looked out over one of the few clear, wide views of the Potomac in the city. The air was so clean inside there weren't any dust motes to dance in the muted beam of light.

Everything on the first floor had been put nicely away, which meant I wouldn't be able to find a damn thing. Since I couldn't remember a single second out of the past three months, though, I could hardly blame that on the cleaners.

I had other things to worry about. That encounter with Andre Miandre bothered me.

Someone had sent him over with that first bill to get me thinking about the Kalis again, but who would have done that? The Kalis? Were they taunting me, trying to bring me to them right away so they could kill me again? Was someone else trying to pit me against them? Anyone who knew me knew I had a recent history of clashing with the Kalis. Sending me off to confront them would be sure to draw my attention from anything else for a while.

Something was wrong here. Someone was trying to manipulate me into doing something. I just didn't know what it was. Yet.

I walked upstairs to my bedroom. The curtains were wide open, and the balcony beyond them called to me. I strolled over, and the patio door that stood between me and the fresh air beyond slid aside.

Just before it did, I noticed a glowing blue dot in the middle of the sheet of glass separating me from the balcony. I knew it right away for what it was.

I looked behind me and saw the laser painting the back wall of my bedroom. Instead of going outside, I dove behind my bed.

Amateur snipers use laser sights to help them pick out their target. Military-grade hardware features UV lasers that are invisible to the naked eye, and the onboard computers on the guns automatically figure in the effect of wind, gravity, rain, and any other factors on where the bullet is going to land. Self-correcting gyroscopes keep the weapon pointed in the right direction. All you need to do is assign a target with the laser and pull the trigger like you mean it.

I expected to hear a hail of high-caliber rounds tearing through the glass and ripping into my bed. A full second after this failed to happen, I remembered what else amateurs used lasers like that for.

I jumped out from behind the bed and dashed into the hallway beyond. Then I threw myself down the stairs to the landing below. I had just turned around to leap down to the condo's first floor when the laser-guided rocket slammed into my balcony.

built-in safety protocols
grammers and overr
Meanwhile, so
ce directly
trajectory
launcher
h='d th
h=d
I

The rocket smashed in through my bedroom window and exploded. The boom deafened me and shook my brain in my skull. Gouts of fire billowed out of the destroyed room and chased me down the stairs. The flames would have swallowed me if I'd still been standing on the landing, but the shock wave from the explosion sent me tumbling down into my kitchen. I rolled with the impact and smacked right into the granite-topped island that separated that room from the dining area beyond. Pain shot through my left shoulder, but I ignored it. Rather than cursing that island, I was grateful for it. It had kept me from rolling all the way into the dining room. The ceiling down here had been blown out by the explosion. This caused it to tip forward from where it was anchored near the stairwell, its far end crushing my living room, which had looked out over the first-level balcony.

Still stunned, I managed to summon the hovercar to meet me outside my balcony. It refused, citing its

, but I pulled rank on its pro-
de those concerns.

eone out there – standing some-
across the Potomac, if I judged the
ght – was likely reloading a rocket
o make sure he'd finished me off. Or maybe
nk that one rocket was enough. After all, if I
n't been in the middle of the stairwell at the time,
d probably have been blown or crushed to bits.

Somebody else came up and started pounding on
my condo's front door. I was staggered enough by the
blast that I nearly answered it. Then I realized that
anyone with a lick of sense would be racing out of a
building that had just been hit by a rocket, not charging toward the explosion. I pulled my service pistol out
of my shoulder holster. It was a Nuzi, just like the one
I'd been killed with. That gun was still being held as
evidence in my murder. This would be the first time I
would fire its replacement.

Whoever was outside kept hammering on the door.
I called up the ID layer to see who it was, and it came
back blank. For an instant, I thought my nanoserver
had been blasted offline, but as my head spun I realized I could see the overlaid outlines of other people
heading for the emergency stairwells just fine.

I waited for the pounding to start again, then mimed
twisting an imaginary knob. The door slid away, re-
vealing a surprised Indian man in a sharp suit. He had
one hand up, catching himself in mid-knock, and in
his other he held a gun. He had the thick, over-mus-
cled form of a bodybuilder who'd been injecting

himself with viral growth DNA for far too many years.

He pointed his gun at me. The blue laser stabbed at my belly.

Before his gun could aim for him, I shot him three times, square in the chest, and he crumpled to the floor. I waited a moment for someone else to appear in the door after him. When no one did, I bolted over and grabbed him. Blood trickled from his mouth, and he could barely breathe, but he was still alive. I knelt down next to him, slapped him across the face, and hauled him into a sitting position. He came to, if just for a moment.

"Kali will take you," he said, his words burbling up to me through a mouth filled with blood. The slitted pupils of his bioengineered cat's eyes dilated wide as he spoke. "Your fate is already written."

I let him go, and he fell back on his head, already too far gone to care about the impact. He'd been the backup plan, I knew. The guy they sent around to make sure the guy with the rocket had done his job. If he didn't report back in a few seconds, they might attack again – or they might just pack up and leave before I could find them. I didn't know which possibility bothered me worse.

I ran back into the condo and weaved my way up the stairs. The ceiling and walls of the second level were on fire. The floor wasn't burning, but it had partially collapsed into the lower level, the section nearest me still held on by unbroken strips of exposed rebar. It made my place look like a ramp leading down to my first-level balcony. If I'd had a jetcycle, I might have been able to try a daredevil jump straight across the Potomac. If I just stepped out onto that surface instead, though, I was sure I would tumble to my doom.

Then I spotted the blue laser beam cutting through the clouds of smoke, dust, and everything else the explosion had knocked loose. The bastards were still out there on the other side of the river, searching for me. They hadn't run yet. That meant they were determined to finish the job.

I wasn't about to let them.

I clicked over to the object location overlay. Through the smoke, I spotted the outline of the hovercar hanging there near the edge of my lower floor.

I could run out the back door and hope that no other Kalis were waiting for me on any other floor or outside of the building, hoping to gun me down in the confusion. With luck, skill, and maybe a little backup, I could probably take them all down. If I did that, though, the people who fired the rocket at me were sure to get away.

I wasn't about to let that happen.

Although I'd only been reborn yesterday, I knew that I could always come back tomorrow. So I did something so incredibly stupid that only an amortal would have dared consider it.

I didn't creep my way down the ramp that my place had become, hoping that I wouldn't somehow slip and fall to my death. Instead, I stuffed my gun back into its holster, charged down that makeshift ramp at top speed and then leaped into the air as I reached the rocket-made ramp's very end.

As I raced down through the wreck of my home, I commanded the hovercar to open up its nearest door and then roll to tilt that door toward my building's roof. I emerged into the daylight from the smoke and debris to see the hovercar still executing that command.

It was too late to stop. Moving like a long jumper, I hurled myself into the air and hoped that I hadn't just made a fatal mistake. If I had, I'd wake up at the Amortals Project again tomorrow and have to go through most of this all over again. At least I wouldn't remember hitting the pavement. No matter what happened with my next body, the pain of that memory would die with me.

I smacked into the hovercar hard. I missed the open door, but only partially. My head and arms got through, but the edge of the opening slammed into my chest, knocking the wind out of me. I felt a rib crack. I ignored the pain and scrabbled for some kind of hold, my feet kicking in thin air like those of a hanged man struggling for one more breath. I managed to snag the edge of one of the seats in the car with my hands, but I couldn't seem to haul myself in.

My weight started to make the hovercar roll back to the level position, which gave me even less to hold on to. My grip on the seat slipped, and for one horrible instant I felt like I had made this body's last mistake. My hands landed on the edge of the door, though, and they held tight. I knew I wouldn't last long there though, even under the best of circumstances.

That's when I saw the telltale blue light shining through the window on the other side of the hovercar and flitting across the machine's ceiling.

Using the override authorization link I'd left open to the hovercar, I ordered it to move forward and to roll hard to its right. It zipped away faster than I thought it would, and it took everything I had to keep my grip on the doorway.

As the machine rolled, the belly of the hovercar came up against me and then lifted me into the air. When the hovercar was nearly upside down, I finally got a grip on its underbelly with my shoes, and I managed to kick myself upward and then down into the passenger compartment.

Somewhere below me, I heard the distinctive sound of a rocket being launched. Seeing me finally get into the hovercar, the assassin must have given up on trying to get a good shot at me and decided to take whatever he could get.

"Shut the door and move!" I said to the autopilot. "Top speed!"

The hovercar jack-rabbited forward, tossing me against the seats. I yowled in protest as my cracked rib threatened to snap. Then the rocket hit.

It couldn't have missed the hovercar by more than a few feet, but it sailed past it and smacked right into the Watergate South again. The explosion rocked the hovercar like a rowboat on a tidal wave, and I felt it falling like a shooting star, arcing across the open sky.

"Up!" I shouted at the autopilot. "Up!"

The hovercar tipped over as it fought hard against the shock wave, depositing me on its glassteel ceiling. This gave me a spectacular view of the Potomac

Parkway rushing up toward me. I closed my eyes and braced for the impact.

The hovercar finally regained control about a dozen feet above the road. By the time it managed to fully reverse its momentum, I could have reached out and touched the pavement with my fingers. After an instant's hesitation while it recalibrated itself, the hovercar shot skyward, navigating its way around the oncoming traffic zipping around us. As we rose, it gently rolled back so that its ceiling was up again. I sat down properly in my seat and ordered the autopilot to head for Roosevelt Island along an evasive semicircular route. While the hovercar executed my orders, I scanned the island's shoreline, zooming in to get as good a look as I could.

I didn't see the rocketeer right away, but I spotted that damned blue laser sweep across the compartment again. If I'd have gone directly at my attacker, he would have been able to take another easy shot at me. With the hovercar moving laterally, though, I hoped it would be harder for him to get a lock.

I looked in the direction from which the laser had come, and I zoomed in my vision to maximum magnification. I spotted a pair of men on the shore of Roosevelt Island. They'd finally given up on shooting at the hovercar and the man with the rocket launcher was climbing onto the back of a motorcycle the other man was driving.

I switched over to the hovercar's manual controls, for which I had to give my authorization again. Most people don't even know how to drive a road car these days, much less a hovercar, but I had decades' worth of combat training with each.

I nudged the hovercar straight toward the bike just as it zipped away. I knew there was only one way off the island: a footbridge that ran into the Washington Memorial Parkway on the Virginia side of the river. Once they reached that thoroughfare, it was only a short hop to disappear into the sprawl of connected buildings that covered most of Arlington. If they managed that, I'd have a devil of a time tracking them down.

I pushed the hovercar hard to catch them. They had a fast bike, but they were land-bound. They had to work their way through the national park's trees, while I could zip above it all. I came in fast and hard over the treetops and overshot them. As I went, I zapped an emergency request for backup to the DC police and any and all federal agents in the area. I didn't expect anyone to be able to respond in time, but at least they could help with the cleanup. This was sure to get messy.

I brought the hovercar in tight and low over the monument to Teddy Roosevelt and waited for the motorcycle to arrive. The memorial featured a bronze statue of the President, a couple of large fountains, and a set of stone monoliths on which the man's most famous quotations were carved. Colleen and I had brought Cal out here when he was young, just to poke around.

My favorite of the quotes was this: "Only those are fit to live who do not fear to die: and none are fit to die who have shrunk from the joy of life and the duty of life." President Emmanuel had cited these words at my memorial service, the one they'd held when they'd thought for sure I wouldn't make it.

The assassins seemed to have wisely opted to avoid the paths and stay hidden beneath the woods' leafy canopy, but just because I couldn't see them didn't mean I couldn't detect them. I flipped up the infrared vision layer, and I spotted the motorcycle's heat signature weaving toward me through the trees.

I opened the door on the right-hand side of the compartment and transferred the controls to that seat. Then I drew my gun and held it out the open door, aiming it in the direction of the oncoming red blob.

The motorcycle burst out of the trees on the edge of the clearing in which the clustered memorial for Roosevelt sprawled. I finally got a good look at the men. They were Indian too, Kalis for sure. The driver was cut from the same mold as the bone breaker I'd killed in the hall outside my condo. He operated the motorcycle like he was wrestling a wild bull, forcing it to do his bidding every inch of the way.

The man on the back was thinner, with shiny black hair. He wore a pair of dark goggles on which the targeting laser was mounted so he could keep his hands free while he used it. They would also let him see the beam at just about any unobstructed range. Right now, he had the rocket launcher slung over his shoulder and ready, and he was looking straight at me.

At any real distance, the man with the rocket launcher never would have been able to hit my hovercar. It's hard enough to fire a weapon like that when you're standing on solid ground, much less when you're bouncing around on the back of a motorcycle charging through the woods at top speed.

This close up, though, it would be hard for him to miss.

ELEVEN

I dove out of the hovercar as the man let loose with the rocket. The rocket flew into the open doorway and exploded inside the passenger compartment. That's probably what saved my life.

The hovercar's reinforced chassis managed to contain most of the explosion, which kept it from killing me directly or slamming me into the ground below. The parts of that terrible force that escaped through the open doorway knocked the hovercar back a few dozen feet before it came spiraling out of the sky to crash to earth. This at least kept it from landing on me.

I fell right into one of the fountains. The water didn't do all that much to cushion my fall, but it protected me from fiery bits of shrapnel raining down from above. I'd only been a bit more than a dozen feet above the fountain, and that little edge made the difference between life and yet another death for me.

I drew my gun while still underwater and came up angry and ready for some payback. The recoil from the rocket launcher had knocked the firer straight off the bike, and he was scrambling to his feet, still clutching the launcher like a lifeline. The driver had circled back around to grab his friend and probably hoped to gloat over my corpse.

I squeezed off three quick shots, and the man with the launcher dropped as if I'd cut his puppeteer's strings. The man on the bike saw his friend fall, and he hunkered down low in his seat and tried to gun it out of there. I took aim and let off a flurry of shots, not at him but his front tire. Killing him wouldn't do me much good at this point. I wanted one of them alive for questioning, and the guy with the rocket launcher had already lost that lottery.

The tire blew, and the man panicked and hit his brakes hard. This catapulted him over his handlebars and into the trees beyond. The bike skidded after him and smashed into him, crushing him between a tree and its unforgiving metal frame.

I leaped out of the fountain and sprinted over to where the wreck of the man lay entangled in the remains of his bike. He'd snapped his neck somewhere in that high-speed mess, and he was dead by the time I reached him.

I cursed and kicked his corpse. He'd nearly killed me and, worse, might have killed a lot of other people with those damned rockets. I sat down on the turf, put my head between my knees, and waited for help to arrive.

I must have done something to drive the Kalis wild if they were hauling out heavy weaponry like this and attacking me in the middle of the afternoon. This wasn't an attack. It was an act of war.

I heard sirens howling off in the distance, growing closer. They almost drowned out the sound coming from the headset dangling from the dead driver's ear. I hadn't noticed the headset in my initial look at the wreck. After I'd seen the man was dead, little else had seemed important. But when I peered over to see where the tinny noise was coming from, I spotted it.

I scrambled over to the man on my hands and knees, grabbed the little silver disc with the hook and fitted it over my ear. It was a miniaturized private radio, a tiny walkie-talkie set to an encrypted channel. Gangs like the Kalis used them for short-range communications because – unlike with regular communications – they made it virtually impossible for someone to tap or track their conversations.

Someone on the other end – a man with a high voice – jabbered at me in Hindi, demanding a report from a man named Meghnad.

"He's dead," I said in English. "They're both dead."

"Who is this?" the voice demanded, still speaking Hindi.

"Tell Patil I know," I said. "Tell him Dooley's coming for him. Tell him not even death can stop me."

The man on the other end of the connection did not speak again.

I pulled the earphone off and tossed it next to its owner's body.

The MPD squad cars arrived a moment later, streaming in from over the river. Although the only way onto the island by land was from the Virginia side of the Potomac, MPD still had jurisdiction here. I was glad of that. There would be less explaining to do. Adamson might not like me much, but I already knew where I stood with her.

The ambulance arrived a minute later. After checking my ID to make sure they'd get paid, the EMTs set to work. They ignored the two dead Kalis, as much for their lack of insurance as the fact they were beyond help.

By the time Querer arrived, the EMTs had fitted me with an Airflex corset for my ribs, and they were gluing together a few tiny lacerations I'd picked up when I landed in the fountain. I'd been too pumped on adrenaline to feel them at the time, but coming down from that now, my entire body felt like one continuous bruise.

"I let you out of my sight for not even an hour, and look what happens," she said.

I didn't bother to smile. "They were waiting for me to come home," I said. "They didn't just send people with guns. They used a rocket launcher and blew up my apartment."

"Someone must have wanted to make a statement." She looked me up and down, appraising the damage.

"Those men were Kalis," I said. "Patil sent them."

She pursed her lips and nodded. "Think he had you killed the other day too?"

I grimaced. I didn't have any proof, nothing that would stand up in a court of law. Lots of people I'd had run-ins with over the years might want me dead – the One Resurrectionists, the Gang of Nine, the Mafia, the Russians, the Monster Crips, half of the firms on Wall Street – but this attack put the Kalis at the top of my list.

That business with the guy looking for change, though, threw a wrench into that smooth-running conspiracy theory. Someone had tried to set me after the Kalis. Would Patil do that? Or one of his lieutenants? Was someone trying to get me to take him down?

Either way, that was what I planned to do. Anyone desperate enough to order a rocket launched into the apartment of an amortal Secret Service agent needed to be brought in. I could worry about the other pieces of the puzzle later.

"I don't know," I said. "But I plan to find out."

The EMTs released me a few minutes later and told me to try to take it easy for a few days. I managed not to laugh out loud at them, mostly because I knew how much it would hurt my ribs.

They offered me some painkillers to take the edge off the aches. I tried to refuse because I wanted to stay sharp. The moment I stood up, though, I realized how much I needed them. Being amortal only meant I could reboot in a new body any time I needed. It didn't do a damned thing to stop my current body from hurting. So they gave me some pills from the onboard prescription dispenser, and a cup of water. The pills didn't do a thing for me at first, but I knew it wouldn't take long for them to kick in.

Then a pair of MPD detectives grabbed me to take a statement. Technically I didn't have to give them anything. I was in charge of this investigation, and I could have just told them I didn't have the time to bother with the local cops. The way I felt, though, I wasn't going anywhere soon, and I always tried to give the MPD folks the respect they deserved.

I told them everything, starting from when I arrived at the Watergate. I gave them as much detail as I could. I even told them the bit about threatening Patil over the walkie-talkie. They just nodded at that and wished me luck.

I started to slur my words together once the painkiller finally took hold. Querer stepped in and made my excuses to the detectives. They understood. Before they left, though, one of them asked me for an autograph, and I gave it to him with a pained smile.

"I've been reading about you since I was a little kid," he said, a bashful smile on his face. "Never thought I'd get to work with you on a case."

"Take it from me," Querer said, "it's not as glamorous as you might think. This is just my second day with him, and I'm already wondering how healthy it is to stand near him."

I gave her a half-hearted snarl. When she offered me an arm to lean on as I limped to her Service-pool hovercar, I admit I wasn't too proud to take it.

She helped me into my seat, then climbed in next to me.

"Where to?" I asked. "I'd ask you to bring me home, but I don't think I have one at the moment."

That pained me more than I could say. Colleen and I had moved into the Watergate after I became amortal. I'd lived there ever since. I'd been there with her, holding her hand, when she died. And now that place was gone.

I wondered about my neighbors. I didn't see much of them these days. Back when Colleen had been alive, we'd known everyone on our hall and been acquainted with half the building, but over the years everyone from those days had died. I'd never gotten that close to any of the newer tenants.

Still, I knew them well enough to greet them by name when we rode in the elevator or passed in the hall. To think that the Kalis might have hurt or even killed some of them made me angrier than the attack on myself. I could always come back, but only a few of my neighbors could say that for themselves.

"Believe it or not," said Querer, "Patrón called in a favor for you. He wants the world to see the President treating you with the utmost respect. No sleazy motels for you."

My head started to swim from the medicine, and I leaned back in my seat as the edges of the pain began to melt away. "Off to the Lincoln Bedroom again?"

"No," Querer said. "It's occupied tonight. Some big-money contributor to the Oberon campaign. I'm taking you to Blair House instead."

Normally, I wouldn't have smiled at being blown out of my condo and made to stay at the Presidential guest house, but the drugs helped spread a wide grin on my face. "Awesome," I said.

Querer giggled at that, and I marveled at the sound. It seemed so girlish I couldn't believe it had come from her.

"Who says things like that anymore?" she said. She mimicked me speaking the word. "'Awesome.' Really?"

I smiled as more of the pain drifted away from me. "Been using it all my life," I said. "Don't see any reason to stop now."

"You ancient." She stressed the last word, making it a label. That's what the mortals called us these days: "the ancients."

"Whippersnapper. Keep the hell off my lawn."

"You don't have a lawn."

"Well, not anymore. Those bastards blew it up."

She stared at me, her face scrunched up in disbelief. "Are we talking about the same thing here?"

I just grinned. "We never are, kid. We never are."

Querer ordered the hovercar to take us to Blair House. "And take the scenic route!" I added.

I gazed out the window as we rose into the air and skated out over the Potomac. The sun was low in the sky behind us, and it bathed the entire city in a golden, nostalgic light. The hole where my condo had been still smoldered, but the fire had been put out. A team of firefighters in hovercars and safety harnesses were still poking around the place, making sure it was still structurally sound. A crowd had gathered out on the lawn below, people huddled together for comfort in the face of such a shocking, devastating event.

From there, we slipped south and then curved around the Lincoln Memorial, moving at a tourist's speed. The entire Mall was restricted airspace, so we had it to ourselves. We floated over the reflecting pool, heading toward the Capitol until we reached the Washington Monument. The hovercar took us in a slow circle around the massive obelisk, and I saw the two seams in it. The first had come about when construction on the monument had to be halted during the Civil War. The stone they used after the war didn't quite match the original material, and you can see the change as a clear line if you bother to look.

The second seam came about for the same basic reason, after that pro-death suicide bomber protesting the Amortals Project blew the top off the structure a few decades back. Despite making a sincere effort, the government couldn't quite match the stone again this time either.

From there, we turned north, toward the White House. As we cut between the somber Eisenhower Executive Office Building and the West Wing, I wondered if the President might look up at us and know what had happened and where we were going. If she saw our lone craft buzzing overhead and bothered to ask about it, I knew the agents on her protection detail would fill her in.

The hovercar climbed into the air as it approached Blair House, just kitty-corner from the White House, to the northwest. It slipped up over the roof and then brought us down to land inside the high-walled courtyard. The team of staffers who normally greeted visiting heads of state came out to meet us with a hoverchair, the kind you see in private hospitals. I reluctantly agreed to let them bring me to my suite in it. Querer followed me up and watched over me until they had me resting in my bedroom.

"We need to get after the Kalis now," I said, protesting the cushy treatment. "We don't have any time to waste. They're not going to sit around and wait for me to come to them."

"You're not going anywhere tonight, Dooley," Querer said. "The rest of us are on the job. Patil can wait for you until the morning."

"Maybe," I said, "but I don't think I can."

Even so, just minutes after she left, I fell asleep.

TWELVE

I probably would have slept all the way until the next morning if I hadn't received a wake-up ping from Blair House's manager a couple of hours later. It flashed in my lenses, starting slowly and then rising in urgency until I finally opened my eyes and responded to it. It's impossible to ignore a light that appears underneath your eyelids, much as you might want to try.

I saw that there was a message attached to the ping, and I opened it. I had a guest waiting for me at the front desk. His name was Ronan Dooley VI.

I checked the time and saw that it was just after 6pm. I sat up and groaned at the aching stiffness that seemed to have seeped into every joint in my body. Despite having been reborn in a fresh body just yesterday, I felt like an old man, and I knew from long experience what that meant.

I responded to the ping and asked the front desk to send Six up in five minutes. I got up, stretched, hit the head, and poured myself a glass of water. Then I moved into the parlor to wait.

A knock came at the door a little while later, and I opened it to see Six and a Secret Service chaperone who'd escorted him to my suite. When I'd started with the Service, we didn't cover Blair House all the time, just when a visiting head of state stayed there. After the assassination of Russian Finance Minister Dmitri Pushkin here during a G40 summit back in 2099, though, the Service took over Blair House security on a permanent basis.

"Come on in," I said to Six. He slid past me into the parlor.

"Thanks for bringing him," I said to the agent. I didn't recognize him, but his ID tagged him as Bryce Hereford.

"Any time, Mr Dooley. We weren't sure if we should disturb you, but since you hadn't left orders against it, we decided to take the chance."

"I'm glad you did."

The agent stuck out his hand. "An honor to meet you, sir."

I returned his smile and shook his hand. I never know how to respond in situations like that. As far as I was concerned, we were just fellow agents, but I could see that he felt differently about it.

That, I realized, was one of the things I liked about Querer. She wasn't impressed with my reputation at all.

I shut the door and turned to see Six already slouched in one of the parlor's overstuffed chairs. He had a hand stretched over his eyes, shading them from me, and he let loose a deep, frustrated sigh.

"What's up, Six?" I asked.

"Nothing." He said it in a way that meant "Everything."

I walked over and sat down in a chair across from him. There were no windows in the room. They'd been sealed off as a security measure and replaced with window-sized wallscreens that looked almost like the real thing. They showed images of the street outside and projected simulated late-evening sunlight that slanted down at us, bringing illumination without the heat.

"How did you find me here?" This wasn't my apartment after all.

"The feeds had it."

"Ah." My movements weren't normally enough to make the news, but I supposed having my apartment blown up might change that.

"I told you we could catch up with each other after this murder investigation is over." I spoke softly, as if he was a rabbit I didn't want to spook.

"I know." His voice was thick and hoarse.

"What's wrong?" I asked again.

Six dropped his hand and looked up at me with red and puffy eyes. "It's my father," he said. "He kicked me out."

I sat back to absorb that bit of news. "What did you do?"

He shot me a hurt look. "What makes you think it was my fault?"

"All right. What did he do – besides kick you out?"

"I broke some of his damned rules."

I nodded, hoping that I was starting to understand. One thing hadn't changed much over all my years, it seemed. Teenagers and their parents still didn't get along.

"Is this something that happens a lot?"

"No!" Six sat up now, indignant. "What kind of person do you think I am?"

I shrugged. "I – I don't know. I don't know you all that well. I don't know your father at all."

"And whose fault is that?"

I knew he was upset and just lashing out because of that. The words still stung, but I tried to ignore it.

"I'm just trying to figure out why your father kicked you out."

"It was because of you, all right?"

I sat back in my chair and nodded. "He found out that you came to see me at the cemetery."

"I don't know how he did it," Six said. "He doesn't track my movements like some of the other parents I know. He's always going on about privacy and how we need to respect each other's rights."

"What about your mother?"

"She's worse about it than he is, always off protesting one thing or another. Sometimes I think that's why we still live in DC. They call the place a cesspool, but they like the easy drive down to the Capitol to lodge their complaints."

"It's all part of the democratic process," I said. "At least they're involved citizens. Most people can't be bothered."

"Yeah, but…" He hunted through his frustration for

the right words to express it. "Doesn't that get you mad?"

"They're not my parents."

He waved that off. "No, not that. I mean, don't all those protesters make you mad? Aren't they dangerous? Don't they get in the way of you doing your job?"

I shrugged. "No."

"Not at all?" He stared at me in disbelief.

"Well, it would be easier to protect the President if nobody ever wanted to talk to her, but that's not the way it works. She needs to be out there and engaged with the people. All politicians do. Otherwise, they can't get elected."

"Yeah, but these protesters, you don't find something un-American about them?"

I shook my head and patted Six's knee. "Not at all. Sure, they have some crackpots mixed up with them sometimes, but most of the time they're just citizens who want to make sure that somebody's listening to their point of view."

Six sat back and ran his hands through his hair. "I just find it so…"

"Embarrassing?"

"Yeah!"

I laughed. "They're your parents. Of course they're embarrassing."

He chuckled at that, and I knew then that he'd be all right.

"So your dad kicked you out just because he found out you'd been to see me?"

Six hemmed and hawed over that. "Well, that was only the start of it. Once he got going on that, he asked me what had gotten me so interested in you in the first place."

"Outside of the fact you're my direct descendant."

"And that I'm named after you – right!"

I waited for a moment, then prompted him again. "Well?"

He frowned as he considered what to say next. He might only be seventeen, but he was far less impulsive than I'd been at that age. He came to a decision and spoke.

"I told him it was because I'd been poking around the Shack."

I cocked my head as if I hadn't heard him properly. "Run that past me again?"

"We have this family cabin in northern Wisconsin, up in the Apostle Islands in Lake Superior. We used to spend a lot of time up there when I was a kid. Whenever Mom and Dad needed to get away from the city, we all piled in the hovercar and headed out there. I spent a couple weeks every summer there growing up."

I remembered the Shack well. My parents had bought it when I was a little boy, and it had passed down to me. I'd given it to Cal sometime after my first revivification, and he'd presumably passed it on to his kids. I'd spent many summers there too, although hadn't been back there in decades.

"Sounds idyllic," I said.

"Sure. Sometimes, though, it was just dull. When I got really bored, I started rummaging around the place, looking for something to do. They have a library in the basement filled with actual books. On paper, you know? I found some books about you there, and I read every one of them."

I stifled a smile at that. I liked the fact that Six had wanted to learn more about me – and that Five apparently had too.

"While I was poking around in the library, I found a hidden door behind one of the bookshelves. I tried to pull the shelf away to get a better look, but even though I could see this door behind it, it was fastened to the wall. I was curious now, so I took all the books down until I found it."

"Found what?"

"The catch. The bookshelf was set up like a door itself, hanging on hinges. Once I lifted the catch, it swung out toward me, and I could see the whole door."

I pursed my lips. From Six's description, that would have been the part of the basement that had been set aside for storage. It sounded like it had been repurposed for more than just that though. Most people didn't go to that much trouble to protect old kayaks and snorkeling gear.

"And what did you find behind that?"

"Nothing." Six scowled. "I couldn't get it open. It had a combination lock built into it. I thought about just popping it off its hinges, but they were on the other side of the door."

"So what did you do?"

Six shrugged. "I put everything back the way I'd found it. I figured I could come back later with some better tools and give it a shot some other time. But then Dad figured out what I'd been up to. He'd noticed that someone had moved some of the books around on the shelf, and he confronted me about it. I'd never seen him so mad."

"Until today?"

"I suppose," said Six. "I mean, he didn't kick me out of the house then, but he wasn't as mad today. More like determined. He sat me down and cussed me out and made me swear I would leave that door alone. He told me to never tell anyone about it either. It was his private stuff, and I had no right to violate that."

"And did you ever mention it to anyone?"

Six flushed red. "Not until just now," he said. "I probably shouldn't have told you about that."

"You're right," I said. "But the secret is safe with me."

Six sighed in relief at that.

"So how does that tie in to what happened today?"

Six grimaced. "I told him why I went to see you. The real reason, I mean."

I realized I was holding my breath, and I let it out slow.

Six put his hands out before him, palms up. "I was tired of all the secrets in the family. I wanted to know what was going on. If I couldn't get into that room to figure things out, then I was going to talk with you instead."

I was confused. "But I don't know anything about that room. That was just a storage room when I owned the place."

"You owned it?" He threw up his hands. "There's another thing I didn't know. But talking with you was the only other thing I could think of to do. When Dad heard that, he just got quiet. He was mad, but he wouldn't let it show. At least that's what he thought. I could see him shaking.

"Then he asked me to leave. At first, I didn't get it. I just walked out of the room and sat down to play some games on the thrid.

"He followed me and hauled me up out of my chair. 'No,' he said. 'You need to leave this house. Now. And do not come back.'

"I still didn't believe it. When my mom came into the room, I tried to explain it to her. I figured she'd understand and convince Dad to take it all back. He refused though. 'It's for his own good,' he told her. She just sat there nodding, tears running down her face."

He fell quiet then. I let the silence grow between us for a while. When I couldn't stand it any longer, I spoke. "And so you left and came here."

"That's about it," he said. "Exactly."

I pondered the situation. While I was happy that Six had contacted me, I didn't have time for this sort of family drama at the moment. Tracking down my killer had to be my highest priority. Every day that passed without me finding my murderer left the trail that much colder.

On the other hand, I couldn't just toss Six out onto the street. He'd been born a hundred and eighty-three years after me, and my blood may have run thin in him, but it was still my blood.

I couldn't bring him back to my place though. The Kalis had seen to that.

I didn't feel like I should let him stay with me at Blair House either. He seemed like a good kid, but I didn't want to have to assign an agent to watch over him, and I couldn't let him have a free run of the place.

Besides, hanging out with me might make him a target. If he'd been with me at my condo this morning, he would have been killed for sure. I couldn't bear the thought of being responsible for his death, even indirectly.

I realized I had only one real choice.

I sent a note to the Blair House kitchen, placing an order for two hot sandwiches and cold drinks to go. They could have them waiting for me in the courtyard in less than ten minutes, and we could eat them on our way.

"Do your parents know you're here?" I asked.

Six shook his head. "I didn't tell anyone. I just grabbed a hovercab and came right over."

"How did you know where I was?"

"When I turned on the thrid to play some games, the news came on first. I saw the report about your condo on the news. We all did."

I winced at the thought of reports of that disaster spinning out of control on the net. Patrón would probably rip off my head and hand it back to me.

"That's part of why I couldn't get my dad to see reason," Six said. "He pointed at the wallscreen and said, 'See? He's dangerous. I don't ever want you to go near him again.'"

"But here you are."

Six shrugged. "When I refused to promise him I wouldn't contact you again, that's when he threw me out. Up until then, I thought I could talk him out of it. I figured maybe Mom would step in and stop him, but she didn't."

He hung his head low and did a poor job trying to hide his sniffles.

"And then you did exactly what he told you not to."

Six wiped his face and looked up at me. His gray eyes seemed to glow at me, just like Colleen's had whenever she'd wept.

"I contacted your office to try to reach you, but they said you weren't there. I tried Agent Querer, and she told me you were here."

I stood up and patted the kid on the shoulder.

"All right, Six," I said. "I've heard enough. Let's get going."

He looked at me expectantly. "Where are we headed?"

I ran my tongue over my teeth. These would be words he didn't want to hear, but I had to say them anyway.

"I'm taking you home."

THIRTEEN

"Come on, Grandpa," Six said. "Think about it. You don't have to do this."

Our hovercar slipped into a parking level about halfway up the towering building in which Six lived with his parents. It sat out on the edge of Alexandria, in a once-modest neighborhood that had fallen on harder times. Here, on the other side of the Potomac, the old DC zoning laws hadn't ever applied, and the oldest and most decrepit skyscrapers in the area teetered here, many held up by steel pillars bolted to their crumbling retrofitted façades.

Six had been saying the same thing to me over and over since we'd left Blair House behind. The only time he'd stopped was when he gave in to his hunger and ate the vat-grown-beefburger and fries or drank from the tube of filtered water that had been waiting for us when we'd gotten to the hovercar.

I had ignored him for most of the ride, assuming he'd eventually give up and move on to something else. It hadn't worked with Cal either. I wondered why

I had thought it might work now. Since we had finally reached our destination, I spoke.

"I can't let you wander around with me. Your father's right. It's too dangerous."

"I'm almost eighteen," he said. "I'm old enough to take care of myself."

I had to laugh at that. "Kid, I'm almost two hundred years old, and if today is any indication, I don't think *I'm* old enough to take care of myself."

"But, Grandpa—"

I cut him off with a wave of my hand. "Your father made a mistake. I'll explain it to him. He'll take you back in."

Although he tried to hide it, hope shone in the kid's eyes. "What makes you so sure of that?"

"He's your father. He loves you. He'll forgive you."

"Just like you forgave Three?"

I closed my eyes and pinched the bridge of my nose, but I didn't say a thing. When I opened my eyes back up, Six gave me a sheepish look.

"I guess that was uncalled for," he said.

"I never kicked Three out of my house. He never lived with me. Two was his dad."

"But wasn't the big falling out between him and you?" He edged forward on his seat, eager to learn more about his family's secrets. At least it got him to stop asking me to turn the hovercar around, if only for a minute.

I looked out the window. A young couple with a squalling baby climbed into a scraped and battered hovercar next to us, and it took off into the sky.

"Not really," I said. "I understood his point of view. Two, though, I think it embarrassed him. He was the grandson of this national hero, and here was his son acting like some kind of revolutionary."

"You couldn't have stepped in and put an end to it?"

I shrugged and looked back at Six. "I tried. It just made things worse. It gave Three a chance to shout at me in front of his father, which only embarrassed Two even more."

Six raised an eyebrow at me. "So here you are getting involved again? What makes you think this will be any different?"

"Hope springs eternal," I said.

"Right," said Six. "That and you."

I opened the door and got out of the car. I put my hand back for Six, and after a tense moment's hesitation, he followed me.

"Lay on, McDuff," I said.

He led me to the elevator, and we took it down to the fifth floor. We got out, hung a right, and strolled along a long hall lined with glowstrips and narrow doors on either side. We passed a few people in the hall, but none of them gave us more than a passing glance. We stopped in front of an otherwise featureless door marked 5150. Six mimed turning a door knob, but the door remained still.

He scowled at me. "See," he said, "Dad's already deauthorized me. They don't want me back."

"Maybe they just want you to knock first."

I gestured him toward the door. He hesitated for a moment, then reached out and knocked on the door three times, maybe just a bit too hard.

Three seconds later, the door slid aside. A middle-aged woman with long dark hair, olive skin, and deep brown eyes flung herself over the threshold and gathered Six into a desperate embrace. She held him tightly, as if trying to convince herself that he wasn't the product of some sort of mental delusion. When she finally seemed satisfied, she released him and held him at arm's length. "Ronan!" she said. "Don't you ever make me worry about you like that again. I've been trying to contact you for hours!"

He tried to look tough about it but failed. "I didn't – I…" He looked down at her, younger than her but taller. "I'm sorry. I blocked you and Dad after I left. I should have answered."

She gave him a gentle scolding with her eyes, then noticed me for the first time. "Oh! And you brought company." She looked at me while she talked to him, unable to recognize me in the hall's dim light. "Why don't you introduce me to your–"

"Grandpa," Six said.

She turned to stare at him. "Grandpa? But both your grandfathers are…"

Her eyes snapped back to me again, and she blanched and stared at me in shock.

I smiled back at her as warmly as I could and stuck out my hand. "Ronan Dooley," I said. "The First. It's a pleasure to meet you."

She kept staring at me until Six cleared his throat. She jumped as if she'd been bit, then took my hand and gave it a firm, fast shake.

"Mr Dooley," she said. "Of course! I'm Lexa, Ronan's wife. Ronan the Fifth, that is. It's a pleasure meeting you too." She continued to shake my hand as she marveled at me. "The First."

I looked down at our hands, and she followed my gaze. "Oh!" she said, finally releasing me. "I'm so sorry. Please." She stepped aside, making way for Six and me. "Come in."

I nodded my thanks to her and followed her son into their living room. It was a nice place, cramped by the standards of the Watergate, but spacious enough for them. The bulk of the place was an open-plan room that served all their common needs. A dining table separated the main living area from the kitchen to the left.

Light streamed in through a wallscreen mounted opposite the door. A foot-tall crucifix hung next to it, much like the one my mother had hung in our house when I'd been growing up.

Looped thrids of preserved family moments played silently on frames scattered along the other walls. I saw Six playing basketball and indoor soccer in several of them, becoming progressively older as he went. I recognized Three in a few of them, as well as a man that must have been Four, plus lots of other people I could not place. I decided not to let my ID layer try.

A long semicircular couch sat before the large wallscreen, and Six's mother guided us to it. As Six and I sat down next to each other, I saw a distant look in her eyes and knew she would be zipping her husband a note. She didn't miss a beat, though, and offered me something to drink.

"A little water would be nice," I said. Six nodded for the same.

She hustled past the dining area to the left and into the kitchen beyond. It was then that Six's father entered the room from a door off to the right.

He looked a lot like an older version of Six, but with dark hair that had grown gray around the temples. Instead of his son's rangy angles, he had become rounded and soft. He bore himself with a sort of weariness I would have thought not suited to a man so relatively young.

Of course, everyone's young compared to me.

He stared first at Six and then at me and said, "Get out." His voice trembled with emotions bound so tightly that it seemed he might burst.

I stood up and put my hands out to calm him down, but he wasn't having any of that. "He's your son," I said to him.

"I wasn't talking to him." Five spat the words like bullets and glared straight at me. "He can stay. You, get the hell out."

I started to speak, but Six jumped up between us instead, facing his father. "Don't talk to him like that, Dad," he said. "Don't you know who this is?"

"Too damn well," said Five.

Lexa came back from the kitchen, a glass of water for me trembling in her hand. "Ronan! I'm shocked. He's not only your – ancestor, he's our guest."

"I know," said Five. "I don't throw out guests. Only family."

He moved in front of me, looming over me, trying to intimidate me. I wasn't having any of that.

"My blood must run awfully thin in you, kid," I said.

He flinched as if I'd stabbed him. I motioned with my chin for him to back up, and he took one step back. I stood up slowly and looked him in the eye. Although he probably didn't realize it, he had Cal's wide forehead and thin nose. Seeing that made me miss my son in a way I hadn't in years. It drained the indignation right out of me.

"Look," I said, holding out my hands to placate Five. "I don't mean to be any trouble here. Your son came to me and said he'd been kicked out of here. I insisted on bringing him home."

Five opened his mouth to say something, but I cut him off. "I can see I'm not welcome here, so I'll be on my way."

"Good," said Five.

Six stood up next to his father and me. "You are too welcome here," he said to me. "I brought you in here as my guest."

He stared at his father, daring him to throw him out along with me.

Five snarled. "This man is not Ronan Dooley. He's a cheap copy engineered to look like him, act like him, even to think that he *is* him. But he's nothing more than a bad bootleg. The real Ronan Dooley died from an assassin's bullet back in 2032."

I got up and walked to the door. It opened before me as I approached it. Before I left, I turned to say my piece.

"I don't know you," I said to Five. "And no matter what you might think, you don't know me. I just wanted to bring your son home to you."

"Mission accomplished," he said in a tone colder than a frozen grave. "Now get the hell out."

Six moved to join me, but I motioned him off. He didn't need to suffer any more because of his affection for me.

I did what the man said, and I walked out. I could hear them shouting at each other as I stormed down the hall.

I got back into my hovercar and sat there for a moment. I wanted to head for Obama Interplanetary and grab the first transport into space. A week in a lunar resort would do me good.

Or maybe I could just ditch it all, quit my job here, and volunteer for one of the Mars settlements. The idea of leaving it all behind and starting over one last life somewhere fresh tempted me so much.

Then I saw Six racing along the roof toward my hovercar. I knew I couldn't stick around – and I couldn't talk to him again either. I'd just be encouraging him to follow me around. Better to make a clean break.

I ordered the hovercar to take me to the Washington Mall. It slipped up into the darkening night, leaving Six to dwindle in the distance behind me.

I used my top-level clearance to allow me to sail in and land in front of the Jefferson Memorial. Most people preferred the other monuments on the Mall. Washington and Lincoln got all the love. Not from me, though. Jefferson was always my man.

When I got out of the hovercar, Querer was waiting there for me.

"How long you been following me?" I asked.

She smirked. "You think you can evade me in a Secret Service pool car?"

"I could if I'd been trying." I sighed at her as I thought about Five and his family. "Thanks for giving me a little space."

"More than I probably should have," she said. "I understand how hard it is to stay away from family, but you did just foil an assassination attempt on your life. Maybe out here in the open's not a safe place to be."

I looked up at the memorial from the bottom of its steps. The interior of the dome glowed with lights filtering out through its Roman pillars, and I could see the bronze statue of Jefferson looking down at us from its center. Still gazing at it, I spoke to Querer.

"Back when I was a kid, there'd been this thing called Moore's Law. It stated that the power of computers would double roughly every two years. This went on for what seemed like forever, but it ran up against its upper limits in the early part of the twenty-first century.

"Before that, lots of people – futurologists, they called themselves – had gone on and on about an oncoming technological singularity that would change everything, something so big that predicting what lay past it would be impossible. The robots would finally figure out they were smarter than us and take over. Aliens would realize we were finally mature enough to join the greater galactic community and would either invite us to join them or wipe out the planet. The dead would rise and take over the world."

"Well, I guess they got that one right," said Querer. "Just maybe not the way they'd expected."

I looked at her and laughed. Her deep eyes sparkled at me.

"Tell me," I said. "Why did I pick you for a partner?"

"Wow, am I really that unlikeable?"

I jumped forward to stomp on that notion. "Not at all. I just wonder if I ever said anything to you about it."

"Only that you couldn't stand me."

"See, that would have been my guess." I stopped when I saw the look of mock horror on her face. "Nothing personal. I just prefer to work alone."

"Right up until the point you get killed?"

"Seems that way."

She wrinkled her brow at me. "Why did you come here?"

"Just someplace to get away. And I like a lot of what Jefferson had to say. For instance, one of the panels in there says this: 'I am not an advocate for frequent changes in laws and constitutions. But laws and institutions must go hand in hand with the progress of the human mind. As that becomes more developed, more enlightened, as new discoveries are made, new truths discovered and manners and opinions change, with the change of circumstances, institutions must advance also to keep pace with the times. We might as well require a man to wear still the coat which fitted him when a boy as civilized society to remain ever under the regimen of their barbarous ancestors.'"

"Wow," Querer said. "Did you memorize that?"

I shook my head. "I had my server look it up."

"Still, quite a quote from a man who's seen more change than anyone else alive."

As those words left her lips, the sniper's bullet took her right between her shoulder blades.

FOURTEEN

Querer fell forward into my arms, blood blossoming on her blouse. My ballistics layer automatically kicked in and calculated the likely angle from which the shot had been fired. According to the glowing line on my optical display, the shooter was somewhere in the direction of the War On Terror Memorial, which stood just around the edge of the Tidal Basin, right on what used to be the southern edge of the FDR Memorial Park.

My first instinct was to call for the hovercar and go after the bastards who'd shot Querer. The way she gasped for breath in my arms quelled that, and the blood seeping up out of her mouth sealed it away. I could come back from something like this, but Querer wasn't an amortal. She only had the one life, and I had to do my best to save it.

I scooped her up in my arms and turned my back to the shooter, shielding her with my body. Then I charged straight up the white marble steps, leaving a spattered trail of her blood behind me as I raced for the shelter of the Jefferson Memorial.

The few other people roaming around the monument scattered before the sight of the bleeding woman in my arms. I hadn't heard the shot, and I doubted any of them had either, but it didn't take a genius to see that something horrible was happening. They wanted nothing to do with that.

I juked to the left and right at random as I went, and I heard the telltale zing of bullets ricocheting off the stone steps around me. Whoever was trying to kill me was doing a lousy job of it. A trained sniper should have destroyed a vital organ in me by now. A true professional, of course, never would have hit Querer instead.

Unless, of course, that's what he was aiming for.

I cursed as I darted between the towering white columns and emerged under the monument's massive rotunda. Were these idiots shooting at me or Querer? Or both?

I called for backup, snapping off a quick note. "Sniper. Agent down." Then I placed Querer on the marble floor and tried to get a better look at her.

Her face seemed as pale as the monument's marble. I had her blood all over my hands, and what wasn't on me or in her was already forming a pool beneath her.

"Hold on," I said. "Help is on the way."

Shaking, she nodded. She was falling into shock. If the EMTs didn't get here right away, she would die within minutes. Even if they raced here as fast as they could, it might already be too late.

I unholstered my sidearm and hefted it in my hand. It felt tiny and pointless, but it was all I had.

"I'll be right back," I told Querer.

She grabbed at my sleeve and tried to pull me back, but her fingers were already too weak. "Don't," she said, her eyes begging more than her lips could manage. "Don't leave."

I knew she wanted someone there to hold her, to tell her it would be all right, but if she was going to live I needed to put an end to this. If the sniper kept on the pressure, the EMTs might not be able to land and help her in time. And there was no guarantee they'd wait for that to happen. I wanted to believe that no one would be insane enough to fire a rocket into the Jefferson Memorial, but I'd seen enough horrible things in my lives to know better.

"I'll be right back," I repeated. I left before she could respond.

I cocked my pistol, stood up into a crouch, then darted for the other side of the rotunda. I figured that the shooter might have his sights trained on the area where I'd disappeared, and I wanted every edge I could find.

I poked the tip of my pistol out around the corner of the back exit and waited. When nothing shot at me, I dared a peek around, setting my eyes to maximum magnification. The ballistics stripe still ran right from where Querer had been hit to the War On Terror Memorial, stabbing through the air like a permanent tracer trail, but I couldn't see the start point. From where I knelt, it disappeared into a stand of trees just on the other side of the Tidal Pool.

I flipped my vision to full spectrum, hoping to pick up something else. A number of heat signatures swarmed around the War On Terror Memorial, but most of them seemed like rubberneckers gawking at the commotion around the Jefferson Memorial, unaware that the shooter was likely standing in their midst. I noticed one of the reddish blobs sitting a bit higher than the others, and I realized that the shooter was actually in one of the trees.

There was no way I could hit the bastard from here, not with my Nuzi. I'd be more likely to hit a civilian with a stray bullet. But at least now I knew where he was.

Checking on the ultraviolet end of the spectrum, I spied a bright UV laser coming right from where I'd figured the shooter to be. This killer was a professional. Unwilling to risk giving himself away with a colored laser sight, he'd used one invisible to the naked eye and was probably wearing UV goggles to see it – or maybe even had full spectrum lens implants of his own.

It was then that I noticed another UV targeting sight playing across the wall next to me.

I spun about to see four Indians in business suits and pale goggles standing behind me. Each of them bore a pair of Yama machine pistols in each hand, and all eight weapons were pointed at me, their UV lasers playing across my face and chest.

They must have been inside the rotunda the entire time, waiting for the shooter to goad me into here. They might have failed to kill me before, but this time, they seemed determined to do the job right.

"Do not move, Mr Dooley," one of the Indians said. She was short, with a sharp face that her pulled-back and braided hair accentuated. She bore herself like an athlete, and the point of the laser sight she had trained on my heart did not waver an inch.

"Shoot me," I said. "Just get it over with and get the hell out of here."

At that moment, I didn't care if they killed me or not, just as long as we wrapped this up before Querer bled out. I could come back later to take care of them, but she didn't have that option.

"I'm afraid it's not quite that simple, Mr Dooley," the woman said. "We come to you with a message."

The others didn't look at her, and they didn't say a word. They just stared straight at me through their goggles. If I tried, I might be able to shoot one of them. On a lucky day, I might get two. I'd never bring down all four.

"I think you've already made your point," I said.

The woman shook her head. "Mr Patil wishes to have a conversation with you on his own terms. This time, you shall not deny him his wish."

"I don't like to chat with people who greet me with bullets."

The woman removed her goggles, which left circles on her face, and she narrowed her dark, gleaming eyes at me.

"You will come with us, or we will shoot your partner. Again."

I glanced at Querer. Her chest heaved and rattled with every breath. She wouldn't last much longer. If these Kalis were still here when the EMTs arrived, she'd never make it.

"If you refuse us, we will kill you," the woman said. She spoke with no hint of irony, every word a promise as if she were reading it from a stone tablet. "And then we will kill her."

I had no doubt she was right. I put my gun back in its holster. "All right," I said. "Let's go."

The woman put out her hand, and one of the men with her stuffed a metallic cap into it. The hat looked like a skier's cap knit out of wire. She tossed it to me.

"Put it on," she said. "It blocks your connection to the net."

I did as she asked, and two of the men with her moved forward to grab me by the elbows. The other stood to the side, keeping his pistol trained on my chest. She fixed the cap's strap under my chin, then spun on her heel and strode away.

The men escorted me down the memorial's front steps, one on each arm and the third following close behind. Sirens wailed in the distance, getting closer with every second. I spotted sets of flashing lights atop a trio of hovercars racing toward us from the north, skirting right over the White House as they zoomed toward the Washington Monument.

I tried to send out a message telling Patrón what had happened, but the cap on my head worked just as advertised. Nothing was going in or out of my skull until it came off. My nanoserver still worked just fine, but the cap had severed my virtual connection to the world beyond.

I looked around but didn't see the Kalis' ride. I wondered if they were planning to execute me there on the steps of the Jefferson Memorial and then go down before Homeland Security's assault rifles in a blaze of idiocy. The woman leading the way, at least, didn't seem the suicidal type, but it's hard to know just how far people are willing to go to deliver a message.

I tried to trip as the men brought me down the stairs, hoping to slow them down, but the two bruisers held me up by my arms and carried me down the last few steps of worn white marble.

When we reached the shore of the Tidal Pool, the woman stepped to the side. The men holding me did not slow down or even hesitate for an instant. Instead, they gripped me more firmly than ever and charged straight into the pool's cool black waters.

I had just enough time to hold my breath before we hit the water. The fingers on my arms did not slacken their grip despite the shock of the cold blackness. I tried to wrestle my way free, but the two men pulled me deeper into the water like twin anchors shackled to my arms.

I opened my eyes and could not see a thing. Then something large and bluish loomed below me in my infrared vision. It grew larger as we drew closer to it. For a moment, I thought it was some sort of structure on the bottom of the pool. Then I realized it was moving toward us.

I blew all the air out of my lungs and tried to breathe in the water surrounding me. If the Kalis managed to take me alive, they would probably torture me worse than they had the last time they killed me, and I knew I'd rather not have to endure that again. My next body might not remember it, but this one would have to suffer through it just the same.

It's harder to drown yourself on purpose than you might think. Sure, people die that way all the time, but a healthy mind knows better than to allow its body to try to breathe water, and you have to override that basic survival instinct to be able to pull it off.

I managed it though. Knowing that death is only temporary takes the edge off the fear of it. I don't like to die. I don't really know if that's me who will be waking up at the Amortals Project or just some incredibly accurate copy. Maybe it doesn't make a difference to anyone else, but it does to me.

Still, I was determined to cheat the Kalis of any fun they might want to have with me. I opened my mouth and inhaled as much water as I could. My lungs rebelled at this and tried to cough the water from them, but they only succeeded in expelling the last dregs of air remaining in my body. When I reflexively tried to breathe again, the only material they could bring in was more water.

A white spotlight that showed up only on my UV vision caught me in it as if I was an escaping prisoner trying to swim to freedom. It blinded me, but the men still pulling me downward kept me from being able to flinch away. Then my brain finally realized it was starving for oxygen. The light raced away from me as my vision narrowed down to a collapsing tunnel.

Then everything went black.

FIFTEEN

The first thing I did when I woke up was force all the water out of my chest. It felt like vomiting, except it came from higher up and hurt much worse. Thinking back, I'm not sure if I woke up and did that, or if doing that woke me up. Either way, I was conscious for the whole miserable experience.

I had been laid out in a fold-out bench with a hole in it for my face, something like a massage table but harder and closer to the floor. Someone had fastened a soft mask of clear plastic over my mouth and nose, and it had sucked all the water out of me, like an oxygen mask set to maximum reverse. Once it had saved my life by removing what felt like several gallons of the Tidal Pool from my lungs, I thought it might kill me by producing enough suction that I couldn't manage to breathe in against it. Then it reversed itself and began supplying me with sweet air. In truth, the air was probably canned and stale, but with my sinuses full of river water I couldn't tell, nor did I care.

A delicate hand patted me on the back. I tried to get up and realized I was strapped down.

"You can't escape us that easily, Mr Dooley." I recognized the voice as that of the Kali woman in the rotunda.

"Call that easy?" I managed that much before I fell into a fit of coughing. The respiratory vacuum might have been done with me, but my lungs weren't. I coughed until I felt like I'd cracked a rib again, and then I coughed some more.

From the feet I could see gathered around me, there were at least three people in the room with me, including the woman. The fourth of my kidnappers probably wasn't too far away.

"Sit him up," the woman said.

I heard a pistol cocked, then felt the tip of its barrel against the base of my skull. The man holding it put his knee into the small of my back and bore down with all his weight, keeping me put while his compatriot undid the straps binding me to the table. Then the man got off my back, and rough hands grabbed me by the shoulders and sat me up. I swiveled onto my haunches and started hacking again.

As I coughed, I glanced around. I was in a small, cramped room not much larger than the back of a stretch limousine, but curved along one axis like a long pipe. Almost everything inside the place was made of white marine-grade plastic, all scuffed and worn but well tended. To the front, where the driver's window would be in a limo, stood an irised-closed door that I guessed led to the cockpit of whatever I was in.

The windows had been polarized white. If I hadn't known where to look, I might not have thought that there were any at all. I'd been in private submarines before, though, and I recognized the design of this one.

That the Kalis had enough money to buy a submarine like this didn't surprise me. I knew they dragged in a staggering and all-but-uncountable amount of money from their rackets. No gang got to run most of DC without being good with numbers. Still, I would never have guessed that they had the imagination to buy a submarine, much less actually put it to use. The fact that they had done so explained a lot. As the head of the Kalis, Sharma Patil was the most wanted man in the region, but he seemed to come and go as he pleased, and no one was ever able to track him. Most of our efforts had been based on land- and air-based travel though. We'd never thought to look for him in the Potomac.

I figured this should have been just one more reason tossed on top of the pile they had for punching my ticket. Yet here I was still breathing. In fact, they'd brought me back to life.

"Why are you doing this?" I asked. "If you wanted me dead, you should have just let me drown."

The woman flashed a mirthless, wry smile. "We're not here to kill you, Mr Dooley. We only want your attention for a short conversation."

I boggled at this. "Most people don't send a sniper's bullet as part of their greeting."

"Would you have come with us willingly if we had asked?" she sneered at me.

"If you'd been polite about it. But killers usually can't manage that."

One of the men raised his arm to backhand me, which was just what I wanted. If I could get him close enough, I might be able to grab his gun before the others could stop me. He froze at the height of his swing, though, when the woman forcefully cleared her throat.

I smiled at her. "Did you go to all this trouble to pick me up for a conversation or a beating?"

"A small talk," she said, "but not with us."

At a gesture from her delicate hand, the lights in the cabin dimmed. A set of thrideo projectors kicked in, and my lenses automatically polarized to see Sharma Patil sitting there in front of me.

He looked like an ancient raja from his homeland. His regal features and bearing seemed to demand respect and obedience from all those around him. He wore sharp business clothes that were more fashionable than any I'd owned in over a hundred years. His tie pulsed with a faint glow that, I was sure, matched his heartbeat, which was strong and steady, not betraying a hint of nervousness at all.

Patil's graying hair swept back from his forehead in a tall widow's peak. Large, wide-set eyes stared out at me from wherever he actually was, and as he spied me a soft smile grew upon his lips. It never touched his eyes.

"Mr Dooley," he said. "I'm so glad we could finally have this chance to chat."

"I wish I felt as amicable about it," I said. "Your

people have a poor way with invitations."

"I do apologize for them, Mr Dooley." His tone showed not a hint of regret. "They are hard people who do hard jobs, and sometimes the niceties do not always come easily to them. Despite that, you should appreciate that they are very good at what they do."

"Like shooting innocents."

"Come now, Mr Dooley," Patil said. "I hardly think Agent Querer is innocent. She does work alongside you, after all."

"I'm not sure what I'm guilty of, but I would think a man in your position would know the dangers that come with guilt by association." I'd tried to nail him on conspiracy charges for associating with known criminals in the past, but the US attorney's office had never been able to make it stick.

Patil shook a long finger at me. "*Touché*, Mr Dooley."

He waited for me to say something, but I wasn't about to indulge him. He'd called this meeting. He could set the agenda. I just stared, memorizing every bit of him. I set my nanoserver to record everything. I'd never been in a face-to-face meeting with Patil before, and if I managed to survive the experience, I knew I'd want to be able to run through the encounter over and over like a quarterback going over last week's game film.

Eventually, the Kali leader spoke.

"I had my people bring you in so I could personally deliver a message to you, Mr Dooley. It is short and succinct, so please listen carefully. I want to be sure I have your full attention."

I nodded at him. The idea that I would ignore him at this point was ludicrous, but I was willing to play along. "Don't be shy."

"Back off."

I dropped my chin forward and stared at him in disbelief. "Are you serious? You think just asking me politely means that I'll suddenly take orders from you?"

Patil nodded softly. "Pardon my manners. I meant, 'Back off, please.'"

I gaped at him. "After what you did to me, you have the gall to ask me to back off?"

"I have done nothing to you, Mr Dooley. I have only sought to protect my own interests."

"By killing me?"

Patil smirked. "For a man such as yourself, such a detail is but a small annoyance. I have no reason to kill you. If I did, you would only come back to haunt me again. You are a ghost made flesh."

"Yet you murdered me – or had me killed. Who did your dirty work for you doesn't really matter, does it?"

It was Patil's turn to look shocked. "You think I had something to do with your horrific public death? How appalling. I may have applauded it, but I had nothing to do with it."

He leaned forward in his chair and steepled his fingers before him. "How long have you been trying to bring me in for my crimes? How many years have I frustrated your efforts? Just how dumb do you think I am?"

"You're the criminal mastermind here, Patil. You tell me."

He shook his head. "What have I done in the past that would make you think I would be so insane? Why would I publicly murder a top Secret Service agent and dare the government to come after me for it?" He pointed at his chest. "People like me, the ones who succeed and rise to the top, don't do it by poking the sleeping elephant. I have always been content to let the elephant slumber, to remain ignorant of my purpose as I tiptoe around him."

"Maybe you've been on top too long, Patil," I said. "Maybe you're getting tired of living."

He smirked at this. "I do not think that I am the one who has grown weary of life, Mr Dooley. This is not our first meeting. When you approached me for a favor back in May, I took a risk and decided to trust you. It wounds me that I cannot expect the same from you."

I narrowed my eyes at him. Despite his classy manners, Patil didn't have the scruples of a three-year-old. "I may not remember much of the recent past," I said, "but I'm sure I'd never ask you for any sort of kindness."

Patil grinned, and it occurred to me that he might not be lying. Also, that I'd just given him more information than I should have. While my murder had been the top topic on all the newsfeeds the day I was killed, the fact that I'd not bothered to back myself up for a few months hadn't been released. I was supposed to be the poster boy for the faithfulness and dedication of the Secret Service, not a bad example of an amortal blithely taking his ability to come back from the dead for granted.

And up until that moment, Patil hadn't realized that fact – but now he did.

He cocked his head and squinted at me, his mouth curled in disbelief. "Just how long was it since your last backup, Mr Dooley?" he said. "How much did you lose?"

"You don't have the clearance for that," I said in my best deadpan.

Patil shook his head. "So the joke is on me. I performed a service for a part of you that's forever dead and gone, beyond anyone's reach. And now I'll never be able to collect upon it. That is unfortunate. I thought we had finally come to an understanding."

"Why would you think that?"

Patil snorted in amusement. "You don't remember? The EMP technology you requested? I suppose you've lost track of that too. More's the pity. Those were not simple items to procure."

"I'm sure I never intended to make good on any debt to you."

"Do you have so little honor, Mr Dooley?"

I nodded. "I'm more of a results-oriented kind of guy – especially when it comes to bringing down crooks like you. A few lies are a small price to pay." I gazed at him, trying to gauge his reaction. "Don't be so shocked. You tried to kill me twice since I was murdered."

Patil shook his head. "You have only yourself to thank for that. You brought it on yourself."

This, I hoped, was my chance to learn more about what I'd been doing during those missing three months. "And just how did I do that?"

Patil folded his hands on his lap. Despite his cool demeanor, his tie pulsed a bit faster now. "Don't play the
innocent, Mr Dooley. We both know how much blood
you have on your hands."

I opened my mouth to protest, but he cut me off. "I
knew – I *knew* – from the moment I heard the news
of your murder that you would assume that I had
been behind it. But I believed you would simply pur-
sue the matter with your traditional doggedness and
quickly discover who the real culprits behind your
murder were.

"Instead, the night you came back, a masked killer
attacked and destroyed my nanoserver farm located in
an underwater facility beneath the Dumbarton Bridge.
At first, I thought perhaps one of my competitors had
decided to launch some sort of offensive against us.
But our security cameras turned up this."

Patil's visage faded away, and an image from a camera mounted high in the corner of a dark, cramped
room replaced it. It showed a score of people reclining
in workstation chairs, their eyes unfocused, their fingers twitching with arcane gestures that only their
nanoservers understood, like ancient wizards engaged
in some sort of spirit walk.

These young men and women were all Indian and
all bore the mark of Kali on their foreheads, guaran-
teeing that anyone who saw them would know whom
they belonged to. This abstract, red-inked image of a
many-armed woman writhed in a hypnotic pattern
beneath their skin. The movements were synced up to
match exactly on each face.

I didn't recognize the facility, but I instantly knew what it was. The Kalis had been running a money laundering operation for decades, filtering cash through a gold-farming operation that sold virtual cash from persistent-world video games to people who didn't want to bother with gathering it themselves. This had been a major issue for the Service since the dawn of the twenty-first century, and we'd never been able to do more than stick our collective thumb in the dike.

The Kali operation was the most solid in the world. It required human operators to run it though. We knew that they had a base somewhere in or near DC, but we'd never been able to find it. It looked like someone finally had.

A man dressed in a dripping, black wetsuit entered the room, a full diving mask covering his face. He bore a dry Nuzi in each fist. The workers roused themselves and reached for guns resting in holsters duct-taped to the sides of their chairs.

The man opened fire before the workers could aim their weapons, riddling their bodies with dozens of bullets. After the first fell, the others refused to surrender, bringing their guns to bear on the man too. He kept firing at them until his guns ran dry. Then he sprang forward, plucked the pistols from the grasps of the first two victims, and let loose with those guns too.

When those pistols were empty, the man stood and surveyed the carnage. Satisfied that no one would interrupt him, he tossed the borrowed guns onto the floor, then removed something heavy from a matte-black dry bag slung across his back. It looked like one of those German potato-masher grenades you see in WWII games and thrids, but bigger, with a thick pipe wrapped in white tape where the handle would be.

The man set the device down on the floor, then tapped the end of it with a gloved finger. Illuminated numbers flashed to life there and started counting down. The man nodded at the device, then turned and left. When the numbers reached 0:00, there was a bang and a flash, and the image went black.

"That little toy hit my facility with an EMP that fried every piece of electronics in it," said Patil. "It will cost me a fortune to fix it."

I allowed myself a faint smile at that.

"Do you have any idea who that was?" Patil asked as the black image dissolved and his image solidified again.

I nodded. I'd turned on my gait recognition layer the moment the scene had started. Because of the foil cap they'd put on my head, I couldn't connect to Homeland Security's main database, but I didn't need to. The layer already had the killer's gait stored in my nanoserver's onboard memory.

It was mine.

SIXTEEN

"Someone faked my gait," I said. "It's been done before, with other people. It's hard to fool the layer's diagnostics but not impossible."

"Of course you would say that. But he used an EMP, one that used the same sort of technology I supplied you." Patil shook his head. "I had thought we were coming to an understanding."

I felt my heart pounding in my chest. It was one thing to die. I'd been expecting to be killed ever since the sniper's bullet had knocked Querer into my arms.

It was something else entirely to realize that someone was trying to frame me – to pin a massacre on me – and not in a court of law but in the mind of one of the most powerful criminals in the nation.

"I have a roomful of witnesses that will place me in the White House at the moment of that incident." I struggled to keep my voice even, to not show how much the scene had shaken me.

"Yes," said Patil. "I wondered how you managed that. To be in two places at once. Did you have someone pose as you in front of the reporters? Or did you somehow manage to blackmail them all into lying for you?"

"There's video of me there," I said. "From several different newsfeeds, and a few private ones too."

Patil scoffed at this. "Faking video is trivial, especially with the resources of the White House behind you. My grandson could manage a decent job of that, and he is merely six."

"How do I know the video from your server farm wasn't faked?"

"You don't," Patil said, his eyes widening. "But I do. That scene came directly from my own surveillance camera. It is unadulterated."

I looked down at my hands. They were not the ones that had pulled the triggers on the guns that had killed all those people. I knew that, but how could I convince Patil of the truth?

"That wasn't me. I swear."

Patil sneered at this. "You've already confessed that lies mean nothing to a man on a mission like yours."

I grimaced. It seemed that my moment of bluntness with Patil might cost me.

"Do you really believe that we could get our hands on every bit of footage from that night in the White House? That no one would say anything about the fact that I didn't show up to my own rebirthday party?"

Patil stared at me as if I weren't really there.

"Sharma." I used the man's first name to grab his attention. "Why would we do something like this? If the Service wanted all your people dead, why wouldn't they just send someone else?"

"Maybe they did." Patil's eyes focused so sharply on me that it seemed like his gaze might slash open my throat. "Maybe that wasn't you. But if not, who was it? And why go to the trouble to impersonate your gait?"

I growled at the thoughts racing through my head. "Someone's trying to frame me. They want you and me at each other's throats."

I remembered the man who'd tried to get change from me back in Georgetown.

"Someone gave me some bills yesterday that had once been mine," I said, "but one of them had passed through one of your businesses shortly before I was murdered."

Patil furrowed his brow. "The implication would be that you were in our custody before you were killed, no? That we Kalis were, in fact, your killers."

"Exactly! Whoever's doing this is trying to set us against each other, probably to draw the heat off them."

"So they can get away with your murder?"

I shrugged. "I have to think the two things are connected."

Patil shook his head. "But why should I believe any of this? Are these yet more lies?"

I reached into my pocket to fish out the bills, and one of the men behind me whipped me across the skull with the barrel of his pistol. I half-spun about to attack him, but the other two men shoved their guns in my face. I put up my hands instead.

"The bills I mentioned are in my pocket."

Patil considered this for a moment, then nodded at the woman. She snaked between two of the men and slipped a hand into my pocket. A moment later, she pulled out the soaking wet bills and held them up into the light. She stared at them, her eyes scanning every detail, until a scowl fell across her face.

"He's telling the truth," she said.

The fact that she had access to the bill-tracking database should have disturbed me, but I was too relieved to worry about it at that moment. I let loose a deep breath I didn't know I'd been holding.

Patil screwed up his face and stared at me, taking my measure. "Anyone who could fake an entire White House party could certainly forge the records for such bills."

"Check them against your own," I said. I didn't know for sure that the Kalis would bother to keep such records. Most merchants just passed on the data to the Treasury department and then cleared their cash cache at the end of every day. The Kalis laundered such a huge volume of money, though, that I could hope that they might be a bit more particular about keeping their own records for far longer than that.

The fact that Patil didn't scoff at me immediately told me I was right. His eyes unfocused for a moment as he looked up the data. He was biting his lower lip when those eyes snapped back onto me.

"Your data matches ours," he said. "Perhaps you are correct. Perhaps someone is trying to set us at each other's throats."

I nodded hard. "Exactly!"

Patil shrugged. "Be that as it may, I do not see why I should not simply kill you and be done with it. Perhaps if I give this mysterious person what he wants he will then leave me alone."

"At least until tomorrow, when I'm revived again."

Patil winced to acknowledge this.

"Let me go," I said. "Let me track down whoever this is and make him pay. That's what you want, isn't it?"

Patil arched a bushy eyebrow at that. "Why, whatever would make you think that?"

I glanced around at the people holding me prisoner. I looked straight at the woman as I spoke.

"If you wanted me dead, I'd already be gone."

Patil laughed at this, the kind of laugh you get from telling an old friend a joke you both already know. "Too true."

He looked me in the eye.

"All right, Mr Dooley. We have an understanding. You will keep out of Kali matters, and I will refrain from trying to kill you."

I shook my head. "What if that's what this killer wants?"

Patil leaned forward as his voice rose in disbelief. "For me to not kill you?"

"No, for me to stay out of your business. Perhaps he's using you as a shield to hide behind."

Patil rubbed his five o'clock shadow with a thin-fingered hand. "Perhaps it is as you say. However, I cannot just give you the keys to my home. That would be unacceptable."

"How about I just contact you when I need something you might be able to supply?"

Patil smacked his knee with an open palm. "Done."

Then he gave me a pitying smile. "If I were you, Mr Dooley, I'd do everything I could to find this killer of yours as fast as you can. If he's foolish enough to put himself between the Secret Service and the Kalis, he's mad enough to try anything."

"I'll find him."

"Please do so fast. You amortals tend to think of time in terms of decades and centuries. Those of us blessed with only a single life never forget that the world can change in an instant."

"I thought Hindus believed in reincarnation," I said.

He smiled at that. "Very good, Mr Dooley, but when we are reincarnated, we come back as something different every time. In this way, we can take a fresh stab at life. The same cannot be said for you, I'm afraid. You carry the same baggage with you every time."

He gestured to the woman, and someone behind me pulled a bag of black cloth over my head. I did not resist.

I waited for several long minutes as the submarine made its way through the Potomac to wherever the Kalis wished to take me. They spoke not a single word, probably communicating through messages sent to each other by nanoserver instead. The silence made for a long, eerie trip.

Eventually, I felt the thrumming of the submarine's engines stop. They had been so soft that I'd not even noticed them until they were gone. Two men then grabbed me by the elbows again and guided me out through a hatchway, one of them pressing down on the back of my head, presumably to keep me from knocking my forehead on the top of the hatch.

The men walked through another hatch and up a ramp. The change in temperature told me that I'd left the sub. They led me up in a winding path that went up two long flights of stairs and along a number of tight hallways. Then I felt something sharp press into my neck, and I fell unconscious.

When I came to, I was sitting alone on a landing in the middle of a long set of stairs. It took me a moment to recognize the place, but I had been there so recently it was hard for me to forget it: the stairwell from *The Exorcist*.

Maybe, I thought again, the people of Georgetown had better reasons than just superstition for staying away from the place. Whatever they were, those reasons had kept the locals from robbing or killing me while I sat there out cold.

I checked the time and saw that it was already past 6am the next day. I'd been out for several hours but still felt like I hadn't slept at all.

I reached up, felt the foil cap still on my head, and tore it off with one swift jerk. Once I did, a slew of messages queued up for my attention. I ignored them all and contacted Patrón by voice. Sometimes he let my calls get caught in his secretarial filter, but I suspected this time I would get right through. While I waited for him to respond, I called for a Secret Service pool hovercar to come pick me up.

"Ronan!" Patrón's voice thundered in my ears. "Where the hell are you?"

"Georgetown." My voice was hoarse with whatever Patil's people had used to knock me out. "I just spent the night in the company of the Kalis. How's Querer?"

"She's— Christ, Ronan, you scared us to death. I thought you were dead for sure. Disappear without a trace twice in the same week. Not even an SOS signal from your eyes."

"I'm fine." I growled to clear my throat, and I headed up the stairs to Prospect.

"You sound half-dead."

"Just tell me about Querer."

"She's going to be fine. I think she's already out of surgery. The bullet didn't hit anything vital."

I closed my eyes and breathed a sigh of relief. "Where is she?"

"GWU Hospital. She should be in recovery right now."

That made sense. The George Washington University Hospital was the closest one to the Jefferson Memorial. Once the EMTs stabilized her, they would have taken her straight there.

"Thanks," I said. "I'm on my way."

"Ronan!" Patrón said. "I want a full report about where you've been all night."

"I'll get right on that," I said, "just as soon as I check on Querer."

We both knew I would never get around to it, but Patrón let it slide. He could give me a hard time about it later, after all this was over. I disconnected from him and stood at the top of the stairs, from which I could see the storefront in which I'd last been killed.

I flipped on my ID layer and scanned the street. The man who'd given me those bills that went through the Kalis wasn't anywhere to be seen. I hadn't thought he would be, but I had needed to try.

At the moment, it seemed like I could cross the Kalis off my list of likely suspects in my murder, although I wasn't entirely sold on that. Patil could have been lying about it, of course, although it seemed like an awfully long way to go to avoid telling the truth to someone you could have just had killed. That didn't mean that someone else in his organization hadn't had me murdered – or hadn't set us against each other.

I'd seen lots of agents make the mistake of thinking of a criminal organization as a monolithic structure, the parts of which always moved in synchronicity with each other and with a unified purpose. It was a convenient way of understanding such a group, but it ignored the true complexity of any human organization. Everyone in any organization is an individual with his or her own wants and needs and plans for satisfying those things. As long as the individual's desires matched up with those of the organization – or, at least, the organization's leaders – then everything worked well. But when those desires diverged, the unity of the organization fractured.

Patil had a number of lieutenants and other flunkies who carried out his orders, people to whom he delegated both power and responsibility. If one or some of them had decided it was time to remove Patil and take over, setting him against me would be the perfect diversion to keep attention off of themselves.

My gut told me, though, that Patil had just as firm a grasp on the Kalis as he ever had. He'd been running the group for a decade now, having taken over from his predecessor via a bloodless coup. Displaying authority without resorting to having to use its power was one of Patil's trademarks. The fact that he'd been desperate enough to send a squad of killers after me indicated that he was shaken more than he would ever care to admit, but that didn't mean that he'd lost his grip on the Kalis as well.

I'd made a lot of enemies over the years, and any one of them might be behind all this trouble. It seemed like I'd slid all the way back to square one.

The hovercar landed next to me, and I gestured for it to open a door before it even touched down. I leaped into the seat, closed the door behind me, and ordered it to bring me to Querer. Visiting her, at least, was something I could manage.

SEVENTEEN

Querer did not look good. She lay in a blue gown in a white-sheeted hospital bed that had the top half propped up to help ensure any loose fluid wouldn't collect in her lungs and stop her breathing. Her right shoulder, between her neck and the actual shoulder joint, was swathed in gauzy bandages and tape. A nasal cannula supplied her with a steady flow of extra oxygen, and a bank of monitors standing near the far side of the bed kept a steady beat of tiny beeps and blinking lights to indicate that she'd not died quite yet.

Alone in the room with her, I gazed down at her sleeping form. The artificial sunlight radiating from the nearby wallscreen made her look older than she was. Getting shot can do that to you too. Nothing ages a person like pain.

Despite that, she had a certain undeniable beauty about her. Here, with her defenses down in every way, she seemed innocent and exposed, vulnerable. She needed someone to protect her, and I had failed at that. I silently promised myself that I would not allow that to happen again.

I reached out to pull a stray curl of hair from where it had fallen across her face, and I tucked it behind her ear. The sensation roused her, and a moment later her wide brown eyes opened.

"Oh," she said with a pained smile. "It's you."

She reached out for my hand, taking care to only move her lower arm, from her elbow down. I put my fingers in hers, and she gave them a soft squeeze.

"You look like hell," she said.

I gave her a wry smile. "Given how you look at the moment, that's a terrible insult," I said.

She copied my smile, then gave my hand another squeeze and let go.

"The bullet went right through my shoulder," she said. "Missed anything vital. Didn't even nick my collarbone. The docs say it's a miracle."

"I don't think they were trying to kill you," I said.

She made a face at that, then winced in pain. "They did a good job of faking it."

I peered at her wounded shoulder. "If they wanted you dead, they would have used a higher-caliber bullet, or one with a soft nose or explosive tip. You would have never known what killed you."

"You say the sweetest things."

I stood there quiet until she waved me toward a chair. "If you're going to stay, then sit," she said. "It hurts to look up at you."

I obliged by moving the chair over to the right side of the foot of her bed, directly in her line of sight, before I sat down.

"So if they weren't trying to kill me, why did they shoot me?" she said. "To get to you?"

I nodded. "Patil wanted to have a conversation with me. They dragged me into a submarine in the Tidal Pool."

"Very persuasive." She considered me for a moment. "Partnering up with the legendary Ronan Dooley has proven hazardous to my health."

"I didn't want a partner. I think I made that clear."

"The fact that you asked Patrón to make me your partner should you get killed – and then that you got killed – makes me wonder how sincere you were about that."

I looked down at my hands, palm up in my lap. "I haven't had a lot of luck with partners. I tend to draw fire, and that's not healthy for anyone who spends a lot of time near me."

Querer arched an eyebrow at me. "That sounds awfully convenient for a man who prefers to be alone."

"I don't mind being around people," I said. "I just don't like to watch them die."

"I'm a big girl, Dooley." Querer groaned as she sat up a bit farther in her bed. "Today's incident aside, I can normally take care of myself."

"I'm sure, but there's little that's normal about my life."

"Don't flatter yourself. You're about as regular an amortal as I've ever met. Most of them are insufferable bastards. There's a certain arrogance that comes with the certainty that no matter how badly you might mess something up you can always start over with a fresh slate."

"And I don't have that? I've been reborn as often as anyone."

Querer smirked. "You ever read *The Lord of the Rings*? Or see the movies?"

"Every chance I get."

"You know the elves in the books, how they are? They take such a long view of the world that they become like aliens to the humans in the story. Amortals are like that. Endlessly patient. Hatching plots that take decades to come together. Playing every side they can find against the middle."

She sized me up with her eyes and nodded her approval. "You're not that patient. You're still among the living, not one of those ghosts that haunt their own lives."

I looked at the wallscreen. It showed the capital waking up to a bright sunrise beaming right down K Street at us.

"I never think of myself as having that much time," I said. "I might. Perhaps the people I work under do, but the people I work *for*, they don't have decades to waste. Or to wait."

Querer smiled at me. "How many times have you saved someone's life?"

I shrugged. "I don't keep track of things like that."

"Give it a guess."

I shook my head. "It's hard to define anyhow. Sure, there are the clear-cut occasions when I stepped in front of a bullet, but that's hardly everything. Did I save a President's life by the decisions I made on an advance trip scouting out a dangerous location? Once

I found a dirty bomb in Union Station and disarmed it. How many lives did I save there?"

"Why do you keep doing it? Saving people, I mean."

I stared at her as if a second head had popped out of the bandage on her shoulder. "Because it needs doing."

"Sure, but there are others who can handle these things too. Are you saying you're the only member of the Secret Service who can properly take a bullet?"

"Of course not."

"Then why not retire? You've certainly earned it. I bet if you turned in your accumulated vacation and sick days you could probably pocket a few years' salary too. Plus, what sort of pension do you qualify for with a hundred and seventy-five years of service under your belt?"

"They cap it at fifty years."

"That hardly seems fair, does it?"

"You're using 'fair' to describe our federal bureaucracy?"

She flung her eyes wide at that. "Are you saying something less than positive about your country, Dooley? Not to mention your employer?"

"Let's just say it's not always the easiest job and leave it at that."

"So," she pressed, "why not retire?"

"It's not that simple. I retire now, I still have a good fifty or more years ahead of me in this body, assuming no one comes after me to kill me once I'm out from under the protective umbrella of the Secret Service. What am I supposed to do with all that time?"

"Oh, I don't know. Enjoy it?" Sarcasm dripped from her tone. "Take a vacation? Wander the world? Find yourself a young lady and settle down? Live the life of the idle rich?"

"Does that strike you as something I would like to do?"

"I don't know, Dooley. I think you could learn to enjoy it. Maybe you could reacquaint yourself with your family."

My face fell at her words. My single attempt at doing that in this century hadn't gone well at all.

"I'm sorry," she said, her voice swollen with sympathy. "It's just that I see you out there, working to save the world, and you're all alone. You don't even have anyone to come home to at the end of the day."

I marveled at her. "They must have you hopped up on some wonderful painkillers to get you talking to me like that."

"Am I not right?"

I took a moment to digest that, hoping she'd say something to fill the void. She didn't, so I finally did.

"I used to have a life. Then I got killed. Now all I have is a job. It's a good job, an important job, and I'm good at it."

I realized I was slouching in my chair, and I sat up straight and looked the wounded woman in the eye. "I protect people. That's what I do."

Then I remembered who I was talking to and what had happened to her the night before. "Or at least I go down trying."

She gave me a forgiving smile for that. "I've been checking up on you," she said. "Before they took you off protective detail, you had been getting yourself killed more and more often."

"I didn't pull any of those triggers."

"You might as well have, the way you threw yourself at assassins. You ever think about doing that?"

"What?" I felt myself start to squirm in my chair and had to concentrate to stop it. "Kill myself? I have a good life. Nothing to complain about."

"You're just in denial. Everybody has something they can bitch about. Just answer the question."

I pursed my lips for a full minute. Then I let it out. "Sure," I said. "I've thought about it. It's a long, lonely life, even when you're not amortal. Everybody thinks about it at one point or another."

I let that lie there between us. When Querer spoke, I had to strain to hear her voice. "Ever act on that?"

I shook my head. "Not that I know of."

"Do you think you might have but now can't remember it?"

"Every time I died, it was in the line of duty. It's all a matter of public record. You can look it up."

"I did." She leaned forward in her bed, despite the obvious pain it caused her. "Are you sure you—" She stopped herself. "Do you remember a woman named Arwen Glover?"

The name brought me up short. It sounded familiar, but I couldn't remember why. I looked her up in my contacts file, and her image slid into the edge of my vision. She was beautiful – stunning, really – with shoulder-length blonde hair and bright blue eyes. The image was from the last time I'd seen her, thirty years ago, but I thought I should have remembered a woman like that for a much longer time.

"She worked with me at the Secret Service," I said. I recalled running into her a few times at headquarters, but that was it. "That was a long time ago though. I haven't seen her since."

I refocused my eyes on Querer, suddenly suspicious about her change in subject. No matter how grateful I might have been for it, she wasn't the sort of person to just jump around in a conversation. Maybe the painkillers had made her fuzzy, but I had to wonder where she was going with this.

"Why?" I asked.

Querer grimaced and wouldn't meet my eyes.

"Why?" I leaned forward in my chair. I wasn't going to let this pass.

Querer rolled her eyes in resignation. "Because she's here."

I stared at her. "What?"

At that moment, a woman burst in through the door. She looked very much like the lady I'd resurrected from my nanoserver's memory, but thirty years older. I stood up to greet her, but she rushed right past me, favoring her right leg just a bit.

As she did, a flood of memories about her shocked me to silence. I hadn't seen her in thirty years, but she looked much the same. She wore her hair the exact same way, although she had let it go from blonde to white. She bore many lines on her face, and while they showed her worries about Querer at the moment, I could see that the deepest ones had come from smiling. She carried herself with the same grace as before, although she moved a hair slower and seemed an inch shorter.

"Amanda!" she said as she reached out to put her arms around Querer. "I saw the report this morning when I got up, and I was so worried about you I ran right over."

Querer held up her arms to keep Arwen from hugging her hard enough to pop her stitches, and the effort made her wince in pain. "It's OK, Mom," she said. "I'm all right."

"All right? You were shot!"

Querer made an either-or gesture with her hands. "I'll be fine. It's not that big a deal."

"'Mom'?" I said.

Arwen snapped around to look at me, unaware that she had stormed right past me. Querer groaned, but this time not from any physical pain.

Arwen gaped at me, displaying her perfect white teeth and her wide blue eyes, which were as bright as ever. "Ronan Dooley?" Her voice was soft but warm.

I put out my hand, and she took it, more out of reflex than will. "It's been a long time, Arwen."

"Yes," she said, staring at me and then down at our hands. "Yes, it has."

I let go of her hand, and it fell to her side. She gazed at me, still astonished, until Querer cleared her throat. Then Arwen hopped around and glared at the bed-ridden woman.

"Why didn't you tell me you were working with Ronan?" Arwen said. "You mentioned a new partner, but you think you might have bothered to tell me who it was."

Looking now, I could see a strong resemblance between the two women. Querer had dark curly hair with deep brown eyes, while Arwen's hair was graying and straight, and her eyes were blue. Their height, their build, the structure of their faces, though, were almost identical.

Querer threw up her hands. "I didn't think it was that important, Mom. The Secret Service is a large organization. I didn't know if you'd ever worked together."

Arwen gave me a sidelong glance as she continued to scold Querer. "Well, I don't know if Ronan would remember me, but I certainly remember him. He's the most decorated agent in the history of the Service, after all."

"Of course, I remember you, Arwen," I said. "I think I had a little crush on you back in those days."

She had the decency to blush at that. "Oh, but I was a married woman climbing the ladder at the Secret Service."

"Which is why I never brought it up back then," I said. "It's too bad we never had the chance to work together."

"Oh, but we did," she said with delight. Then, concerned, she cocked her head to the side. "Don't you remember?"

EIGHTEEN

I frowned. "I'll be two hundred years old next month," I said, "but I think I would remember something like that."

"Unless you somehow forgot to back yourself up again," Querer said in a dry tone.

Arwen gazed at me expectantly. I found I could not look away. I hadn't been lying when I said I had a crush on her back in the day, although it hadn't been nearly so little as I'd made it out to be. She'd wormed her way into my thoughts for weeks.

But then I had forgotten about her almost entirely. What, I wondered, would make me do something like that?

I thought back to thirty years ago. That would have been 2138. I turned 170 that year. I died that year too.

I'd been working the cybercrimes division again in those days. I'd foiled an attack against Senator Lee during the 2136 Presidential campaign, and Patrón had decided to take me off protection until the public – or at least the crazies who were likely to focus on me as a target again – had forgotten about me. I'd seen the wisdom in that, although I hadn't been happy about it.

"I remember meeting you in late 2137," I said to Arwen. "But I don't recall us being assigned to anything together. Your office was on the floor below mine in those days."

Arwen frowned. "But nothing else?" I could see the effort she made to keep her voice steady.

I shook my head. "Now that I think back on it, Querer – Amanda – is right. I lost about six months of my memories back in 2138. After that, Patrón had Mangold – remember him? – bring me in for my backups every week, whether I wanted to or not. That went on until Mangold retired fifteen years later, and Patrón never bothered to give anyone else the assignment."

"Well," Arwen said in a hoarse voice, tears welling in her eyes, "I suppose that explains a lot."

"What is it?" I said. I wanted to help her, but I had no idea what she was so distressed about.

She collected herself, then faced me head on. "I used to wonder why I never heard from you after all that happened. You went off to go save the world, and the next thing I knew you were dead and being brought back to life at the Amortals Project."

"What happened to you?" I asked. "Why didn't I ever see you again after that?"

Arwen reached down and rubbed her right thigh. "I took a bullet in this leg, and Patrón insisted I retire. He made sure I received full disability payments, so I didn't have to work again."

"So you just quit?" said Querer.

Arwen looked over at her daughter. "I was pregnant with you when that all happened. I nearly lost you when I was shot. That scared me enough to keep me home for a long time. Raising you alone took a lot of work."

"What happened to your husband?" I asked. I didn't recall ever meeting him, but I noticed that Arwen wore no wedding ring on her hand now.

Arwen gave a helpless frown. "We married young, and it didn't go well. After I got out of the hospital and came home, he realized that he'd been scared for me but not at all for himself. He didn't love me anymore, he confessed, and he left. He didn't know I was pregnant at the time. Hell, I barely knew myself."

I checked Querer's reaction. She was busy ignoring her mother and staring out the wallscreen instead. She'd clearly heard this tale before.

"Anyhow," she said, sweeping away the wistfulness in her face with a forced smile, "that's all ancient history now."

"To you," I said. "To me it's all new. Like watching reruns of a thrid you missed when it came out."

Arwen smiled at that, and this time it wasn't forced.

"So what did we work on together?" I asked. I didn't want the conversation to end quite yet.

"I don't know all the details about it," Arwen said. "Some of it was above my clearance. I just went where I was needed and did what I was ordered."

"That's the best kind of agent. We could use more of those in the Service."

"I read about it," said Querer. Arwen and I both turned to look at her in surprise.

"I didn't think you'd have clearance to read that report," I said. "I barely do, and I was in the thick of it."

Querer smirked at me. "I didn't break any laws. I'm a good little agent too. I read the parts that weren't auto-redacted for my level. Even that much makes for an amazing story."

"It's just the job," I said. "We work with some pretty amazing people. 'Standing next to history,' I've heard it said."

"Yeah," Querer said, "but a plot involving the Pro-Deathers, the President, and the Pope? That doesn't come along but once in a lifetime – even for you."

I put a modest smile on my face and kept my mouth zipped.

"What?" Arwen said. "Oh, Ronan, what happened? Can you tell me about it?"

I hemmed and hawed about it. "Technically, no. It's all classified at the topmost level. Actually, it's above my level, and I shouldn't even know about it. In fact, I barely do."

"That's what you get for not backing up," Querer said. "You would think you'd have learned that lesson."

"Old dogs and new tricks," Arwen said. "He didn't grow up with amortals running around like you did, honey. He didn't have a role model to follow."

"Fortunately, most of them don't follow his example, or we'd have huge gaps in our national history."

I put up a hand to silence the comments. "I did my job, and I saved a lot of lives. That counts more than any memories of it."

"Or so you were told," said Querer.

"You remember Father G?" I said.

"The man leading the protesters outside the White House? Sure."

"I met first met him during that incident. He was our informant."

Querer goggled at that. "That Pro-Deather? But why? He hates amortals, doesn't he?"

I shook my head. "He's a good man, just a little misguided. When he found himself getting wrapped up with the One Resurrectionists behind the assassination plot, he knew he had to do something to stop them. He came to me and told me everything."

Arwen nodded. "If only he hadn't been too late."

"What do you mean, 'too late'?" Querer asked, a hint of indignity in her voice. "Dooley saved both the President and the Pope. Doesn't that count for something?"

Arwen reached up and touched my cheek with more tenderness than I thought I deserved. "Yes," she said, gazing into my eyes, "but not in time for Ronan to save himself."

I tried to smile at that but found I couldn't manage it. "I got better," I said.

Remembering herself, Arwen retrieved her hand and looked away.

"Do you think maybe they have something to do with it this time around?" said Querer.

"Who?"

"The One Resurrectionists. They certainly have a history with you. Maybe you were investigating another plot of theirs and got too close."

I rubbed my forehead as I mulled that over. I'd had a long night, and I was still in the blood-spattered clothes I'd been wearing when the Kalis hauled me into the Tidal Pool.

My first thought was that Querei was overreaching. I'd seen nothing since my revivification to indicate that Father G or the One Resurrectionists or any other religious movement had been behind my murder. I couldn't just go around accusing every old enemy of killing me, working them over until one of them cracked.

On the other hand, I didn't have much else in the way of a plan.

"What do you think?" I said to Arwen.

She blushed. "Oh, don't ask me," she said. "I've been out of the game far too long. You can't possibly care what an old lady like me might think."

"Can the false modesty, Arwen," I said. "I don't remember enough of you, but I know you're one of the sharpest agents the Service ever had. And I may only look like I'm thirty, but I haven't really been that old since your great-great-grandmother was in diapers."

She covered her mouth to stifle a laugh at that. "All right then," she said, becoming serious. "I think it's a definite possibility. How many other leads do you have?"

I looked at Querer, and she shrugged at me. "At the moment?" I said. "None. The Kalis looked promising, but they turned out to be a dead end."

Arwen frowned. "And you're not going after them for shooting my daughter?"

I put up my hands. "The Service will, for sure. And we'll help them out as much as we can. My murder investigation is still ongoing, though, and I doubt Patrón will take us off of that."

"Take *you* off of that, you mean."

I admit, I didn't know what she getting at.

She saw my confusion and explained. "You're not going to take my daughter back out into the field with you in this condition. She's just been shot."

"Mom!"

I had to hand it to Querer. She could have handled this like an embarrassed teenager. I've seen many people who were far older than her deal with their parents like that. When you get multi-generational families of amortals, you can find a man over a hundred years old who still can't keep his cool around his parents.

Querer, though, was too together for that. She just laid down the law, clear and simple. "My status as an agent and my assignments are not up to Dooley to decide. That falls to Director Patrón."

Arwen began to protest, but Querer held up an index finger to cut her off.

"The doctors here say I'm doing well and should make a full and fast recovery. They want to keep me here a while for observation, and then – if you're up for it – you can take me home. I'll contact Director Patrón at that point and work with him to determine my next step, whatever that may be."

"But, honey, you've been shot!"

Arwen unconsciously rubbed her hand on her leg as she spoke, right at the spot that still caused her to limp. I could see her trying to keep herself together, but it was a struggle.

I sympathized with her. I'd watched my wife and son fall ill and die, and there's nothing to make you feel more helpless than seeing a loved one in pain – especially when you know that the same fate might never befall you, that you'll never join them in whatever peace they might have found. Someone could have saved them the way they saved me, but just like with ninety-nine percent of the population, that didn't happen, and there was nothing I could do about it.

"Yes, Mom, and it hurts, but I'm going to survive. It won't be enough to put me on disability. With any luck, I'll get a decoration, though, just like yours."

Arwen smiled despite herself at that. "Imagine that," she said. "Matching mother-daughter medals."

I put a hand on Arwen's shoulder. "Don't worry about it," I said. "I'm sure Patrón won't put her back into the field until she's ready."

"These are hard times though," Arwen said. "He might think he has to dig deep to find the help he needs." She shook her head. "And between you and me, I never trusted him much anyhow."

"Hey," Querer said. "What about me? I'm sitting right here."

"Oh, you." Arwen dismissed her daughter with a wave of her hand. "Like you ever listen to me anyhow."

"I wouldn't worry about those One Resurrectionists much," I said. "Over the years, they've proved mostly harmless."

Arwen tried to interrupt me, but I pressed right on. "Sure, there have been a few outliers over the years, rogue elements that have crossed over the line, but most of them are good people who just happen to think that our government is doing something evil. We've had those around since 1776."

"Don't be flip with me, Ronan," Arwen said, tightening her mouth into a stern face. "These rogue elements may have been behind your murder. That's nothing to joke about."

I put up my hands. "You're right! I can't argue with that. I'll be sure to check them out right away – mostly because I don't have any other leads at the moment."

"And the Kalis?"

"I'll make sure to light a fire under Patrón to find the people who shot your daughter and kidnapped me. That's a dangerous bunch that needs to be brought in."

"Whatever's going on, this isn't like Patil," said Querer. "From all I know of him – and you'd know better than me – he likes to be the quiet mastermind, skimming his money off the top and making sure everything runs as smooth as glass."

I nodded. "Whoever killed me sure knew how to push Patil's buttons. He never shows his face to people unless there's serious trouble. For him to shoot you in the line of duty–"

"Don't forget how he blew up your apartment."

"Exactly. He's desperate, and that makes him dangerous."

A notice that I'd received a message from Six popped into my vision. I'd set my nanoserver to filter out all non-emergency messages, but I'd always made an exception for family. This was despite the fact that nobody from my family had tried to contact me for decades. I'd forgotten I'd even made that exception in the first place, but that's what let Six get through.

I ignored it for the moment.

"What about yourself?" asked Arwen. "Doesn't it bother you that someone's trying to kill you?"

I weaved my head back and forth, unsure. "Of course it does, but I – I don't take it personally."

Arwen glared at me as if I was insane. "You can't be serious."

I shrugged. "You know how it is when you're an agent. Most of the killers aren't after you, just the person you're protecting."

"Well, yes, but that's not the case here."

My system pinged me again with another note from Six. This was one was flagged red and urgent. I ignored it again. Now wasn't a good time.

"True," I said to Arwen. "But as an amortal, I know – and my attackers know – that death isn't permanent. It's just a temporary setback. The people after me can't really kill me. They can only slow me down."

Arwen could not repress a scowl. "Ronan Dooley, that is the most absurd pile of rationalizations I've ever heard."

"Maybe," I said, "but I was honestly angrier when they shot your daughter than any time they were gunning for me."

A third ping from Six popped up, this time flagged as an emergency. I closed my eyes and sighed. When I opened them, I saw Arwen gazing at me, her anger softening.

"I'm sorry," I said. "My very-great-grandson is messaging me about an emergency. I need to take this."

She reached out and gave my arm a sympathetic squeeze. "Go." She glanced over at Querer. "When it comes to offspring and emergencies, I certainly understand."

NINETEEN

"What is it?" I asked Six by subvocalization as I strode out of Querer's room. I made my way toward the elevator that would take me to the parking slips above the hospital.

"Didn't you read any of my messages?" the boy asked, his voice cracking with stress as he spoke. He was on the edge of panic.

"I figured it would be faster to chat. Just take a deep breath, then fill me in."

"It's Dad," he said, ignoring the bit about breathing. "Five. He took off."

"Is that unusual?"

"No, not that part. But after the way he talked to you, I got curious."

"Uh-oh. What happened?" I got into the elevator and ordered it to the proper parking level.

"He has a private closet in his bedroom. He keeps it locked. I broke into it."

"You defeated it yourself?" I was impressed. Getting through an electronic lockset and reinforced door wasn't something most civilians could accomplish without an axe.

"It wasn't that hard," said Six. "Dad doesn't trust electronics. He just had a padlock on it."

"So how'd you get it off? Was it a key or combination?"

"It's a combination, but I didn't bother with that. It had the lock straps mounted on the outside of the door, so I just undid the screws holding those down."

I could hear how pleased he was with himself for figuring that out. I only wondered how long that should have taken. Five had probably trusted the outer doors to keep any intruders out. He hadn't bet on his son's curiosity eventually getting the better of him.

"So what's the problem?" I asked.

"Dad didn't believe keeping electronic records. He still kept everything on paper. The closet was full of boxes of it. I don't remember ever seeing that much of it in one place outside of a museum."

"And?"

That hauled Six up short out of his babbling, but it also derailed the circuitous train of thought he'd been riding. "What?"

"And what did you find?"

"Oh! Grandpa, you wouldn't believe it. The entire place was filled with all sorts of stuff from something called the One Resurrection."

My heart skipped enough beats I thought it might never start up again. When it did, it hurt.

"Are you sure?"

"Oh, yeah," Six said. "I see their logo sometimes when we go to church. I recognized it right away."

"Wait. What?" The doors of the elevator opened, and I rushed out into the parking structure to find my hovercar. "Where do you go to church?"

Other than for funerals, I hadn't been in a church for years. At my age, I didn't get invited to weddings much anymore.

"The National Cathedral. It's not the closest place, but Dad says it's the best."

"You're Episcopalians?"

I don't know why the thought bothered me so much. Perhaps it's because I knew such news would send whatever remains were left of my long-gone mother spinning in her grave. It was one thing to fall away from the Catholic Church. It was something far worse to take up with another denomination.

"I guess so," Six said. Caution crept into his voice. "I don't really go all that often. Dad drags me there on Christmas and Easter, but I usually sleep in on Sundays."

"So you're a Chreaster?" I smiled despite my misgivings about whatever Five was up to. "I suppose that still beats me."

"Grandpa," Six said. "What's all this mean?"

I hesitated. "Hopefully nothing," I finally said. "The One Resurrection is a group of papists who believe that only God should have the option of bringing somebody back to life. They're opposed to amortals on moral grounds."

"That sure sounds like Dad."

"They're mostly Catholic, although I suppose they wouldn't turn away Episcopalians or anyone else who cared to join. Your father may be – clearly is – mixed up with them."

"Is – is that bad?"

"Hard to say. It depends on what they've been doing lately, and on how much your father had to do with it."

"How are you going to figure that out?"

I found the hovercar waiting where I'd left it, and I gestured for its door to open.

"That's my job, kid. I'm usually pretty good at it."

"What – what about–? You did just get killed though."

I sat down in the hovercar and pinched the bridge of my nose. "That, Six, is what happens when I'm too good at it. I'll let you know what I find out."

"Thanks, Grandpa."

"Don't mention it. Literally. Don't tell a soul what you just told me, OK? Not even your mother."

"Got it."

"Put all that stuff back where you found it. Replace the lock. Go to your room and stay there."

Six laughed. "If they find me there, they'll know something's up."

"Then get out and do what you do. Just keep your nose clean."

"Wow. 'Keep my nose clean'? Who talks like that?"

I smirked. "You done good, kid. With luck, I'll be able to keep your dad's nose clean too. Good night."

"It's morning, Grandpa."

"Sure. For you."

Six laughed again. I hoped I'd helped him feel better, even if only a little. "Good night too," he said before breaking the connection.

I ordered the hovercar to haul me back to Blair House. Once I got there, I took a shower, changed into some clothes that didn't smell like the bottom of the Potomac, and wolfed down a fantastic breakfast that I barely took the time to taste.

Then I started to hunt my great-great-great-grandson down. I first tried checking Five's footprint on the net, only to find he didn't have much of one at all. I managed to turn up a few instances of youthful indiscretion: pictures of him at parties, nothing serious. Other than that, though, he kept a suspiciously low profile.

Five did not have any implants. He apparently had a phone, although he normally kept it turned off. I tried searching for his location by that but had no luck. I even tried calling him and confronting him directly, but as many times as I pinged him he never picked up the connection.

In my experience, only three types of people cut themselves off from the rest of the world like Five: Luddites, criminals, and the insane. I'd talked with him, and while he may have hated me, I didn't think of him as certifiably ready to be fitted for a white dinner jacket with wraparound sleeves.

That left technological drop-out or crook. The fact that Five lived in Alexandria with his wife and son meant he wasn't one of those guys who drop out of civilization to live in a cabin in the woods and send bomb-laden hate mail to mid-level bureaucrats.

That brought us down to one possibility: Five was up to no good.

There's a broad range of criminality, of course, from speeding on the highway to plotting mass murders. Most of humanity falls somewhere between those two extremes. Few of us are so innocent that we don't bend the occasional rule, and even fewer of us stand ready to destroy the entire world.

The question then was this: what was Five doing that he wanted to make sure no one else could find out about it?

I decided I'd go back to basic investigation work and follow the lead I had. Six had found One Resurrection literature in his father's closet. It wasn't a crime to side with people who didn't agree with the concept of amortality, but the fact that Five felt he needed to hide his association with One Resurrection – even from his own family – told me there was more to it than that.

The problem with One Resurrection was that it wasn't an organization so much as a movement. It had no central offices, just a homesite on the net. People joined in it to whatever degree they liked. They could chip in some comments or a few bucks, maybe design some placards or posters to promote their point of view, or they could dedicate their lives to the cause.

A little research showed me that Father Luke Gustavo was still listed as one of the leaders of the One Resurrection movement, despite the fact he'd secretly betrayed part of that group decades ago. Although he wasn't the named head of the group, no one else was either. He was one of the hottest firebrands in their forums, preaching fire and brimstone sermons about the hubris of humanity and the folly of treading into territory properly reserved for God. Lots of people agreed with what he had to say, and those that disagreed with him on the forums received a verbal evisceration with a heaping scoop of humiliation for dessert.

The forum comments about my murder were mostly positive. They offered up a prayer for my certainly damned soul and hoped that my new self would somehow see the light – or meet a similarly horrible and deserved end. Some of the commenters were thrilled about the killing and wished they had done the job themselves.

A couple of the posters actually took credit for my murder, each separate from the other. Rather than receiving the congratulations and adulation they expected, though, they fell into an argument that quickly devolved from calling each other liars to questioning which lower forms of life had served as the other claimant's parents.

Reading between the lines of their rants, I could see that neither of them had been involved in my murder in any way. The fact that they were so excited about it that they wanted to take credit angered me. I tried to not take it personally, but images from the snuff thrid kept flashing back in my head, and that made it just about impossible.

I'd been killed many times before, but the mainstream media had always hailed me as a returning hero. I'd purposely not hunted down the crackpot opinions because I knew they'd only make me mad. Now, though, I had no choice. The investigation had brought me here, and I had to follow through. The fact that I was chasing my own progeny through this muck washed all that anger with sadness and regret.

The worst part was that none of this had brought me any closer to finding either my murderer or my not-so-great-great-great-grandson.

I tapped into Homeland Security's Total Intelligence Engine and put in an order to find Five.

TIE was the greatest achievement ever made in the field of law enforcement. It gathered together every bit of information generated in the nation and synthesized it into a single, searchable database. That included every bit of data on the net, over a full alphabyte of information and growing every second.

Collecting all that data was the easy part. Sorting through it was insane. I still remember the days before the internet. The first computer I every programmed was a DECwriter II. Instead of a screen, it had a dot-matrix printer for its display. Anytime you wanted to see what the computer was doing, you had to print out a new display again.

We've come a long way in the last two hundred years.

Moore's Law might have petered out back about the time I lost my first life, but you wouldn't know that from the way Homeland Security worked. TIE had the most incredible supercomputers in the world working for it every instant of every day. It was a bit over my head, but supposedly they just kept adding supercomputers in parallel with each other every time they needed to add more capacity. So far, it seemed to have worked.

I had TIE pull up Five's record and then search every security camera in Alexandria for footage of him leaving his home. It came up with nothing. Facial recognition came up blank. Gait recognition came up blank. Olfactory sensors failed to find his scent. As far as TIE was concerned, Five was still sitting at home.

Of course, there are ways to get around TIE, but they require conscious effort. You can wear a mask or a hat to obscure your face. You can defeat gait detection just by putting some gravel in one of your shoes. You can spray yourself with perfume or step in something conveniently found on most sidewalks in the city to cover your scent. You trade for things you want instead of using money.

"Aw, Five," I said to myself, "what have you gotten yourself into?" The fact that Five was actively hiding from TIE made me even more nervous for him.

Just because he had gone under deep cover at the moment, though, didn't mean he always had. I had TIE bring up all of Five's recorded movements over the past six months and search for patterns.

From the analysis, Five was a creature of strong habits. He spent most of his time either at home or at work. Despite the fact he'd graduated with a degree in biology, he had worked for a private company called Failsafe Security as a security consultant for over twenty years, which likely explained how he skilled he was at evading TIE when he wanted to.

He couldn't keep that up forever though, not if he wanted to be a part of civilization, which is why TIE had any trail on him at all. He seemed to have few if any hobbies or pursuits. He commuted from his home to the office and back, and he regularly went to church and back. Just as Six had said, Five attended the National Cathedral. I wondered about that, as there were plenty of other churches located closer to their place in Alexandria. Christ Church, which had been there before the founding of America, was only a stone's throw from their home.

Maybe Five was a fan of architecture. I'd been to the National Cathedral many times, and you can't find a better example of Neo-Gothic architecture in the country. Walking into it gives you the sense of awe that a smaller church just can't hope to match.

I had TIE overlay Six's movements atop Five's. The two of them overlapped mostly at home, but rarely anywhere else. I removed Six's layer and added Lexa Dooley's instead. Five's wife moved around a lot more than her husband and was clearly not concerned about anyone following her. She also attended church with him, nearly every Sunday. There was something about that fact that stuck out at me. I checked the frequency of Five's trips to the church versus Lexa's. He ended up there two or three times as often as her.

According to TIE, Five's visits to the cathedral happened at irregular days and times. It looked as if someone was deliberately trying to avoid creating a pattern of visits, which didn't make much sense if Five had lawful reasons for being there. If he was a church deacon – or whatever the Episcopalians called the laypeople who gave their reverends a hand – then he should have attended *regular* meetings there, not ones randomly scattered about the calendar.

Of course, these were only the visits I knew about. Five could clearly avoid TIE when he wanted to. Or could he? The cathedral was a national monument. It might be too challenging to move in or out of it unseen.

Then I realized what Five was doing: establishing a pattern of movement. If TIE saw him coming and going from the National Cathedral on a random but regular basis, then it wouldn't raise any alarms if he went there at any other time he wanted to as well – like when he *really* needed to be there.

I signaled the Blair House staff to get my hovercar ready. Then I left for the National Cathedral to see if I could find a missing man hiding at his favorite spot.

TWENTY

It was mid-afternoon by the time I reached the National Cathedral. Unlike much of the city, it stood open to the sun. Congress had long ago named it a national landmark and had forbidden developers from encroaching too closely upon it.

I came up Massachusetts Avenue, skirted around St Alban's School, and parked the hovercar on an uncovered section of Wisconsin. As I was about to get out of the car, Patrón pinged me. I'd blown him off for most of the day while I puzzled over my murder case and the troubles with Five, wondering how the two might intersect.

While Patrón was technically my superior, nobody on the planet had seniority over me. Perhaps I abused that privilege too often, but I considered it my prerogative to be able to ignore my boss when I felt I needed to. This time, though, Patrón had figured out I was in the hovercar, and he pinged that instead. Being from the Secret Service pool, the hovercar instantly recognized Patrón's authority and patched the call into its audio system.

I could have run from the car if I'd liked, but that seemed to be pushing it too far. I figured I'd take my lumps from Patrón now rather than later if he was that determined to reach me.

"Dooley!" he said. "I've been trying to reach you all day. Is something wrong with your nanoserver?"

"It's working fine," I said struggling to keep my tone even. "What do you need?"

"I'd like an update about your murder investigation, up to and including what the hell happened to you last night. In detail."

"It'll be in my report."

"I am not going to wait for you to go back and fill in the blanks when this is all over. This is an important investigation, and I have people of every rank in the government breathing down my neck over it. Spill it, Dooley."

I grunted at him. "I'm in the middle of the investigation right now. I don't have the time to sit down and route all the relevant data to you."

"Dooley—" He raised his voice the way a mother does before chastising a recalcitrant child.

I cut him off. "Look, Patrón," I said, "do you want me wasting time telling you how I'm going to catch my killer, or would you rather I do my job and actually catch him?"

"So you think it's a man?"

"Think what you like," I said. "I'm very twentieth-century. I still use 'him' as a generic."

"Damn it, Dooley, toss me a bone here. Give me something to bring back to the President."

I had been about to stand up and shut the door on the hovercar. I stopped and blinked at that. "What does she care about this? Doesn't she have bigger things to worry about?"

"Maybe she has a crush on you."

"Not cute," I said. "What's going on here?"

Patrón snorted. "For a man as old as you are, I'm still shocked sometimes by how naive you can be, especially when it comes to yourself."

"Speak English. Or Spanish. Or Mandarin. Or Hindi. Something that makes sense."

Patrón hesitated while he composed his thoughts. I recognized this from countless conversations with him over the years, and I patiently waited for him to be ready. When he finally spoke, it was with the tone of a primary school teacher trying to explain how to plot suborbital flight plans to a nine-year-old.

"Do you realize who you are?"

"Back at the Amortals Project, they told me I was Ronan Dooley when I woke up there."

"No. I mean, do you recognize your place in the world?"

I knew where he was going with this, but I wanted to make him follow through with it. "I'm a Secret Service agent, and I'm trying to do my job, but my boss keeps pestering me to chat with him like a teenage girl."

"You're the world's oldest man. You're the original amortal. You're the model for the rest of us, the hero who started it all. When someone murders you – not just murders but *desecrates* you – it scares the rest of us."

"Oh, come on. None of you were killed. And if you were, so what? You'll just come back again tomorrow."

"I didn't say it was logical, Dooley, but emotions rarely are. The fact remains that the most powerful people in the nation – hell, in the world – are now scared. They want action. Results. And I need to give it to them."

"You?" I didn't like the direction he'd turned with this. "What about me? I'm the man on the job."

"For now." Patrón paused a moment to let that sink in. "I gave you this case as a courtesy, because of your long service with the Service and because of our nearly-as-long friendship. I had to override a lot of objections to make that happen, and after a few days with no results, their voices are growing louder."

"You call having the Kalis blow up my condo, then kidnap me after shooting my partner, 'no results'? I think you're using a different dictionary than I am."

"You know damn well what I mean. These people, including the President, want your killer's head on a silver platter."

"And if you don't get his, you're going to have to settle for mine." I didn't bother trying to keep the bitterness from my voice.

This was the reason I'd never aspired to be director of the Secret Service. I'd been offered the position more than once, but the top job isn't about running the Service as much as it's about dealing with politics. I knew enough about myself to know that I had no stomach for such things. I'd have been forced to resign within my first month, and since my amortality is attached to my job, I wasn't keen to risk that.

"Of course not," Patrón said. "This is exactly what I mean. You're all but untouchable, and you don't even know it."

"But now I do. Thanks."

"Dooley." Patrón's voice sounded at least as weary as I guessed him to be. "All I'm saying is that if you can't find your killer soon, then I'm going to have to assign you some help."

"Isn't that what Querer's for?"

"In case you hadn't noticed, that's not going too well."

I'd had too much of this. I needed to walk. I got out of the car and closed the door behind me. The hovercar pinged me for permission to transfer the conversation to my nanoserver, and I reluctantly agreed. I needed to thrash this out with Patrón, or he would wind up thrashing me.

"If you don't have results by tomorrow, I'm going to have to send in the big guns."

I shivered at that. "No," I said. "You wouldn't. That's a PR nightmare."

The "big guns," as Patrón called them, were the Secret Services' special forces, the Special Power Armor Team. They flew around in hover-armor suits equipped with missiles, rocket-propelled grenades, and rotary machine-guns. Their usual tactic was to kill everything in sight, then kill it again just to be sure.

"People don't like to see them on protection duty,"

Patrón said, granting me that point, but then following it up with one of his own. "But that's not true when it comes to other operations. Footage of the SPAT in action against your killers would be PR gold. Think of the message it would send."

"That we're so desperate to bring in criminals that we need to bring in a squad of flying tanks?"

"That we're ready to defend our people and our country with devastating firepower against which no one can hope to stand. The deterrent value alone will be staggering."

I groaned. "Just let me handle this, all right? I have two words for you: collateral damage. Talk about loose cannons. You send the SPAT into action against civilians, and you'll end up with blood everywhere at the best and dead innocents at worst."

"You're not helping your side of the argument."

"Just–" I struggled to find the right words. Last night finally seemed to be catching up to me. "Just let me handle it."

"Where are you now?"

I didn't feel like telling him, but I knew he could call up the information on the hovercar I'd rode here in, instantly.

"Heading into the National Cathedral."

"Really?" Patrón paused. "Going in for your first confession?"

"I have nothing to confess," I said. "I'm three days old. I'm as innocent as I've ever been."

"Just keep out of trouble, Dooley. We don't need you kidnapped again."

He made it sound like it was my fault those Kalis had grabbed me and pulled me into the Tidal Pool.

"I'll do my best."

"And report in to me when you get out. That's an order."

"Is the President actually in the room with you and listening in on the conversation, or are you just mugging for the hidden cameras she's placed in your office?"

"No comment. Now get moving."

I stopped and craned back my neck to take in the facade of the National Cathedral. The gothic spires of gray stone stabbed up into the sky above me, defiantly archaic in a postmodern world. Sculptures of countless forgotten saints loomed over me, looking out over a city that swarmed around them without affecting them one bit except by the slow erosion of acid rain.

I climbed up the wide, long Pilgrim Steps and entered the towering building under an arch filled with nude people emerging from the roiling sea. My culture layer identified it as a tympanum sculpted by Frederick Hart, entitled "Ex Nihilo." My nanoserver translated the Latin as meaning "out of nothing."

I knew the feeling.

I cranked the culture layer down as I walked into the building, or I knew I would be overwhelmed. The kind of artistic detail that goes into constructing a cathedral can stun you with its naked glory – which is the idea, really. Trying to absorb several weeks' worth of footnotes in a short walk can drive you to the brink of madness as you contemplate how so many people dedicated their lives to building this place.

As I made my way into the nave, a volunteer guide greeted me, a tall woman with Asian features and green eyes. "Welcome to the National Cathedral," she said. "Our next tour begins in about thirty minutes. If you like, you could wander about and meet in the transept when it's time."

"Actually," I said, "I'm here looking for someone."

I shut my mouth then, realizing that if I asked after Ronan Dooley V she might associate the name with his famous ancestor and recognize me. Since I didn't know who in the cathedral might be part of whatever Five had become involved with, I didn't want to tip my hand that soon.

Instead, I described Five in detail, right down to his graying temples. The woman nodded as I spoke.

"You're looking for Ron?" she asked. "He's one of our volunteers. Can I ask what this is about?"

I smiled warmly. "Just a distant relative dropping by for a visit. His son told me I might be able to find him here."

"Right," she said with delight. "I'm sure he'll be thrilled to see you." She peered down the center aisle of the cathedral and pointed through the transept to the place where the choir stood during services.

"The last I saw Ron, he was walking that way," she said. "He was with Father G, and they were heading for one of the meeting rooms in the basement."

I used an easy smile to cover my surprise at hearing the priest's name, and the fact that he was here with Five. I reminded myself that while this was the home base of the Episcopal Church in America, the National

Cathedral made a point of welcoming people of all faiths – even radical Catholic priests.

"Thank you," I said.

She offered me a printed guide to the cathedral. I stared at it for a second, amazed that anyone still bothered with such things. Then I took it and moved down the central nave toward the transept.

The arched stone ceiling towered above me in a way that inspired vertigo if I looked up at it for too long. With space at such a premium in DC, most ceilings hung low, barely over eight feet from the floor. This seemed like either an awesome tribute to God or a stunning waste, depending on which side of the faith line you fell.

Sunlight streamed in through the multicolored stained-glass windows that lined the nave's southern wall. I looked up to see my favorite, the one that Colleen had adored too: the Space Window. I looked for the piece of moon rock embedded in it and found it with my naked eyes, no layers required.

For me, the only thing in the cathedral that topped the Space Window was the grotesque of Darth Vader's head that hung high up on the north side of one of the three-hundred-foot-tall towers. That probably has to do more with my twentieth-century youth than anything else. When I was a kid, the idea of colonies on the Moon and Mars seemed like science fiction. I never would have believed that tourists would go to such places on vacation. I still didn't have a working lightsaber though.

I played the tourist as I walked, pretending to take

in all of the amazing art and architecture but really keeping my eye out for people looking for me. The cathedral had no thrid cameras in it, a real anomaly in public buildings. Every bishop over the decades had been adamant about keeping them out. They wanted only the eyes of God watching over their flock, not those of Man.

That didn't mean, though, that men and women actually in the building with me couldn't keep an eye on me. While the cathedral's security system may have been archaic, that didn't mean it wasn't effective. At least they didn't have the all-too-common problem of over-reliance on technology. I'd seen more than one place stripped to the walls when the owners had placed too much faith in their automated security systems.

I strolled through the transept and stepped up to the choir box. Gothic arches of polished wood surrounded it on all four sides, smaller versions of the stone ones that topped the cathedral's exterior. A rope of burgundy velvet blocked off the choir box's front entrance.

Rather than attract attention by hopping the rope, I turned left and headed into the north transept. A beautiful rose window called "Last Judgment" hung high before me, the northern daylight bringing its blues, reds, and yellows to glowing life.

I wound my way past a tiny chapel to my right. A small altar sat inside it, backed by a trio of wooden arches under which had been painted an image of a risen Christ surrounded by doves and winged angels. It stood empty, and I disturbed no one in it as I passed.

I found the stairs to the lower level just beyond that, hidden behind a stone screen, and I took them down. As I emerged into the crypt level, I almost ran into Five.

"What are you doing here?" he hissed, his face a mask of rage and frustration. "You shouldn't be here."

"It's a public place in a free country," I said stepping backward.

"America hasn't been free for a long time," said a voice behind me. I knew who it was before I turned around to confront him, but before I could say a word to Father G he shot me in the chest.

TWENTY-ONE

Fortunately or not, Father G's weapon of choice had been a taser. The darts stuck right in my shirt, and the jolt of electricity that shot between them made all of my muscles flex as hard as they could at once. I fell over on my back, fighting my muscles to relax just enough to let me writhe in pain.

While this was happening, the law enforcement part of my brain noted that the taser used a dischargeable set of darts that featured their own disposable shock battery. That meant that the priest's taser likely had several more sets of darts ready to fire at me, should I try to get up and move.

I didn't think, though, that it was going to take more than that first set to keep me down. My body might only have been a few days old, but at that moment I felt like I was ready to die.

"What the hell did you do that for?" Five said.

"Just step back, son," Father G said with a growl. "And don't blaspheme. You've done quite enough damage here already, I think."

"I did the damage? You just shot a federal agent. How long do you think it'll take for them to figure that out and get here?"

Father G knelt down, turned me over onto my front, and pulled my arms behind my back. Then he clasped a pair of cold metal cylinders around my wrists. Stunned as I was, it took me a while to realize they were chained together. He'd fitted me with a pair of manacles that had to be older than I was.

"Shut your mouth, son," Father G said. "Accept the blame that's rightfully yours and beg the Lord for penance."

"What are you saying?"

"If you hadn't led the man right to our door, I wouldn't have had to tase him."

Five grunted in anger. "No one followed me here. I guarantee it."

Father G rolled me over on to my back. The numbness from the jolt was starting to wear off, which made everything hurt worse than ever, but at least I could move again.

I tested the manacles. They were solid, and they kept me from moving my hands more than a foot from each other.

I was in serious trouble. I didn't want to call in Patrón, but I wasn't sure I had a choice. I checked my connection to the net and found it wasn't there.

The thought that the tasing might have fried my nanoserver sent a shiver through me. I'd come to rely on my implanted net connection over the decades, and the procedure to replace it wasn't simple. Plus, there was the fact that I'd been cut off from any backup while in the hands of a mad priest who'd already shown his willingness to attack me. And my only help was a descendent who'd long since proven how much he hated me.

"He's going to have the entire Secret Service knocking on our door in a matter of minutes," Five said. "We should evacuate now."

"Don't be silly," Father G scoffed. "The man's lying here under a yard of stone. His communication signal can't possibly reach him down here."

That bit of news relieved me more than I wished it had. I ran a routine diagnostic on my nanoserver, and it came back online. The tasing had disrupted it for a moment, but now it seemed to be running fine. The priest had been right though. My link to the net was blocked. I had no way of calling for help.

"Help me get him on his feet," Father G said. He grabbed me under one shoulder, and Five grabbed me under the other. Then they leveraged me up until I was standing.

I let my knees buckle under me. I might not be able to call for the cavalry to save me, but I didn't need to make it any easier for them to shove me around.

They hauled me along anyhow, my knees just off the ground and my feet dragging behind me on the old stone floor that had been worn down over the years by countless feet. I wondered if a tourist might spot them carrying me away in chains and say something, but no one else was around. They must have cleared the crypt for whatever they were doing down here. Maybe they routinely turned any curious people away one by one, and I just happened to walk straight into their security detail.

Father G leaned close and hissed in my ear. "Keep quiet, and I won't have to tase you again."

I grunted in agreement with this. I wanted to say something sharp, but my tongue felt too dull to pull it off.

The two men hauled me deeper into the crypt level, taking a right and then a quick left. This brought us into the Chapel of St Joseph of Arimathea, dedicated to the man who donated his own pre-purchased tomb for the burial of Christ.

I'd been in here long ago with Colleen, playing the tourist family with Cal. It hadn't changed much over the years. When we entered the room, the men dragged me down a short set of stairs into the center of the sunken chamber, the lowest point in the entire cathedral. They sat me down in a chair after struggling to get my bound arms to fit around the back of it.

There were others here too, men and women, well-dressed and clean-cut folks who all gaped at me with a mixture of shock and contempt. There were ten of them in all, including Five and Father G, and they'd clearly been in the middle of a discussion when I arrived.

In the center of the room, someone had set up a thrid display that showed the central part of DC. The image centered on the White House but also included everything from the National Cathedral down through to the Congressional Cemetery. Everyone in the room was wearing polarized glasses to be able to see it properly, which told me that they were just as much Luddites as my captors. When Five and Father G brought me in, someone pressed a button on the display, and it flickered into nothingness before I could study it in detail.

"What in God's name do we have here?" a woman said as she spotted me. She had deep chocolate skin and short, kinked hair pasted against her scalp. Her eyes and lips were wide and soft and could have been kind and friendly under other circumstances. Instead, they showed nothing but a hint of well-buried cruelty.

"Do you really need an introduction, Ruby?" said Father G. He reached down and pulled my head back by my hair, exposing my face.

The others in the room gasped, but Ruby kept her cool. A ghost of a smile reached the corners of her lips as she regarded me. She gestured to a pair of people to head out the door, and they left the way we came in, presumably to take up the guard post that Five and Father G had abandoned. Then she strode over to me and crouched down so that she could peer into my eyes.

"To what do we owe the pleasure of your company, Mr Dooley?"

I shook my hair free of Father G's grasp with a snarl.

"You're all under arrest," I said. I glared at Ruby and then gazed at everyone else, my nanoserver recording their faces as I took in the room. The walls here were made of cut limestone at least a foot thick. The arched ceiling above me had to be far thicker than that. With the guards at the stairs keeping everyone out, I could scream at the top of my lungs here, and no one above would ever hear even the faintest echo.

Ruby stared at me with those round, brown eyes of hers and then opened her mouth and laughed. "I'd been told you were a brave man, Mr Dooley, but I had no idea you were so funny as well. It's a real privilege to meet you."

"Assaulting a federal officer is a serious crime. Those that manage to survive the arrest usually get handed a one-way ticket to the Moon to work in the Darkside Penal Colony."

Ruby wasn't about to crack, I could tell, but the others weren't likely to be so immune to the threat of prosecution. I'd listened to the rants from the One Resurrection before. They called for nothing less than the overthrow of the government and the ending of the Amortals Project. Still, it was one thing to call for revolution and another thing entirely to have the guts to fight for it.

When I looked at them, though, none of them turned away, which meant I was in serious trouble. Only Five refused to meet my eyes.

"Do you really think we can be intimidated by a shackled man?" Ruby asked. "If anyone should be afraid here, it's you, Mr Dooley."

"I didn't think you believed I really am Ronan Dooley," I said.

Ruby gave me a smile that never came close to touching her eyes. "I don't, but if you do, I will call you that for the sake of convenience. After all, these days no one else is proud to carry that name."

Five groaned at that. "Let's cut the drama and just figure out what we're going to do with him," he said. "We can't keep him down here forever."

Ruby nodded, granting Five that point. "We only have to manage it for another couple of days at most," she said. "After that, his life will be moot."

"And who's going to guard him for that long?" Five asked. "We should just leave him here and scatter. Someone will find him, but by that time we'll all be long gone."

Ruby shook her head. "He's gotten too close to us already. He's seen too many of us. If he gets out of here with the data in his head, the Feds will be able to chase us all down."

When she turned her head to gaze at me, I felt like she was a hungry panther sizing me up for a meal. "Unless, of course," she said, "we kill him now."

Five took a step back from me. "I– I don't think that's a good idea. This isn't about killing people. It's about forcing them to stick to one life."

Ruby frowned. "No great changes ever came without bloodshed, Ron," she said. "I thought you understood that. Now I'm not so sure."

That angered Five. "I've been with the movement longer than you, Ruby. I understand it just fine. It's never been about taking out our aggravations directly. It's not his fault he's amortal, right? Especially not him."

Ruby reached behind her back and pulled a pistol from a hidden holster. It was plastic, designed to be able to evade magnetometers and most other easy detection methods. Even the bullets would be made of a special metal-plastic alloy.

"What's the harm?" she said. "They'll just send out another one tomorrow – one without the memories of all our faces."

"That's not how it works," said Ron, "and you know it."

She slid back the action on the pistol, chambering a bullet. Then she pointed it right at my head.

"Go ahead," I said. "I'm not afraid of people who shoot prisoners. I'll come back, hunt you down, and blow your head off myself."

"Oh," Ruby said, "I'm not going to do it."

She reversed her grip on the gun and held it out for Five. "He is."

Five blanched. At that moment, he reminded me of Cal. I'd taken him to Cedar Point in Sandusky, Ohio, to ride the roller coasters on a blustery day. He had just been tall enough to get past the signs that said, "You must be this tall to ride this ride," and he'd been so excited to finally tackle the big-kid coasters. When he finally got into the front car of the Top Thrill Dragster, though, he looked up at that 420-foot peak and turned the same color as the whitecaps blowing in at us on Lake Erie. It was the utter fear of getting exactly what he'd been asking for and realizing just what that meant.

"No," Five said. "You can't ask me to do that."

Ruby stuck out her bottom lip. "I don't know, Ron. Some of our members have come to me about you, asking me if I think we can really trust someone who's a direct descendent of the most notorious amortal around. I always tell them, 'Sure. Ron's good people.' Plus, there's the irony of having Ronan Dooley's great-great-great-grandson taking up our cause. If that doesn't get people's attention, what can?"

Ruby lowered the gun and stepped closer to Five, speaking in a low voice. "But they keep coming to me with these questions. They keep voicing their doubts. And I keep allaying their fears. But some days, Ron – some days I find myself wondering the same thing. How could a man with such close ties to the federal poster boy for amortals be ready to stand with us when the revolution comes?"

Five didn't say a word. He didn't look at Ruby or me or anyone else. He just kept his eyes on that plastic gun. He stared at it as if it were a wild animal that might bite him if he made any sudden moves.

"You know what I do when I get those thoughts in my head?" Ruby said. Her voice was barely more than a whisper now, but it echoed in the stone-lined chamber as if she were standing in front of a microphone in an empty arena.

Five shook his head, but his eyes never left that gun.

Ruby took Five's hand, lifted his fingers between them, and pressed the pistol into his palm. She held it there until his fingers closed around it.

"I pray, Ron," she said. "I pray long and hard and hope that God will help me find an answer, a way of ridding myself of these doubts. And so He has."

She leaned in close now and spoke in Five's ear. "Shoot him," she said. "Kill him, and kill all doubts about yourself with him. Then you'll be one of us. With God, body and soul."

Five shuddered at her words. He stared at the gun. He hefted it and felt its weight in his hand. He held it up before himself and examined it in the light, his hand around the grip, his finger on the trigger.

"All right, Grandpa." He said my name, but he was talking to himself. "All right. If I have to, I will."

He turned to look me in the eyes. I could see tears welling up in him – and hate. This time, though, the hate wasn't just for me, but for everyone in the room. Everyone in the world. For his whole life that had brought him inevitably and inexorably to this moment, which he hadn't even known to try to avoid. He could barely stand any of it.

For a moment, I worried he might turn the gun on himself. That wouldn't have saved me though. Ruby would have just picked it up – or drawn one of the other guns I was sure they had – and murdered me herself.

Instead, he brought the pistol up and pointed it right between my eyes. I braced myself for the shot, but it did not come.

Five's gaze darted all around the room, and I wondered if he might try to shoot Ruby and the others instead. He couldn't possibly kill them all, though, and we'd both die in a bloodbath if he tried.

He had to shoot me. It was the only way.

"Do it," I said to Five. "Kill me."

I caught his eyes and held them in my gaze. Then I spoke to him slowly and carefully. "Do what you have to do."

He wiped his eyes with his free hand, then gritted his teeth and got ready to squeeze that trigger.

I closed my eyes to make it easier for him, and I waited for death to take me once again.

TWENTY-TWO

The gunshots echoed so loud they hurt my ears and set them ringing. For a second I thought I'd been killed and just hadn't realized it yet. I might have died eight times already, but with the exception of the first death, I didn't remember any of them.

Maybe this was how it worked. The bullet hit you, but death removed the pain.

I wondered what might happen next. Would I find my soul pulled up out of my body and drawn up to heaven – or down to hell? Would it hover around for a bit and then get yanked over to the Amortals Project to slip into my new body instead? Or, worst of all, would I just lie here trapped in my lifeless body, unable to say or do a thing as they scooped me up and put me in the ground?

I opened my eyes then and saw that I was not dead.

Five stood there before me, his eyes wide with shock and pain. Blood stained the front of his shirt, and I knew it was not mine. He opened his mouth to speak, but no words escaped it, only more blood. Then he pitched forward and fell on top of my lap.

Struggling again to free my hands so I could help Five, I looked up to see Ruby gaping in shock as if Christ Himself had entered the room to save my life. I peered past her to see a telltale blur somewhere near the one of the gated entrances to the chapel. It had to be a federal agent – probably Secret Service but just as likely seconded from the FBI. No one else on American soil had access to the kind of stealth technology that rendered suits of powered armor both invisible and silent.

My Friend or Foe layer kicked in then. Every one of the One Resurrectionists started to glow green, while the outline of the agent in the stealth armor turned red. Even if the revolutionaries hadn't been such Luddites, their nanoservers wouldn't have been able to pick up the encrypted "friend" signal the agent was broadcasting, but because he and I were on the same side I could see his outline as clear as a lit match in a pitch-black room.

Not knowing how trigger-happy my savior might be, I did the only sensible thing. I tipped my chair over and threw myself to the floor, pulling Five over with my legs as I went. As I bounced off the polished marble, the agent let loose a barrage of bullets.

By now, the others in the room knew that something was wrong, and they'd started to dive for cover. Some of them pulled plastic pistols of their own and tried to return fire, shooting blindly in the direction of the door. Even if their desperate attacks actually managed to hit the intruding agent, I knew the slugs would only ricochet off his armor. The force of a lucky shot in the right spot as the agent was moving in the wrong direction might be enough to knock him off his feet, but it had no chance of actually hurting him.

Two of the terrorists raced for the room's other exit, a pair of doors in the wall opposite the one through which the agent had stormed. I knew that if they reached it they'd have a good chance of escaping while the stealth-suited agent dealt with the other One Resurrectionists they left behind.

As they flung themselves up the steps that led to their freedom, though, I spotted another blur in the left doorway, and I knew they were doomed. The triple crack of a carefully controlled burst of bullets from that direction confirmed my prediction.

Next to me, lying on the floor and bleeding out fast, Five opened his eyes, saw me looking at him, and gave me a weak smile. He struggled to say something, and despite the painfully loud reports from the gunfire, I cranked up my auditory levels so I could hear his words and activated my Lip Reading layer to help make out what he said.

No sound escaped from him. The blood pooling in his lungs made sure of that. But he mouthed two words to me, and they meant everything: "I'm sorry."

At that moment, I would have done anything to trade places with him, amortal or not. I'd lived nearly two hundred years, and Five had only made it to about a quarter of that. It wasn't fair. The inherent injustice of it appalled me. How many descendants had

I outlived? I'd given up counting years ago. How many more might fade away while I continued on? How long might it be until I watched Six die too?

I didn't care how far apart from Five I'd fallen. I didn't care how much he might have hated me. I'd have put that damned plastic gun to my own head and pulled the trigger if it would have brought him back.

"Stop!" I shouted. "Stop it, Goddamn it!"

I sent out a cease-fire order over the Friend or Foe layer. I shouted at the shooters over and over to end their attack. It did no good. By the time I opened my mouth, it was already too late.

The gunfight seemed like it took forever, but it was over in a matter of seconds. It ended when the last echoes of the gunshots faded into nothing and were replaced with cries of anguish. There weren't nearly as many such sounds as I would have hoped. Five, at least, would never make any noises again at all, and several of his associates had fared just as poorly.

"Agent Dooley?" a male voice said, apparently springing from nothing.

"Yes?" I had strained my voice raw with shouting.

"Sir, are you hurt? Can you get up?"

I closed my eyes and pushed back the grief welling in me over Five's death. I still had a job to do here, and I could not break down in front of these agents.

"I'm fine, but my wrists are shackled."

"All clear," another disembodied voice said. This one was feminine. The echoes in the rock-lined room made it impossible even to tell from which direction it came. "All hostiles are either down or secure."

"Deactivating stealth mode," the man beside me said. The blur before me flickered like a torch in a tornado, then fell into focus.

The man kneeling next to me was young, maybe twenty-five. He wore a full body-formed suit of composite armor of an indeterminable color that proved hard to look at for long. I could see his face through the now unpolarized shield that still covered it, forming a transparent layer of protection. The man's eyes were hard and serious. That comforted me some. He and his partner had just brought down or killed a number of people, after all, and if he'd been grinning like a fool I'd have been worried for myself as well.

"I'm Agent Williams. That's Agent Rice." He nodded at the woman who now stood visible in the aisle between the chapel's simple wooden pews, holding her assault rifle over the few figures that still squirmed with life.

"We're with Homeland Security, Special Forces," Williams said as he helped me off the chair and to my feet.

"Which unit?" I asked.

Williams answered without a hint of irony. "That's above your clearance, sir."

I nodded at that, then flexed my arms against my shackles. They still held as firm as ever.

"I called for a locksmith as part of the clean-up crew," Rice said. "They should be here any minute."

"Can't you handle that yourselves?" I asked.

Rice hefted her assault rifle in front of her. "This is the only tool I have that might work, sir. I don't think you'd care for the results."

I scanned the room, assessing the situation. The men and women who'd been in the room with me had scattered at the sound of the first shots, and they'd knocked over or aside many of the wooden pews and tables placed around the room.

Gaping holes from stray bullets pocked the mural showing the burial of Christ after the Crucifixion. A young woman had run this way and realized she'd trapped herself in a dead end. Her back against the wall, she'd tried to return fire at the stealth-suited agents. Now she lay here, her blood smeared against the mural, her eyes open and glassy.

Opposite her, four people had gone in the other wrong direction, back through the pews until they reached the wrought iron gate in front of the columbarium, inside which rested the ashes of many famous locals. That included the noted teacher Anne Sullivan and her most famous student, Helen Keller. The irony that these people had been killed there by someone to whom they were deaf and blind would have been, I'm sure, lost on them.

Of all the One Resurrectionists that had been plotting something here mere minutes ago, I saw only one of them still breathing: Ruby. The woman who'd forced Five to point a gun at me lay on the floor in a pool of blood. I couldn't tell if any of it was hers, but she was clearly not having a good day. One of her legs was bent at what had to be a painful angle. She'd mercifully fallen unconscious. I felt like grabbing her ankle and twisting it until she woke up.

"She was the only one not armed," Williams said, standing next to me. "She should survive. The medics will be here to help her soon."

I counted up the One Resurrectionists in the room. One near the mural, four near the columbarium, two shot down as they tried to escape through an open doorway, Ruby, and Five.

That made nine. There had been ten.

Father G was missing.

I grabbed Williams by the shoulder. "One's gone. A priest. Did you see one leaving as you came in?"

"It's a church," he said with a grimace. "There were lots of people upstairs. We swept past them in stealth mode."

"I saw a few clergymen," Rice said. "What did your man look like?"

I shot them an image of Father G from my nanoserver. I pulled it from the glimpse I got of him just before he tased me.

"His name's Father Luke Gustavo. He goes by Father G. He probably should have been locked up a long time ago."

Rice groaned and nodded. "He was walking out the south doors when I came in," she said. "I had to wait for him to pass through before I could enter the cathedral."

I hung my head. I would have buried it in my hands if they hadn't still been bound behind me.

"Would one of your captors have a key to your shackles?" asked Williams.

"Yes," I said. "But I'm sure it's in the pocket of Father G."

"I'm sure the rest of our team can find him, sir," said Rice.

"Can you communicate with them down here?"

Rice flushed, then turned on her heel and sprinted up the stairs and out of the chapel. As she left, a medical team entered through the other doorway. They wanted to focus on me, of course, but I jerked my head toward Five.

"See if there's anything you can do for him instead."

"But, sir," a brave medic said.

"That wasn't a request," I said. "I'll be fine."

A Hispanic woman in blue coveralls entered with a case of tools slung over her shoulder. She raised her eyebrows when she saw me, then set to work without a word. Within seconds, she had me free.

"Don't see too many of these anymore," the locksmith said. She hefted the shackles in her hand as I rubbed my freed wrists. The links of the chain clanked against each other.

I nodded, but I wasn't really listening to her. I was watching the medics work on Five's body, giving it their best effort to somehow pump life back into him, humoring me although they knew it would be pointless.

I couldn't think about the shackles or Father G or the One Resurrectionists any more. I couldn't even think about my murderer, somewhere out there, roaming free. I couldn't think about any of it.

The only thing that kept popping into my head was Six and how I was going to have to break this to him and his mother.

TWENTY-THREE

"What the hell happened down there?" Patrón said. He sat behind his desk, his hands flat on its flawless, blank surface. He glared at me as if he might be able to see straight through me if he could only concentrate hard enough.

"It's all in my report," I said. I'd thrown together the bare minimum on my way over from the National Cathedral and zapped it out ahead of me via the net. "Read it."

I hadn't sat down when I came in. I didn't want to feel that comfortable yet. Maybe ever.

At Patrón's request, Williams and Rice had escorted me to Secret Service Headquarters in their transport. They'd dropped me off outside one of the parking slips, placing me in the hands of a pair of agents that I knew I had met before. I couldn't be bothered to call up my ID layer so I could be polite enough to call them by name. I didn't care who they might be. They worked for the Service with me, and they were taking me to Patrón's office. That's all I needed to know.

Patrón had never been the warm and reassuring type. If he thought one of his people needed someone to talk to, he'd send them to chat with a shrink. He didn't have time for such things. Compassion made him squirm.

"If I wanted information from something that thin and useless, I'd chat with the President." Patrón scowled at me. "Give me the real skinny, not that nugget of indigestible pap you scribbled out in the opening throes of your incipient post-traumatic stress disorder."

I shrugged. "Chasing the Kalis wasn't getting me anywhere. I thought the One Resurrectionists might have had something to do with my murder, so I went to check up on them."

Patrón rubbed his eyes. When he stopped, he stared right at me. He looked older than I'd ever seen him – at least since he'd lost his first life.

"And what was your direct descendant doing there?"

I shrugged again, perfectly aware of how useless that made me appear. "Seems he fell in with the wrong crowd. You know how kids are."

"What the hell's that supposed to mean?"

"Nothing at all."

"It better not." Patrón fidgeted in his chair. "Not all of us have been disowned by our descendants."

I glared at him with murderous eyes. "You want my report, or you want me to go down that path with you?"

He turned red and looked down at his hands. They were perfectly and recently manicured. I would have put money down that he'd had his toes done at the same time. He'd come a long way since his days in the field.

When he raised his head again, he'd lost some of his fire. "All right, Ronan," he said. "Let's start over. What happened down there?"

I sized him up. This was not the Patrón I'd protected Presidents with. Back in the day, we'd spent countless hours whiling away the long, dull stretches that come with any sort of protection work. The danger in that kind of work was that you'd let the boredom lull you into a false sense of security. Boredom was what you wanted. You had to come to love it, to treasure it. Once you'd experienced the alternative, it wasn't hard to do.

Patrón and I had helped stave off the worst effects of boredom on each other by talking for hours, playing games, becoming friends. We'd kept each other sharp, although we'd long ago stopped playing poker together after I'd established myself as the superior player. He had a subtle tell that I'd spotted and relentlessly exploited. When he was bluffing, he'd become dead serious, and his right eye would twitch twice. It never happened when he simply didn't tell the truth. I'd seen him lie better than any sociopath in the name of national security. His tell only came out when he was trying to intimidate someone with something he didn't really have, like a pair of pocket aces.

But that had been many years ago. Too many for me to want to count. Neither one of us was the same.

"I spotted Father G leading the protest outside of the White House when I left it the other day," I said. "That got me to thinking about him and the One Resurrectionists and the way they've always had me at the top of their hit list."

"But this is an organization that's never displayed any violent tendencies before." He raised a hand to cut off my objection. "That double assassination plot was hatched by a splinter group. We never were able to link them back to the Ones."

"True, but they've often advocated violence, or at least suggested it. They usually go right up to the edge of calling for open, armed rebellion and pull up short, but it never seemed like it would take too much to push them over the edge."

"Could you have been investigating them before your murder?"

"Anything's possible," I said. "That one's more than a bit likely. Even if I hadn't been, they know me and might have been willing to claim credit for my murder if they thought it would help their position."

Patrón frowned. "They did have a great deal of illegal ordnance for a supposedly peaceful group. They were clearly planning something."

"I suspect that once forensics gets through examining the crime scene, we'll have plenty of leads on that. You should also raid every one of their workplaces and homes."

"Already on that," said Patrón. "Teams are moving in on each of them as we speak. Except for Ronan the Fifth's place. I figured you'd want to take care of that one yourself."

Silence fell between us, and I let it fester and grow.

The quiet became too much for Patrón, and he broke.

"Ronan," he said. "I'm sorry about your great-great-great-grandson, but I have to ask. Is it a coincidence he was there?"

I smirked at him. "You think I sent him in there as some sort of mole. Just so I could have him and Father G tase and shackle me – and so some of your trigger-happy yahoos could shoot him dead."

Patrón raised his right hand from the table so he could stab his index finger down at it. "That was a legitimate removal," he said. "Agent Williams' recordings show you in clear and present danger of losing your life."

I gritted my teeth. "You just don't get it, do you?" I said. "I'm amortal. You know what that means?"

"I'm amortal too, Ronan. I know what it means. I read the Amortals Project's brochures too. You're a valuable asset, and Williams acted to protect that, just as I had ordered him to."

"No, you really don't get it at all. When you're an amortal, it doesn't mean your life is more precious. It's *less*. I get as many shots at a decent life as I want. Most people only get one. That makes their lives vital. It makes ours disposable."

Patrón dismissed my words with a wave of his wrist. "So, the greatest minds in the world – the most important people in the world – they're something you can just wad up and throw away."

"They're a renewable resource," I said. "It's simple economics. Our lives are less rare than those of regular folks. Therefore, they're worth less."

"You don't really believe that."

I leaned forward and stabbed my own finger at Patrón's desk. "You're damned right I do. If I'd been killed in that fight, I'd be waking up again in the Amortals Project. I'd have a few less memories, but I'd be much better for the wear."

"The other people in that room were all expendable."

"Including my great-great-great-grandson?"

Patrón winced at that. "If he was working with the One Resurrectionists, he wasn't your relative any more, Ronan. He was an enemy of the state. You lost him long ago."

"Maybe I wouldn't have. Maybe I'd have had the chance to turn things around with him – if you hadn't sent in an assault team to rescue someone who, by definition, didn't need rescuing."

"Or maybe he was just a distraction from you doing your god-damned job!" Patrón slapped his hands down on his desktop to punctuate his words.

"I was following a lead," I said. "I didn't have many left."

Patrón glowered at me. "You went from your partner's hospital room to stumble straight into a nest of armed insurrectionists – and you got your multiple-great-grandson killed over it. What the hell is wrong with you?"

"I didn't pull that trigger," I said. I felt my anger at Patrón growing. How dare he try to push me around like this? "I would have traded places with him in a heartbeat."

"And that's just the problem," Patrón said. "The Dooley I know would never have let himself get drawn into a situation like that. You're taking too many chances. You're falling right over the edge."

His nostrils flared as he spoke. "The shrinks here tell me you're suffering from post-traumatic stress, survivor's guilt, and a general death wish. They figure the reason you're cutting everything so close to the line these days is that you want to die, permanently, and you're pissed off at Uncle Sam for refusing to let that happen."

Patrón looked like he was doing everything he could to keep from spitting at me. He fought back adding in one more thing but couldn't help it. "You ungrateful bastard, you."

I stared at my old friend. This, then, was the real bone of contention between us: that he'd had to work so hard to become amortal and I'd just had it handed to me.

I'm not saying he wasn't right about the death wish. More than once I'd wished the USA would just let me die, but it had never seen fit to release me from my amortality. To be fair, I had never asked. It was one thing to die, but another entirely to demand that it be made permanent.

I'd seen it happen before. Mostly it came from people who'd just watched their spouses or their kids pass on. They couldn't bear to go on without them, and they insisted on being removed from the Amortals Project.

It was hard to be put into the project, but even more difficult to leave. It required a battery of tests and evaluation by a panel of psychiatrists who were all interested in cracking open your soul and hunting around inside for any flaw they thought they might be able to cure. Even then, there was a waiting period.

Once, a CIA agent named Jeremy Wilson – a top man in line for the director's job – gave up fighting the bureaucracy and took the matter into his own hands. He showed up in Langley and started shooting every amortal he could find until the black ops team they sent in finally stopped him.

They didn't bring him back.

I felt my hand twitching. Maybe it was my trigger finger. I was still coming down from the adrenaline that had been pumping through me in the National Cathedral, I knew, but that didn't make me feel any more stable.

I snarled at Patrón. "I'm sorry you had to work so hard to become an amortal, but I don't care. I didn't ask for this. I don't particularly want it."

Patrón stood up, leaned over his desk, and snarled right back at me. "I can have that revoked. All I have to do is fire you, and it's all over: you're on your last life, Ronan."

I pulled out my sidearm and hefted it in my hand.

Patrón stood back and put his hands out, palms facing me. "Go ahead," he said. "You think if you shoot me, I won't remember this conversation, right? And we can just go right back to the way it used to?"

He pointed at his eyes. "You think I'm not recording this? Every word? You think I won't find out what you've done?"

"Shut up," I said.

I looked down at my pistol. I'd carried a Nuzi for decades. Other agents went with fancier guns with more bells and whistles. I preferred a gun that did what it was supposed to, one that I could rely on in a fix. The more complex you made something, the more likely it was to fail.

My life had gotten more and more complex over the years. I'd tried to keep it simple, but it had grown more complicated despite that. Legends had risen around and about me without my input. My old enemies bred new ones, foes I wasn't always sure I could comprehend. I lived in a world in which almost every person born in the same century as me was long dead – including everyone I'd ever really cared about – and I didn't much care for the few friends I had left.

It was time to call Patrón's bluff.

"Go ahead," I said. "Fire me. I dare you."

Patrón gaped at me. "Are you serious? You think I won't do it?" He turned deadly serious.

I stared into his eyes and saw the right one twitch twice. "You don't have the balls. You never did have the stomach for dirty work. You have other people do it for you. That's why you're the director and I'm still an agent."

I held the gun up in front of me, showing it to him. "I don't mind getting my hands bloody."

Patrón's eyes flew so wide I could see the whites all the way around them, and his face grew crimson.

"You think you're such a hard-ass?" he said.

He grabbed his shirt and ripped it open. The buttons went flying everywhere, tik-tik-tikking across his desk to the floor. He stabbed a finger into his chest, right over his heart.

"Go ahead!" he shouted. "Shoot me! Right here! Right now!"

Spittle flew from his face as he raged at me.

"Here's your big chance," he said. "The one you've wanted for decades. Kill me, you bastard! I dare *you!*"

I weighed my pistol in my hand. Then I came to a decision. I pitched the gun onto his desk. It dug a deep scratch in the polished top.

"You pathetic wreck," I said. "You can't provoke me into killing you. And you can't fire me. I quit."

Patrón snatched up the gun and pointed it at me. "You can't quit," he said. "I refuse to accept your resignation!"

I turned my back on him, hoping he'd shoot me before I reached the door. He didn't.

As I left, I looked back over my shoulder. "Consider it an indefinite leave of absence then. I've had a death in the family."

TWENTY-FOUR

Five's funeral was about as miserable an affair as I could ever remember attending. It was as hot a day as I'd ever suffered through during a DC July. Black clouds blanketed the sky, trapping the heat in like an army blanket, and the rain that slammed down from them did absolutely nothing to cool things off.

I had gone to Five's apartment to break the terrible news personally to Lexa and Six. They had not taken it well, which offered me some small comfort. Even if I never had the chance to properly get to know Five, at least I could see that his family had loved him deeply.

Lexa screamed and cursed at me and even threw a glass at me. Six just sat there and stared at the wallscreen, his eyes unfocused, lost. Then he got up and held his mother and let her collapse in his arms.

I walked out and left them alone. Times like this, family meant the most to anyone. While I technically qualified, I wasn't any closer to them than any random stranger in their building.

I contacted Six later that night and helped guide him through the funeral arrangements. One thing about living almost two hundred years is that you spend an awful lot of time burying people much younger than you. I knew more about funerals than I'd ever hoped to learn, but it came in handy at that moment.

Five's death shattered Lexa. She'd been happy for her husband to work in a safe job and do safe things and plan for a safe retirement that both of them could enjoy together. The thought that he'd died in a gunfight and wouldn't be around for the latter part of the life they'd planned together crushed her flat.

To his credit, Six would have stepped up without any help from me. He had plenty of backbone, and although he might have been a bit of a slacker till now, he recognized responsibility when life handed it to him, and he ran with it.

I didn't ask to attend the funeral. I didn't think it was my place. Six headed me off on the question anyhow, requesting that I give his mother some time and space before she had to be in the same space with me again.

She surprised us both by asking about me on the morning of the funeral. She told Six that she wanted me to attend. If I couldn't be there for most of Five's life, she at least thought I should be there to see him off.

The funeral was held, of course, in the National Cathedral, directly above the chapel in which Five had been killed. Presiding Bishop Wilma Wrightly, the head of the entire Episcopal Church, held the ceremony herself. Because of the connection to me, a few newshounds went and recorded the event surreptitiously. I wondered if Patrón would take the time to watch it himself or assign another agent to watch it and file a report.

Despite being on my self-imposed leave of absence, no one had bothered revoking my clearance or limiting my access to my Service-related layers. As I entered the cathedral and shook the rain off my coat, I activated my ID layer and scanned the attendees. No one came up flagged as a Secret Service agent, of course. Nor were there any federal employees in the place beside myself. Three people showed with no tags at all, which could have meant a number of things.

They could have been undercover agents from the Service or some other federal agency. They might have been part of Five's Luddite sect – although I doubted that. It would take a lot of guts and far fewer brains to show up at the funeral of a man who'd been shot to death by federal agents, no matter how close a friend he might have been. Or they could just have been poorer folks who couldn't afford a nanoserver and had no record of priors. That was unlikely but not impossible. Seeing how well and conservatively dressed the three people in question were, my money was on federal agents.

It disheartened me to see how few people had showed up to the funeral. In all, there were only two dozen people.

"Where is everyone?" I said to Six in a hushed tone as I sidled up next to him in the front pew, coming in from the side near the wall. He stood between me and his mother, who sat on the aisle. She wore a black dress and veil, and she stared straight at the coffin in the transept and did not look up to greet me.

"Dad didn't have many friends," Six said just as softly. He was as somber as I'd ever seen him, even after getting kicked out of his home. He wore a new black suit that still had a tag dangling from one wrist. I reached over and tore it off.

"Thanks," said Six. "Dad mostly kept to himself. He didn't have any brothers or sisters, and his parents died a while ago. I think—" He cut himself off and looked away from me.

"What?"

"I think he had a hard time living down his name."

I arched an eyebrow at that. "Sure, it's unusual. It's Irish. I managed just fine with it."

Six gave me a weak smirk. "It's not the name itself," he said. "It's who had it first that makes it hard to carry. You cast a long shadow, Grandpa."

It had been a long time since I'd thought about that. Cal had mentioned it to me after he'd gone off to college. "It's not easy being the son of a hero, Dad." And he hadn't even had to bear the name.

"I'm sorry," I said. "I suppose it's only grown longer over the years."

"Think about it like this," said Six. "You're a hundred and eighty-two years older than me. For you, it would be something like being named Thomas Jefferson VI."

I goggled at him. He was right. "How long have you been waiting to use that little bit of trivia?" I asked.

The hint of a smile curled at the edges of his mouth. "Just since Dad kicked you out of our place. I was thinking about you a lot that night, and I looked up everything I could find."

I groaned inside. "Just remember, not everything you read is true. Not even most of it."

"I figured that," said Six. "Those rumors about you disarming a dirty bomb in Union Station had to be fake, right?"

I didn't say anything. Six wrinkled his brow and stared at me. "Right?"

I pointed to the bishop entering the transept. "I think the funeral's about to begin."

Six grabbed my arm, his voice quiet and urgent. "What about the ones linking you to Heidi Klum?"

I kept my eyes on the bishop. "I was never unfaithful to your great-great-great-great-grandmother."

"She's been gone a long time, Grandpa."

His eyes fell on his father's casket as the bishop's procession walked past it, and he fell silent. Colleen might have been well over a hundred years gone, but Six hadn't been without Five for even a hundred hours.

I barely paid any attention to the actual ceremony. I'd been to far too many funerals in my time, and I was sure I could preside over one myself by this point. I kept my head bowed, and lost myself in thought, following Six's bodily cues and my own muscle memory as to when I should sit or stand. At least I didn't have to kneel.

Speaking about Colleen made me wonder what she

would have thought about all of this if she'd still been alive, somehow made amortal too. I suspect – no, I know – that she wouldn't have allowed me to drift apart from our descendants. I would have been as much a part of Five's life as I had been with Two, my first grandchild.

I'd never retired from the Service, so I'd never played the part of the doting old man who lavishes attention on his grandchildren during his golden years. I'd avoided the golden years entirely by getting shot and revived as the first amortal. I'd gone from sixty three years old to twenty overnight.

That had put a horrible strain on my marriage. Colleen had never been any more self-conscious about aging than any other woman I'd known, but the fact that I was suddenly more than forty years younger than her shook her to her core.

"Would you rather they had let me die?" I asked her once, during one of our most heated arguments.

"Ronan *did* die!" she said. "You're not my husband! You're just some changeling child slipped into his casket before we could put him in the ground!"

"If you really believe that, then why don't you leave me?" I asked. "How can you live with me? How can you pretend to be married to me if I'm not really your husband?"

She fell into a sobbing, helpless heap. "I can't help it." She whispered to me, "I loved him so much. I can't bear the thought of him being gone."

I knelt down next to her then and put my arm around her shoulders. She looked up finally and put a hand on my cheek. I hadn't realized it was wet with my own tears until then.

"You may not be my husband," Colleen said. "But you're all I have left of him. And you remind me so much of him that it breaks my heart to look at you."

I pulled my arm back, but she clung to me then. "But it hurts even worse to think of life without you. That you'd be out there living as Ronan without me while I sat here weeping for him. So stay," she said. "Please stay."

I'd done everything I could after that to convince her that she was wrong, that I was still her husband, the man she'd fallen in love with so many years ago. I don't know if I ever convinced her, or if maybe I just needed to convince myself, but I know that many of those years were happy ones for us.

Ten years after I first came back, we celebrated our fiftieth wedding anniversary. Colleen was seventy-three years old at the time. I was the same age, although I looked thirty. She used to look at the photos of the party we held and laugh and laugh and laugh.

The cancer came for her soon after that. It started in her ovaries, and it spread fast. By the time we found it, it had metastasized so far into her that the doctors could barely tell where the disease ended and Colleen began. Despite that, she took a long time dying. She fought for every last minute of her life: chemo, hospitals, quacks. She did everything she could to spend every possible second with me.

I took a leave of absence from the Service so I could

nurse her through everything. Cal and his wife Kira
helped out as much as they could, and their kids
stopped by whenever work, classes, or their own children permitted. In the end, though, there was nothing
any of us could do to stop it.

I had tried. I pulled in every favor I had. I begged,
pleaded, wheedled, threatened, charmed, and cajoled.
I tried to line up amortality for her as well, but we
couldn't possibly afford it. On my government salary,
I couldn't even make the payment on a single month's
premium for amortality insurance, especially given
how sick Colleen was at the time. No one would give
me a loan that would cover the payments. I had no
way to ever pay it back.

I even begged every President I'd ever served under
to intervene on Colleen's behalf. None of them came
through. They pointed out that they didn't really have
the power to grant amortality, and even if they did
they wouldn't have used it. If they decided to save my
wife, then where would it end?

I found myself weeping for Colleen all over again.
Six put an arm around my shoulders.

"I miss him too," he said to me.

I couldn't bear to tell him the truth.

I remembered holding Colleen's hand as her life left
her. Just before that, she looked up at me and gave me
the best smile she could manage. The painkillers only
went so far.

"Ronan," she said. "When I'm gone, I want you to
move on."

I tried to protest, but she just shushed me.

"Please," she said. "Go on with your life. Enjoy this amortality of yours for as long as possible. Find happiness for yourself wherever you can. Never forget me – but never let me get in your way."

And I never have. Here I am, at our great-great-great-grandson's funeral, and all I can think about is her and how much better a job she would have made of all the time that somehow fell into my lap.

TWENTY-FIVE

At first, I hadn't noticed that the bishop had stopped talking. My grief over Colleen had swallowed me once again, and I felt like I might drown in it. I heard someone next to me clearing his throat.

"I repeat: would anyone from Ronan's family care to say a few words about him?" the bishop said. The woman's voice was filled with such compassion. I knew she only wanted to give Lexa and Six a chance to remember Five in front of his family and friends, but they didn't want to take her up on it.

Six grabbed me by the shoulder. "Go ahead, Grandpa," he said. "Say something. Please."

My first instinct was to yank my arm away in shock, but I managed to stop myself. I stared at the young man, trying to see if he was toying with me. The facade of lightheartedness he'd shown before the funeral had melted away. A boy who'd lost his father stood before me now, the ceremony having stripped away his false bravado.

"But he..."

I had been about to say that Five had hated me, but then I glanced past Six to see Lexa standing behind him. I could barely see her face behind the black veil that covered it. Her voice was lower than a whisper, but I heard it as plain as a shout.

"Please," she said.

I opened my mouth to say that I was sure that Five would have appreciated it far more if his wife or son were to speak at his funeral instead of me. Then I closed it when I realized that they weren't able to manage that. They couldn't bring themselves to stand up there – not yet – and they needed someone to represent Five's family here for them. That duty fell to me.

I thought that I should beg off in honor of the fact that Five hadn't cared for me at all, but then I remembered something I'd learned long ago. Funerals aren't for the dead. They're for the survivors. And these two people, the ones who'd been closer to Five than anyone, needed me to step up for them.

I nodded, and Lexa and Six stepped out into the main aisle to allow me to walk past them. As I did, Lexa reached out and squeezed my hand in gratitude, and that proved to be enough to steel my resolve.

I walked up to the pulpit, a massive thing of white stone on which someone had long ago carved a scene showing the signing of the Magna Carta. I ascended the stairs, and the bishop stepped back from the front of the pulpit and motioned for me to move forward.

I cleared my throat as I took the bishop's place, and the hidden microphone pickups grabbed that sound and amplified it so that it echoed along the cathedral's stone walls. I blushed as I gazed out over the small group of people assembled there for Five's funeral. Every set of eyes looked up at me, their owners ready to absorb whatever wisdom I could impart to them that might help them understand the tragedy that had taken Five from us before his time.

I spotted the Secret Service agents standing there – plus another one standing in the darkness in the cathedral's far corner. For all I knew, they had us surrounded, and at that moment I wanted little more than the thinnest excuse to chase them all out of the place with their tails between their legs.

Then I looked down at Lexa and Six, though, and I knew that I could not do that to them. They had no real idea of what Five had been wrapped up in – just that it had been bad enough to get him killed – and I didn't think they could bear having a fight break out in the middle of his funeral. No matter what else Five had done in his life, to them he'd been a loving husband and father, and that's what I needed to honor today.

I cleared my throat again and began to speak.

"I don't have anything prepared to say today," I said. "I didn't ever think I would wind up here, at this pulpit, talking to you about my great-great-great-grandson."

I faltered for a moment. I bowed my head and tried to collect my thoughts, but it was like trying to put back together a shattered vase – or to collect a dying man's last breath.

I rubbed my eyes then tried again.

"Despite the fact that he's my direct descendant and bears my name, I didn't know this Ronan Dooley all that well. It's a miracle of sorts that I was ever able to know him at all.

"When I say that, I'm not talking about the miracle of amortality. I'm speaking about the way that a family can drift apart. It's hard enough, it seems, for one generation to be able to relate to the next, so you can imagine what sort of distance the years put between me and Five, as I called him.

"I treasure the fact that I did manage to meet him and talk with him before his death. 'Untimely' is about the kindest way you can speak of his demise. I'd only just started to get to know him when he was taken from us. I'd never even talked with his father – who died several years ago – at all.

"I can't say that we reunited and it was perfect from the first word between us. More like the opposite of that. But it was something. It was a contact of some sort when we'd had none at all before. It may not have been an auspicious start, but it was at least a start.

"I do know this. From even the little time we were able to share, I know that Ronan Dooley the Fifth was a good man and that he cared for his wife and his son more than anything in the world. He and his son may not have always seen eye to eye, but that's because they both cared so deeply, each in their own ways, but always for each other.

"I only wish that he had been with us for longer."

I paused there, unsure if I should say more. But I couldn't help myself.

"People often ask me what it's like to be amortal, to know that no matter what happens, no matter what I do, I'll always get another chance. And I usually give them a pat story, something about how it's wonderful to know that I'll always live to screw it up even worse."

A few people chuckled at that. The bishop standing behind me was one of them. None of the Secret Service agents showed any emotion at all.

"But today I'll tell you the truth. It feels awful.

"It feels like cheating. It feels like someone slipped me a 'get out of jail free' card when I have to watch everyone I ever cared about get marched off to prison.

"Some people might call it survivor's guilt, sure, but it's more than that. It's the feeling I get when I look down at a casket like Five's and I can't say, 'It should have been me.' After all, I should have been dead a century ago."

I stopped for a moment there, afraid I'd been rambling. I looked down at the Bible sitting closed on the pulpit in front of me, a massive tome of gilt-edged pages bound in crinkled red leather.

It didn't have any answers for me. It never had.

I looked back up and saw Six staring up at me, holding his mother's hand as they mourned the man who had meant everything to them both. I wanted to stop there, but I knew I had to say something more.

I cleared my throat and tried again.

"When I was a boy, which was during a period you probably read about in your history books when you were in school, I complained to my father once that he wasn't being fair. 'Life isn't fair,' he told me.

"I thought about that for a long time. Life isn't fair. He was right about that. But I didn't understand why people used that as an excuse to make it worse for each other instead of better.

"Then I realized that complaining about it was silly, childish even. Life isn't fair. Fairness has nothing to do with life. We here, all of us, nothing is fair among us. Some of us are born smarter, some faster, some friend-lier, some meaner, some wealthier, some poorer. There's no control over that. It's mostly genetics and history mixed in with a healthy dose of random chance.

"It's not about fair or unfair. It's about doing the right thing. About being good to people and making the lives of those around you not fairer but better. That's really all you can hope for out of life, no matter how long it might be.

"I know that Five spent his life trying to make things better for his wife and their son. He had ideals, and he strove to live up to them. No matter how tragically that may have ended, I respect that, and I love him for it.

"I only hope that when I finally do meet my end – and because nothing lasts forever, I someday will – I hope that someone can step up to my casket and say the same about me."

I gazed out at the people in the pews, all of them looking right back at me.

"We should all be so lucky," I said.

With that, I turned and left the pulpit. The bishop shook my hand as I headed for the staircase and gave me a friendly clap on my shoulder.

As I walked back to the front pew, I stopped at Five's coffin and placed my hand on it. I had only planned to rest it there for a second, but I found I could not leave. I stared at my hand as if it were stuck there.

Then I bowed down and kissed the coffin gently. It smelled of fresh lilies.

When I got back to the pew, Lexa and Six both hugged me, and I sat down between them. No one else got up to speak.

The bishop wrapped up the ceremony soon after that. I stood in the cathedral's entryway with Lexa and Six and helped them accept condolences from Five's friends as they left. The entire time, I felt like it should have been Five standing there at my funeral instead.

If I'd had a choice, I would have walked away, but I couldn't leave Lexa and Six there to handle this alone. When it was over, Lexa embraced me again. Then she stepped back, holding me by my elbows and looked up into my face.

"I have Ron's will," she said as she lifted the black veil from her face. "You should read it."

I waited for it to appear in my nanoserver, but she reached into her pocket and pulled out a few folded pieces of paper instead. I took them from her, feeling the smooth texture of the paper's surface in my hand.

"Should I read this now?" I asked.

She nodded, her resolve bracing her cheeks and eyes.

I unfolded the papers and scanned them. They started out with the standard stuff: *"I, Ronan Dooley V, being of sound mind and body,"* etc. Then they segued into what he wanted to have done in the case of his demise.

None of it surprised me at first. His requests included a funeral at the National Cathedral. He gave most of his worldly goods to Lexa, with a few personal items culled out for Six. It was all as I expected, as straightforward as could be.

Then I reached my name.

TWENTY-SIX

"To Ronan Dooley, Sr, I do hereby bequeath the property on Madeline Island and all of the contents therein. He is to scatter my ashes there after my cremation, and this is to be accomplished as soon as possible after my death."

I read the passage three times, just to make sure I had it right.

I gaped at Lexa and Six. "He's giving me the Shack?"

They both nodded, a ghost of a smile weakening the grief on their faces.

"I used to take Colleen and Cal up there when we were young." I thought back about the place, confused. I hadn't been there in years, and I'd even forgotten why. "I – I gave it to Cal."

"And he gave it to his son, and to his, and so on," said Lexa. She put a hand on my arm. "Now Ron would like for it to come back to you."

I turned to Six. "I can't accept this," I said. "It should go to you."

Six shook his head. "If Dad wanted you to have it, then he had his reasons." He allowed the clouds hanging over him to part just a bit. "Besides, you can give it to me in your next will."

"How long will it take for the cremation?" I asked Lexa.

She bowed her head for a moment, battling her grief. When she raised her chin, she was ready to talk about any details that I needed.

"The funeral home said they could have it done by late tomorrow," she said.

I stared down at the paper again and discovered I was smiling.

"I can't wait to get back there," I said. "It's been far too long."

Six craned back his neck to peer into the sky. "It's July. The weather there should be just about perfect. Much better than the sweaty shit we get around here."

"Ronan!" Lexa shot him an exasperated snort, but he just rolled his eyes. "Not in front of your grandpa," she said.

"I'm sure he's heard much worse," Six said.

"See," I said, "this part of family I don't miss."

Both Lexa and Six froze. Then they burst out laughing so hard that fat tears soon rolled down their flushed cheeks. I joined with them. I couldn't help it.

"That's just what Ron liked to say," Lexa said once she could catch her breath.

I sighed. "I suppose we don't just hand down our genes," I said.

Something over Lexa's shoulder caught my eye. One of the Secret Service agents was climbing into a hovercar parked on Wisconsin Avenue. Seeing that gutted the good humor I'd found right out of me.

"I'm going to leave for the Shack immediately," I said. "Can you two follow me up there once you have Five's ashes?"

"I want to go with you," Six said. "How long has it been since you've been up there? I could show you around."

I shook my head, thinking about that mysterious locked room Six had discovered. "This is something I need to do alone. We don't know everything about what Five was involved with – or who. I could be walking into a trap."

"But, Grandpa, I can help."

He seemed even more pained than he had been at the funeral. There he'd tried to keep himself together in front of all those people. Here, though, with just his mother and me around, he looked like he might crack.

Lexa wrapped an arm around him. "No," she said softly. "You can't."

He looked at her and started to protest, but she shushed him with a finger on his lips.

"No," she said, tears welling in her eyes too. "I just lost your father. I can't lose you too. It would be too much for me to take."

"It's all right," I said to Six. "I can handle this. And even if I can't, I what's the worst that could happen to me?"

Six wiped his eyes. "You could come back and not remember us at all."

The kid had a point.

"No problem," I said. "I'll back myself up before I leave."

"Promise?"

I grabbed the young man by his shoulders and put my arms around him. "Yes," I said as I kissed the top of his head. "I don't want to lose you either. I promise."

I said my good-byes then, and made my way back to my hovercar. I had it fly me back to Blair House, where the government was still letting me stay. I might have been on a leave of absence, but that didn't mean I had another place to live yet. Since I'd lost my condo in the line of duty, President Oberon had made it clear that I could stay in Blair House as long as I liked. I intended to like it for a long time.

While I was packing for the trip, Patrón pinged me. I took the call, and his image leaped into my vision. He looked both determined and flustered.

"I don't work for you anymore," I said, hoping he'd take the hint.

"I didn't accept your resignation."

"But I'm not taking your orders any more. Call it what you like."

He did not seem pleased. "I hear you might be leaving town, Ronan."

"Your agents stuck out at the funeral like piñatas, Patrón. Didn't anyone ever tell them that eavesdropping is rude?"

I kept packing, tossing the few clothes the Blair House staff had scrounged up for me into a duffel bag I'd taken from the place's lost-and-found locker. It had been sitting there for over a decade, and the Czech diplomat it had once belonged to wouldn't miss it.

"Where are you going?"

"I'm getting the hell out of DC for a while. I've been here too long."

"Do you mean in DC or on the planet?"

I fought the urge to spit at his image. "I'm not heading for Mars, if that's what you mean."

"It wasn't, Ronan."

"Get to the point then, *Winston*." I said his first name like it was a curse.

"I want to know where you're going."

I scoffed at him. "Aren't you just going to track me?"

He smirked at that. "Make it easy on me. For old times' sake. Then maybe I won't have to hang any more piñatas around your neck."

I hesitated. Patrón had the entire resources of the Service at his command, and he could tap Homeland Security for help whenever he wanted it, including the datastream from TIE. I didn't plan on letting anyone follow me, but being evasive about it would only make him more determined to do it anyhow.

"I'm heading up north," I said. "I'm going to crawl into a hole and not come out until I'm ready."

"Like a bear hibernating for the winter."

"I prefer to think of it as a caterpillar creeping into its chrysalis."

"So you're a butterfly in this scenario?"

"I just want my wings."

He put his head in his hands for a moment, then mimed pulling his hair out of his head. "For someone who had eternal life handed to him, you sure have a lot of desires."

I put the last of my gear in the duffel bag and zipped it up.

"I never asked for amortality, Patrón. I just can't seem to kick the habit."

He shook his head at me as if I was a spoiled child who just wasn't quite mature enough to see how good I had it.

"I need you to come in for a backup before you leave, Ronan. I should have insisted on it before accepting your request for leave, but it's time to make up for that now."

"I didn't request anything. I quit."

"That's not how I filed it. You're still on payroll. You're still an amortal. Report in for your backup before you go."

"I was already planning on it."

He raised his eyebrows. "Given your track record on this matter, I find that difficult to believe."

"You're right," I said. "I wasn't lying before, but I am now: I'll be right over."

"Don't mess with me on this one, Ronan. In case you've forgotten, someone slaughtered you not too long ago, and we still haven't figured out who. They might try again. Backing yourself up is only reasonable."

I sighed. I'd been planning to stop by the Amortals Project before I left town. I'd promised Six that I would, after all. But the way Patrón was telling me it was in my best interests brought me up short. He didn't care about my interests, I knew, except when they matched up with his own.

I looked Patrón straight in his eyes, so dark they were almost black. "So now I'm reasonable?"

"This comes from the President herself," he said. "I am relaying to you a direct order to come in for a backup. Today."

I rocked on my heels as I considered this. "Well," I said, "why didn't you just say so?"

I cut off the conversation and headed for the door. From Blair House, the hovercab whisked me away to Reagan International, and I hopped a suborbital that had me in Chicago in under an hour. From there, I rented a hovercar and aimed it east. I zipped through the monstrous maze of starscrapers spearing out of the central part of the city and scooted into a parking slip near the Sears Tower – which it will always be to me, no matter how many times they might sell the naming rights.

When I'd first come to Chicago as a kid, I'd gone to the top of the Sears Tower to peer out of the observation deck of what was then the tallest building in the world. Today, several other Chicago buildings dwarfed the Sears Tower, blocking the view from it in most directions, except for one line of sight that stabbed straight east toward Lake Michigan.

I pulled out a pocketknife I'd picked up in the airport, then crawled under the dashboard and pried open the fuse box. Once inside, I ripped out the fuses that provided power to the GPS system and the mobile net connection, plus anything else that wasn't essential to keeping the hovercar in the air.

Once that was done, I ordered the hovercar to head east. Minutes later, I was out over Lake Michigan, zipping over the crinkled surface the color of dark lapis, a thousand feet below. I shut off the autopilot and took over the controls myself. I liked feeling them thrum softly in my hands. Then I shut down the nanoserver in my head. It asked me three times if I was sure, and I confirmed my choice each time.

I couldn't remember the last time I hadn't had my nanoserver up and running. When the Kalis kidnapped me, they had cut me off from the net, but that had still left my nanoserver going. It had isolated me but not stripped me of my onboard tools.

I felt utterly naked – and free.

I didn't need the nanoserver to show me where I was going. I knew the way by heart.

I tipped the hovercar's controls to the left and swung it around to the north. Then I brought it low, no more than fifty feet above the gray-capped waves zipping beneath the hovercar's hull. I goosed the hovercar up to its top speed and skimmed over the lake until land rose up from the waters before me. Then I turned to follow the curve of the Wisconsin shoreline.

When I spotted Sturgeon Bay, I cut across the channel that sliced through the thumb of Door County and found the Wisconsin mainland again. I chased along that until I reached Escanaba, nestled there on the shoreline of Michigan's Upper Peninsula. I turned inland and skipped over Escanaba to pick up the remnants of Highway 2. With the advent of the hovercar, it had fallen into such disuse that most of it was

now overgrown with brush and pine trees. Still, I
could pick out enough of the gray concrete peeking
through the lush greenery that I could follow it.

Highway 2 led me all the way across the UP,
through Iron River and Watersmeet and into Wake-
field and Ironwood. From there, I tracked it into
Wisconsin. When I reached Odana, I steered the hovercar north once more and soon spied Madeline Island
heaving up out of Lake Superior's chilly waves.

When I made it to the island, I slowed down and
dropped to just a dozen feet above the ground. I found
the remains of the road that hugged the island's south
shore and followed it to the northeast. When it turned
due north, heading straight into the heart of the island, I went with it. I wound my way through a maze
of long-unkept roads that had never been much more
than strips of gravel. I found North Shore Road and
turned northeast, pointing myself toward the deeper
waters of Lake Superior, moving farther away from
civilization with every second.

Before I ran off the end of the island, I spotted
the narrow driveway to the Shack, and I turned left
onto it.

Just like that, I was home.

TWENTY-SEVEN

The Shack was a misnomer, the opposite of what it really was, like calling a fat man Slim or a tall man Tiny. A cabin had once stood on this land, little more than an old logging shack, and my parents had used it as a vacation home. Calling it rustic was being kind to it. It had no electricity or running water, and to heat it we had to haul in propane tanks from La Pointe, the only town on the island.

I'd come here every summer growing up, treasuring the isolation, the solitude the place offered, as well as the chance to reconnect with nature. I swam off the dock, fished, hiked, played with my dog, and baked myself in the sun. I learned to sail a boat here and used my little Sunfish to wander all around the Apostle Islands, poking around among the lighthouses and woods, the beaches and the bluffs.

When I was in college, my parents had the cabin torn down, and a glorious new house went up in its place. It stood three stories tall and drew water off its own well. It brought electricity in from the buried cable near the gravel road.

After my parents retired, they spent most of the year up here. They did everything they could to take the property off the grid. They replaced the roof's cedar shingles with solar panels. They mounted a set of wind turbines on the roof and down on the end of the dock. They kept the propane furnace as a backup but heated the place mostly with captured electricity and wood fires burning in the three separate fireplaces.

I used to bring Colleen and Cal up here for at least a week in the middle of every summer, often right about this time of year. After Colleen died, I passed it on to him. That was part of the deal I'd had with my parents: to bequeath the Shack to my kid, just as they'd done for me. I wasn't about to let the fact that I might not ever die put a crimp in that. When Colleen passed away, I figured that both of Cal's parents had died at least once. It was his turn.

I hadn't come back here too often after that, especially after Three and I had our falling out. It was not a place for an old ghost to haunt but for a family to enjoy.

I parked the hovercar on the old volleyball court I'd installed in the front yard back when Cal was in junior high, and I listened to the hiss of the door as it opened. The scent of pine assaulted me as I stepped from the hovercar. I stood tall and inhaled deeply through my nose as the late-afternoon summer sun instantly set about roasting the stress out of me.

I waited for my nanoserver to automatically polarize the lenses in my eyes, but then I remembered I'd shut it off on my way here. I shaded my eyes with my hand instead and gazed up at the old place. It looked surprisingly good. The windows were clean, the lawn had been mowed, and the porch had been swept.

I wondered if Five had hired a caretaker to manage the place or if he'd just spent a lot of time up here himself. When I'd run a check on his movement patterns through TIE, though, it hadn't shown any out-of-state trips. Of course, as a security expert, Five might have been able to manage getting up here undetected, much as I'd tried to do.

I was still wearing my suit and tie, and the warm Wisconsin July had me sweating through my shirt. I'd change into casual clothes once I settled in. I suspected that Five had some shorts and T-shirts here I could borrow. He wouldn't miss them.

As I walked up to the front door, a young dog – a puppy, no more than a few months old – came barreling around the corner of the house, charging straight for me. When I first glimpsed him, my hand darted to my sidearm, just in case whatever was coming at me proved dangerous. As the dog drew closer, though, I dropped my hand and laughed. The puppy slowed down and wagged its tail, its pink tongue hanging out as it panted in the heat.

The dog was the spitting image of my old Airedale, Murphy. He had a black and brown coat of coarse, curly hair trimmed short and neat for the summer, and his tail hadn't been docked, the way the breeders always did for show dogs but had neglected to bother with for our family pet.

Most Airedales look alike to the untrained eye, of course, but I'd spent enough time with Murphy to be able to tell him apart from any others in an instant. This one seemed like a ghost from my past, but when he came up to nuzzle my hand for a good scratch, he felt as solid as ever. I knelt down and gave the dog a good scratch. He even smelled like Murphy.

The Murphy I'd known and loved, though, had been dead for over a hundred and seventy-five years. We'd buried him in the woods here ourselves.

Satisfied with the scratching, the dog whirled away and trotted back off around the house, no doubt hunting for something to chase.

I hefted my pistol in my hand. It felt good. For some reason, it reminded me of prowling around these woods with Murphy and a baseball bat, which at that young age I'd thought would be enough to protect me against any rampaging bears we might find.

Suspicious now, I crept around the side of the house and peered in through the windows. The shades were down in some, while others were too high to reveal anything to me but a ceiling. No lights burned inside, but it was barely early evening, with several hours of sunlight left in the day. The house's air conditioner wasn't running, but the breeze coming in off the lake would make it tolerable enough inside that you wouldn't need it. Most of the windows in the place were raised open a few inches and likely locked in place, enough to let some air in but not so far that anyone would be able to creep inside.

I put my ear up to one of the windows, but I heard nothing. No radio playing. No soft snoring. No footfalls creaking on a loose floorboard. No guns cocking.

Still, my gut told me someone had to be around. Either way, I wasn't about to waltz in the front door and risk getting shot. That would throw me back to square one. For a moment I regretted not backing myself up as Patrón had ordered me to.

I crept around to the other side of the house, making my way along the wraparound screened porch that looked out over the lake below. There I found the door that led straight into the basement. Beside it there stood a window with a weak latch that I'd known about since my youth. The entire time I'd known the place, no one had ever taken the time to fix it.

I popped out the screen in that window as quietly as I could, then I grabbed the lower sash. I pushed it in and jiggled it to the right a bit, then shoved it up. The window opened as smoothly as ever.

The basement mudroom behind the door sat dark and silent, the only light in it filtering in over my shoulder. Confident that no one in the upper floors could possibly have heard me jimmy the window open, I shimmied my way in, headfirst.

I was only halfway through when I felt the tip of a metal cylinder press right into the back of my skull.

"Son of a bitch," a voice behind that cylinder said. It was male and confident and weathered with age. It sounded like my father. "How stupid can you get?"

I knew there was no way I could spin around and shoot the man before he could perforate my skull. I considered shoving myself forward or back, but with my belly hanging atop the windowsill, I didn't think I had even a nanite's chance of getting out of the way before the man shot me.

I tried it anyway. I'm amortal, right? What did I have to lose?

With a roar, I twisted around and tried to bring my gun to bear on the man. He grabbed my wrist with one hand and zapped me in the side of my head with whatever he was holding in the other. A surge of electricity coursed through my skull, and then everything went black. While I figured out I hadn't been knocked unconscious but blind, my attacker twisted my Nuzi out of my hand.

I fell out of the window and into the basement in about as graceless a way as I could imagine. I nearly broke my neck on the floor, but I managed to contort myself fully onto the bare cement without doing myself any more harm.

I heard the sound of my pistol being cocked. I tried to scramble away, but I ran into a wall. I recognized it as the corner of the mudroom, and I started to stand up and feel for the door that led into the rest of the house.

"Sit down!" the man barked.

I froze, waiting for a bullet from my Nuzi to put an end to this part of my life. When it didn't come, I slowly slid back into the corner. Having the two walls against my back felt oddly comforting.

"The blindness is just a side-effect," the man said. "Your vision will clear in a minute."

Within seconds, I could pick out the man's gray shape. The light streaming in through the window silhouetted him in its frame. He was about my height, although he seemed a little thicker. That was all I could make out. I held up my arm to shield my eyes – and perhaps out of some insane hope I might protect myself against an incoming bullet.

"I'm a federal agent," I said. "This place will be swarming with armed operatives in minutes."

"Probably," the man said. "But if that's true, then it's already too late for me to do anything about it, isn't it?"

I knew I could call the Service for backup in an instant. All I had to do was turn my nanoserver back on, and they'd spot my signal. Assuming Patrón was still trying to track my movements, he'd have someone out here in short order. If I actually asked for help, it would arrive even faster.

The man uncocked the pistol. With a practiced move, he pushed the clip release and let it drop out of the Nuzi and into his other hand. Then he worked the gun's action to eject the bullet still sitting in its chamber. He tossed me the clip and flicked the extra bullet along after it. Just barely able to track the clip's arc, I caught it in midair, then scooped up the spare round and popped that back into the clip.

"Just calm down," the man said as he stuffed the pistol into the waistband of his shorts. "I'm not going to shoot you."

"This is my house," I said. "You're trespassing."

The man snorted in derision. "Don't kid yourself,

Ronan. You haven't owned this house for over a hundred years."

"The owner died. He just willed it to me."

The man cursed. "That's just like Five. Too damned smart for his own good." His voice welled up with regret. "This complicates things."

"You knew him?"

The man growled. "Better than you ever did. You still haven't figured it out, have you?"

I squinted at him, still unable to make out his features. "That's what I came up here for. To get some answers."

The man laughed. "You came to the right place. Can't guarantee you're going to like them though."

"Let's start with an easy one," I said. "Who are you?"

The man hesitated. I could almost smell the circuits overheating in his head. He rubbed the palm of his hand across his forehead.

"It's a simple question," I said.

"For most people, maybe." He gestured toward the stairs. "Let's go up and have a little chat."

"I'm not going anywhere until I know who I'm dealing with."

"You want to play it that way? The man who is holding all the bullets but nothing to shoot them with?"

I hefted the clip in my hand and wondered how much damage I could do by throwing it at him.

"Who are you?" I said again.

"Are you still looking for the man who killed you?"

My heart felt like someone had stabbed it with an icicle. "Officially, no," I said.

"And personally?"

"Always. Until I find him."

"So, now you can stop."

I froze. I didn't want to move a millimeter. I'd been looking forward to this meeting ever since I came to back in that crèche in the Amortals Project, but I hadn't seen it happening like this.

I'd tried to put some distance between myself and that victim I'd seen on the thrideo. I never would have let something like that happen to myself. The torture and humiliation that man – that victim – had gone through, that had happened to someone else.

Because of that, I'd set out to solve *a* murder, not *my* murder. Or so I'd told myself. That helped give me some perspective on the incident. Otherwise, I might run screaming into the night.

Now, though, confronted by my killer – and him having the upper hand on me once again – some ancient part of my brain informed me that I'd been a fool. That it had all been a front. That I needed to flee from this man, or I would go through all that again.

And this time, the protective layers would be stripped away. I'd not just have to watch and listen to every last detail. I'd have to feel the pain, taste the blood, smell the fear. Whoever followed after me – in my next life – he might be able to extract some measure of vengeance, but I was clearly doomed.

But why, then, had the killer unloaded my gun?

Why not keep it and shoot me? If quick death wasn't good enough for me, then what horrible things did he have planned?

Maybe he was just waiting until he could prepare another set of cameras to record it all again. I glanced around the room, searching for the telltale glint of light off a lens. I came up empty, but that might only mean he was saving my murder until later.

Who the hell was he?

"Turn on the lights," I said, my voice barely a croak. "Please."

"Are you sure you're ready for that?" he asked.

I nodded carefully. I might not like the answer – and it might not help my successor, who would never remember any of this – but I had to know. Even if the truth died with me – even if it killed me – I had to know.

The ceiling light – a single bare cluster of tiny LEDs packed together like the glowing facets of an insect's eye – flashed on. The blindness had left me, but it took a moment for my eyes to adjust to the stark and brilliant illumination.

The man stepped forward into the light. He wore khaki shorts, sandals, and an old college T-shirt with the logo nearly worn off. His tanned skin showed the glow of fresh exposure to the sun. His dark hair swept back from his forehead, the area around his temples having gone a solid white that extended all the way down through his full and bushy beard. Crows feet surrounded his deep, dark eyes, which glinted with wisdom and determination.

I knew that face peering down at me. I knew the wry smile on those lips. I just couldn't believe he was standing there before me.

"Dad?" I said.

The man's smile widened, showing all his straight white teeth. "No, Ronan," he said with a soft laugh. "I'm you."

TWENTY-EIGHT

I sat there and stared at the man, my mouth wide open, my heart feeling like it might have stopped. I rubbed the bump on my head, wondering if the blow I'd taken there had knocked me out without my brain letting me know about it.

"I'm dead," I said. "You killed me when I came in the door. This is some kind of misfiring of the last few active neurons in my brain."

The man knelt down before me, reached out, and slapped me across the face. "That feel like a death-dream?" he said.

I rubbed my cheek. The sting from the slap helped refocus my brain. I swung my fist at the man. He blocked it and slapped me again.

"Concentrate here," he said to me as he stood back up. "This is as serious as it gets."

I glared at him as he backed up a few steps. "What the hell is going on?" I asked. "You can't be me. I'm sitting right here."

He smiled again at that. "I'm not exactly you," he

275

said. "I'm not your father – our father – either. I'm
your predecessor."

I goggled at him. "You're the me that forgot to back
himself up for three months and then got himself
murdered in a gruesome way?"

He shook his head. "That's not quite it."

"Then how, exactly, is it?"

He ran a hand over his beard. "I'm the man who figured out a way to make sure he never had to back
himself up again."

He reached down to offer me a hand up. I was too
stunned to refuse, and I let him pull me to my feet. He
clapped me on my shoulder. "Let's go to the den. I
don't know about you, but I need a drink."

He gestured for me to lead, so I did. I knew the way.

My head swam as I climbed the stairs, and not just
from whatever he'd used to zap me. I clutched the railing to make sure I didn't fall. I didn't understand how
this could be, how my earlier self could be here with me.
It violated everything I knew about my life – or lives.

Once I reached the first floor, I let my feet guide me
straight to the den. Like the rest of the house, it was paneled in rich golden woods that complemented the
reddish color of the log-ribbed exterior. The fireplace set
into the room's inside wall was dark and cold. I'd
warmed myself by it more nights than I could count. Hot
as the weather was right now, I felt frozen, and I wished
I could start a blaze in that hearth to thaw me out.

The man who claimed to be me left the door open
behind him as he followed me in. He crossed the room
and went straight to the double doors concealing the

wet bar and liquor cabinet. Once inside, he uncorked a bottle of thirty year-old Glenlivet and poured a few fingers for each of us into short, square glasses.

He handed one of the glasses to me and motioned for me to take one of the pair of overstuffed red leather chairs that sat near the window opposite the fireplace, across a weathered wooden table from each other. I'd played countless games on this table with my parents: chess, euchre, mahjong. As Cal got older, we'd continued the tradition, only with newer games, like *Magic: The Gathering* and *Settlers of Catan*.

My old copy of *Settlers* still sat there on the table. The man caught me looking at it as he brought the bottle of scotch over to join us.

"I started out letting Cal win..." he said.

"But he picked up on it pretty fast," I finished.

I slammed back the scotch and held out the empty glass for a refill. The man winced at me as the liquor burned down my throat.

"That's a sipping whisky," he said.

"I needed a bracer."

He nodded as he tipped another stiff double into my glass. I picked it up and gazed into it as if it answers I needed might be swirling inside it.

The man raised his glass in a toast. "May you be in heaven half an hour before the Devil knows you're dead."

"Sláinte," I said. This time I sipped the scotch, and the burn came slow enough for me to enjoy it.

We both sat there in silence, savoring the drink and dreading leaving that quiet moment for the next.

"So," the man said finally, "I suppose you have a lot of questions."

"A few," I said, "but I think I've figured it out."

"Good," he said with a smile. "That will make it easier."

"Sure." I smiled right back at him. "I've gone insane."

"That would be the simplest answer. Sadly it's wrong."

"That complicates things." I put my drink down on the table. "Bring me up to speed."

The man took a sip of the scotch, set it down, and began to speak. "It all started thirty years ago, but I wasn't around for that."

"I remember farther back than that."

He put up a hand to stop me. "You're still thinking about this as if we're the same person. We're not. That's just a clever fiction the Amortals Project sold to everyone to keep us excited about amortality."

"We share the same genes and the same memories, but we're not the same?"

"If you have two copies of the same book, are they the same thing? As a book, it's distinguishable from any other title, but the copies are essentially the same. They're interchangeable, sure, but they're also two separate items.

"So we're more like twins."

"But separated at a hundred and ninety-nine years old rather than at birth."

"But – but…" I wanted to protest but couldn't put my complaint into words.

"Yeah," he said softly, "I know."

I looked down at my chest. I couldn't believe it. Despite myself, I was wondering about my soul.

"It seems so silly, but—" I couldn't finish the sentence.

"I know," the older me said. "I haven't been a church-goer since long before Colleen died. I'm about as areligious as you can get, but the Amortals Project always implied that the soul transfers from one body to the other."

"They never actually said it? I could have sworn I'd heard that from them."

"Maybe from a technician, who might have even believed it, but not in any of the official material. They're very careful about it. I checked."

I stared at him. "Then what the hell are we?"

He shrugged. "Damned good copies of the original."

"Aren't we supposed to attack each other now out of some twisted sense of jealousy?"

"You played too much D&D as a kid."

"So, how long have you known?" I asked.

My other self smirked. "Five approached me about it right after my last backup."

"Five was involved in all of this?"

He nodded sagely. "For almost thirty years."

"I didn't think we got along with him at all."

"You remember the last time you died before this week?"

"But that wasn't me. You just—"

He cut me off with a sigh. "Just roll with the mutating definitions, all right? Do you remember it?"

I nodded. "That was the whole business with the One Resurrectionists, right? We worked with Arwen Glover on that."

"Yeah, although we don't remember any of that. Ever wonder why that is?"

"Just another case of us not backing up often enough." I stared at him intently as he raised his eyebrows and pursed his lips. "Or not? What was it then?"

I put my glass to my lips again and downed the rest of the scotch. My older self filled it again straight away.

"What's your real question here?" he asked. "What have you spent every day of your very young life trying to figure out?"

"Who killed me?" I squirmed in my seat. "Or who killed the last me, who I thought was you? Wait. Who was that then?"

"A clone," he said. "One that had never been activated."

I gaped at him. "You stole it from the Amortals Project."

He gave his head a tight shake. "They have that place locked down tight. Also, if a clone of me went missing, they would have figured out what happened right away."

I cocked my head at him. "So the real question, then, isn't who killed me – or someone who looked an awful lot like me. It's why?"

"So I could disappear."

I nodded. "Sure, I get that. Hell, I've wanted to do that many times myself. But there must be easier ways to walk away from it all. Ways that don't involve bootlegging a clone and murdering it in a gruesome way."

He sat back in his chair, and I realized that even though we were much the same person, he didn't fully trust me. Thinking about it, I didn't entirely trust him either.

"And how the hell could you do that? You grew a copy of yourself and you killed it?"

He shook his head. "It wasn't alive really. We never imprinted it. It might as well have been brain dead."

I knew that for the massive rationalization it was. "What was with the eyes? And all the bullets? Wasn't one enough to kill something that wasn't alive?"

He sighed at my sarcasm. "The clone didn't have my implants. My lenses, my nanoserver, all the rest. If my corpse showed up without those, Paul Winding would have spotted the discrepancy right away. I had to leave enough for him to identify me but no more."

I pushed my drink away. The way my stomach was roiling, I couldn't take any more of it. "But why record it? Why the thrideo?"

He took a long sip of his drink and waited for me to figure it out.

"You just wanted me too mad to think. You've been behind all of this, haven't you?" I said. "You gave that homeless guy the money to ask me for change. You sent the Kalis after me – and me after them."

He put down his glass. "I needed time. I knew the killing wouldn't be able to fool you or Patrón for long, so I tossed a few red herrings in your way."

I got out of my chair and began to pace the room. My father used to do the same thing in this room when we'd play chess and he was waiting for me to figure out my next move. It felt right.

"How long have you been planning this?"

"Me? Only since Five approached me about it."

"So he grew the clone for you?" My head spun. "Is that what's in that room in the basement that Six told me about?"

He nodded. "The science behind force-growing clones from cells to adulthood in a short time is tricky. Only the Amortals Project has mastered it. We had to be patient about it."

I blinked. "So who started all this? Five?"

"No, it was our past self, the one right before me. While investigating the One Resurrectionists, he figured out that they were right. The Amortals Project is an abomination."

"Sure, but that abomination gave birth to us. Like it or not, we wouldn't be here otherwise. A lot of very powerful people could say the same thing."

My past self shook his head. "While the fiction about souls and such bothers me, that's not the real issue here."

My eyes widened in shock. I would have put good money on our former self having launched all this to expose exactly that horrifying crime. "That's not enough?"

"Copying the dead, that's just a tool. It's nothing. We've been able to clone creatures for over two centuries. Putting old memories into them, that was the big trick that made this all possible, but it's still just a tool, a new kind of science. No, it's what you do with the tool that matters."

"Which is what?"

"There's a conspiracy, a group of amortals that have been running the country – the world, really – since the dawn of the twenty-first century. They're in charge of the Amortals Project. They decide who lives and who dies."

TWENTY-NINE

"A shadowy cabal with the power over life and death?" I stopped pacing and turned on him. I couldn't keep my incredulity from my voice. "Are you out of your mind?"

My past self's mouth tightened into a flat line across his face. "It sounds insane, but it's true. They're called the Brain Trust. My past self discovered this while he was working with Arwen thirty years ago. They learned about it when they foiled the Brain Trust's plan to kill the President and the Pope."

"Why would this Brain Trust want to assassinate anyone? I thought the President and the Pope would have been charter members."

He snorted. "Shadowy cabals have a tendency to implode. President Westwood had blackmailed and intimidated the others into backing his run for the White House, and they were ready to get rid of him."

"What about the Pope? He's not amortal."

"Exactly. But if they could kill him and turn him into one to 'save his life,' think about how that would roil the Catholic Church."

My stomach churned at the thought.

"But our past self put a stop to all that," he said. "He threatened to expose the Brain Trust, and with Patrón's help, they killed him for it."

I sent my mind back to those days, searching my memories for something that just wasn't there. I realized, though, that this had been the point at which my friendship with Patrón had soured. At the time, I'd attributed it to the stresses of the job, but now that I knew what had really happened it all made far more sense.

"And then they just brought him back without any of those troublesome memories." I shook my head. "But why didn't it end there?"

"Before they killed him, he and Arwen decided to do something about it. They needed someone outside of the government to give them a hand, so they brought in Five. He'd already been a part of the One Resurrectionists, but he was only involved with the political protests, not the faction that had been prodded into doing the cabal's dirty work for it."

"So we asked him to step up his game and join our plot instead?"

"Essentially, yes."

I put out a hand to steady myself on a chair. "Why?"

He folded his hands on the table in front of him. "Do you know how they backup your memories?"

"They hook you up to this helmet full of wires, and they analyze and capture all of your brain activity, then copy it into a supercomputer." I waved my hands to show that I knew I was cutting out several important steps.

"That's what they tell you, but that's not it at all."

The phone in the corner of the room rang.

I stared at it. I hadn't heard an actual phone ringing in more decades than I cared to count. I hadn't noticed the phone when I walked into the room because it had always been there: a cordless model attached to a landline. My father had installed it, and I'd never bothered to throw it away, perhaps out of some twisted sense of nostalgia for a time before we were all tethered to the net. It seemed my descendants had shared or at least respected that.

After my father died, I'd hooked the phone up to a VoIP modem. As an experiment, Cal had reprogrammed it to bounce the signal through a large number of random redirects and anonymizers to make the line untraceable. He thought since his father was a "spy" that it would be fun. It had proved useful more than once over the years, although mostly to keep the people back at HQ from knowing where I was on vacation.

The other me got out of his chair and answered the phone. "Hello, Arwen," he said. "I'm going to put you on speakerphone."

He pressed a button on the cordless handset and put it down in the middle of the table. Arwen's voice came through it clear and strong, although a bit delayed, like talking to someone in the Lunar Colony.

"Are you both there?" she said.

"Yes," we said in unison.

I glared at my other self over that, and he shrugged an apology at me.

"I can't tell you boys how thrilled I am to see this all finally coming together. It's been a long wait."

"Nine's not quite up to speed yet, Arwen," my older self said.

"Nine?" I asked.

"I came up with that for you," Arwen said. "You're the ninth person to be known as Ronan Dooley the original."

I closed my eyes and rubbed my forehead. This was all making my skull spin.

"I suppose that makes me Eight," said my older self.

"If you like," said Arwen. "I still think of you both as Seven's sons."

I groaned. "Isn't this going to get confusing if we start talking about Five and Six? Can't we use Greek letters or something?

"That would make you Iota," said Arwen, unable to suppress a giggle, "and Eight would be Theta."

Eight smiled. "Theta's an ancient symbol for death." He looked at me. "I don't think Iota fits him though."

I shook my head, barely able to believe I was playing the codename game with these two. "Don't we have other things to talk about? Is this why you called, Arwen?"

"Omega," she said. "I think you're an Omega."

Eight grinned. "If all goes right, you'll be the last of us. That works."

"Whatever," I said. "Arwen? What did you really call about?"

"Right!" she said, remembering. "My friend on the inside tells me that you two are about to receive some unwelcome visitors."

"How long do we have until they arrive?" Eight asked.

"I'm not certain," Arwen said, "but it's on the order of minutes rather than hours."

"We need to get out of here," I said to Eight. "Now."

"Good-bye, Arwen," he said to the phone. "I'll be in touch once we get settled."

"Good luck," her voice said. "To you both."

Eight stabbed the disconnect button with his finger, then glared at me.

"Did you call for help on your way in?" he asked.

I shook my head.

He made a frustrated noise. "Damn it. They must think you're dead."

"How you do figure that? I just got here." I ran a hand through my hair. "Are you sure you didn't kill me back there? It would explain a lot."

He stared at me until recognition dawned on his face. "No, but I might as well have. Patrón must have been tracking your nanoserver."

"I turned it off back in Chicago," I said, confused.

He smirked at me. I wondered if I looked that smug when I did it or if it was something that had come to him lately.

"It doesn't have to be powered on for them to be able to track it," he said. "It works even when you stop breathing."

"So I come up here, and he sends in the troops? Why?"

"Because he thinks you're dead."

"But why would he?" I rubbed my head where he'd zapped me. I had thought he'd hit me with a taser of some sort, but tasers don't make you blind. "What the hell did you do to me?"

He fished the device out of his pocket. "It's a HERF gun. A short-range, narrow-focus EMP generator. Fries any electronics in its area of effect. Permanently."

"No," I said, horrified. I tried to turn my nanoserver back on. It had been one thing to voluntarily cut myself off from the net and from all my layers. I'd always known I could turn them back on. To have them permanently removed, that was something else altogether.

I smacked myself in the back of my skull as if my head had some sort of loose circuit. "No, no, no, no, no."

"Did you go blind?"

I stared at him. "Yeah."

He nodded. "They superpolarized when I killed your nanoserver. When they depolarize naturally, you can see again."

"Why?" I said as I grabbed him by the front of the shirt. "Why did you do this to me?"

I felt violated. I'd been connected to the net since before my first death. I felt naked without it. When I'd severed the connection voluntarily, I'd felt free. Now I just felt like a barefoot child walking through the snow.

"It had to be done," he said. He glanced out a window at the sky. "I just didn't think they'd move on it so fast."

I shook my head at him and choked back the urge to throttle him. I pushed him away from me.

"I have a rental," I said, heading for the front door. "I untethered it from the net. We can use that to get out of here."

"And go where?" he said as he chased after me. "If they catch us together, it's all over. Better we split up."

"You have your own hovercar?" I asked as we emerged from the Shack.

"In the garage." He pointed to a separate building nestled into the woods on the far side of the clearing in front of the house.

"Anything incriminating inside?"

"Tons," he said, "but nothing that should give anyone a clue about what's up – for a while, at least. Here."

"What about the cloning room in the basement?"

"Set to self-destruct if anyone without our DNA manages to open it. We don't fool around."

He tossed me one of a pair of ancient walkie-talkies he'd scooped up on his way out of the house. Each was a voice-activated headset you plugged into your ear, like the ones the Kalis that blew up my apartment had used. Cal and I had played laser tag while wearing these when he was a kid.

"They're scrambled," he said. "Use channel five."

As we left the cabin, Murphy came running up to us again. He stopped short and gazed up at the two of us, confused, then started to sniff around.

"You cloned him too?" I asked, scratching the dog behind the ears.

"Five started him going the moment he hauled the spare body out of the crèche. He thought I'd appreciate having an old friend waiting for me."

I heard a roar coming down out of the evening sky above us. The sun still hung low in the west. The east had darkened with the oncoming night, but not enough for any stars to show yet – except for one, but it wasn't a proper star. Patrón had bypassed the standard channels and sent his team after us in a federal orbital transport. It arced out of the indigo sky like a shooting star aiming straight for us. It would be here in under five minutes. There was no way to avoid it.

"Go," I said, smacking Eight on the back. "Get your vehicle and get out of here. I'll draw them away."

"Thanks," he said, a wry, satisfied smile on his lips. "I need the room to finish up all the preparations. Once everything's ready, I'll see you in DC."

He set off at a run toward the garage. Murphy glanced up at me, his ears canted high with curiosity, then went chasing after Eight. I watched them go as I made for my rental. I'd never had a chance to see myself like this, other than through thrids. He moved the same way I did, although a hair slower. Still, he knew his business and every step showed he was determined to get it done.

I gestured for the hovercar's door to open, and I jumped in. I grabbed the controls and brought the machine straight up into the air. An alarm blared until the hovercar managed to close the open door, by which time I was already a hundred feet in the air.

"You there, kid?"

I fumbled for the walkie-talkie, which had slipped under my seat. The hovercar wobbled as I did. When I finally got my hand on it, I saw that it was on and already set to channel five.

I fumbled with the headset until I got it jammed in my ear. "Roger," I said.

"It's Ronan, actually," he said.

"Cut the jokes. That transport will be here in no time, and we both need to be as far away from the Shack by then as we can."

"Already on it," he said. "Which way are you headed?"

"I'm going to head deeper over the lake. Make them think I'm bolting for Canada."

"Won't that bring the border patrol down on your... Ah," he said, getting it. "That's the idea. You want all the attention you can grab."

"Up to a point, yeah."

"I'm heading not-north then. Good luck."

"Hey," I said, not quite ready to let him go that easy. "What were you about to tell me before Arwen called? About how they backup your memories."

The channel remained silent long enough that I wondered if he'd dropped his walkie-talkie or shut it off.

"Still there?" I asked, letting my irritation seep into my tone. "Come on. Don't leave me hanging."

"There is no supercomputer for them to copy your memories into," he said. "No computer could possibly capture and record every neural connection in a human brain. Not even close."

I frowned as I coaxed the hovercar higher into the air. In the sky behind me, I watched the transport follow its inexorable arc toward the Shack.

"So how do they do it?" I asked.

"They copy them directly into your clone."

I felt like someone had punched me in the throat.

He continued. "They force-grow your clone to adulthood and then copy your memories into it. They leave it trapped there in storage until you die. When that happens, they just wake up the clone and send him on his merry way."

"You can't be–" I stopped myself. No one would joke about this. No amortal, for sure.

That meant that the Amortals Project – the US Government – had set up a program that kept copies of thousands of the wealthiest and most powerful people in the world in suspended animation until they were needed. I had been one of those clones, kept unconscious for who knew how long. I hadn't been reactivated in thirty years.

"I was kept on ice for thirty years?"

"Probably less. Once force-grown, clones age just like anyone else. If you were the first backup after I was activated back in '38, you'd be in something like your fifties now, and you don't look it."

I felt nauseous. The shoreline of Isle Royale peeked up over the edge of the northern horizon as I zoomed toward it. Canada lay just beyond that, somewhere beyond the curve of the globe.

"How many? How many copies of us did they make?"

"I don't know for sure," he said. "It could be that they make a new clone for each backup, but that seems like a waste. My guess is that they create a new one at least every five years."

So many questions churned in my mind. What did they do with the obsolete clones? What if they couldn't overwrite a clone's memories? Then they would have to use a fresh clone each time. For Secret Service agents like me, who were supposed to backup weekly, that would be fifty-two new clones a year. That would make me the latest in a line of over three hundred life-ready clones.

"They have to be able to overwrite memories," I said. "Otherwise, it's insane."

"Having them create and murder at least five clones between you and me isn't enough? The original entered amortality a hundred and thirty-six years ago. That's at least twenty-seven copies of us made, only eight of which ever saw the light of day."

"Oh, God."

"He didn't have anything to do with this. Check your six. The transport's left the Shack and is heading your way."

I scanned the sky behind me and spotted a small speck of metal glinting orange in the sun's dying rays and growing bigger with every passing second. I didn't have long.

"Think of it," he said. "If they had to come up with a new clone every week, that would be over seven thousand clones of us floating around. But we didn't come in every week, of course."

"Think of the lives we saved," I said. I couldn't bite back my bitterness.

"Think of what they might be doing if they can actually rewrite the memories of clones. What's to stop them from doing that to an activated clone?"

I wondered if I could open the hovercar's door at this altitude to be sick.

"How many gaps in your history do you have?" he asked. "Would you even notice if a decade went missing?"

"We can't trust our memories," I whispered to myself.

"No," he answered. "We can't trust anything."

The deafening roar that had come racing up behind me finally became too painfully loud for my stunned mind to ignore. I looked behind me and saw the massive transport taking up half the sky.

THIRTY

The transport bristled with rotary machine-guns and red-tipped missiles, all of which pointed directly at my tail. It grew closer as I watched it, looming over my tiny hovercar like a leviathan about to swallow me whole. Then, an instant later, it pulled past me, nosing high overhead. Its bulk hovered over me, the wash from its jets rattling me right down to the roots of my teeth.

I spotted a woman sitting in the glassteel blister that housed the transport's belly gun. She pointed straight at me, and then stabbed her finger down at the ground.

For an instant I wondered why the transport's captain hadn't just radioed his demands to me directly. Then I remembered that my nanoserver was shot and that I'd disabled the hovercar's communications equipment. After fussing with the fuse box for a moment, I switched the hovercar's communications gear back on, and the dashboard leaped to life. A hoarse male voice blared in my ears. It belonged to someone who was used to having people follow his orders.

"...approaching Canadian airspace. If you do not respond *immediately*, we will be forced to blow your craft from the sky. You have thirty seconds to comply."

I waited.

"One last time. Agent Dooley. This is Captain Henry Moloke of the United States Air Force. By the authority of the Department of Homeland Security, I hereby order you to land your aircraft. You are approaching Canadian airspace. If you do not respond *immediately—*"

"What seems to be the problem, officers?"

Captain Moloke sighed in relief. "Thank God," he said, his voice soft and grateful. Then he spoke firmly again. "Please identify yourself."

"Agent Ronan Dooley of the United States Secret Service. My passport is in order, captain. Go ahead and check my credentials."

"Actually, sir, you are currently broadcasting no credentials. Is your nanoserver functioning correctly?"

I grimaced. "Not at all."

"We can have that repaired once we get you back to DC."

"No need for that," I said. "I'm on vacation up here. I'm sorry someone put you to the trouble to find me."

He hesitated. "I have orders to bring you back to Washington immediately, sir."

"On what charges?"

"I'm not a police officer, sir. I don't need a warrant."

I nodded. There had been a time when the US military wouldn't have been permitted to take action against a US citizen inside the country's own borders.

That had been so long ago that I barely remembered it, but I still missed it.

"It doesn't have to be like that," I said.

"My orders are 'bring him back, willing or not,' sir. I'm sorry."

I stared down and saw Isle Royale scudding beneath me. A little bit farther, and I'd have made it into Canada – for all the good that would have done me. At the most, it would have delayed Patrón getting his hands on me for a few days while he wrestled with the extradition requests.

Still, I wasn't about to go quietly. Eight needed more time to make a clean getaway, and I wasn't about to let him down.

"No, captain," I said. "You don't need a warrant – but you still have to catch me first."

With that, I slammed the hovercar into reverse. The transmission screamed in protest and tried to leap straight up through the dashboard to tell me what it thought about being treated like that, but the hovercar managed to switch direction anyhow.

My seat's autobelts deployed and grabbed me from several angles around my middle to keep me in my seat. I smiled, as that was just what I had wanted. I planned on needing those straps even more soon.

As the transport zipped straight past me, its powerful wake buffeted my hovercar about like a ship on a stormy sea. The transport's rear gunner pointed his lasers at me and fired off a wide-spectrum burst designed to burn out my retinas. On most people it would have blinded them and forced them to land. In my case, my lenses darkened in plenty of time to protect me. Turns out they didn't need my nanoserver for at least that basic function. Here's to superphototropic materials.

I knew the gunner would wait a moment before firing again, just to see how well his first attack had fared. I used that hesitation to buy me some space, and I threw the hovercar into a barrel roll that spun me off to the left, spiraling away from the transport in a long, sharp arc that drew me closer to the Canadian shoreline.

I glanced back to spy a thin cable tipped with a magnetic coupler sailing through the space where I had just been. If I let the transport get that close again, the gunners would catch me and haul me in for sure.

A new voice came in over the hovercar's communications system now, one with a distinctly Canadian accent and politeness. "Attention, please, unidentified hovercar. You are about to trespass into Canadian airspace. Please break off and return to the United States on the bearing now being transmitted to your hovercar's autopilot."

I ignored that, along with the plaintive beeping that now sprang from the autopilot. If I'd been scared – or stupid – enough to give in and turn the damned thing back on, Captain Moloke would have taken over my autopilot and put me down on the nearest open patch of land still in the USA. I'd have been stranded there for all of the thirty seconds it would take for his troopers to surround me, rip my hovercar open like a garbage bag, and haul me aboard their transport.

That was probably how it was still going to end, but I didn't need to win this game. I just had to run out the clock. That gave me the advantage I needed. I shut the hovercar's communications system off again. It would only serve to annoy me, I knew.

I flirted with dashing into Canada and seeing if I could cause an international incident. I pointed my hovercar straight for the border and gunned it. About then, I spotted the trio of Canadian fighter jets break off from where they'd been cutting a broad circle to the north and come right at me. I might have been able to make it across the border, but I had no illusion that I'd get much farther than that.

One of the Canadian jets let loose with a barrage of tracer bullets that sailed through the air between us like shooting stars. They angled far to my left, clearly only meant as a warning. Still, I was flying a rental hovercar. It wouldn't take much to bring me screaming down.

I was pretty sure their orders were to bring me in alive. There's not much use in killing an amortal. Patrón wanted to know what I was doing, and it would be a lot simpler for him to just ask me rather than have me die in an "accident."

Of course, that didn't mean I couldn't die in an honest accident.

I yanked up hard on the hovercar's controls, starting into a full vertical loop. When I reached the apex of the loop and was upside down, though, I flipped the craft over and dove forward, executing a perfect Immelman turn.

This put me pointed nose-to-nose with the transport, which had come about and chased after me once I'd pulled out of my barrel roll. From here, I could see straight into the transport's cockpit blister, in which I spotted a dark-skinned man I knew had to be Captain Moloke. His white eyes grew wide in his dark face. His teeth gleamed as he shouted for me to break off from this suicidal game of chicken I'd turned his chase into, but I couldn't hear a word coming from him. I turned the communications console back on.

"– off, damn it!" Moloke shouted, audible over the blaring proximity alarms going off in his cockpit. "Now!"

"I'm amortal, captain," I said, the gap between us growing smaller with every passing instant. My hovercar's alarm finally kicked in too, and I had to bellow over it to be heard. "How about you?"

I saw Moloke flinch at that and pull the controls in his hands back and to the right. That was all I needed, just a hint of the direction in which he planned to go. I nudged my controls down and to the left. My hovercar zoomed past the oncoming transport, clearing its hull by a matter of scant feet.

Unfortunately, I hadn't figured the transport's belly gun blister into my movement. By the time I spotted it, there was no time to react. The roof of my hovercar smashed into the gun blister's glassteel hemisphere. Both had been reinforced against collisions, but even a glancing impact at opposing top speeds was enough to cause problems. The hovercar's roof caved in, stopping just shy of crushing my head. The impact knocked me off course and threw the craft toward the ground below, spinning out of control. The weapons blister cracked open like an egg. The gunner inside came cartwheeling out, still harnessed into her gun mount, which had broken completely free.

I wrestled with the hovercar's controls, straining at them with all my might. If not for the hovercar's autostabilization system, I never would have recovered before I slammed into the ground rushing up toward me. As it was, I managed to haul the hovercar out of its steep, chaotic dive and sweep back into the transport's wake, swinging into line far below it.

I spied the gunner hurtling down toward me. She'd managed to free herself from her gun mount, but her parachute had automatically deployed before that and gotten tangled in her harness. She yanked at it, desperate to pry it free before she ran out of time, but I could see that she had zero chance of managing that.

I put my hovercar into a steep dive set to intersect the gunner's path, then matched velocities with her. She spotted me coming and looped her thumbs through her harness's quick-release rings, then pulled. She sprang free from the fouled chute.

I forced the hovercar to open its passenger door. The collision with the transport had already damaged it, and the roaring winds finished the job and tore it free from its hinges.

The surface of the lake below raced toward us as the gunner kicked off from her gun mount, aiming for the open door. I gave the controls a nudge to help her out, and she grabbed onto the door's mangled frame and hauled herself in.

"Hold on!" I shouted as wrenched the hovercraft's controls back and over as hard as I could.

The gunner yelped as her legs tumbled about the hovercar's cabin, but she managed to keep a death grip on the passenger's chair with her arms.

Looking down at the waves, I could see I was too late. I had saved the woman from the fall but not the landing. No matter how hard I hauled on those controls, we were going to crash.

Something hard thumped into the back of the hovercraft, but I ignored it. The oncoming waters had all of my attention.

I knew I was probably going to die then and there, but that didn't bother me as much as the thought that I'd killed this gunner too. Even if she was trying to help bring me in so that Patrón could do to me whatever he had planned, she'd only been doing her job. She didn't deserve to die. Not permanently.

She screamed as the waters reached up to devour us.

I felt something pull at us, slowing us down. The autobelts bit into my arms and shoulders, and the gunner growled as she struggled to hold on. I knew then that the thump I'd heard had been a magnet-headed cable slapping into the back of the hovercar, tethering us to the transport.

Although hope leaped in my heart for an instant, this last-ditch effort to save us wasn't enough. We hit Lake Superior hard, and its chilly black waters rushed in through the open door and enveloped us.

THIRTY-ONE

I woke up in the Secret Service sick bay back in DC. At first, I thought that I'd died in the crash and been revived again. Then I realized that I wouldn't have remembered the crash if that had been the case.

Of course, if they'd been able to keep me from brain death long enough to back me up, then I might be in a whole new body. That had happened to me the first time I'd been revivified, way back in 2032.

New bodies didn't hurt as much as mine did though.

A young nurse stood at my bedside. He put a finger to his lips. "Don't try to speak right away," he said. "You swallowed a lot of lake water. You're lucky to be alive."

"What–?" I croaked. I'd tried to ignore his advice, but my throat hurt too much to cooperate with me.

He gave me a restrained, professional smile and handed me a sleeve of purified water that had been sitting on my bedside table. I took it gratefully and raised it to my lips. A slight squeeze sprayed water into the back of my mouth, and its cold stream trickled down the back of my throat, loosening things up as it went. A few sprays later, and I was ready to speak.

"What happened to the gunner?" I asked.

The nurse raised an eyebrow in ignorance.

"The woman in the hovercar with me?"

"She's fine," Patrón said as he walked into the room. "Glad to see you awake." His sullen demeanor said he was anything but.

I felt a sudden desire to throw off my blankets and beat Patrón to death, for all the good it would do. As an amortal, he'd just be back again soon enough and not remember a damn bit of it – except what the nurse and the security cameras would tell him.

I pushed that wish away and offered Patrón a weak smile instead. It didn't take much effort to feign the weakness. As much reason as I had to hate Patrón at the moment, he didn't know that, and I wanted to keep it that way.

"What happened?" I asked.

Patrón gave me a gruff glare. "How much of it do you remember?"

I rubbed my neck. I considered feigning amnesia, but since I'd already asked about the gunner's fate, I doubted I could get away with it. "Most of it, I think. Last thing that's clear is hitting the water."

"The rental company wasn't very happy about that," Patrón said. "I hope you're insured."

I couldn't help laughing at that. Every amortal was insured to the gills. No one who could afford amortality wanted to spend eternity paying off debts that insurance could have helped with. I wasn't wealthy, but as far as that went I was no exception.

The laugh hurt my ribs, and I winced in pain.

"You did nearly as good a number on yourself," Patrón said. "Fortunately, Uncle Sam has you covered there."

"But I was on sabbatical."

He waved that concern off. "You're still an employee of the Secret Service – and an amortal. It's far more expensive to boot up a new body for you than to handle your medical bills."

"Glad to hear it's all in the name of fiscal responsibility," I said.

Patrón let himself laugh at that. Then he turned deadly serious.

"Ronan," he said, putting a hand on my bedrail, "what's going on?"

"I'm not sure," I said. "I decide to head up to the old family cabin, and suddenly I have a special forces squad sent out to bring me in."

"We were concerned about you. Your signal went dead."

"I tried to quit. You wouldn't let me. I wanted to be alone."

He shook his head. "No amortal should ever be that alone."

"You had to send in a fully armed transport to remind me of that?"

"Your nanoserver went dead."

"I turned it off."

"*Dead* dead."

That explained it for sure then. When Eight zapped me in the head, that set off an alarm back at the head office. Patrón scrambled the transport into the air right after that.

"You're not supposed to be able to track a nanoserver once it's off."

He sucked at his teeth. "That's true for most people. Not for amortals. We need to know if you're alive and where you are at all times."

"So much for privacy. Or civil rights."

Patrón grabbed me by the shoulder. "Don't give me that shit," he said. "You know how things work around here. You've been a part of the US government for almost two hundred years."

"I did have a life before the Service."

"Not as far as I'm concerned. So, tell me: what happened out there? What made you jackrabbit as soon as the transport popped over the horizon? And who else was there?"

"Nobody but me," I said. It was, in a way, the absolute truth.

"Don't mess with me, Ronan. I'm not in the mood for it today. The damned One Resurrectionists are rioting in the streets right now, with your old friend Father G leading the charge. I don't have the time to deal with your personal dramas too. I can have a team of interrogators out here in under fifteen minutes. They'll be able to force the answers out of you."

I fought a need to spit in his face. "You don't have the authority to do that to me."

"The hell I don't. As the head of the Secret Service, I have a standing Presidential order that permits me to abridge any and all civil rights when dealing with matters of the security of the President and the First Family."

"I'm no threat to the President. I've been part of the Secret Service during twenty-five administrations. I'm untouchable."

Patrón dropped any facade of pleasantness, much less friendship. His eyes turned as cold as I'd ever seen them.

"No one is untouchable," he said. "The Amortals Project was first established to protect the life of the President, and for that reason it's always been a part of the Secret Service. Anything that threatens the Amortals Project is a matter of national security, and I will not permit any personal attachments, no matter how strong or old, to get in the way of that."

He glared at me now and leaned over my bedrail to get into my face. "Now come clean with me, Agent Dooley. This all smells worse than the Potomac. Tell me what's going on."

My fist clenched on its own, and I considered punching him in the face with it.

"How long have you been amortal?" I asked him instead.

"Quit trying to change the subject."

I put a hand on his chest and pushed him back out of my face, sitting up in the bed as I did.

"You remember back in the old days? When people in power actually died? You knew that as long as you were patient, things would change. Things would get better."

"Are you threatening me?" Patrón snarled.

"Civil rights got better. Global warming got better. Technology got better. Right up until 2032, when the Amortals Project finally got its start. Then it all stalled out. The big breakthrough – the final victory over mortality – killed everything else. Progress ground to a halt. The world fell into stasis. There was no pressure to get anything done, to improve upon anything. All that mattered to the people who could do anything about it was maintaining the status quo."

"That's our job!" Patrón said. "We keep the people in charge in charge. That's how we keep order."

"Maybe order's not always such a good thing," I said. "America was founded on revolution, not preservation."

Patrón nodded at me like he finally understood. With every word he leaned closer to me, farther into my face. "You're advocating chaos. Destruction. Death!"

"I'm nearly two hundred years old," I said. I could smell the meat from his lunch on his breath. His closeness set my teeth on edge. "I've died more than anyone else in the world, and I keep coming back. It's not right."

"You sanctimonious jackass." Patrón sneered at me. "You've had the world handed to you on a platter, and like a spoiled brat you just want to knock it aside."

"I got killed saving the President!"

Patrón leered down at me, his voice dripping with disgust. "Shot right to the top, eh?"

Before I even knew it, I'd punched him. Beat as I was, my fist flew up from my bed and smashed Patrón right in his nose. I felt the little bones in it crunch beneath my knuckles, and he staggered backward, clutching his face. Blood ran out between his fingers, coating his chin and neck and staining his shirt and tie.

The adrenaline coursing through me popped me out of the bed. I stood there in my hospital gown, my feet bare, my hands up and ready before me. If he came back at me, I was going to pound him into a pulp.

Instead, Patrón drew his gun.

"Get back!" he said in a scratchy voice. His eyes were watering so badly that I was surprised he could see at all. The way the barrel of his gun waved about the room told me that maybe he couldn't.

He cocked the pistol with his thumb, and I dove behind the bed.

"What the hell is going on in here?"

Querer appeared in the doorway and then dove away as Patrón, startled by her appearance, snapped off a wild shot at her.

"Hold your fire!" she shouted. "Hold your God-damned fire!"

Patrón cursed. "Querer?" he said waving the gun back toward the bed. "Dooley's gone mad! He's trying to kill me!"

I scrambled around the far side of the bed as fast and as quietly as I could.

"So you shot at *me*?" Querer asked. I saw her peering in from the bottom of the doorframe, keeping low in the hopes that Patrón wouldn't shoot in that direction.

He turned toward her, and that's when I launched myself at him. He heard me coming and half turned before I slammed into him. I grabbed the wrist of his gun hand as I tackled him to the tiled floor, keeping the weapon pointed well away from both Querer and me.

I smashed Patrón's hand into the floor until he cried out and let go of the gun. He snarled at me like a cornered rat and brought his blood-coated free hand around to grab me by the throat.

"Kill you!" he said. "Bring you back, and kill you again!"

I brought back my fist to smash it into Patrón's nose once more. This time, I planned to hit him hard enough to drive the bits of shattered bone into his brain. If someone was going to die here, it was not going to be me.

That's when Querer stepped back into the room and shouted, "Freeze!"

Surprised, both Patrón and I did just that and saw that Querer had taken her sidearm out and pointed it right at us as we'd struggled on the floor. It didn't matter who she was aiming at. Tangled as we were, if she fired at one she'd hit us both.

A squad of internal security guards appeared behind her, their weapons also drawn. They stabbed their arms into the room around Querer, making her seem like a lethal-armed goddess.

Patrón and I glared at each other for a long, taut moment. As the adrenaline drained out of me, I felt even worse than I had when I'd awakened in that bed.

With his nose bent and his face bloodied, Patrón didn't seem much better.

"Truce?" he muttered. I nodded my assent, and we let each other go.

The agents stood there, their guns still trained on us, as we got to our feet. As I stepped away from Patrón, back toward the bed, I saw most of the barrels follow me there. Only Querer kept her attention on Patrón as well.

Patrón pointed at me and opened his mouth to speak.

Something made a loud bang outside the building. It was so powerful that I felt it vibrate my bones.

Then everything went dark.

THIRTY-TWO

"What the hell?" I said. "What now?"

My night-vision kicked in, but there was little light to see by down here in the sick bay, even magnified, just the glow from some of the medical equipment still running on battery power. I switched over to infra-red and saw that the agents behind Querer had fanned out into the hallway in the standard crouch-and-cover formation, in case we were being attacked.

Patrón stood where he was. His nose glowed in the infrared spectrum, the injury I'd done to it causing heat to spill out of his face.

I tried to connect to the net and see what was going on, but Eight's zapper had done a real number on my nanoserver. It still wouldn't come online. I could access the built-in controls on my optics, but that was it.

"Damned Resurrectionists," Patrón said.

Querer spoke up. "They set off an EMP," she said. "It's taken out everything within about three miles of the Washington Monument. Every bit of unprotected electronics is dead."

"Where did they get something like that?" one of the agents in the hallway said.

Patrón cursed. "What the hell's the point? What do they think they could accomplish by doing this?"

"Other than leaving us in the dark?" I asked.

The building's back-up generators kicked in then, and the lights came on again.

"So much for that," Patrón said. "You'd think they'd have done better research about government defenses."

"They're not trying to pierce our defenses," I said. "They just want to cause chaos."

"And why would they want to do that?"

"Because you want order."

"What happened in here, sir?" an agent named Kim Lee asked. He still had his gun out and was pointing it at me, his hands trembling just a bit. He was speaking to Patrón though.

Patrón looked down at his gun on the floor, then scooped it up. He weighed it in his hand as if he didn't recognize it anymore. Then he reached up with his other hand and felt his nose. He growled in pain. Then he pointed his gun at me.

"Agent Dooley is under arrest," he said.

"On what charges?" said one of the other agents, a woman I barely knew, although she often smiled at me in the halls. Her name was Susan Dosi.

"Assault and battery, for sure," Patrón said. He spat blood on the room's bleached, white floor. "Perhaps attempted murder as well, and whatever else we might care to toss in after that."

The other agents in the room blanched at his words. While Patrón might have been the director of the Secret Service – and therefore their boss – they knew me either personally or by reputation. They must have found it hard to believe that I'd turn against my old friend.

I'd known him long enough to know better.

Patrón unfocused his eyes for a moment and then cursed. "The White House wants all hands on deck to protect it against the riot." He glared at me. "I don't have the time for this now, Ronan, but I'm not through with you."

"I can secure Agent Dooley, sir," Querer said. "He's supposed to be my partner, after all."

Patrón nodded at her. "All right. You take care of him. Don't let him out of your sight. The rest of you, come with me." With that, he strode out of the room at a half-jog, the other agents in the area following in his wake.

Querer watched after them until they disappeared down the hall. Then she turned to me. "You've looked better," she said.

"It's not every day I crash a hovercar into a lake and survive," I said. Then I remembered that the last time I'd seen her, she'd been in a hospital. "How are you?"

She rotated her shoulder and winced. "I'm fine, as long as the painkillers are working, which they aren't."

"Let's get out of here," I said, rolling out of bed as gently as I could. Everything about me ached.

"I'm supposed to be guarding you," Querer said, "not escorting you back to Blair House." Her gaze flickered up to a high corner of the room and back. I knew there was a camera there.

"We don't have time for those games now," I said. "The fact that this riot started now is no coincidence."

"No, I doubt that it is."

"What's really happening out there?" I asked.

She grunted as she came to a decision. "We can talk about it outside," she said. She reached into a wardrobe near the door and pulled out a fresh suit of clothes for me. "After you get dressed."

I joined her in the hall a minute later, fixing my tie in place.

"Much better," she said. "You almost look human."

"Let's go."

"Patrón told me not to let you out of my sight," she said, taking my arm. "And I don't plan to."

We strode through the building, each of us trying to ignore our pains. We exited onto H Street and turned left.

"No hovercar?" I said.

"After that crash, I don't think I trust you in one anymore," she said. "Besides, MPD is sure to be clamping down hard on any non-emergency transports in the area. The White House is only seven blocks from here."

"But that's not where we're going."

She shook her head. When we reached 10th Street, we turned south, heading for the Amortals Project, only two blocks away. I didn't know exactly what we'd find there, but I knew that's where we had to be. Eight had put his plan into motion, and although he hadn't bet on me being involved, I was determined to play a part in it.

The streetlights were out and the various signs and ads were all gone too, which made the city much darker than usual. A pair of people down the street made their way around the place with flashlights, but otherwise, the street was deserted. I could hear the sounds of the riot going on just a block or two from here, the noise from it echoing back toward us through the labyrinthine system of wide streets buried under the never-ending buildings that sprawled above.

"Over here," Querer said. "We need to talk."

She hauled me across the street and ducked into the hotel that took up the entire block north of the Amortals Project. I'd protected the Prime Minister of Ireland here once, and I remembered it well.

"It's not safe to chat here either," I said. "What about TIF?"

"The power's out in the whole building," she said. "The hotel is private property, so its electronics weren't hardened against the EMP. Its cameras went down with everything else."

"We don't have the time to stop in for a drink," I said. "We have places to be."

"We have a few minutes yet," Querer said, pulling me along by my arm. "Trust me."

I permitted myself the smallest smile as we strode into the deserted lobby. A doorman shined a flashlight at us, but I waved it off with a flash of my badge. As we sauntered over to a pair of overstuffed chairs, he went back to watching the door and hoping the rioters wouldn't make it this far away from the White House.

"Why don't you tell me what's going on?" I said as we sat down. "Now."

"Ronan." Querer stared into my eyes, her hands on her knees, which nearly touched mine. She took a deep breath and held it for a moment. Then she spoke three words I never thought I'd hear from her: "I'm Arwen's clone."

My spinal fluid turned to ice. The moment she spoke the words, I had no doubt that they were true. I had known that the two women – Querer and Arwen – were remarkably similar, but I had expected that from a mother and daughter. When Querer spoke to me there in the dim light of my monochromatic night-vision sight, though, the small, cosmetic differences in their looks could not distract me. Querer normally affected a bit of a deeper voice with a hint of the kind of gentle southern twang a kid might pick up in the Appalachians. When she let all of that go, though, you couldn't have told the difference between the two of them, even with a sonic analyzer. Their voices were identical.

I reached out for her hand and spoke to her in a low whisper, tamping down my emotions to keep the tremor from my voice.

"What," I asked, "have you done?"

She leaned in closer to me, making sure the doorman couldn't hear us by chance. "The clone that Eight killed wasn't the only one that Five prepared. In fact, it wasn't even the first. The first clone Five made was of Arwen. He let it – me, I mean – grow in the cloning crèche in the Shack for nine months, and then he gave me to her to pass off as her own baby. She'd been faking the pregnancy the entire time, so no one was surprised when she left the Service to concentrate on being a good mother."

"But why?" I asked. She raised an eyebrow at me, and I scrambled to explain myself. "Not that I'm not glad you're here right now, but why would Five do that?"

"He knew that Eight was going to need help, preferably someone on the inside of the Secret Service. By the time the plan came together, Arwen would be too old, maybe even dead. The life expectancy for mortals drops a bit every year, you know."

"But why not just make an adult clone of Arwen too?"

Querer smiled again and squeezed my hand. "Five only had the one crèche."

"So he cloned you and copied Arwen's brain into you? As a baby?" This didn't make any sense. I wondered for a moment whose side Querer might really be on. If she was about to betray me, though, it made even less sense for her to let me out of the sickbay just like that, defying Patrón's orders.

"No. Five didn't have a good way to back up a brain. Cloning is hard enough. Do you know how the amortal backup works?"

I nodded. "Eight explained it to me. They copy the synaptic patterns from one brain into its clone."

"Right, but you can't do that with an immature brain. A baby's brain doesn't match up with its adult version. They wanted to try, but they had to wait."

I gawked at her. "They had to wait until you were an adult?"

Querer bowed her head. Her voice was so low I had to strain to hear it, even once I leaned in close. "I had no idea. Arwen raised me as her daughter, and that's just what I was – until she told me the truth on my twentieth birthday. She explained it all to me, and then she gave me a choice."

"To become Arwen or to remain yourself?" I could barely imagine the enormity of such a decision, especially from the perspective of someone so young.

"Here I was, faced with the fact that I'd been born – created, really – for a reason. Since the day I came home with Arwen, though, she'd always treated me as if I weren't her clone but her daughter. When it came time to tell me the news, she couldn't bring herself to do it. She'd already resigned herself to the fact that they needed to come up with some other way to help Eight."

"But Five pressured her into it?"

I glanced over Querer's shoulder and saw the doorman eyeing us. We couldn't stay here much longer. The last thing we needed was for him to contact the MPD or – worse – Homeland Security.

She shook her head. "He did it himself. He found me when I was at college and told me the truth. When I confronted Arwen about it, she broke down and confessed everything."

Querer's voice grew thick. "She didn't want me to do it, but Five got angry about it." She ran her hands

through her hair. "Five had cobbled together his own
equipment from black-market parts and plans. Couple
that with the fact that twenty years of living meant
that my brain wasn't a blank slate, and you had a
recipe for disaster. Integrating everything clanking
around in my head probably would have driven me
mad."

She looked up at me then, her eyes wide and bright.
"I refused. He stormed out. None of us talked for years
after that."

She wiped her eyes. "Part of it was that Five didn't
believe that I'd go through with it – that if I didn't
have Arwen's memories, I couldn't possibly be dedicated enough. But he was wrong. Do you know
why?"

I shook my head. I was still trying to absorb all this.

"Arwen had always raised me to stand up for myself
and for everyone around me, to make sure the right
thing got done. It didn't matter that I didn't have her
memories, that I wasn't there when she saw the things
she saw. She told me about it. She made sure I knew
about what the amortals   especially the so called
Brain Trust – have done to our country. To our world.
How they've raped us of everything that made America so great. It doesn't matter if I'm me or Arwen or
something in between. Someone has to do something
to tear them all back down."

I reached out and squeezed her hand. "And now
that's just what we're going to do," I said. "Tonight."

THIRTY-THREE

"We've both just been in the hospital," Querer said, her voice sounding as weary and battered as I felt. "I don't know about you, but I ache all over. And the center of town is embroiled in a full-scale riot. I don't know if I'm up for this."

"This is the time," I said. "This is the night. That riot is no coincidence. Five set this all up for us. We have to do this now, or we'll never have as good a chance again."

"Five's dead," she said. "The Service destroyed his little cabal."

"Not entirely. Father G got away, and from the looks of things he's been awfully busy ever since."

Querer shook her head. "It's a shame that Patrón sent the SPAT into the National Cathedral after you. A part of me always thought of Five as my father. He was the man who had the most to do with my birth."

I bowed my head. "I barely knew him. The few moments we had together it seemed like he hated me."

"He had to do that, you know. I'm sure it wasn't any fun for him either. Think about it. He reconciled with one version of you thirty years ago and then had to keep his distance from the next you for the rest of his life. Then, to try to help Eight stay free, he has to be a bastard to you again."

"He did a good job of it," I said. "He had me convinced I probably deserved it."

"No one said you didn't."

I had to peer through the darkness to see Querer's barely repressed smile.

"Five planned for this before he died," she said. "He knew the risks. He knew he might never live to see all those years of planning pay off. That's why he set it up to go on without him. Just in case."

"Father G must have been in on this from the start."

"Not really." Querer frowned at that thought. "Five just used the One Resurrectionists as part of his plans. Father G's a true believer. I don't think Five ever revealed his real motives for working with him. Can you imagine? The man would have been preaching about it right outside the White House gates."

"Then why's Father G leading this riot right now?"

"Because I told him to. Five set up a series of messages for me to send to Father G in the event of his death. One of them was prepared to kick-start everything the day we were ready to move. When Patrón brought you in, I knew it had to be now, and Eight confirmed it."

"What was the message?"

"Three words: 'Initiate Project Delta.'"

More Greek letters. *Delta* meant change, and that's what we seemed headed for. I rubbed my eyes and wondered how we were supposed to make it happen.

The doorman started toward us. I pushed myself to my feet and put out a hand to help Querer up too. She waved me off, managing it herself, only groaning a little.

"Can I help you folks?" the doorman said.

"Just hiding out from the riot for a few minutes," I said.

He grimaced. "One of our security guards on the roof tells me it's getting closer. I'm going to have to lockdown the lobby now. You're welcome to stay, but if you do, I can't let you out until all this is over."

"Thanks," I said, "but that means we need to be on our way."

I escorted Querer to the front door. As we left, the doorman locked the door behind us, working the mechanism by hand. Outside, we turned to the right, heading south again. The Amortals Project building loomed just down the street.

"I remember when that block used to hold Madame Tussauds," I said staring at the nondescript entrance. It had been redesigned to look just like any other facade in the area, decorated in Governmental Boring. The only indication of what the place housed was set in classy lettering on a set of understated brass plates bracketing the entrances. They read: "The Amortals Project." Nothing more.

"Has it changed much?" Querer asked.

"In some ways, very much." I stopped to steel myself for this, thinking of the thousands of clones stored somewhere inside, mindless copies of powerful people walking around somewhere else in the world. "In others, not at all."

When we reached the corner of 10th and G, I stared down G to the west. Five blocks off, the Treasury Building blocked my direct view of the White House, but the sky over the complex beyond Treasury was lit up like a crime scene. Spotlights scanned the stars above, scissoring back and forth across the night.

Closer, on this side of the Treasury Building, I could see people with flashlights, lanterns, and even torches roaming the streets. I wondered if some of them had pitchforks too. There had to be hundreds of them just on G Street, smashing windows, chanting and hollering over the blaring alarms and the dopplering of police hovercar sirens racing up and down the streets, trying to restore order.

The smell of tear gas rolled down G Street toward us. As faint as it was where we stood, it must have enveloped the White House in a thick, white fog. Somewhere in the distance, the chatter of machine-gun fire echoed, braided through with screams of anger, terror, and despair.

"Five sure knew how to plan one hell of a distraction," I said, my voice thick with some mixture of grief and pride.

Querer took my arm and guided me down 10th Street. I let her. My brain felt overloaded, too stuffed with too many details, too many years of spotty memory, too many emotions threatening to pull me over the brink.

I wondered how Father G had managed to get so many people to take to the streets and put their safety on the line to protest against the White House. Then I remembered the gatherings he had going on outside of the place when I had left the rebirthday party there in my honor. He'd been preparing his people for this for weeks, maybe years, getting them riled up and then holding them back until they were not only ready to burst, they were demanding it.

I thought of all the years of pent-up frustration the mortals in this city had to deal with. They'd watched the rich and famous – politicians, actors, athletes, pundits, Wall Street barons – gradually separate themselves from the common folk for years, then decades, and now centuries, with the faces rarely ever changing, the gap growing to the size of an unbridgeable canyon. You might as well have tried to walk to the Lunar Colony from here instead.

I started wondering why more of them hadn't joined in.

Querer reached out and put her hand on the door of the Amortals Project. "We're here."

I stared up at the doorway. I'd been inside this building so many times in my life that I'd long since lost count. I'd come back to life here eight times – that I knew about for sure. I didn't know how well I could trust anything at the moment, most of all myself.

"But what's the plan?" I asked. "Just go on in and shoot things up until they stop working?"

Her wan smile drifted toward me. "Something like that."

She reached into her pocket, pulled out a pistol, and handed it to me.

"We have top-level clearance," she said. "We can bring in anything we want."

"My nanoserver's down." I grimaced at this crippling fact. "The security system won't recognize me."

"The building's connection is down too. During a blackout, the system reverts to secondary means of identification."

"Facial recognition," I said, understanding. Five had planned this right.

I put the pistol in my pocket. "We can't bring down the entire project with a couple of guns."

"We don't have to. If we can get access to the clone maintenance system, we can bring the whole thing down from within."

It dawned on me what she meant. Clones were kept stable and growing via a special cocktail of chemicals and gene-therapy viruses. It was a delicate, computerized balance. If we could mess with that, we could kill every clone in the complex in no time at all.

The thought of ending so many lives at once turned my stomach. I'd seen a lot of death in my time – caused quite a bit of it, too – but contemplating the murder of so many innocent souls stopped me cold.

Querer grimaced at my pained look. "It's the only way, Ronan," she said. "We have to stop this."

I blinked, but just for an instant. Then I patted my pistol and nodded at her with only a hint of a shudder.

"Chances are we'll blow it all and wind up dead instead," I said. "Right?"

"You ready to die?" she asked as she pulled open the door.

"Ready?" I said. "I think I'm starting to look forward to it."

"See," she said. "Admitting you have a problem, that's the first step toward beating it."

"Beating what?"

"Your addiction to death."

Just as Querer was about to enter, I put my hand on her shoulder to stop her. "You don't have to do this," I said to her. "I can handle it. Alone."

She narrowed her eyes at me. "You think this isn't my fight too?"

"You're not an amortal." Her eyes grew wide and indignant. "Not officially, anyway. You die, and that's it."

"That's it for you too, Omega."

I winced at the name. "Call me, Ronan. Please."

"Clone or not – amortalization contract or not – I'm an American," she said, her voice as hard as the gun in my pocket. "And I'm a Secret Service agent. I swore to protect my nation from threats of all kinds." She glared into the building. "I've never seen a greater threat."

"I didn't mean to offend you," I said. "I just – I can do this. There's no reason for you to get killed too."

At that, she softened a bit around the edges. She let the door shut behind her, then reached out and caressed my cheek. "That was one thing Arwen loved about you," she said. "Or that she loved about the you before Eight, at least. You're so old-fashioned."

I leaned into her hand. "Did they really love each other?"

Querer nodded wordlessly, her eyes brimming with tears she'd never let spill over. "Very much," she said when she could speak.

"And the Amortals Project stole that from me. De-stroyed it. Erased it." I gazed into her eyes. "What does that mean for us?"

A wry smile touched her lips. "It means we have to find our own way," she said. "Just like it should be."

I took her hand from my face and held it in mine. Then I leaned in to kiss her. Her lips were soft and full and moist.

"All right," I said as we parted. "Now, I'm ready to die."

THIRTY-FOUR

Just as Querer had predicted, the security system recognized us and let us right in. A pair of guards stood watch at a desk inside the marble-lined foyer, and they barely looked up at us as we came in. Despite the power being out elsewhere in town, the Amortals Project was running along like nothing had changed. There was some sense of calm, I supposed, that went with having the best automated security system in the nation keeping you protected.

As we walked past the guards' desk, though, one of them turned to me and said, "A pleasure to see you again, Mr Dooley."

The building's internal net must have been working fine. The other guard held out a hand to stop us, and Querer and I hauled up short.

"I know we have standing orders to allow you in for a backup at any time," the second guard said. "With the riot going on right now, though, this may not be a good moment."

"I don't know, boys," I said, forcing a grin onto my

face. "It sounds like the perfect time to me."

That earned me a pair of polite laughs.

Querer shook her head. "We're not here for a backup," she said. "We just want to speak with Juwan Winslow."

"He's still here?" I asked Querer, surprised.

"Some days it seems like Dr Winslow lives here," the first guard said. He waved us on. "You'll find him in his lab. I'll let him know you're coming."

I started to say, "No need," but Querer grabbed my arm and pulled me along.

We strode down the hallway with a purpose to our step. I knew the way by heart, but the lack of a colored stripe on the floor leading me to my destination threw me a bit. I wondered if getting my nanoserver fixed was an option or if Eight had done such a number on me that I might never be connected to the net again.

This both dismayed and delighted me. I worried about everything I would miss without my layers to assist me, but at the same time the idea that I was freed from my electronic tether to the rest of the world made me feel light and easy.

When we reached Winslow's lab, the doors opened automatically to admit us, then slipped closed behind us again. The place was just as I'd remembered it from my countless visits here for backups. For most people, those were normally run in another room, but as Winslow's first successful amortal, I received special attention. He often brought me in here to check me out personally and to catch up with each other's lives.

The room was entirely white and lit as brightly as an operating room. Cloning crèches lined the back wall, all of them empty at the moment. Supposedly they were waiting for the news that an amortal had died so that they could be shoved into action, growing a new replacement body. Now, though, I knew that this was just where Winslow would have the already prepared clones moved to in anticipation of waking them up.

Lab equipment of all kinds lined the sets of polished workbenches that occupied the middle of the room. Server arrays churning through computations ran along the wall on the left, and a massive wallscreen took up just about every inch of the right.

Whenever I came here, I half expected to see a Tesla coil or a set of Jacob's ladders surrounding Winslow as he bellowed at the ceiling, "Give my creation *life!*" The reality was always far less fun.

I'd first met Winslow when I'd woken up in his original lab, which hadn't been nearly so clean and modern as this place. Of course, that had been a hundred and thirty-six years ago. The lack of radical new technology developed over the past century may have slowed progress, but it hadn't frozen it solid.

The Amortals Project had grown from a crackpot's dream into the most vital government program in the world. The amount of money people were willing to pay to live forever was staggering. I often wondered how any of them could then afford more than a cardboard box for a bed.

That day I'd first seen Winslow, he'd been in his early fifties. His dark goatee had gone gray, as had the short-cropped hair on his head. He'd worn glasses in those days – an affectation even then – gold-rimmed circles that caught the light and lent his eyes a redundant sparkle of intelligence. Today, his wrinkles were gone, and his hair and even his brown skin seemed darker and healthier. He'd been killed in a car accident about two months ago and come back fresh and clean, with just as much energy as ever.

Querer and I sauntered in and waited for Winslow to acknowledge us. After a full minute, he finally looked up at us over a phantom pair of spectacles that he did not have on his face. He seemed annoyed at first blush, but when he recognized me he broke into a wide smile that showed all of his teeth.

"Ronan!" He got up and walked around his desk to greet me with a warm handshake. "It's been far too long, my boy." He rolled his eyes up, embarrassed. "Actually, it's not even been a week, has it? How have you been?" He gave me a chuck in the shoulder. "New body holding up all right?"

"Just fine, Juwan." Try as I might, I couldn't bring myself to return his warmth, and he sensed this.

"What is it?" he said. "Come on in and have a seat. We can talk."

He showed me to an oval conference table that sat in front of the wallscreen. He took the chair at the head of the table and motioned Querer and me into ones nearby.

"You haven't introduced me to the lovely Miss Querer." He spoke to me but stuck his hand out to Querer. "It's a pleasure to meet you."

"That's *Agent* Querer, thank you."

He flashed what I'm sure he thought was a charming smile. "Of course, my dear. No harm intended."

She grimaced in reply.

Nonplussed, Winslow sat back in his chair. He was used to being in control – of the conversation, of the Amortals Project, and perhaps, in some sense, of the world. Sensing he was losing that, he made another grasp at it.

"So," he said, "what is it that brings you to me on such a dark and dangerous night? I hear we're having a riot near the White House. I have my machines revved up and ready to go just in case the worst should happen."

"It's about the Brain Trust," I said.

Winslow's warmth drained out of him as if I'd shot him through the heart. He stared at me, concerned, for a moment, then Querer, then back to me.

"Which brain trust is that then? I – I'm afraid I don't know what you're talking about."

"*The* Brain Trust," I said. "The group of people who maintain control over the Amortals Project and the clones you create for it."

"Oh," he said, feigning disinterest. "That. I suppose I've heard some people use that term for our board of directors, although I don't really see the humor in it."

"I don't either, Juwan," I said, "but we're about to break this wide open. I came here to give you a chance to get in front of this."

"Right," Querer said, nodding as she recognized my tactics. "To get your side of the story, sir."

Winslow stared at me, then grimaced and stared at Querer for even longer. Then he glanced up at one of the corners of the room over my shoulder, where I knew a hidden security camera sat.

"Hold on," he said. "I think this conversation requires more than our standard level of privacy."

Querer glanced around the room. I could tell she was identifying the various recording and security devices with her optic layers. After Juwan shut them all off, she nodded at me. "We're clear."

I put a hand out on the table toward Winslow. "So, Juwan. Tell me what's going on."

"How much do you know?" Sweat broke out on his brow.

"Everything," said Querer.

He gave her a sick smirk. "Can you be more specific?"

I took a shot at summing it up. "The Brain Trust usurped the Amortals Project and is using it as a means of controlling the most powerful people in the world."

His smile wavered and disappeared. "There's a lot more to it than that, of course."

"How much?"

His face contorted with regret. "Ronan. You have to know I never intended– I was trying to do something good. To solve the problem of mortality. To beat death."

"And so you did."

"For some of us," Querer chipped in.

Winslow flinched at that. "I suppose that's part of the problem. When the vast majority of the world still lies in death's hands, those who have escaped its clutches have that much more power."

"That's even more true for those who control the means of escape," I said.

"You wouldn't believe what the Brain Trust has forced me to do over the years. I've tampered with the minds of every great leader in the world. At least those trusting enough to join the Amortals Project. I've edited their memories. I've affected their loyalties."

He stood, unable to keep himself in his chair any longer. Querer stood too, ready to move in case he rabbited. I stayed in my seat, hoping that my stoic stance would help calm him down.

"It's not all been bad," he said. "Some good has come from it. We've had nothing but peace between the US and our allies for the past hundred years."

"But not so much with our enemies," I said.

"True, but we've made new allies too. The promise of eternal life is a huge temptation for anyone, even our enemies. The Pax Americana has spread to cover more than half the globe."

"But our enemies are more entrenched than ever," said Querer.

I didn't like the way the conversation was heading. The more Winslow thought of himself as the worst criminal the world had ever seen, the less likely he would be to cooperate with us.

"Why don't other countries have their own Amortals Projects?" I said. "You'd think that once they knew it was possible, they'd do everything they could to crack it."

Winslow wavered before he answered. "For one good reason. Well, two really."

He counted the reasons off on his fingers. "First, we don't let them. One of the top priorities of the NSA and CIA is to make sure that no other country gets its hands on the technology. It's given us more of an edge than the atomic bomb, and our government is determined to make sure that we don't lose that.

"Second, the way it works is so— It is the most tightly held secret in the world. Only I and a handful of my protégés here really understand everything about it. Not too many more even know about the reality behind it, much less how it works.

"Third," he said, ignoring the fact he'd mentioned two points, "the Amortals Project gave us TIE, which no other nation has. Without that level of intelligence analysis, they can't possibly hope to catch up with us, ever, and we always know about it long before they can really give it a good shot."

I sat straight up in my chair at that. "What does TIE have to do with the Amortals Project?" I asked.

Winslow gaped at me. "You – you don't know?"

I shook my head. I glanced back to see Querer doing the same thing.

He ran a hand over his face. "I don't know whether to laugh or cry."

My stomach flipped over. How deep did this thing go? "Try telling us the truth."

He stopped as if I'd stood up and slapped him in the face.

"Come on, Juwan," I said quietly. "This is your chance. It's time."

His chin trembled. I thought he might burst into tears. Instead, a weak laugh leaped from his lips.

"No," he said. "I've thought that before, many times, but it's never been true. Not once." He slumped back down in his chair. "You just don't know how it is, how powerful…"

"You're wrong," Querer said, leaning over the back of my chair to speak to Winslow. "This is the time. It's now or never. Everything is in motion, and we're never going to have a better chance to fix this."

"Oh, I've heard about the riots," Winslow said. "You think shutting off the lights in downtown DC and letting people run wild through the streets is going to change anything?" He shook his head as he looked up at her. "You really are so young."

Querer stepped around from behind me to talk to Winslow directly. "Turn on your wallscreen," she said, folding her arms across her chest. "Tap into the newsfeed."

"What difference will that make?"

"Look and see," she said. She stood before him, proud and defiant, daring him to deny her this simple request.

His shoulders slumped as he gave in. His eyes unfocused for a moment as he accessed the wallscreen's control layer. "Which feed should I tap?"

"Any of them," she said, turning toward the screen. "All of them."

A talking head appeared on the wallscreen, standing in the reinforced press station set up on the edge of the south lawn of the White House. Behind her, the White House gleamed like a beacon in the night. Spotlights crisscrossed the sky behind it, picking out unmanned hunter-killer drones circling the place, ready to slaughter any of the rioters who dared to get too close.

The words "Breaking News" scrolled across the bottom of the screen, white on a field of red. The newscaster projected beauty and grim determination as she spoke.

"– again, we have word that someone has broken into the White House and taken the President and the First Gentleman hostage in the Oval Office. There are reports of shots fired. The assailant is allegedly none other than the amortal Secret Service agent who has saved the lives of more Presidents than any other: Agent Ronan Dooley."

THIRTY-FIVE

Winslow's jaw dropped open so hard that he choked. I had to leap over and pound him on the back until he could breathe again. When he managed to speak, he said, "What the hell is going on, Ronan?"

I looked down at him and shrugged. "I'm just as surprised as you." His eyes were so wide I thought I could see his lens implants reflected there in the light.

"All right," I said, sitting down again, "maybe not that surprised."

Winslow spluttered at me as he struggled between feelings of betrayal and rage. "If you're here, then who is that in the White House?" he asked. "Is this all some kind of hoax?"

Querer intercepted that one. "Not at all. That's Ronan Dooley in the White House, and he is attacking the President."

Winslow gave me a look hard enough to shatter diamonds. "Then who are you?"

I put up my hands in surrender. "You tell me, Juwan. I just woke up here a few days ago. It's been a pretty hard start for a fresh life."

He wrinkled his brow at me, then gasped in horror. He began turning green. "Oh. Oh, God. You weren't killed. Your old body, that is. When we activated you, he wasn't dead. Oh, God."

He pushed his chair back from the table and put his head between his legs. I wondered if he was going to vomit, but he managed to hold his stomach together for now.

When he finally sat back up, he had turned pale, and a thin sheen of clammy sweat covered his skin. "I knew this would happen," he said. "I mean, eventually it had to. We'd make a mistake in verifying a death, and we'd suddenly have two copies of a patient walking the streets."

"Nothing like this has ever happened before?" I asked.

Winslow groaned. "There was that one time when that trillionaire went missing while trying to climb Olympus Mons. After an exhaustive search that turned up the bodies of every other member of the expedition, we officially called him dead and activated his next body."

"But he survived?"

Winslow shook his head ruefully. "After TIE found out about it? Not for long."

I squirmed in my seat.

"That was on Mars, though, with the new body still here on Earth. With you–" He threw his hands into the air. "Everyone in the world is going to see your old self taking the First Family hostage. There's no rug on the planet large enough for anyone to sweep that under it."

Querer shushed us and pointed at the screen. The woman there spoke again.

"We now have video from the scene at the Oval Office. The assailant entered the place during a press teleconference, waited for the right moment, and then attacked. Watch."

A video captured by an observer's optical feed zoomed onto the screen. At first, it all seemed perfectly normal. The President sat at her desk in the Oval Office, framed by the US flag on the left and the President's flag on the right. She was speaking to the nation about the riots in DC.

"There is no reason for alarm," she said. "We have plans in place for dealing with just such a cowardly terrorist attack as this, and the Department of Homeland Security is already implementing them. Order will be restored shortly, and the criminals responsible for instigating these troubles will be swiftly brought to justice."

As she spoke, I entered the room from the right, coming in through the west door, beyond which stood the President's private study.

It was really Eight, of course. He'd shaved his beard and colored his hair to look younger, like me. I thought maybe he was wearing makeup too.

The observer glanced in Eight's direction. Dressed in the standard Secret Service dark suit and tie, he looked tired but determined, much like I felt at the moment. Seeing that the interruption was only from a Secret

Service agent – someone who was supposed to professionally blend into the background – the observer
looked back to the President. She had continued to
speak, not missing a beat at Eight's entrance.

"I will personally monitor the situation every moment until it is resolved," she said. "Keep calm and, if
you live in the District of Columbia, please remain in-
doors until further notice. I will bring you new
developments as they happen. Until then, goodnight,
and God bless America."

As those last three words left her lips, Eight appeared behind her with a gun in his hand. He pointed
it directly at the back of her head and spoke clearly
and loudly. "Madame President, I'm here to arrest you
for your numerous crimes against the people of America. Please put your hands behind your head."

At first, the President laughed. She clearly thought
someone was playing a joke on her. Despite the fact it
was an awful gag at a terrible time, she was determined to be a good sport about it. A lifetime politician,
she was painfully aware the incident was being
recorded and broadcast live to feeds around the planet,
and the last thing she wanted to do was appear weak
or humorless.

She turned around to see what sort of madman
would have had the insane temerity to pull a prank
on her in the middle of a press feed. As her eyes fell
on Eight's face, she relaxed for a moment, then forced
a friendly scowl on her face.

"Very funny, Agent Dooley. April Fool's Day was
three months ago, but I suppose you don't remember

that." She delivered the line so smoothly I wondered if one of her speechwriters had fed it into her teleprompter layer on the fly.

"This isn't a joke, ma'am. Somebody else should have done this a long time ago, but I guess it falls to me."

The First Gentleman came steaming into the picture then from somewhere behind the observer. "This isn't funny, Dooley," he said, oozing menace. "Give me that gun, and your badge along with it."

The President glared at her husband for stepping in, and she opened her mouth to chastise him for it. At that moment, Eight pointed his gun at the ceiling and fired a round right through the Presidential seal embossed there.

The video devolved into chaos as the observer scrambled for cover behind one of the couches that sat at the other end of the Oval Office.

"I am not joking," Eight said. He enunciated every word as if he was talking to idiot children. "The next person who fails to follow my orders will take a bullet for it."

The observer scrambled for the door, grabbed the handle, and found it locked.

"Don't bother trying to get out," Eight said. "The gunshot activated the automatic lockdown procedure. It'll take the agents outside a few moments to disengage it."

"What in the name of God do you want?" the President asked. She tried to keep her cool, but instead she sounded like an irritated mother.

Eight ignored her. "Mo!" he called out to the observer. Although I couldn't see the man, I knew it had to be Mohammed Sanza, the President's Chief of Staff. "Come back over here and look at me. I have a message for the American people."

Sanza turned around slowly and saw Eight holding the gun on him. He backed away as far as he could go.

"Come here," Eight said, louder. He stabbed the gun at one of the chairs in the conversation area.

"The Secret Service will be here in an instant," the First Gentleman said, his voice cracking.

"If they know what's good for them, they'll stay outside for now," Eight said. He knew they'd be following Mo's news feed and listening to his every word. "I'm sealed inside one of the best-protected rooms on the planet. The walls are lined with steel, and the windows can withstand anything shy of a missile."

"Just put down the gun, Ronan," the President said, playing the good cop to her husband's bad cop. "You've been through an awful lot lately. Turn yourself in, and we'll make sure you get the help you need."

"If the agents on duty are smart, they'll try to gas the entire room. It's sealed, and they have full control over the ventilation system." Eight sniffed the air. "As soon as I start feeling drowsy, though, I'm going to start shooting."

From the way Sanza gasped, I'm sure this shocked him. Eight wasn't talking to anyone in the room though. His words were meant for the protection team outside that was no doubt looking for a way to get at him.

"You're bluffing," the First Gentleman said. A former athlete in a life long ago, he moved in his fresh body like a panther on the hunt. He strode forward and reached out to take the gun from Eight's hand.

Eight shot him in the gut.

Paul Oberon – Secret Service codename: Mr Claus – folded over like someone had hit him in the stomach with a bat. He toppled backward, clutching his middle with both hands, trying to keep in the blood already seeping through his white dress shirt.

The President screamed at the sight, then got up from her desk to race to her husband's side. "Paul!" she said. "Oh, God! Paul!"

She fell to her knees next to him and cradled his head in her hands. He looked up at her with eyes filled with shock and horror. In all his many years on the planet, he'd never been shot. He'd died a few times – euthanized once he'd worn out his current body – but he didn't remember any of it, of course.

"He'll be fine," Eight said. "Won't you just activate another one?"

Gina Oberon lowered her husband back to the floor and spun to her feet, fixing Eight in a fiery glare. "You *monster!*"

I have to give the President credit. After that perfectly understandable outburst, she screwed up her face and got serious again. "Agent Dooley, as your Commander-in-Chief, I order you to put down your firearm and surrender!"

Eight ignored her. "You two weren't even married," he said. "Sure, somewhere there's a marriage license and wedding photos and all the other bits of proof that two people named Paul and Gina Oberon were once married in front of thousands of witnesses, but here's the catch."

He stopped and glanced at Sanza to make sure he was getting all of this.

"He's not the man who married Gina Oberon – and you're not that woman either. You're cheap, vat-grown copies living out an authorized sequel to someone else's lives."

The President gaped at Eight. "You're insane."

"Look at me, ma'am," he said, treating each word as if it was as fragile as an egg. "I'm not the Ronan Dooley whose rebirthday party you attended a few days back. I'm the man he was supposed to replace."

"That's a lie," the President said. "Don't say that!"

Eight kept the gun on her and turned toward Sanza again. "The Amortals Project has been a lie from the start. Open your eyes, America."

The President made a cutting motion across her neck, signaling to Sanza to stop broadcasting.

Eight kept talking. "You're being used. We're all being used. Take a look at the world around you, America, and make up your own–"

The feed cut off then, going entirely black.

The talking head appeared back on the screen. "And those are the stunning developments taking place in the White House at this very moment. We have reporters located in the White House Press Room, waiting to hear more information. As soon as they have it, we'll bring it right to you."

The wallscreen went black then too.

THIRTY-SIX

"I've seen enough," Winslow said in a weary voice. He sat back in his chair and rubbed his eyes. Despite the youth of his body, he sat hunched over like an old man worn with age, like every one of his years had caught up with him.

"Do you get it?" Querer said. "If this isn't the time, then there is no other. There may never be."

Winslow looked at his hands. "These aren't my hands," he said, his voice filled with both wonder and regret as he turned them over and examined them front and back. "They never really were."

"I know this isn't what you wanted, Juwan," I said. "You never intended it to turn out like this."

He stared at me. "How long have I known you?" he said. I couldn't do the math that fast, but I knew his nanoserver would feed him the number. "A hundred and thirty-six years?"

I grimaced and realized I'd been holding my breath. "No, Juwan." I shook my head. "We just met."

With every nod of his head, the regret in his frown grew deeper.

"All right," he said finally. "You're right. It is time. Come with me."

He turned and walked off to a door set between two of the crèches lining the far wall. Querer and I stayed on his heels.

When Winslow reached the door, he stopped and put a hand on it. "We're about to go through the rabbit hole here," he said. "Are you sure you're ready for this?"

"Give me the red pill," I said.

Winslow gave me a proud frown that made my stomach flip. Then he spoke to the door. "Alpha twenty thirty-eight."

It slid aside, and Querer and I followed Winslow into an elevator. The door closed behind us, and the car began moving down.

After what seemed like the longest elevator ride ever, the door slid open. Winslow stepped aside and ushered Querer and me into the room before him.

Over the decades, I've been all around the world and seen many strange things. I've watched people suffer and thrive, kill and die. When I was born, America wasn't even as old as I am now. It's hard to surprise me.

Still, I wasn't ready for this.

We stepped from the elevator onto a hoverlift that hung in the air in the middle of a dim, cavernous warehouse of a room that seemed to stretch on forever. It was filled from its distant floor to its towering ceiling with countless racks filled with rows and columns of crèches. Each of these stood upright and – as I could see in the soft glow of the bluish monitor lights that rippled throughout the place – each contained a hibernating human being that had never known anything of the life it stood ready to live.

I stood there on the floating platform and stared, trying to take it all in, to wrap my head around the inconceivable.

"All these people," Querer whispered. Silent tears cut tracks down her cheeks.

Robots floated about the place on inbuilt hoverboards that glowed blue beneath them. They fluttered from crèche to high-tech, coffin-like crèche like worker bees searching for pollen. A spherical robot detached itself from a nearby crèche and approached us, folding a pair of spindly metal limbs in close to its body like a preying mantis. It rose to match our eyes, and it peered at us through a pair of unblinking lenses

"We have guests." The robot's voice was deep and resonant. It sounded natural yet was devoid of nature.

I recognized it immediately. "That's President Emmanuel. His voice."

Winslow ignored me. "Yes, Minder. You already know Ronan Dooley. He is one of our clients."

"And the other is Amanda Querer, who I have not met before. My pleasure. Will she be joining us?"

"As an amortal?" Winslow said. "Not quite yet."

"That's disappointing," Minder said. "I feel she would make an excellent addition."

Other robots detached themselves from their work and floated closer to us. Many of them looked much like the one hovering in front of us, but others were shaped like missiles or rafts or horns. One even had something that looked like a motorcycle seat on top of it so that you could ride it like a horse.

"Dooley Nine is defective," the robot said. "Is he here for repair or replacement?"

"Neither," I said, holding up a hand between myself and the robot. "I'm doing fine."

"Your nanoserver is dysfunctional. I can replace it. The surgery is minor."

For a moment, I actually considered it. Until I had no access to the net, I'd barely realized how much I'd relied on it. Still, even if we'd had the time for it, I didn't think I should hand myself over to this robot for my care.

I shook my head. "That's not why we're here."

"I'm just giving them a quick tour, Minder." I could hear an edge in Winslow's voice, one I hoped the robot could not detect.

"My offer to implement repairs stands. Approach any terminal when you are ready, Dooley Nine." The robot cocked its body to one side as it spoke, like the head of a curious puppy – that spoke with the President's voice.

"Thanks." I fought with the urge to follow that up with "sir."

The spherical robot moved off, and the other robots parted before us so that we could move farther into the room.

"What was that?" Querer asked.

Winslow sucked at his teeth. "Minder controls the entire Amortals Project. I handed those responsibilities over to it more than a century ago."

"It's a supercomputer of some kind?" She watched the robots retreat.

"That's impossible," I said, staring around as we moved deeper into the seemingly endless racks of crèches. "No computer system could possibly handle all of this."

"Obviously there's one that can," said Querer.

"No," Winslow said softly as he gazed down at his feet. "Ronan is right."

"What does that mean?" I asked, afraid of what the answer might be.

Winslow gave me a sad smile. "Patience," he said.

Our hoverlift cruised straight between the crèche stacks, then veered left. It continued in this direction until we reached the room's far wall. There, the platform brought us up to a room that hung from the ceiling like the passenger compartment on the bottom of a blimp. The lights inside it blazed like the sun in the room's chill darkness, and my optic implants had to shade it out until we were inside it.

The room was open on two sides, but for a waist-high railing. Wallscreens made up the other two sides, and they glowed and pulsed with streams of data.

A set of four hoverchairs floated in from the darkness and arranged themselves in the room for us. As he sat down, Winslow motioned for Querer and me each to take one, but I preferred to stand.

"What's going on here?" I asked Winslow as soon as he'd settled in.

"It's both simple and complicated," he said.

"Let's start with simple."

"All right." He grimaced, took a deep breath, and then spoke. His words were calm and clear, and he enunciated each one in his best didactic manner, but they were insane.

"I founded the Amortals Project because I wished to defeat death. Not every one of my experiments succeeded, but despite that a few of those failures lived. I didn't have the heart to destroy their remains, but it didn't seem right to just let them lie there fallow.

"I implanted nanoservers in every body I worked with as a matter of course. They form the cybernetic bridge I use to transfer the memories from one living brain into another. While silicon-based computers facilitate the transfer, the memories are stored in entirely organic matter."

He watched our faces the entire time, trying to read our expressions. We gave him nothing.

"You don't find this at all shocking?" he said.

"The man currently holding the President hostage in the Oval Office filled me in," I said.

"Really?" Winslow was the one shocked instead. "That's far above his security clearance level."

"And ours, I assume."

He frowned. "Only a handful of people know the whole truth, and none of them would normally be inclined to share."

"There's nothing normal about any of this," said Querer.

"Still, how did he find out?" Winslow asked. "Our security is flawless."

"I told him," Patrón said.

I whipped my head around to see my boss riding one of the saddle-backed robots. He wore a loose, white shirt and pants that fit him like pajamas, the exact kind that I'd woken up in every time I'd come back to life in one of the crèches up in Winslow's lab. He carried a pistol of black steel in his hand, and he leveled it at me.

"What in the world?" Winslow leaped from his chair and stood on unsteady feet. He stared at Patrón but did not speak to him. "What's going on here, Minder? Is Director Patrón dead?"

"No." President Emmanuel's voice emanated from the wallscreens to either side of us. "The director of the Secret Service is dealing with the hostage situation in the White House. He requested the activation of his latest backup."

"You're Goddamn right I did," the Patrón floating in front of us said as he dismounted from the robot carrying him and joined us in the command center. "I saw through the older Ronan's deception right away. There's only so much that hair dye can hide."

Winslow gaped in horror. "But, Minder, that's against your core programming."

"True," the computer said. "As Director Patrón said, though, the situation was desperate. I was able to override those restrictions in the name of national security concerns."

"Don't act so surprised, Juwan," Patrón said with a jaunty grin. "This isn't the first time Minder has overridden his programming to preserve America's interests. But I don't expect you to remember that.

After all, it's been thirty years since that incident."

"I think I'd remember something like that." Winslow trembled as he spoke.

"Sure," said Patrón. "If I hadn't arranged for your memories of that to be erased." He hefted the gun before him. "I had to kill you to make that work, of course, but it seemed like a small price for you to pay to keep your country safe."

"That's when my past self figured out what was going on here, wasn't it?" I said. "And you killed him for it."

"Don't give yourself so much credit, Ronan," Patrón said. "You're not that smart. Of course, neither am I."

"How's that?" asked Querer.

"I told Ronan all about it back then," said Patrón. "I thought for sure he'd see how things had to be and would back my play for the good of the nation. Instead he grew a backbone and threatened to blow it all wide open."

"You killed me." I raised a hand to my chest and watched Patrón's eyes follow my movement.

Querer and I had put our guns away when we'd entered the command room. My gun still sat in its holster. If I went for it, Patrón would gun me down before I could get it clear, for sure.

Patrón frowned. "It was a damned shame, too," he said, "but I needed to make sure I tied off all the loose ends. A lot of good people died that day." He gave Winslow a pointed look. "But they all came back in better shape than ever, and none the wiser for it. Now it's looking like '38 all over again."

He turned to me. "First, though, I want to know how you did it. I scoured your home and office. I hunted down and destroyed every record you made. There's no way you should have been able to find out what happened, what I did."

I put my hand on the butt of my gun and remained silent.

Patrón raised his eyebrows at me and giggled in disbelief. "Oh, you still don't know, do you? The man terrorizing the President right now might, but you don't have a clue."

"I sense that this is causing you a great deal of distress, Agent Dooley," President Emmanuel's voice said. "Allow me to explain the crux of the matter."

A life-sized image popped up on one of the wallscreens. It showed President Westwood standing in the Oval Office, arguing with Patrón as I watched from nearby.

"You can't do this," the President said, stabbing a thick finger into Patrón's chest with every word. "I forbid it."

"But, Mr President," the Patrón on the screen said. "Be reasonable. This isn't something I can do anything about. None of us can. Not without bringing down the entire government. It's too late."

The President's face flushed with rage. I had never seen him so upset. He was a man who was used to getting what he wanted, even before he ascended to the Presidency, and he wasn't about to let Patrón defy him.

"Then bring down the government," the President said. "Break down the whole goddamned thing." He turned and walked back to his desk. "I'm calling a press conference immediately. I'm ending these atrocities of yours right now."

"Mr President," Patrón said.

The President ignored him. "Oberon?" he said over his communications link. "Get your ass into the Oval Office right now. We have a situation on our hands, and I'm going to need you to help me spin it."

"This is my favorite part," the Patrón standing near me in the flesh said. "Watch."

"Mr President." Patrón pulled his pistol and pointed it at the President.

"What?" The President turned as he snapped at Patrón, and he stared down the barrel of the gun pointed at his face.

"I'm sorry."

In the background of the scene, I could see my past self moving, trying to throw myself in the path of the bullet. Even now, though, I knew I'd be too late.

The gun barked in Patrón's hand, and the top of the President's head disappeared.

THIRTY-SEVEN

Everyone in the command center jumped at the crack of the gunshot, except for Patrón. He made a cutting gesture across his throat, and the video playing on the wallscreen disappeared.

"You killed the President!" I said.

Patrón chuckled. "That's just what you said in '38. Back then, I couldn't convince you it was for the greater good, and I had to shoot you too."

I fought back the urge to launch myself at the bastard. The gun he held pointed at my chest helped with that.

"But Ronan was given the Medal of Honor for saving President Westwood back then," Querer said.

"I don't remember any of it, of course," I said, keeping my eyes always on Patrón. "I won the award based on his testimony."

"What can I say?" Patrón rolled his eyes. "I felt like he deserved something for all his trouble."

"That footage has to be fake," said Querer. "How could you get away with something like that? There's a limit to how much can be covered up. It was in the Oval Office!"

"He had help," Winslow said. "More than you could imagine."

"What, like the entire Secret Service?"

"Far more than that," Patrón said with a vicious grin.

"But how?" I asked. "TIE monitors every bit of information generated in the White House. It should have figured it out and shut you down instantly." That was when I figured it out.

"Unless," I said, "TIE is on your side."

"Actually," Patrón said, "it's more like I'm on *its* side. Isn't that right, Minder?"

"Absolutely," Minder's voice said.

My heart froze. If Minder, the computer system behind the Amortals Project, also controlled TIE, just how powerful must it be? I wished I could have called up my calculator layer to do the math, but my gut told me that such a computer would have to be several orders of magnitude ahead of the best supercomputers on the market today.

"Where could you possibly find that much processing power?" I said.

"Where indeed?" Winslow asked. His gaze wandered out of the room to scan the racks of clones arrayed throughout the massive cavity in which we sat.

"Oh, no," I said. "You can't be using all those people."

Winslow got to his feet. "It didn't start out that way. I never meant for any of this to happen."

"What?" said Querer. "What did he do?"

"What's the most powerful processor you have on you?" I asked, struggling to keep my voice even.

"My nanoserver," Querer said without an instant's hesitation.

"Wrong," said Winslow. "It's your brain. A human brain contains something on the order of a hundred trillion synapses, about a billion in every cubic millimeter. That's far more than any nanoserver could ever hope to have. Even that massive array up in my lab only equals about a single human brain."

"Are you saying that TIE is made of people?"

"No," I said, staring out at the tens of thousands of clones lying in their crèches. "He's saying it's made out of *them*."

Querer gasped in horror, but Patrón's cackling quickly drowned that out.

"Ironic, isn't it, Ronan?" Patrón said. "All those scientists struggling for so many years to design an artificial intelligence, and we had the all-natural answer right in our hands. All those untapped brains ready to be used."

I turned to Winslow. "You did this?"

He shuddered. "It struck me that if we could use the brains for storage, we might be able to tap their processing power too. I started out with just a few of them running independently, but I slowly added more and more of them in parallel."

It was my turn to shudder. He'd taken human beings and turned them into computers.

"And you used them to run TIE?" I said.

Winslow nodded. "I started out employing them for the Amortals Project. You'd be stunned how high the processing requirements are for maintaining so many clones. But as I linked more of the clones together, I saw that we had more capacity than we could possibly use."

"But whose idea was it to use that to build TIE?" Querer asked, her forehead crinkled with dread.

Patrón cackled again, and I edged closer to him. I didn't know if I could reach him before he shot me, but I aimed to give it a try if I got the chance.

"That's the best part," Patrón said. "Go on, Juwan. Tell them."

Winslow's lips trembled. "It was Minder's idea. It suggested that deploying part of its processing power to form a seamless intelligence gathering project would be the most efficient use of it as a resource."

"Minder?" I asked. "You mean the system that runs the Project?"

Winslow grimaced. "Here's where it–" He stopped to compose himself. "As a scientist, you always have these crazy dreams, these wild notions of where your work might go, where it might take you. But this, this rocketed far past anything I could have even conceived."

"How's that?"

"For lack of a better phrase, Minder woke up. It achieved its own form of superintelligence, a massive hive mind it self-constructed out of the unconscious minds that made it up."

"It's an artificial intelligence?" Querer's voice sounded tiny in the little room hanging above the huge chamber.

"Not exactly," Minder said in President Emmanuel's voice. I jumped when I heard it this time. "The connections between the individual brains may be artificial, but I am mostly organic. I am a self-aware, human collective consciousness."

"This is how you're doing this?" I said to Patrón. "This is how you and the rest have held onto power for so long? You take people and make them pieces of your machine?"

"Do you have a better use for them?" he said with a smirk.

I took a step toward him, my hand on the butt of the pistol Querer had given me. "They're not circuits," I said. "They're people, and you're the coldest bastard I've run across in a long damned time."

Patrón pointed his gun at my chest. "I see that you're upset, and I understand why. Believe me, I do. Several of my clones are part of Minder, just like yours. Hell, I was one of those clones until just a few minutes ago myself."

The thought of so many of my clones – maybe even all of my backups, as far as I knew – being absorbed into Minder's hive intelligence infuriated me. I ignored Patrón's pistol and stepped closer to him.

"Think about it, Ronan," he said. "The Amortals Project has kept you alive for nearly two hundred years. Theoretically, there are no limits. You could live forever. Isn't that worth it? Those clones won't ever know what's happening to them. To allow them to be a part of Minder is less cruel than letting them live and die without ever having a conscious thought at all."

"This is an atrocity," I said with a snarl. "It has to end now, and if you have to end with it, then so be it."

Patrón grimaced. "Come on, Ronan. It doesn't have to be like that. I'll give you the same choice I offered you thirty years ago: join me. Be a part of the solution."

I flinched at that. "I think I've been a part of that problem long enough."

Patrón shook his head. "I don't mean like that. I mean, come on in to the inner circle. Play a part in running the world. If you don't like how things are, you can work to change them, to change other people's minds, from within. You can be a part of the Brain Trust. Hell, within a decade or so, I could see you running it."

"Excuse me," Minder said. "I thought you would like to know. The Secret Service just stormed the Oval Office."

An image of the scene inside the White House splashed across one of the wallscreens, filling it from edge to edge. In it, the President sat in her chair behind her desk, and Eight held a gun to the President's head. Her mascara had run, giving her raccoon eyes. Rather than being frightened or sad, she was furious.

"Freeze!" someone shouted over the sounds of many feet stampeding into the Oval Office at once.

"Kill him!" President Oberon screamed at the agents bursting into the room. "Shoot to kill him now!"

Rather than try to beat the agents to the punch, Eight put his hands up into the air, his gun still held loosely in one of them. "I think I made my point," he said.

The agents didn't care if he was surrendering. They unleashed a barrage of bullets at him. The reports echoed in the airtight office with enough noise to make me think Armageddon might have come early.

The lead slugs slammed Eight into the bulletproof glass behind him, splashing it with burst after burst of blood. He danced with each impact until one of the bullets caught him in the head, removing much of his skull. He collapsed then, the agents still pumping bullet after bullet into his fresh corpse.

I didn't see any of that then, although I heard about it later. I already knew how that story was going to end, and I didn't want to have to bear witness to my own slaughter twice in the same week. While everyone else gawked at the sequel to my first snuff film, I threw myself at Patrón.

The scene in the Oval Office had distracted him. By the time he saw me coming, it was already too late.

I brought my forearms up and slammed into Patrón with a block that would have been perfect on any offensive line. I caught him square in the chest, folding his gun arm against him. He stumbled backward and caught his heel on the lip of the open side of the room in which we stood. Still gripping his pistol, he careened straight over the edge and tumbled away into

the darkness, firing wildly as he went, his bullets ricocheting off unseen walls.

He screamed the entire way down and stopped only
when the floor made him.

"Nice work," Querer said. She leaned over the edge
of the platform and stared down into the darkness that
had swallowed Patrón. "I was three seconds away
from trying that myself."

"My God," said Winslow. He shook with relief. "Is it
really, finally over?"

"It saddens me that you felt the need to commit that
pointless act of murder," Minder's voice said.

A new image appeared on the wallscreen that had
been showing the Oval Office. It framed a light-dap-
pled crèche containing another clone of Patrón.
Dressed in the thin, baggy disposable clothes found in
hospitals and mortuaries, he looked like a dead man
in a polished, glass-fronted coffin, or a strange visitor
from another planet, about to be released from his
rocket ship and unleashed on an unsuspecting world.

A number of the lights framing the clone turned
from blue to red. The new Patrón opened his eyes and
glared out at the world he'd been summoned to save
from me.

THIRTY-EIGHT

"We're just going to have to kill him again," Querer said. She chambered a round into her pistol as we watched the new Patrón emerge from his crèche. A saddle-backed robot entered the image, and he mounted it.

I shook my head. "That's going to get old quick. Given the number of clones he probably has stored here, we're going to run out of bullets before he runs out of bodies."

I turned to Winslow. He stared up at me with troubled eyes. "Do you have any control over this system?" I asked.

He blinked as he thought about it. "Not much. Minder handles everything. I turned over all responsibilities to it years ago."

"Can you stop him from activating more clones?" Querer asked. "Just lock everything down?"

"It doesn't work like that," Minder said. "Each crèche is controlled individually, and they're locked from the inside." I couldn't help but hear a bit of mockery in its steady voice. Another part of me wondered if Minder was trying to give me a hint.

"That's right," said Winslow. "It's a failsafe that gives the clones a means of escape in case of some unforeseen disaster. We wake up the clones remotely, and each one's first act is to open the crèche door from the inside. This way, though, if something disastrous was to happen to the facility, they could each, in theory, manage to escape on their own."

I smiled. "Then all we have to do is something disastrous." I pointed to the other wallscreen. "Can you wake up the nearest Patrón clone and show me where it is?"

"Of course," Winslow said. He stood before the wallscreen, and a graphical interface sprang up before him. His hands began to dance along it as if he were a priest performing some ancient ritual of resurrection known only to him and his gods. "It's over there." He pointed to his right. "Top row, about eleven o'clock."

I peered out through the open side of the platform and spotted a crèche framed by red lights in a sea of blue. I raised my gun and pumped three bullets into it. The lights all went out.

"What are you doing?" Patrón bellowed from somewhere below. If he'd come directly to the platform from the crèche, he should have reached us by then. That meant he must have taken the time to plan some sort of surprise for us. I could only hope I'd interrupted him.

"Do it again," I said to Winslow.

The scientist nodded, and his hands swung across the wallscreen again, issuing orders and authorizations.

"Stop it!" Patrón shouted from the darkness below. His image burst onto the wallscreen opposite Winslow. His skin was flushed with horror and anger. "Stop killing me, now! Minder! Stop him!"

"Dr Winslow has the primary authority to activate clones. I am – I am struggling with the decision to relieve him of that process. He is our creator and has been a faithful member of the Brain Trust. It is not something I am willing to do lightly."

I shot a quizzical look at Querer and then at Winslow. He nodded back at me and arched his eyebrows in a knowing way. Then he pointed out toward the crèches again.

"This one's three rows down at 2 o'clock," he said.

I spotted the red lights on the crèche in question and shot three more bullets into it.

"Goddamn it!" Patrón said. "Stop!"

The image of Patrón pulled back a bit to show him dismount from his carrier robot. He knelt down next to the messy remains of the Patrón that I'd knocked off the platform. He stepped over the corpse to reach down and scoop up the pistol that Patrón had still been firing when he hit the cold concrete. He hefted it in his hand and checked its action.

"Fine," Patrón said. "You want to play that way? Minder? Can Dr Winslow stop you from awakening clones?"

"No," Minder said. "He doesn't have that ability."

"Excellent," Patrón flashed a savage grin. "Find every copy of me in the Project, and release them all."

Querer gasped. "Can't you do anything about that?" she asked Winslow.

He shook his head. "No. Not at the moment."

I held up a finger to signal Querer to wait. She stared at me in disbelief but then closed her mouth. She was going to have to trust me on this, and I loved the fact that she already did.

Patrón laughed as he remounted the carrier robot and swung up into the air. The sound echoed off every wall in the entire massive complex. "Get ready for us, Dooley! We're coming for you soon!"

I gazed out over the rows and aisles and stacks of crèches and watched as dozens of sets of blue lights changed to red. I held up my pistol for a moment but then decided to save my bullets.

"How's it going now?" I asked.

"Much better," Winslow said, sweat breaking on his brow. His hands flew around the wallscreen, darting about faster than a hopped-up hummingbird. "That loosened Minder up quite a bit."

Querer gawked at me. "Does that mean what I think it does?"

Winslow nodded. "The clones comprise Minder's hive mind, but not every clone is of the same mind. It's much like its own internal democracy, although one in which the strongest personalities in the largest numbers hold the most sway. Remove all the Patróns from the collective, and Minder becomes much more reasonable."

"Very true, Dr Winslow," Minder said. "I stand ready

to implement your orders upon your confirmation. First, though, your life is in immediate danger. Please move ten feet to the left immediately."

Instead of following Minder's advice, Winslow froze. I started toward him, but before I could reach him Querer grabbed my hand and pulled me back. As I snatched my arm away from her, a long burst of bullets lanced through the wallscreen in front of Winslow and cut him down.

I returned fire through the ruined wallscreen, letting loose with everything my gun had left. I received a satisfying howl of pain for my troubles. I leaped toward the wall and jammed my eye up against one of the holes. Through it, I saw Patrón clutching at his side, where a bright red stain had blossomed on his loose white clothes.

"We can't stay here," Querer said. "He'll just keep taking cheap shots at us until we're dead."

"I don't plan to," I said. I followed Patrón's progress as he arced around toward one of the open ends of the platform and then turned to dive down beneath it.

"Let 'em go," Winslow said in a voice so soft I almost couldn't make out the words.

Querer tossed me her pistol, then knelt down next to him to examine his wounds. His life seeped out of him from a handful of holes in his arms and chest. She looked up at me, grim as I had ever seen her, and shook her head. He would bleed out long before anyone could help him.

"We can't, Juwan," I said. "He's not going to just let us walk out of here alive."

"No," Winslow wheezed. But then he could not say any more.

I strained my ears for any sound of Patrón's approach, and I kept whipping my head back and forth in an effort to look out both of the open sides of the platform at once. If he decided to fire through the wallscreen again, that would hardly do me any good, but it was the best I could do.

I glanced at the holes in the wallscreen and saw a message displayed there in glowing red letters emblazoned on a black field. "Release all Dooleys?" it said. "Please confirm."

I pictured dozens of my clones streaming out of their crèches to beat the horde of Patróns roaming about the place to death. This seemed like a good idea. I smacked my hand on the wallscreen to set the wheels in motion.

Nothing happened.

"Minder?" I said.

"Yes, Dooley Nine?"

"The wallscreen seems to be broken. Can I give you orders verbally?"

"Of course, Dooley Nine. Would you like to confirm Dr Winslow's command? I can have every one of your clones on the floor in under five minutes."

I drew a deep breath to bark out a "Yes!" but Querer leaped up and stopped me with a "No!"

"Think about it," she said. "What happens if you do that? After all the Patróns left Minder, it swayed to your side. If you let loose all of your clones, how is that going to change Minder this time?"

She was right. I couldn't just let all my selves go. If I did, I'd be playing right into Patrón's hands.

I closed my mouth. As I did, Patrón rose up from beneath the edge of the platform, his gun leveled right at me. I had Querer's pistol at my side, but I knew I'd never be able to aim and fire it before he shot me dead.

"Minder!" he said. "I hereby confirm Dr Winslow's command. Release all of the Dooley clones now!"

"I'm sorry, but I can't do that. Dr Winslow established a clear chain of succession for me to follow in the event of his untimely death."

Patrón aimed his pistol right at my head. "And where do I fall on that list?"

"You don't," Minder said. "At all."

Patrón snarled, first at Minder and then at me. He nudged the carrier robot closer until it hovered right at the edge of the platform, as close as he could get without dismounting and joining us there. He jabbed his pistol at me.

"Do it," he said. "Let them all go. I want to kill as many of you as I can at once, Ronan. And I want to see the rest of them rot in a third-world prison for the rest of their unnatural damned lives."

I hesitated. I couldn't just let Patrón have his way. If I did, he'd be sure to shoot Querer and me dead anyhow.

"Do it, or I'll shoot her first." He aimed the gun at Querer. "You can watch her die, and your clones won't even know who she was."

"Don't you dare," Querer growled at me.

"I'm going to count to three, Ronan," Patrón said. "Then I'm going to start shooting. I can worry about how to clean all this up after you're dead."

I looked into Patrón's eyes, and I saw his right one twitch twice.

I knew right then that he was bluffing. He was out of bullets.

"Minder," I said. "There's been a change of plans."

Patrón smirked at me. He thought he had me dead to rights.

"What can I do for you, Dooley Nine?" Minder said.

"Release all of the Dooley clones – and everyone else."

"What?" Patrón's eyes flew open wide. "No! Belay that order, Minder!"

"Can you please confirm your order, Dooley Nine?" asked Minder. "You do realize that this will result in my dissolution?"

"No!" Patrón said. "Stop it, Minder! It's suicide!"

Minder said nothing.

Patrón brandished his empty pistol at me. "Don't you dare," he said to me. "Don't you damn well dare! I'll make this death of yours the worst of all."

I gave him a pitying look. "If you could do that, you would have already."

Horror dawned on Patrón's face as he realized I had seen through his bluff.

"Minder?" I said. "I hereby–"

Before I could complete the sentence, Patrón came screaming at me at the top of his lungs as his carrier robot lurched forward. Determined to stop me by any means necessary, he hurled his empty pistol at my head.

I batted it out of the air with one hand as I raised Querer's gun with the other. Then I shot him right through his twitching eye.

The carrier robot hauled up short as its rider tumbled backward off it and into the open air beyond the platform's edge. This time, he fell without any noise but the sickening crunch he made when he landed.

I got on top of the carrier robot, and Querer leaped on behind me. I looked out at the crèches beyond and saw countless copies of Patrón leaving their now open crèches behind. Some tried to hail other carrier robots. Others had already given up and started climbing down from their crèches on their own.

"Dear God," Querer said. "What do we do now?"

They couldn't touch us now, but if we gave them a chance – if we gave any one of them the chance – they'd kill us both. With my face splashed across the newsfeeds as the man who'd tried to assassinate the President, I'd have the entire nation lend the Patróns a hand in trying to hunt me down.

Whether someone was holding a gun to my head at the moment or not, there was only one choice.

"Minder?" I said. "I hereby confirm my orders. Release the clones. Set every last one of them free."

Minder didn't say a word.

I grabbed the robot's saddle and tried to direct it toward the exit. With my nanoserver fried, though, I had no way to communicate with it. I couldn't get it to do anything. I slapped the top of it in frustration. I hadn't come all this way to be stuck here now.

Then the robot started moving. When it slipped forward off the platform and zoomed toward the exit, I turned back to grin at Querer, who I knew had set the robot on its current course for me. She hugged me like she might never let me go.

When we got halfway to the elevator doors, the lights on every crèche in the room turned from blue to·red.

And then countless slumbering people, unaware even that they had been asleep, awoke for the first time in their lives, all at once.

ABOUT THE AUTHOR

Matt Forbeck has worked full-time on fiction and games since 1989. He has written novels, comic books, short stories, non-fiction (including the acclaimed *Marvel Encyclopedia*), magazine articles, and computer game scripts. He has designed collectible card games, roleplaying games, miniatures and board games. His work has been published in at least a dozen different languages.

Matt is a proud member of the Alliterates writers group, the International Association of Media Tie-In Writers, and the International Game Developers Association. He lives in Beloit, Wisconsin, USA, with his wife Ann and their children: Marty, and the quadruplets, Pat, Nick, Ken and Helen. (And there's a whole other story.)

www.forbeck.com

AUTHOR'S NOTES

Amortals has been a long time coming. I first came up with the idea way back in 1994 after I learned about snuff films, movies in which real people allegedly are killed. This was back in the days before the Internet, and these illegal shows used to be passed around on VHS tapes, supposedly giving viewers a real look at the horrors of death.

I never saw any of these films – never wanted to – but the idea of them stuck with me. I wondered what would it be like to see *your own* snuff film, and what would you then do about it? The first chapter of *Amortals* charged into my mind and stomped around the place, demanding that I write it down.

The title popped into my head along with the opening bits of the story. Ronan Dooley, who would play both the victim and the detective, would no longer be mortal, but since he could be killed he wasn't exactly immortal either. No, he was *a*mortal.

After that, I came up with the basic framework for the story, including the first three chapters and an outline of the first book, plus a couple sequels. I pitched it to Ace Books and White Wolf Publishing, and collected a matched pair of rejection letters for my efforts. Then I set it aside for many years while I concentrated on starting up a roleplaying game company – Pinnacle Entertainment Group, which published the western horror game *Deadlands* and my own dystopian superhero game, *Brave New World*.

Once I left Pinnacle at the end of 1999, I wanted to take another shot at writing novels, but I was too busy working as a freelance writer and game designer to manage it. This is one of the great paradoxes of being a working writer. When you depend on your writing to bring in regular money from contract work, it's nearly impossible to set aside several months of your life and income to write something that has no guarantee it will ever get published.

I solved that problem by starting to write tie-in novels instead. The publishers of these books commissioned them ahead of time, giving me an advance up front along with a guaranteed sale. My first, *CAV: The Big Dance*, was a short, small-press novel that came out in 2002.

I used that as a crowbar to open up other doors, and Wizards of the Coast published my first mass-market novel – a middle-grade *Dungeons & Dragons* fantasy called *Secret of the Spiritkeeper* – in 2004. I followed that up with another 10 novels based on various games, including *Blood Bowl*, *Eberron*, and *Mutant Chronicles*.

Still, I had that itch to write *Amortals*, and while I could ignore it for long stretches of time, it never went away. I pitched it to Solaris back in 2005, and while the managing editor there – one Marc Gascoigne, now the head Angry Robot himself – liked it, he couldn't get the rest of his team to sign off on it.

When I first pitched the book to Marco, he said, "That sounds an awful lot like *Altered Carbon* by Richard K. Morgan." To which I said, "What by who?"

I bought the book and read it right away. It's excellent. If you like *Amortals*, go get it. You'll love it.

Altered Carbon is set in a future in which you can have your mind backed up to an onboard storage system and then reloaded into any available body set up to accept it. The hero is brought back into a body and has a limited amount of time to solve a murder. If he fails, he's sent back into a virtual prison to finish his sentence for previous crimes. Sound familiar?

When, in 2009, Marco started up Angry Robot Books, he invited me to pitch him some novels. I sent him a stack of them, each only a couple paragraphs long. He pulled out the one for *Vegas Knights*, and said, "I like that one. Do you have any more?"

I went back to my pitch for *Amortals* and polished it up. Remembering that Marco had mentioned *Altered Carbon* after reading the pitch before, I told him that Morgan's book may feature many of the same notes as *Amortals*, but they're entirely different songs.

He agreed, and by now you've hopefully already enjoyed the results.

A LOOK UNDER THE HOOD:
The Original Pitch For Amortals

As a published author, I'm often asked how one gets a book accepted by a publishing house. Here's the pitch for *Amortals* that convinced Angry Robot to pick up the book. You may notice that several things changed in the process of writing the manuscript. For instance, I melded Morton North and Amanda Querer into a single character.

AMORTALS

A novel proposal

By Matt Forbeck

matt@forbeck.com

High Concept

In a not-too-distant future in which scientists have solved the problem of mortality by learning how to backup and restore a person's mind into a vat-bred clone, a Secret Service agent wakes up and is put to work solving his own murder.

Set-Up

Biotechnology has evolved to the point that the wealthy or important can have their memories electronically backed up. Upon their death, these memories can be loaded into an identical clone prepared for this purpose. Or so it seems.

The wealthy can pay for this procedure and have stopped funding medical research. The life expectancy of the poor plummets, creating a canyon between the haves (who continue to amass wealth without even the abatement of death) and the have-nots (who can't afford even their shortened lives).

Amortals explores the nature of identity, the fallibility of memory, the disposable world in which we live, and the malleability of history, both personal and otherwise. It's dark and gritty and filled with political commentary veiled by the pseudo-distance that SF provides.

Main Characters

Ronan "Methuselah" Dooley: The best Secret Service agent in the country – and the oldest man in the world. He was nearly killed saving the President, and he underwent the first test of the amortal procedure to save his life.

Morton North: Dooley's new partner in the field, the latest in a long line. He's still in his first body and can't afford his next.

Amanda Querer: Dooley's last partner, a career agent with no hope of amortality.

Winston Patrón: The head of the Secret Service and a close advisor to the President.

Sharma Patil: Leader of the Kalis, an Indian mob that dominates organized crime in DC.

Plot

The story opens with Ronan Dooley's vicious murder. We pull back to see North and Patrón, discussing the case with a Dooley who's very much alive. It's been several weeks since Dooley's last backup, and he's missing all of his memories of that time – and his partner Querer along with them.

With North's help, Dooley must reconstruct his missing past and learn what he was up to so that he can determine who killed him. He suspects he got too close to the Kalis, and they murdered him for his efforts. They filmed his murder to send him a message to back off.

As Dooley delves further into the plot, he figures out that his last case involved a plot to assassinate the President that he foiled. He follows the trail all the way up to Patil, who denies everything. He's in charge of organized crime, not anarchy. He's learned to milk the system for everything it's worth, and he has no interest in tearing it down.

Soon enough, Dooley discovers that Querer is still alive – and apparently has gotten involved in the assassination plot. Believing that she's gone into deep cover, Dooley argues with Patrón that they need to give her the space she needs. Patrón gives Dooley 48 hours to prove that Querer hasn't gone rogue.

The deadline comes and goes, and Dooley must throw the rest of the Secret Service off Querer's trail while he finishes tracking her down. Once he catches up with her, he discovers that she has gone rogue but that she's not the leader of the plot. He is.

Investigating the assassination plot, Dooley's last self realized that the conspirators were right. The government had been carving up his memories to make him more pliable – and presumably they'd done the same with every other amortal on the planet.

The current Dooley must decide whether to help his old self, bring him in, or kill him to cover up the fact that he seems to have gone mad. It's then that the older Dooley reveals that the plot against the President is only one part of the scheme. Killing an amortal doesn't do any good – unless you destroy the facility with all of the spare bodies as well.

THE ORIGINAL SYNOPSIS

I wrote this back in 1994 for when I started pitching it around for what I hoped would be my first novel. I tossed this away before I started in on the version that became the book you hold in your hands.

THE AMORTALS
A World Synopsis

The world of the Amortals is our own in the year 2126. The story is set mostly in Chicago, the third largest city in USA, Inc. In order to keep up with the economic world pressure and to pay off its skyrocketing debt, the United States incorporated itself in 2026, on the 250th anniversary of the Declaration of Independence. The new government bears a great deal of resemblance to our own, but instead of a Constitution, USA, Inc., is based a document known as the Articles of the Incorporation. Most other nation-corps have similar documents upon which they have been refounded.

Under the new system, one share equals one vote. Only residents of the US can own stock in their nation, and every citizen is awarded one share at birth. Other shares can be purchased or awarded over the course of a stock-holder's life. State and local borders no longer exist except as convenient means of referring to an area. Due to the fast and cheap means of communicating available in the future, USA, Inc., is single, undivided entity.

Every four years, a general election is held to choose the President. All other governmental offices (like those of the five hundred district representatives, each with a constituency of one million stockholders) are filled by employees. Open interviews are established for each position, and the most qualified applicants are awarded the positions.

The current President of the Corporation has been in power for fifty years. He is an amortal, of course, and barring any horrible scandal, he is likely to remain in power for the foreseeable future.

The process of granting amortality was developed in the years before the Incorporation. It has had a profound effect on the entire world.

Once it became clear that they had the potential to live forever, people in power started to take a more long-term look at their world. It was decided that the biggest problem facing the world was a lack of resources. Since the supply side of the equation was uncontrollable, simple economics dictated that restrictions would have to be made on demand. To that end, world-wide birth control was instituted by introducing massive amounts of birth control drugs into all of the planet's drinking water treatment plants.

The only way to have a baby is to get a license. These are only given out to those prospective parents that have completed parenting courses and a battery of physical and genetic exams. Those lucky enough to win a license (or rich enough to simply purchase one) are then given an antidote to the birth control drug and permitted to have a single child.

Amortality is a rare thing in this society. Only one in a thousand people is either wealthy enough to have purchased it or fortunate enough to have been awarded it as part of a compensation package (like our protagonist, Ronan Dooley). At first, only the rich ever became amortal, but it soon became apparent that some people were simply too valuable for those in power to allow them to die. They were irreplaceable, and so steps were taken to ensure they would never be gone.

Those who have "earned" their amortality are stuck in a kind of indentured servitude. If they want to keep living (at least beyond the natural life span of the incarnation they're currently on), they have to keep working for their employer. There is no retirement plan.

This upsetting of the natural order has made many people extremely angry, particularly those that are doomed to die working for the same people their great-grandparents worked for. A resistance movement known as the Underground has arisen to try to put an end to amortality and bring things back to the way they were. They are supported by a number of religious organizations that have always claimed that it was only God's prerogative to cheat death.

It is this organization that Dooley and his wife Miranda get involved in. It's a powerful group, but it's hampered by the fact that it must remain secret to avoid persecution, as well as by the fact that its members are all "short timers".

One of the main reasons the Underground has formed is because of the staggering gap between the haves and have-nots. The rich have all of time stretching out before themselves in which to grow even richer. The poor can look forward to nothing but a timely death. This dichotomy has made the rich even more jealous of their position than they are today. After all, to fall from on high in this world means not only to be poor, but to lose your amortality. People are willing to fight even harder to preserve for themselves not one, but several lifetimes.

Correspondingly, since they no longer have any real fear of death, the rich have horribly neglected the poor. Diseases like AIDS kill large portions of the population. After amortality became available, funds for researching for a cure for such illnesses became a low priority. If an amortal was mortally ill, the solution was as simple as a new body. Those in poverty don't have that option, but they haven't enough power to make those capable of doing anything about it care.

The cities are in decay, having been long since abandoned by most rich. One exception to this is downtown Chicago, in which the wealthy have simply raised themselves above it all. No mortals are allowed to live above the fiftieth floor in any of the city's skyscrapers, and most are forced to suffer in quarters so cramped as to make the housing projects of the twentieth century look roomy.

Gangs rule the streets. Drugs have been entirely legalized, but they're as addictive and costly as ever. Without any of the treatment programs of the wealthy, many of the poor fall into the endless cycle of stealing from each other to get their daily fixes.

Meanwhile, far overhead, in skyscraper mansions connected by soaring walkways, the rich look down on the poor and feel only fear that they should ever fall so low.

Life with the rich is a song. Sex is open and free. Foods and fashions are exotic. The arts flourish.

On the underside, though, it's just the opposite. Fear of getting hurt or ill and not being able to pay for a doctor (health insurance exists, but is exorbitant) makes most people a lot more cautious than they might normally be. People with gunshot wounds, whether sustained in a fight or as a bystander, are routinely put out of their misery. The streets are dotted with crippled victims who were not so fortunate.

The rich never see the streets, though, and neither do many of the poor, at least those of the poor well-off enough to consider themselves "middle-class". With modern technology, most workers rarely have to leave the safety of their tiny apartments. They telecommute to work, and most of their needs are met by delivery services staffed by well-armed drivers. These "webheads", as they're known, often side with the rich in questions about what to do with the truly poor. Although the webheads may not have much, they're head and shoulders above the souls that roam the streets.

The time for rebellion is ripe, but the people have few footholds in the world above them. Lately, though, things have gotten so bad that some of the wealthy (or potentially so) have sided with the Underground out of simple principle. Miranda is one of these people. With her help, Dooley will become one of them, too.

And then the tide may finally be turning.

THE ORIGINAL FIRST CHAPTER

Dooley came to and suddenly realized that was the last thing he wanted to do. His skull felt like a jackhammer had woken up inside of it, found itself trapped, and was trying its best to bang its way out. He felt like death warmed over – no, worse.

He tried to open his eyes, but they were crusted over with the blood that had streamed down over them from the many cuts on his head. A gloved hand slapped him across the face, knocking the crusts loose and starting the blood flowing again. With a herculean effort, Dooley managed to wrest his eyes open.

He immediately closed them again. The man was still there, the man who had done this to him. He mumbled a prayer to some forsaken god under his breath. The fisted glove slammed into his face again.

Dooley tried to say something again, but the teeth got in his way. He spat out the loose pieces of bone and began to whimper. He was lost and confused. He didn't know who the man was or why he was hurting him. He only knew that he wanted it to stop.

He struggled for a moment before he realized he was tied to the wooden café chair he was sitting in. His legs were fastened to the chair's, and his hands were bound behind his back. The cord had already cut deep into the skin on his wrists, and it was starting to gnaw against his bones. He pulled against it desperately but only succeeded in flaying his skin further.

The tears rolling down his cheeks finally dissolved the crusts on his eyelashes altogether. He opened his eyes to see that he had vomited on himself. He felt the urge to do so again, and although there was nothing left in his stomach, that didn't stop him from retching foul air.

He wanted to tell his torturer to stop, to leave him alone. He'd do anything, say anything, tell anything. He just wanted the pain to end.

But he found he didn't have the words.

He coughed and hacked and spit up blood. He was bleeding internally. Some of his organs had been ruptured.

He felt like he might drown in his own fluids before the man could hurt him again. He hoped that he would.

Unfortunately, while Dooley had been consumed by his pain, the man had circled around behind him. He kicked the top of the chair hard, toppling it forward onto the floor with Dooley along with it. Dooley's knees smashed into the concrete, followed quickly by his forehead and his already broken nose.

He wanted to pass out, to find some sort of escape, but unconsciousness would not come. Just when he thought he might finally return to its solace, the man grabbed the back of the chair and hauled Dooley upright again, jolting him awake.

Dooley opened his eyes all the way this time, blinking away the blood and sweat that stung his eyes. He was in a large room. The walls were far enough away that he couldn't see them in the darkness. A single, bare incandescent bulb shining overhead lit the area in which he was sitting, casting what little he could see in sharp shadows. Blood and vomit pooled on the concrete around him. Something cylindrical and silver sat on the floor in front of him and to his left. It lay just inside the edge of the light. All else was darkness.

He could hear footsteps circling him in the void outside the cone of illumination that was his universe. Boot heels trod purposefully out past the edge of the light as if the man was trying to find a way in. Dooley wished with all his might that the light would keep the man away, that he was trapped in the darkness, leaving Dooley safe under the bulb's care.

The footsteps came around in front of Dooley and stopped. A voice came out of the void. It was muffled, electronically masked. Still, it sounded strangely familiar, but try as he might, he could not place it.

"Are you ready, Dooley?" it asked him.

Dooley's head was spinning out of control. He tried to answer, but found he couldn't. His tongue lolled in his mouth like a useless, old rag. It was dry as a carpet in a desert cave. He licked his cracked and split lips and tried again, but all he could manage was another whimper.

"Come on, Dooley. This isn't like you." The voice laughed sadistically. "Where's that rapier wit of yours now, old man?"

Suddenly, Dooley was consumed with anger. This man was toying with him, teasing him, torturing him. Dooley started to scream unintelligibly, venting his frustration at the man as if he could wither him away with the sheer ferocity of his emotion.

The man just cackled lowly, the mask making the sound into something inhuman.

Just as quickly as it began, Dooley's fit ended. He slumped forward exhausted, his rage entirely spent.

The blood trickling down his wrists had made the cord slick. He indulged himself in an instant of hope, but it was dashed as he found that the bonds had bitten too far into his flesh for him to ever have any chance of freeing himself. He had gored his wrists, but it had done him no good. He was as trapped as ever.

"Do you know why you're here, Dooley?" the voice said. "Do you know what you've done that would justify such pain?"

Dooley looked up, straining to see the man's face in the darkness. There was nothing. He could see nothing. He shook his head back and forth in his misery and moaned and moaned.

The voice came again, deep, black, and clingy, shattering

Dooley's hopes that he would ever be able to get away from it. It stuck to his brain and burned like napalm. The flames were inextinguishable. Not blood nor tears would ever put them out.

"You messed with the wrong people. You put your nose in where it didn't belong." The voice paused dramatically. "You did your job, Dooley. And for that, you're going to receive the ultimate reward."

The tip of a gun broke out of the darkness and into the light. It was long and thin and black and cold. It seemed to absorb the light as it hit it, sucking it slowly from the cone as it inched forward.

It was perfect, flawless. The only thing that Dooley saw that was darker than the barrel was the hole that ran right down its middle. That hole seemed to suck at the light, to pull Dooley in closer and closer to its black promise.

"You," said the voice. Dooley had almost forgotten the man was there. "You are going to die."

Dooley's eyes flew wide at the tone of sheer menace in the man's words. This was it. It was all over.

Then his executioner stepped into the light, right behind his automatic rifle. He was dressed all in dull, flat black, from his high-laced boots to his full helmet. The only part of it that reflected any light at all was the helmet's face-plate, and this was like a mirror.

Dooley stared into the shiny visor, hoping to be able to somehow penetrate it, to be able to see through it and let his eyes fall on the face of the man who was going to kill him. But all he could see was his own battered face staring back at himself hopelessly.

For a moment despair took him, and he cried like a child, wailing for the rest of his life that would not be. His murderer stood there stolidly, implacably. He was entirely unmoved.

When he had cried himself so hoarse he couldn't make any more sound, Dooley looked up at the man and started crying again, soundlessly this time. He knew the man was waiting for him to finish, so he decided he would never stop. Eventually, entirely exhausted, he stopped.

Slowly, he looked up at the man again, his stomach tight with fear, but his heart filled with resignation. The darkness was invading the light, eating it, stealing it away. Dooley looked at himself in the faceplate.

At one time, he had been handsome. Bloodshot brown eyes stared back at him from a drawn, pale face almost completely covered by fresh, red blood. His nose was broken, and his left cheekbone had been smashed. His curly brown hair was matted down with thick, black fluid.

He laughed once at the sight of himself, a short, humorless sound. A smile followed it. Many of his teeth were missing. He winced at the pain, but let the smile turn into a grin.

He laughed again, louder this time. Then once more and again. Soon he was cackling wildly, tears streaming down his cheeks, washing thin trails of white down his red, red face. The man in black never even moved.

When he finally stopped, he looked directly into the center of the gun. He watched it intensely, trying to see deeper and deeper into it as if he was trying to reveal the deadly secret that lay nestled at the end of the chamber. Then he let out a deep sigh, forcing the air out of his lungs and leaving it out in the light.

In the silence, the sound of the gun being cocked was clear and crisp, like the crack of a foot on a dry twig on a dark night.

"Goodbye, Dooley," the killer said. "I'll be seeing you around."

Dooley didn't react at all.

As he was staring into the gun's muzzle, transfixed by the purity of its darkness, it suddenly flashed with the brightest light he had ever seen. It was followed quickly by an impact that hit him right between the eyes. Once through the front of the skull, the bullet, barely slowed at all, exploded, blasting out through the back of his head, letting the light from the bulb spill down inside his brain.

The darkness took him entirely then.

He never even heard the gun's report.

COMING SOON

Here's an exclusive first look at Matt Forbeck's superb urban fantasy, *Vegas Knights*, coming soon from Angry Robot.

ONE

"Luck is for losers."

I hated it when Bill said that. I hated the tone, the words, the way it made me feel like just that: a loser.

"Shut up," I said. "I can't think with you jabbering at me like that."

I ran a hand through my shaggy hair and stared down at the cards before me. I ignored the five laid out face-up in the middle of the table. I couldn't do anything about them. The two hole cards face-down in front of me worried me though, and I hadn't even looked at them.

Bill slapped a hand on the polished wood. The cards jumped off the table a fraction of an inch and settled right back down where they'd been. Nothing about them changed a bit.

"You think it's hard to concentrate here, in a hotel room?" Bill sneered at me. "Just imagine how much worse it's going to be on the floor in a real game with real money on the table."

"We won't be playing for chips?"

"Chips are money, Jackson," he said. "That's one of the tricks the casinos play on you to keep you coming back. Losing a stack of black chips doesn't seem like that big a deal. But that stack's worth all your textbooks for the year."

I glared at Bill now. He stared back at me with his blue eyes under his dark, close-cut hair. Everything about him was razor-sharp, from the edges of his sideburns to the creases in his khakis. He was only nineteen, a few months older than me, but he always seemed far more sophisticated.

"You're not helping, brother," I said. I turned and reached for my laptop.

Bill leaned over the table. "What are you doing? That can't help you."

I launched my video chat program. "I'm going to call Ultman."

Bill slammed the laptop shut, almost pinching my fingers. "No. What's the professor going to say?" He put on his best Indian accent. "'I told you not to do anything foolish, Mr Wisdom'? 'Bring him back to Ann Arbor, Mr Chancey'?" He gagged. "Are you going to listen to that?"

I rubbed my eyes and sighed. "This is crazy," I said. "I can't believe I let you talk me into this."

Bill pulled the laptop away and tossed it on one of the beds. I glanced out past it to the view out of the room's wide, tinted window, which was curved to fit inside the casino's outer wall. The sun had fallen behind the mountains to the west, turning the sky into bands of bright orange at the horizon, fading to star-speckled blue-black high above.

I'd never seen mountains before the plane trip from Detroit Metro to McCarran today. The guidebook on my smartphone called the range hunkered off to the west of Las Vegas the Spring Mountains. They looked close enough to walk to, although intellectually I knew it would take me at least a good day's hike just to reach their feet.

"It's a good plan," said Bill. "It's going to work. How can it not work?"

I smirked at him. "You want a list? I've seen enough movies. We're going to screw this up, and a couple gorillas in dark suits and glasses will take us into a back room and beat us half to death then offer us a free ride to the airport."

Bill groaned. "You're always so negative. You have to think positive. We're not going to screw this up."

"I'm positive we will."

Bill made a fist. "Thinking like that will get us killed."

I put up my hands and walked to the window. When we'd checked in three hours ago, the hotel tower had faced the strip. I wondered how long it would take for it to make a complete spin.

"Forget it then," I said. "It's not worth it. It's just money."

"Just money," he said. "So you're rich? Your grandma doesn't have to work to send you to school? That out-of-state tuition isn't taking a bit out of her retirement fund?"

I winced. Bill knew how poor I was, especially compared to him. I felt guilty every day about taking my grandma's money, but she wouldn't let me not. "A man's nothing without an education," she'd told me. "Just see how your daddy and granddaddy turned out. We ain't gonna have that from you."

Bill just wouldn't let up though. "How's that scholarship working out for you?"

I turned and scowled at him. He knew. "I'd be doing fine."

"If what?" he said. He stuck out his chest, daring me to say it.

"Forget it. I ain't going for it."

He pumped his fist at me in frustration. "Magic isn't the problem, Jackson. It's the solution."

"It's stealing. It ain't right."

"So now you got morals." He rubbed his forehead. "You didn't seem to mind taking money from those frat boys last week."

I knew he was going to bring that up. "They had it coming. Besides, it was just beer money. They could afford it."

Bill tossed up his arms. "And these casinos can't? Have you looked at this place? It's a garden in a desert!"

He walked over to the wardrobe, opened it up, and started rummaging through it. "Look at this hotel," he said. "Revolutions is fifty stories tall, and the whole building spins on an axis.

"Check out the Luxor. That light that spears out of the top of the pyramid, you can see that from space. The Stratosphere is over a thousand feet tall, and it has rides on top of it. The Mirage has a working volcano sitting out in front of it.

"Do you have any idea about the kind of engineering that goes into building something like that? Do you know what it costs to keep it all going?"

"Do you?"

"A hell of a lot more than we could ever take out of here in a single night. The profits on a place like this are astronomical. And half of them go to the mob."

"You believe that, you've been watching too much TV."

"Think what you like, Jackson," he said. "You could take enough money from these people to pay for your entire education, and they wouldn't notice it."

I knew he was right, but I shook my head anyway. "That ain't the point. I can't do it anyhow. It – it just don't want to work."

"You can do it," Bill said. "You've done it before. You're just psyching yourself out."

He pulled a pistol out of his duffel bag.

"What the hell are you doing with that?" I took a step back and bumped into the tempered glass behind me. We were thirty-three stories up in a rotating building, and the windows here were all sealed up good.

"It's insurance." Bill flipped out the pistol's empty cylinder with practiced ease, like a gunslinger from the early days of this lawless town. He slipped a single bullet into it, slapped it back home and gave it a spin.

"Against what? The bellboy?"

"All sorts of things." He pointed the gun at me. "Right now, it's against friends cutting their own throats."

"Put the gun down, Bill," I said. "It ain't funny."

"I'm not joking." He cocked the pistol. "Change the cards."

"How the hell did you get that through the airport?" I glanced around for some way to escape. Only one door led out of the room, and Bill stood between me and it.

"I'm a magician, Jackson." Bill snorted. "How do you think I did it?"

He pulled the trigger, and my heart nearly stopped. The hammer clicked on an empty chamber.

"Put it away, brother." I held my hands over my chest. "Someone's going to get hurt."

He cocked the pistol again. "Just change the cards. Then I put it away."

I walked back to the table. "How did you get your hands on a gun?" I asked. "Tell me you haven't had that stashed in our dorm room all year."

"I'm from Detroit," he said, like that explained every-thing.

"I ate in your family's mansion for Thanksgiving, Bill. Grosse Pointe Woods ain't hardly the hood."

"Just change the card."

I looked down at the table. The cards were still there, mocking me: the three, six, and jack of clubs, the queen of diamonds, and the ace of spades.

I put a hand on the top of my two pocket cards, and I stared at their backs so hard I thought I might burn a hole straight through them.

"Feel anything?" asked Bill.

"I don't always. Sometimes it just happens."

He grinned as he shook his head. "Too funny. For me, it's like a synapse bursts in my brain, like a little orgasm."

"That what I hear you doing in the bathroom at night? Playing with your wand and doing magic?"

He pulled the trigger.

The click made me jump about a foot. "Knock that the hell off!" I said.

"Just shut up and change the damned cards!"

I reached down and turned them over, exposing the two of hearts and the two of diamonds.

Bill clucked his tongue at me. "A pair of deuces? That's the best hand you can come up with?"

"That's not what I was trying for."

"I know," he said. He pulled the trigger again.

I tried not to flinch — I didn't want to give him the sat-isfaction — but I just couldn't help it.

"That's half the chambers," Bill said. "And you say you're not lucky." He pulled back the hammer. "Three more tries."

I wondered if I could catch the bullet. The great stage magicians had done it for decades, ever since there had been bullets to catch, and they'd just been using tricks. I knew real magic.

If I couldn't change a couple of cards, though, I couldn't see how I might manage to catch a speeding bullet in my bare hands.

"Clock's ticking," Bill said.

"You told me there weren't any clocks in the casinos."

"We're not on the — just change the cards!"

I turned the hole cards facedown again. I pictured the faces of the cards in my mind, and I imagined them turning into something else. I turned them back over.

They were the two of diamonds and the two of hearts.

"Dammit," I said. "I could have sworn something happened there."

I was so frustrated, I didn't even move when Bill's pistol clicked on an empty chamber again.

"They did change, you idiot," he said. "You flipped them."

"What?"

I did a double-take at the cards. He was right. The heart and the diamond had switched positions.

"What'd you pull the trigger for then?" I asked.

"Rearranging the cards may be good for Three Card Monte," he said, "but this is poker. The big leagues. No-limit Texas Hold 'Em."

I nodded. I hated him at that moment, but not just for the gun. I hated him for being right.

"Two more chambers," he said. "One of them has to be full.

That gave me a fifty percent chance of taking a bullet if I missed the next try and no damned chance of lucking out at all if I missed the one after that. I'd been fortunate so far, but eventually my luck would run out. I had to make this work.

I flipped the cards over and stared at their backs again. We'd picked up a few used table decks in the hotel store after we'd checked in. They bore the red, white, and blue roulette-wheel logo of the Revolution Casino and Hotel laid over a background of the original US flag with the circle of 13 stars. Two of the corners had been rounded off to make sure no one could try to use them to cheat in a game.

I pictured the card faces in my mind, and I saw the two of diamonds change to the five of diamonds. I left the other deuce alone.

I flipped the cards over, and they'd done just what I'd seen. I turned to smile at Bill and instead found he'd pointed the gun right in my face.

"What?" I said, more disturbed by his angry grimace than the pistol. "It worked! I got me a straight."

I pointed at the cards in order: *ace, deuce, trey, four, five*. It was the lowest possible straight, sure, but still a straight.

"You dumb ass," Bill said. "Is that really the best you can do?"

"Come on," I said, my voice cracking just a little. "That'll beat anything that anyone else could come up with. Even a tiny straight like that beats a pair, two pair, or trips."

"What about a flush?"

I froze, then looked at the cards again. There were three clubs there. "A straight doesn't beat a flush?" I asked. "I always get that mixed up."

Bill stabbed the gun at me and pulled the trigger. I had just enough time to say, "Don't!" before the hammer fell on the last empty chamber.

"That's it," Bill said, cocking the pistol again. "Your luck's run out. You get one last chance. Do it right, or die."

"You suck," I said. "You know that."

He leveled the gun at my chest. "You don't think I'd do it."

"No." I shook my head. "I know you would. That's why you suck."

I flipped the cards back over and tried to ignore him, to concentrate on changing the cards. I could have chosen any two clubs, of course, but I wanted to get the best possible hand. In my mind, I changed the cards into the ace and king of clubs.

I found it hard to focus on those two cards, though, knowing that Bill was pointing a pistol at me. I figured he was just bluffing. He wouldn't really shoot me. He knew what he was doing, and I trusted him. He was just trying to motivate me, to get me paying my full attention to the cards, but I couldn't stop thinking about that bullet sitting in that final chamber.

I thought I'd done it right, but I wasn't sure. I just had to trust, to hope, that I'd managed to make the cards switch. I reached down and flipped them over.

Bill poked the gun at me as he leaned over to look at the cards on the table: the ace and king of clubs.

I'd never been so happy to see two cards in my life.

"Woo-hoo!" Bill threw his hands in the air. "You did it! I knew you could!" He offered me a high-five, and I slapped his hand hard enough to make it sting.

He shook his hand out, cursing. "What was that for?"

"That damned gun. Were you really going to shoot me?"

Bill gave me a sheepish grin. "Of course not," he said. He reached into his pocket and produced a bullet. "I palmed the bullet. It was never even in the gun."

We both laughed at that, me mostly out of relief. Then he tossed the gun onto the table, and it went off.

The bullet smashed into the wall next to Bill's bed, and the recoil sent the gun spinning back off of the table to land with a dead thud on the carpeted floor.

"Shit!" Bill said, his hands trembling. "I'm… I'm sorry, Jackson. I don't know how – that's impossible."

I looked down at the ace and king of clubs, which the gun's misfire had knocked to the floor as it skidded off the table.

"That's the thing about magic," I said. "Nothing's impossible."

TWO

"Card, sir?"

I looked up at the dealer, a dark-haired man in a pin-striped suit and fedora, the men's uniform here at Bootleggers, one of the hottest new casinos on the strip – or so Bill had said. The dealer's name tag read: "JUSTIN: ATLANTA." He peered at me over his wire-rim glasses and his dark soul patch.

Justin had been peeling cards out of a six-deck shoe with the detached resignation of an assembly line worker at the end of his shift. Everyone else at the Blackjack table hung on the turn of every card, but Justin didn't seem like he could care less.

It wasn't his money.

Bill and I had each brought five hundred dollars to the table. For Bill, that was just pocket money, but for me it represented all my textbook money for the term. I'd borrowed some of the books I needed for the seven weeks from the start of the Winter semester to the beginning of Michigan's spring break, but I hadn't bothered showing up to most of the classes anyhow. Bill and I had been cramming on our magic studies instead, getting prepped up for the biggest test of them all: nine days in Las Vegas.

On the walk over from Revolutions, Bill had insisted we go over the plan again. I didn't want to – I was sick of thinking about it – but he told me he could see how nervous I was. I wondered if he was trying to calm his nerves or mine.

"Just repeat the Blackjack plan back to me," he said as we walked out the front door and down the steps carved to resemble those of the Capitol Building in DC. "I want to hear you say it.

I groaned but went along with it. I liked playing Blackjack, but studying it so hard had stripped all the joy out of it for me.

It's a simple game. The dealer gives everyone two cards face up, then gives himself one face down and one face up. You're not playing against the other players, though, just the dealer.

Whichever one of you who gets closest to twenty-one without going over wins whatever you bet. Face cards count as tens. Aces can be used as either one or eleven. If you get 21 on the deal, that's Blackjack, and it pays 3:2 odds, or a hundred and fifty percent of your bet.

When it's your turn, you can either ask the dealer for another card ("Hit me") or stay pat ("Stand"). If you take a hit and go over 21, you bust out and lose your bet.

After you go, the dealer flips over his hole card. If his total is seventeen or more, he stands. Otherwise, he has to take hits until his hand is seventeen or over, or he goes bust.

There are a few other wrinkles. You can split pairs to make two hands and bet on each of them. You can double down on lower hands, which means you double your bet and take one card, but after that you have to stand.

Blackjack offers some of the best odds of any casino game, especially if you pay attention to the cards that have already been played. If you're clever, you can then figure out what's left in the dealer's six-deck shoe and use that to push the odds even farther in your favor.

This is called card counting. It's what Dustin Hoffman's autistic character did in Rain Man. Regular folks use things like plus-minus systems to help them keep track of whether or not a deck's running high on face cards – which favors the player – or low.

There's nothing technically illegal about any of this, but the casinos hate it. If they catch you counting cards, they ask you to leave, then send your photo to every other casino in town to make sure you can't play there either.

We didn't want that.

"We play the same table," I said as we strolled north on Las Vegas Boulevard. "We keep our bets the same. We never vary, and if one of us leaves the table, the other one does too."

"Right," said Bill. "We don't want them picking us out as the latest version of one of the MIT card-counting teams."

The clown sirens of Circus Circus beckoned us on our left, while the flashing lights of the Riviera and the new Thunderbird called to us from across the street. The art-deco tower of Bootleggers shone like a beacon at the end of the block.

"We don't try to change the first cards dealt to us," I said, "just the ones we take as hits. We stand pat on seventeen or higher."

During our practice sessions back in Ann Arbor, we'd tried messing with the cards during the initial deal, but it was too hard to keep track of each set long enough to concentrate on them. At least it was for me.

Bill raised an index finger to correct me. "Unless the

dealer is showing a face card or an ace."

"Right. Then we take a single hit."

Bill checked his expensive watch. I never wore one, preferring to rely on my phone. One less thing to carry.

"It's 9pm," he said. "Just before the shift change in the Blackjack pit at Bootleggers. We play for an hour, and the next time they change dealers after that, we leave."

"How do you know all that?" I asked. "You talk like you grew up in a casino instead of some rich suburb."

Bill grinned. "That's what the Internet is for. It explains the rules to you."

"And you gotta know the rules to play the game."

Bill shook his head. "To win the game."

Bootleggers looked like something Donald Trump would have come up with if he'd finally realized he was the reincarnation of Al Capone. The main entrance looked like the red-carpeted front of the glitziest theatre in 1920s Hollywood. The hotel tower behind it stabbed into the night, hundreds of spotlights illuminating its limestone-clad sides and neon-traced corners that curved toward setback after setback in layers like the crags of a mountain spire. It all culminated in a monster of a circular sign that read "BOOTLEGGERS" in a tall, thin, curved font with neon letters that had to stand thirty feet high.

At the entrance, a doorman dressed in a pinstriped zoot suit over black tuxedo shoes with white spats held open the speakeasy-style door for us. Bill had the place mapped out in his head, and he took us straight to the Blackjack pit — a collection of green-felted tables under brassy lights with green-glass shades – and we got to work.

At least Bill did.

We sat down at a half-crowded table and put our money on the felt. Bill tossed down his cash with authority: five crisp, new hundred-dollar bills. I pushed my stack of crumpled twenties to the dealer who took pains to smooth and count them carefully and in full sight of the hidden security cameras that watched every table. Then he counted out two stacks of twenty green twenty-five dollar chips and pushed one of them to each of us.

A small red sign near the dealer noted that this table had a twenty-five dollar minimum bet. With a confident smile, Bill pushed four of his chips forward as his bet. Trying not to gulp loud enough to be heard, I did the same.

I'd wanted to start out easier, with minimum bets, and work our way up. Bill had argued against it. "We can't ramp up too fast, or we'll draw attention," he said. "If we start big, it's not so steep a climb."

The fact that this only gave me five chances to blow it before I was tapped out didn't budge Bill a bit.

"That's only a worry if you're going to lose," he said. "That's not in the cards. Not for us."

I'd expressed my doubts about this, which ended up with Bill pulling a gun on me in our hotel room. I knew he was just trying to motivate me, but that bullet sneaking its way into the pistol still scared me. I believed he'd palmed the bullet, but that doesn't mean he couldn't have accidentally killed me.

How did the bullet get in there then? Had one of us subconsciously used our magic to load it into the chamber? If so, one of us wanted me to die. I wasn't sure which one of us would make the worse answer for that question.

Then I came up with one: it might have been us both.

With thoughts like that troubling me, it's maybe not surprising I lost the first four hands. Try as I might I couldn't get the right cards to fall for me. Not once.

On the fourth hand, the dealer pulled a blackjack, which

took everyone's bet. That wasn't my fault. Even Bill lost his money on that one, although he was still up three hundred dollars already. But it put me down to my last four-chip stack.

I thought about parsing out my stack and just betting a single chip at a time. Although it would break with our plan, it would keep me in the game for at least another few hands. That had to be worth something, right?

I pulled the top chip off my tiny stack and glanced at Bill for confirmation. He gave me a noncommittal shrug. I didn't see any hatred, anger, or even frustration in his eyes. It was something worse: resignation. It said, "Of course you blew it. I knew you would."

I may not have been able to pull out the cards I wanted when I wanted, but I knew one thing. I wasn't going out like that.

I shoved all my chips forward.

Justin dealt the cards. Mine both came up aces. I groaned. That gave me either two (playing both cards as ones) or twelve (playing one card as one and the other as eleven), since the third option — using both aces as elevens — would bust me out.

The dealer's up-card showed the ace of diamonds. "Insurance, anyone?" he asked, offering us a side-bet that would keep our original bet safe if he happened to have Blackjack.

None of us took him up on it. It was a sucker's bet. "Only card counters and idiots take insurance," Bill had said during one of our practice sessions. "You're neither."

I couldn't have paid for the insurance anyhow, even if I'd wanted to. I had nothing else to bet.

Despite that, I held my breath as Justin peeled back the corner of his hole card to take a peek at it. For an instant,

I thought he'd flip it over to show a ten or a face card, then sweep up the last of my money along with everyone else's bet. Instead, he put the card back down and kept playing.

"Card, sir?" That's what he said when he got to me.

Players in the zone – ones who are good at the game and are there to win, rarely speak, and the dealers don't talk to them. They don't need to. They used distinct and simple hand signs to show what they want. This makes it easy for the dealer to know exactly what they mean and for the eyes in the sky to keep track of it all.

When my turn came around, I'd kept my hands on the rail in front of me. I'd been trying to concentrate on the next card out of the shoe, and I'd forgotten to scratch the table to signal the dealer to hit me.

"You should split those," Bill said. "You always split aces."

"I can't," I said. I nodded at the blank space on the green felt where my starting stake had once been.

"Would you care to purchase more chips, sir?" Justin asked.

I grimaced and shook my head.

Bill grabbed a short stack of chips from his pile and shoved them next to mine. I gaped at him. After all the crap he'd given me up until now, I figured he'd just let me go broke and then be stuck watching him win for the rest of the week.

"You can't bet on my hand," I said.

"It's a loan," Bill said. "Not a bet. Split them."

"Sure you're not just wasting your money? I can't pay that back if I lose."

Bill smiled. "So don't lose."

I pointed at the cards and asked the dealer to split them. Justin moved them apart, and I pushed Bill's chips over to one of the aces, and my stack over to the other.

I stared at the plastic shoe and the first card sitting in it, the one the dealer would slip out of there and place next to my first ace. I willed for it to come up a face card. I visualized the jack of hearts – and that's just what landed next to my ace.

"Blackjack," Justin said. He reached into his tray of chips and put a stack of four green chips right next to mine.

The dealer's complete lack of enthusiasm did nothing to dampen mine. I wanted to jump up and let out a war whoop, but I refused to let a single success distract me. I still had another hand to win, and it was Bill's money riding on it, not mine. Somehow, that meant even more to me that I not lose it.

"Can I double down on that ace?" I asked.

Justin nodded. I moved my the chips I'd just won from him over to double my bet on my remaining ace. With the double down, I'd only be allowed a single extra card, but I only needed the one.

I stared at the deck and reached out with my mind again. I pictured the king of diamonds, the One-Eyed King, the Man with the Axe.

The dealer reached for the shoe, drew a card and flipped it over in front of me.

Hello, Your Majesty.

**Brace yourself for VEGAS KNIGHTS,
coming soon from Angry Robot,
as a paperback and eBook.**

ANGRY
ROBOT

Teenage serial killers
Zombie detectives
The grim reaper in love
Howling axes **Vampire**
hordes Dead men's
clones The Black Hand
Death by cellphone
Gangster shamen
Steampunk anarchists
Sex-crazed bloodsuckers
Murderous gods
Riots **Quests** Discovery
Death

Prepare
to welcome
your new
Robot overlords.

angryrobotbooks.com

LAVIE TIDHAR
THE BOOKMAN

J. ROBERT
KING
ANGEL
OF
DEATH

DAMAGE TIME

COLIN HARVEY

ANDY REMIC

KELL'S
LEGEND

Triumff
HER MAJESTY'S HERO

Mr. DAN ABNETT

TIM WAGGONER

> MOXYLAND
> Lauren Beukes

KING MAKER

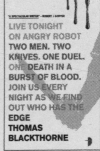

"A SPECTACULAR WRITER" — ROBERT J. SAWYER

LIVE TONIGHT
ON ANGRY ROBOT
TWO MEN. TWO
KNIVES. ONE DUEL.
ONE DEATH IN A
BURST OF BLOOD.
JOIN US EVERY
NIGHT AS WE FIND
OUT WHO HAS THE
EDGE
THOMAS
BLACKTHORNE